Hilda Vaughan was born in 1892 in Builth Wells, Breconshire, and became, through her writing, closely identified with the neighbouring county of Radnorshire, where her father was county clerk. She served in a Red Cross hospital during the First World War and was organising secretary of the Women's Land Army in Breconshire and Radnorshire.

Educated privately, Vaughan attributed her intellectual awakening to her neighbour, the Squire of Cilmerry Park, S.M.P. Bligh, himself a published author. While taking a writing course in Bedfordshire, she met Charles Morgan, then drama critic for *The Times* and later also a novelist. They married in 1923.

Hilda Vaughan's first novel *The Battle to the Weak*, published in 1925, is set in a rural Radnorshire community, and portrays both a traditional way of life and the struggle of individuals, men and women, to achieve independence and engage with the wider world. Vaughan went on to write ten novels of varying style, including *The Invader* (1928) and *The Soldier and The Gentlewoman* (1932), as well as two plays and short stories, including the novella *A Thing of Nought* (1934), which reflects the star-crossed lovers theme of her first novel. She died in 1985.

THE BATTLE TO THE WEAK

A THING OF NOUGHT

HILDA VAUGHAN

PARTHIAN
LIBRARY OF WALES

'...and the race is not to the swift,
nor the battle to the strong'

Ecclesiastes

Parthian
The Old Surgery
Napier Street
Cardigan
SA43 1ED
www.parthianbooks.co.uk

The Library of Wales is a Welsh Assembly Government
initiative which highlights and celebrates Wales' literary
heritage in the English language.

Published with the financial support of
the Welsh Books Council.

www.libraryofwales.org

Series Editor: Dai Smith

The Battle to the Weak first published in 1925
A Thing of Nought first published in 1934
© Hilda Vaughan 1925
Library of Wales edition 2010
Foreword © Fflur Dafydd 2010
Publishing Editor: Penny Thomas
All Rights Reserved

ISBN 978-1-906998-25-7

Cover design: www.theundercard.com
Cover image: *Angels in their Anguish* by Clive Hicks-Jenkins 2010

Printed and bound by Gwag Gomer, Llandysul, Wales
Typeset by Lucy Llewellyn

British Library Cataloguing in Publication Data

A cataloguing record for this book is available from the British Library.

LIBRARY OF WALES

FOREWORD

Much of my early education left me completely oblivious to Welsh women writers writing in English. Even though R.S. Thomas was studied on the syllabus, and Dylan Thomas was referenced repeatedly, when it came to the women I was only aware of a handful of writers, and most of those, I was told, wrote in Welsh, not English. Towering above them all was the writer Kate Roberts, hailed as 'Brenhines ein Llên', (Queen of our Literature), whose short stories of hardship and endurance often left me and my friends feeling disheartened for days. And so for escapism, we would turn to our English lessons, where we could read rather of the trials and tribulations of Jane Eyre and the Bennett sisters; scenarios that seemed to communicate something profound, interesting and exciting about the human condition, and more so about love, which was, of course, a major preoccupation of ours in those early days of womanhood. On the corridors of a Welsh-speaking school we'd talk in English literary riddles and quotes so that the boys would not guess at our intentions, and when our hearts were inevitably broken, and the dark clouds of disappointment and doubt would appear; that would be when we would revert back to Welsh, and start quoting Kate Roberts.

And so for me there seemed to be Kate Roberts at one end of the spectrum and Jane Austen and the Brontë sisters at the other and, in my mind, very little lay in between. But of course, all the while, Hilda Vaughan and her contemporaries lay in between, or maybe I should say, side by side, for Vaughan was in fact an exact contemporary of Kate Roberts, with only a year's difference between them – Roberts having being born in 1891 and Vaughan in 1892. Both died in 1985.

The Battle to the Weak, therefore, was my first encounter with the rather elusive literary figure of Hilda Vaughan, and I could not help but wonder what my impressionable, teenage self would have made of her. In the days where author images were scarcely featured on books, I was first struck by Hilda Vaughan's portrait, which stared at me from the back of the crumbling, weather-beaten 1925 edition. She is staring almost expressionlessly at the camera, not giving too much away; hair slicked neatly to the side, beads hanging from the neck, seeming far more glamorous, more aristocratic, than sharp-eyed Kate. But like Kate Roberts herself, she also had a well-known husband, and beneath the photo one is informed that 'in private life Hilda Vaughan is Mrs Charles Morgan, author of *Sparkenbroke*', and the instant this is revealed the fact ceases to be private, and Hilda Vaughan herself is partly obscured by her literary husband. In searching the portrait again for signs of this rather more demure figure of 'Mrs Charles Morgan', I catch something else in her gaze, a certain wryness, perhaps, which acknowledges the patriarchal conventions of her time, yet dares the reader to dip into the book, to discover her not as a wife or a member of a well-known family, but simply as an author and a storyteller.

And it is well worth doing so. To call this novel 'A fascinating story of farm life, laid in Breconshire on the borders of Herefordshire' as the original 1925 edition does, is almost to understate its narrative prowess and descriptive beauty. It is indeed a novel rooted to that very location and in some ways carries with it the classic traits of border experience, with tensions played out between complex characters with unsound identities – but it is also a diverse and rich novel which could speak on behalf of any part of rural Wales during that period. Above all, the reissuing of *The Battle to the Weak*, gives us an opportunity to appreciate afresh the gifted, subtle storytelling of one of the prominent voices of the Welsh borders, one whose use of language and narrative devices indeed transcends any period, and imbues the novel with a modern touch, making it feel contemporary and fresh. The sense of place is captured succinctly, effortlessly almost, and time and time again one is left reeling by the finely tuned sensory descriptions, the world that 'is without form or void', the house that is like 'a button mushroom with snowy top and flesh-coloured stem', as Vaughan creates wonderful optical illusions with the deftness of a watercolour artist. She conjures character in very few brushstrokes – and when Esther comes bounding down the path of 'crushed cockle shells', we are instantly drawn to the lovely, dutiful, fascinating Esther, who, like any credible character in a work of fiction, undergoes many changes throughout the novel, and who finds herself hardened by circumstance, unwilling to yield to love in her later years.

And yet, the first flush of love she feels towards Rhys Lloyd as an impressionable eighteen year old, certainly would have engaged with the younger reader in me who felt so enamoured of Austen and Brontë. Looking back objectively on it now, I can see the disparity between my world and Austen's, not only in terms of the period but in terms of the values of the English gentry of the late eighteenth and early nineteenth century, so far removed from my own world. Of course, this may have been part of her appeal, but in reading *The Battle to the Weak*, I was struck by how a novel like this would have resonated entirely differently with my group of friends, brought up as we were in the rural area of the Teifi Valley, many of us living on farms or friendly with farming families. Esther and Glenys are almost robust, rural antidotes to Jane and Elizabeth Bennett, and their emotional journeys, though darker, are also so much more illuminating in the long term.

The whole range of woman's experience is to be seen in this rich tapestry of a novel – from the passionate Glenys and the poor, suffering Annie Bevan, to the misguided yet well-meaning Megan, and Vaughan is careful to eschew happy, straightforward endings for her characters. Their fates are all brought about through their dealings with men, and these are never simple or clear cut, with the battle between the sexes often involving a hearty struggle of values before a truce can be reached. We see also a similar pattern to Megan Lloyd's life in Vaughan's crafty and sophisticated story, *A Thing of Nought*, also reissued in this Library of Wales edition. Here again is a female character pining for a man who has been sent overseas on his travels, and yet driven to forget him, and eventually forced into an unhappy marriage. But the more compact form of the short story allows a more mystical, otherworldly narrative to flourish on this particular canvas, one which haunts the reader for days.

Esther finds herself at an emotional border towards the end of the novel; as Vaughan contemplates a tentative happy ending for her heroine. Like Jane Eyre, Esther is called to her suitor's side in illness and injury, and finding him in this state, emasculated and dependent, finally accepts herself as his equal, feeling that: 'Rhys the suitor, for whom she felt deep admiration and awe, had never been so dear to her as was this Rhys, the sick child who had spoken so fretfully and who had fallen asleep in his chair.' Like Jane Eyre, Esther becomes empowered here, finally finding the familiarity for which she has been searching, the homeliness she craves, and there may also be something quintessentially Welsh in this, too, not a world away from the understated denouements of Kate Roberts' stories.

Although there was no question of Hilda Vaughan replacing Kate Roberts on our syllabus (it was, after all, a Welsh-language syllabus), one wonders whether, in fact, Hilda Vaughan's alternative voice would have made an interesting addition to our English classes back in the 1990s. Esther Bevan may be denied the privileges of the Bennett Sisters and the education of Jane Eyre, but she is, in many ways, a shrewder, more sharply drawn character, who embodies the land around her, and who would have spoken more directly to generations of young women brought up in rural areas. As Rhys Lloyd states towards the end of the novel: 'She's of the land... maybe as that is how she is bein' so dear to me. My nature is rooted in hers like, same as 'tis rooted in the soil from which both of us is springing.'

Fflur Dafydd

CONTENTS

THE BATTLE
TO THE WEAK

PROLOGUE

For an hour after sunrise, a shepherd who stood upon the summit of the Garth might have believed himself returned to the first days of creation. For 'there went up a mist from the earth, and watered the whole face of the ground'. Later in the day it would be possible, from this point, to look westward into the bleak country of Wales and eastward over the richer pasturage of Herefordshire. Now the world was without form and void; the valley beneath and the hills beyond were alike hidden.

The mist thinned slowly as time passed. Presently the upper slopes of the hillside became visible like the sea coast of an island itself half-submerged, and the higher patches of lightness admitted a dominant blue from the sky. From one of these – a picture of dull pastel in a billowy frame – emerged the quivering outline of a farm.

A man on horseback stooped from his saddle to kiss a

girl who carried a baby in her arms. As he straightened himself he glanced over his shoulder at his house and its outbuildings. Whitewash still fresh spoke of a new tenant, and, though his pride of ownership had already lost its first fine savour, John Bevan had not ceased to talk long and loud of 'My farm', 'My stock', and 'My house'. He surveyed them now with obvious pleasure; then turned once more to the frail figure of his wife. 'She is bein' my missus, too,' he reflected. 'Not lookin' her best now, she isn't, but when I was marryin' her there was a lot as 'ould have liked to have her, and I was cuttin' 'em all out.'

When he had first seen her, faintly flushed by the excitements of the yearly pleasure fair, her delicate prettiness had appeared to him like that of a wild rose. Since then she had faded fast, and her expression threatened to become peevish. Seeing her daily, he had scarcely noticed the change, but she knew it was creeping upon her. Her manner was the more timid because she understood that what small influence she had over him would vanish with her physical attractions.

'Payin' less and less heed to me he'll be, and all along o' the children I do bear him,' she reflected, as she watched him ride off briskly down the cart track which led from Pengarreg to the valley below.

Straightening herself, she carried her bundle back into the kitchen where she put it in the wicker cradle beside the hearth. She was glad to have disposed of it, for the next baby, to whom she must give birth in three months' time, demanded the whole slight stock of her vitality. She was thankful that Esther seldom cried, and proud of the child's appearance, which even John Bevan's unmarried sisters

4

were forced to admire. Yet she was disappointed and shocked at finding so little pleasure in her motherhood.

'I do wish as I were not havin' another so soon,' she sighed, looking down at the round little head, covered with golden-red fluff, soft as a duckling's down. 'I don't seem to take no delight in Esther now, like what I did when she were first born.' She turned away listlessly from the cradle. 'And indeed I don't know how to come around the work in this great big old house. I was a deal happier in the small little one as we were havin' the first year o' our marriage. Times 'on't never be like that no more. The boss he do seem to think more o' his drink than he do o' me since he comed into his grandfather's money.'

With a deepening line of worry between her brows she began to clear away the breakfast. A saucer slipped through her fingers, and falling on to the stone floor broke to pieces with the tinkling sound of ice.

'Oh dear, oh dear!' she cried. Little Esther opened her round grey eyes and stared solemnly.

To her the room was a vast place in which giants moved to and fro about their mysterious business. Sometimes they came and clapped their hands and smiled at her, and she smiled back at them, a slow, fat smile that produced a dimple in each of her cheeks: but for the greater part of her time she lay unheeded, gazing at the strange sights, and listening to the noises around her. She had already begun to distinguish the sounds of pain and anger, and her mother's exclamation of distress awoke a dim response in her. She tried to say the word they had been at such pains to teach her, but it was unheard in the clatter of crockery. She tried to struggle out of her cradle,

5

a new and exciting accomplishment, but she was wound up in a thick shawl and could not extricate herself. Her impulse was to cry; but, as that seldom brought her attention or relief, she lay still, whimpering slightly, and fighting with fat little pink hands to free herself from bondage. In the attempt she grew sleepy. Her mother had gone from the room, and it was profoundly quiet. A sheepdog slunk in at the open door. Having sniffed the floor for crumbs, he came to the cradle-side, wagged his tail shyly, and licked the clutching fingers. Once more Esther became wide awake, and this time she crooned with delight; but at the sound of a human footfall, and the fear of a blow, the big warm creature that was soft to touch was gone. The world was full of bright things at which Esther grabbed, trying to hold them because they pleased her, or to convey them to her mouth in order to find out if they were good to taste. Some of them, like the sunshine on the wall, could never be caught, and others were snatched away from her by the giants. She did not know why the friendly dog had gone. She was lonely and began to cry, but after a while her sobs turned to deep breathing and she fell asleep.

Annie Bevan had started a dozen of her tasks and finished none. Already she was exhausted, though the long summer's day lay before her. She dragged herself into the kitchen, and, noticing that the fire had gone out and would have to be re-lit, dropped on to a chair, laid her arms on the table, and hid her face in them. 'Three months more,' she thought, 'and me goin' weaker all the while.'

Meanwhile the man, riding along on a showy pony, was intent upon his day's outing. The moist cool air was fragrant with the meadowsweet beside the track, and with the honeysuckle which festooned the rocks and stunted may trees on the open hillside. The river valley beneath him was still shrouded in mist, so that he appeared to be riding down from the sky into a bank of white clouds. As the first rays of the sun touched them, the dew-drenched grass slopes about him began to glitter and sparkle with millions of prismatic points of light. Even to him, whose pleasures were mainly of the grosser sort, the beauty of that morning made its appeal, quickening his sense of well-being and filling him with new fire. He threw up his head and began to sing his favourite hymn – 'Jerusalem the golden, with milk and honey blest'. The words echoed from the far side of the narrow dingle down which he had begun to ride, and died away long after they had been uttered. He enjoyed making so much noise where he alone could be heard. The sound of his singing seemed to fill the universe. He flung back his shoulders, filled his lungs, and sang on lustily in a rough bass voice, lingering over the words he liked best – 'The shout of them that triumph, the song of them that feast'. So pleased was he with the performance that, having bawled out the hymn once, he began it over again; but when he reached for the second time the line 'And they who with their Leader have conquer'd in the fight', which he had rendered with great spirit on the first occasion, he had entered the mist zone, and an impenetrable curtain muffled the sound of his singing. It was light, yet he could scarcely see where he was going. Even the pricked ears of his pony were dim as though seen from a distance. He was forced to drop the reins on her neck and to let her find the way for him. He shivered with cold, and abruptly ceased to sing, feeling less secure than he had done in the importance of his own personality. His face assumed a sullen look, and he rode on quietly until he reached the valley where the track he had been following joined the main road to Llangantyn. There he gathered up his reins, turned at right angles, and trotted along briskly, for it was now level going. Only the click-click of iron horseshoes on a metalled highway, and the quiet murmuring of a river, unseen in the fog, broke the stillness.

Suddenly ahead of him loomed up another figure on horseback, riding in the same direction but at a more sober pace. He urged on his pony and overtook his fellow-traveller.

'Lloyd the Henallt, is it?' he cried as he came abreast of him. 'Well, well, and where are you off to so early?'

The man thus addressed was of a type still to be found among the Celtic peoples of Wales. His skull was long and narrow, and his black eyes slightly oblique. He was short and thin, and his yellowish complexion suggested kinship with the Portuguese. Clean-shaven, but for trim black side-whiskers, he wore a dark suit and a bowler hat, the badge of well-to-do respectability. There was nothing in his expression to indicate that he was pleased at the prospect of having company on the road, but he greeted his neighbour civilly enough.

'Good mornin' to you, Mr Bevan. What are you thinkin' o' the weather? Is it likely to take up now?'

''Deed, I don't know. It do look likely whatever with this old mist so thick first thing in the mornin'. But wherever are you off to?'

'Oh, goin' into Llangantyn, I am.'

'What for at this time o' day? There's no one ill up at your place, is there?'

'No, indeed; we're all keepin' pretty fair.'

'Maybe you're wantin' the vet, then?'

'No, no.'

'Well, you can't be goin' shoppin' at this hour?'

Elias Lloyd hesitated and shot an angry glance at his persistent questioner. At last he said reluctantly 'To tell you the truth now, I'm catching the mail down to Aberyscir.'

'You don't say! Doin' the very same as myself, then.'

Elias Lloyd turned his head sharply and peered up through the mist.

'Are *you* goin' to Aberyscir today?'

'Yes, indeed. They do tell me the cattle market there is bein' a deal better nor ours in Llangantyn. Wantin' to buy a cow, I am, so I did think to go and look for one there.'

'You are givin' yourself a terrible long journey to buy one old cow.'

John Bevan laughed. 'Oh, you aren't one to go from home, only on some partic'lar business, or to tend chapel. You don't understand a man likin' to treat hisself onst in a while. Havin' plenty o' money I am to afford an outin' since I comed into Pengarreg after grandfather,' and he glanced down patronisingly at the man whose brother had been the bailiff there in the late owner's time.

'Havin' to be tight on the money, the Lloyds is, no doubt,' he reflected. 'Not bein' in so good a position as what *I* am.'

'Maybe,' Elias Lloyd ventured, 'as I could be buyin' a cow for you – savin' you the expense of the journey...?'

9

'Crafty old fox,' thought John Bevan. 'Thinkin' to make his bit out of it.'

'You're wonderful kind, Mr Lloyd,' he answered, clapping him heartily on the shoulder, 'but indeed I'm looking forward to the trip. And what is takin' you to Aberyscir?'

'Oh! A small little matter o' business.'

'Oh indeed! Wantin' to buy summat, are you?'

'No, I'm not wantin' to buy nothin'.'

'Well, damn you, man, what are you bein' so close about? Anyone 'ould think as you was goin' to make your will.'

Elias Lloyd shifted uneasily in the saddle. 'Havin' a sale o' sheep, I am,' he announced after an interval of silence.

'Well, fancy my not hearin' o' that before! I wasn't knowin' as you carried enough sheep at the Henallt to have a regular sale like.'

''Tis my brother's sale as well as mine.'

'Your brother? Not the one as was bailiff to grandfather?'

'That's the only brother I'm havin'.'

'But he is livin' in a small little cottage alongside o' your place. He's not havin' much land to keep sheep on.'

'Enough for a few, whatever.'

'What do make you have your sale so far from home?'

'Well, indeed, I'm knowin' some good buyers down by Aberyscir.'

'Well, well.'

Conversation languished.

As they neared Llangantyn, the mist grew more transparent, and, lifting suddenly, hung in quivering trails

10

upon the hills on either side of the valley. Flat pastures came into view, gay with the lush grass of early summer, in which the placid cows stood knee deep. The river that had come dashing down from the mountains, foaming and furious, broadened out, and ran smoothly between low banks.

'Rich land here,' observed John Bevan.

Elias Lloyd grunted his assent. Side by side they rode over the stone bridge, and into the sleepy little town. The shutters of the shop windows creaked and groaned as they were taken down, as if they were unwilling as the townsfolk themselves to be disturbed in their late slumbers.

'Now is the time to be showin' these old townies as honest farmers are astir,' cried John Bevan, eager for an opportunity to show off his horsemanship. 'I never did see such a late-risin' lazy lot,' and he set his pony at a gallop that sent sparks flying from the cobblestones, and made the clatter of hooves echo through the streets.

Opposite the Greyhound Hotel he pulled her up, so regardless of her mouth that she reared and came to a standstill on her haunches. Flinging himself off, he shouted for the ostler, and swaggered into the bar, pleasantly conscious of the superiority of such an entrance to that of the sober Methodist, who rode quietly into the yard, dismounted slowly, and led his own horse into the stable. A couple of drinks further strengthened John Bevan's self-esteem, and he strode off to the railway station, humming to himself so gaily that passers-by turned to stare at him.

The twenty-mile journey to Aberyscir was accomplished leisurely in an hour and a half.

The narrow streets of the old-fashioned town were

11

crowded to suffocation, and the high-pitched voices of a Welsh crowd, engaged in the congenial pursuit of bartering, made a deafening clamour. John Bevan, coming from an anglicised border county, could not speak his own language, and despised his fellow-countrymen who were able to do so as much as they despised him. But he could shout as loud and gesticulate as freely in a bargain as the best of them; and when he had struck his man's extended hand with a dramatic gesture of finality signifying that the deal was made, he led away the cow he had bought, satisfied that he had done a creditable morning's work. He had some difficulty in finding the drover who was to take her home for him with other cattle bound for Llangantyn. The delay made him thirsty. Talking to the bystanders in the heat and dust of the market made him yet thirstier, and when he succeeded in tracking down his man and disposing of the cow, he adjourned with several dealers to the nearest public house, and stood them round after round of drinks. They left him at last, flushed and elated, with his hat pushed back on his head, and his huge red hands thrust deep into his pockets. Out into the street he strolled, jingling his money and wondering whether he had better take the next train home.

'There's work to be done there,' he reflected, 'and it 'ould pleasure the Missus wonderful to see me back early.'

A dealer leading a colt shouted a greeting at him as he passed. A fine colt! John Bevan with his eye for a horse must needs go to look at it. He was back in the smithfield before he was aware of it, and engaged in a lively piece of banter with a young woman against whom he had jostled.

'Damn it all,' he thought, 'there's a bit o' life to be

12

seen here. Best enjoy myself now as I've got the chanst.'

The late afternoon found him entering another public house for a last drink on his way to the railway station.

'No more nor one,' he told himself.

A hand was laid on his arm, and looking down he saw the stunted figure of Ben Davies, a neighbour of his from the Llangantyn district.

'Why, Mr Davies,' he cried, before he had recalled that the man was a noted mischief-maker whom wise folk avoided. ''Tis good to meet someone here as can talk a word o' English. Come and have a drink, man.'

Nothing loth, the little cringing fellow followed him to the counter and began to administer compliments. For the sake of these John Bevan stood him another drink, and another, and because by that time he was himself becoming fuddled and ready to give anything to a man who pleased him, or to knock down one who did not, he forgot about his train home and his good intentions, and settled himself down to enjoy one of his drinking bouts.

'You're a good fellow, Ben Davies,' he said, as though he defied his listener to contradict him. 'I don't see it fair to say nothin' against you like what some o' them old Methodists do do. Give me a man as can drink – like the gentries; my friends is all bein' gentlemen.' And he laughed loudly.

Then Ben Davies saw his opportunity for getting even with Elias Lloyd who had denounced him at a chapel meeting. With eyes craftily narrowed and head on one side, he began: 'You are bein' in wonderful good spirits today, Mr Bevan.'

'Come you, we must all be havin' a joke sometimes.'

13

'Jokes is all very well; but I could be tellin' you summat – but *there* – I mustn't be sayin' nothin', or I'll be gettin' myself into trouble. I 'ould be likin' to serve you, Mr Bevan, since you are bein' that kind; but I'm a poor man, and we must each of us be thinkin' of our own skin.'

'Whatever do you mean, man?'

'What I am sayin', Mr Bevan. Wantin' to act like a neighbour to you, I am.'

'Well?'

'But 'tisn't hardly my business. And, mind you, 'tis only hearsay. I don't know nothin' for certain.'

'Out with it, man.'

'You 'on't never be mentionin' my name if I do tell you?'

'No, no. Speak up, can't you?'

Ben Davies sidled up closer.

'Are you seein' anything strange with Elias Lloyd's sheep, the ones as he and his brother is makin' a sale of today?' he whispered.

John Bevan stared down at him. 'I haven't been lookin' at his old sheep. What are they to me?'

Ben Davies shrugged his shoulders as though disclaiming any responsibility. 'Maybe they aren't nothin'.' He finished his drink and wiped his mouth with the back of his hand. Then he added: 'But maybe as they are.' There was another pause. 'All I do say is as some o' the wethers do look as if they'd had their ear-marks altered so as they shan't be recognised.'

John Bevan made a clicking sound with his tongue. 'Stolen?' he suggested vaguely looking round the crowded room and wishing that someone would strike up a song.

14

He wanted to join in a chorus and to beat time upon the counter with his fist, but he was not sufficiently drunk to start singing alone.

'Stolen,' repeated Ben Davies ominously. 'Stolen, sure, to be. I wonder now whose sheep they may have been?' After a while he added: 'What 'ould you be doin' now, if someone was to steal sheep o' yours, Mr Bevan?'

'I'd be killin' 'em just.'

'And serve 'em right too. 'Tis a wicked thing robbin' a neighbour.... Was you countin' all your sheep when you did come into your property after your grandfather?'

'Not just at first I wasn't. The snow was lyin' that deep when I took over the place.'

Ben Davies shook his head. 'Pity. Pity indeed.'

John Bevan stared at him for a full minute, and the colour heightened in his already flushed face.

'Are you meanin' as them sheep was stolen off o' *me*?' he demanded.

Ben Davies shrank away from him. 'I 'ouldn't like to say so, Mr Bevan.'

'Well, I'll be findin' out whatever.' His voice rose to a shout. 'I'll never be restin' until I do know the truth. And if those sheep was bein' mine...'

He left the sentence unfinished, and brought down his clenched fist upon the counter so that the glasses danced. A number of strangers standing near turned to stare at his angry face.

'An ugly customer that,' whispered one.

'Ah! But he's a fine swampin' lad. Look at the shoulders he's got on him, and a neck like a bull, just. Them big red-haired fellows is terrors to fight. I've known a lot o' 'em, all

15

with the same hissy tempers. You mind them fierce-rollin'
eyes he's got too. I 'ouldn't like to handle a colt with eyes
like that, and men and horses is bein' wonderful sim'lar.'

'Ah, well! Them noisy ones is mostly bein' bested by
the quiet little 'uns. Look at that small little sneakin' chap
with him – for all the world like a weasel after a big dull
old rabbit.'

'I don't believe,' thundered John Bevan, 'as the man is
born as 'ould dare to rob me under my very nose.'

The mocking grins which spread over the listeners'
faces goaded him to fury.

'If that's what you do think, I'll soon be showin' you,'
he shouted. 'Out o' my way, you.'

He flung out into the street. The loitering crowd there
impeded his progress, and he swore under his breath as he
elbowed his way through it, whilst the sweat poured down
his face and the dust made his eyes smart. In spite of his
haste the Lloyds' sale was over, and the last lot of sheep
was being unpenned when he burst into the smithfield.

'Holt,' he cried, 'I do want to look at your sheep.'

A grey-bearded farmer looked him up and down with
evident disapproval.

'No use, man. I've only now been buyin' 'em, and I'm
not wishful to sell again.'

'I don't want to buy the damned sheep.'

'Then get out o' my way, can't you? Time's money to
honest folk.' And muttering something about drunken
fools, the farmer shouldered past him, and shouted to the
boy in front of the flock to go on.

'Stop those sheep,' roared John Bevan, as they pattered
out of sight round a bend in the road leading out of the

smithfield. 'I do demand to see their ear-marks.'

'That you 'on't do,' said their new owner. 'I've paid my deposit on the sheep to one man, and I don't want no bother about their belongin' to another. I can see right enough what you are gettin' at. You leave me and my sheep alone.'

He hurried away, pursued by drunken shouting.

'Damn you, you old fool! You can't stop me to look at the sheep. They're bein' mine, I tell you. I don't care who do know it. I'm an honest man. I've been robbed. *Robbed*, d'you hear? A swindlin' hypocritical neighbour o' mine's robbed me. That's why he was bein' so close about his business here this mornin'. I didn't think at the time, but 'tis plain as daylight now. *I'll* teach him to steal my sheep, *I'll...*'

The farmer whom he had followed down the street turned and faced him.

'Look here, there's the policeman comin'. You go and tell him what it's all about.' And he left him standing alone, his feet planted wide apart, his hat pushed far back on his head, swaying slightly as he stood. Seeing the policeman's eye upon him, he ceased to shout and tried to pull himself together. Since he had no evidence that the sheep had been stolen, it would be wise to make enquiries into the matter before raising a scandal; but the effort needed to control his temper made him rage the more. Clenching his fists until his nails bit into the horny palms of his hands, he staggered off in search of the auctioneer, and having, with difficulty and delay, collected the names and addresses of those to whom the sheep had been sold, returned to the public house in which he had left Ben Davies. Other farmers from Llangantyn had joined the

17

company and greeted him with derisive laughter.

'Well, well,' cried one of them. 'I was allus hearin' as you did think yourself too sharp to be bested by no one. Fancy an innocent old Methodist stealin' the sheep off o' your grandfather's farm atween the day as he come to die and you was takin' over the place!'

'I don't say as they *was* stolen for sure,' put in Ben Davies. 'I 'ouldn't like to make no trouble.'

The others greeted this as a good joke, and their laughter, though for the moment it was not directed against himself, infuriated John Bevan. Between them they enraged him to such a pitch that at last they ceased to enjoy the fun of seeing such a boastful man made to look a fool, and became alarmed for their own safety. So they agreed with him that Elias Lloyd and his brother were unparalleled rogues, for whom no punishment could be too severe. John Bevan, meanwhile, drank more and more beer, and became, with each tankard, more fuddled and furious.

On the journey home he muttered and nodded, his head hanging foolishly first on one side and then on the other, his bloodshot eyes half-closed. Now and then a violent jerk would awaken him, and glaring around him he would announce that he intended to break every bone in the bodies of Elias Lloyd and his misbegotten brother.

Meanwhile the chapel deacon, having heard the tumult of his neighbour's arrival at Aberyscir station, had wisely kept out of his way. When they alighted at Llangantyn he was quick to reach the Greyhound Hotel, and in a few minutes he had left the town, and was urging his grass-blown pony homeward.

The river flowed serene and silvery in the quiet evening

18

light. The dusty white road was deserted. The hills on either side of it were growing dark, and the level pastures beside the river were an emerald velvet. The mood of this still twilight hour was soothing even to Elias Lloyd, who ordinarily cared little for beauty and was more concerned with the jealousy of God than with His gifts. His pace slackened as he approached the steep track which led up to his farm on the hillside. With feet shaken clear of the stirrups and reins dropped on his pony's neck, he jogged along with his mind for once empty of fear or wrath. He had not reckoned on John Bevan's ability to sit a horse at full gallop when he was almost too drunk to stand upright, and the thunder of hooves on the road came as an unexpected warning that he was being pursued.

'That drunkard, sure to be,' he thought. 'I'd best be givin' him the slip quick. He's dangerous tonight. By mornin' he'll be forgettin' the lies some mischief-makers have been tellin' him in market, and if he's still bein' inclined to quarrel, I'll go and reason him out of it. If there was maybe *one* or perhaps two o' his sheep got put in with my brother's by mistake, he can't never prove it.'

Without stopping to look over his shoulder he seized the reins, thrust his feet hurriedly into the stirrups, and urged his fat pony forward. The drowsy valley was filled with the clamour of iron beating furiously upon stone, and a cloud of dust arose. But fast as Elias Lloyd rode, John Bevan gained upon him.

'Come on, damn you, come on,' he shouted, striking his pony blow after blow with his stick.

With terror-stricken eyes and nostrils distended, she galloped on, labouring for breath and flecked with foam.

'Now I've got you,' yelled her rider as he came abreast of his quarry. 'Now I'll learn you to go stealin' my sheep, you bloody hypocrite – you!'

Elias Lloyd swerved out of the way just in time to avoid a shattering blow, and as the other rode at him again, he wheeled his horse round and shouted with all the vehemence of extreme fear: 'Don't you be hittin' me now. Holt, for the Lord's sake! Holt! There's some mistake, man.'

'Mistake,' roared John Bevan. 'You dare to call it a mistake – stealin' my sheep and making o' me a laughin' stock amongst strangers?'

And he rode at his enemy once more, and tried to seize his horse by the bridle. In doing so he almost rolled out of his own saddle, and the two terrified ponies reared and plunged. Elias Lloyd, always a poor horseman, and helpless now with fright, clung to the peak of his saddle. At that moment, his antagonist, quick to recover himself, struck him in the face with all his force. Elias Lloyd uttered a loud cry, swayed, and fell. His panic-stricken animal galloped away towards the mountainside on which it had been bred, and John Bevan, on his own sweating pony that quivered under him as if she were about to drop with exhaustion, sat looking down at his victim. Sobered by the sight of what he had done, he leant out of the saddle.

'Are you hurted?' he asked foolishly.

The injured man groaned, and covered his face with his hands.

'You are not dead whatever,' the victor muttered in a tone of relief. Now that he had experienced the satisfaction of striking someone, his anger had abated, and the matter

of the sheep was forgotten. 'Shall I be helpin' of you up?'
he enquired; but Elias Lloyd staggered to his feet unaided.

'My face is all broke to pieces,' he groaned. From
between his fingers there oozed blood.

'Indeed, I'm sorry as I was hittin' you so hard,' John
Bevan confessed.

Elias Lloyd withdrew his hands, and looked up with a
face distorted with pain and fury. 'May the Lord requite
you for this,' he shrieked. 'May you be desolate and
rewarded with shame.'

'I've said as I wasn't meanin' to hit you so hard.
Indeed, and I'm terrible sorry for what I've done.'

'Get out o' my sight, can't you! Oh, the pain! Oh Lord,
'tis terrible! Do thou requite mine enemies for this.' He
raised his voice as if he were praying in chapel. 'Let them
be as the dust before the wind, and the angel of the Lord
scatterin' them. Let their way be dark and slippery, and let
the angel of the Lord persecute them. Let hot burning
coals of fire fall upon them, let them be cast into the fire
and into the pit that they never rise up again.'

John Bevan turned and rode away sullenly, but the
deacon, his face and hands smeared with blood, continued
to stand in the deserted road and to curse his neighbour
aloud in the words of Holy Writ.

The steep hill on which were perched the homesteads of
Pengarreg and the Henallt overlooked the road to
Llangantyn. At the foot of the hill, confronting each other
from opposite sides of the road, were the church and the
chapel. A diminutive schoolhouse, a blacksmith's forge and
two or three labourers' cottages completed the village of

21

Lewisbridge. The oldest building in the place was the church, ivy-covered and guarded by three yew trees. The newest was the red-brick Calvinistic-Methodist chapel, which glared impudently at its rival from across the way. The two places of worship were emptied at the same hour on Sunday mornings, and the separate streams of black-clad men and women mingled upon the common highway. They were indistinguishable from each other. In earlier years the younger churchwomen had been made conspicuous by their coloured clothes, but soon the less strict among the Methodists had followed their example, and gay ribbons were no longer peculiar to the establishment.

On the Sunday after his encounter with Elias Lloyd, John Bevan slouched out of church with his hands thrust into his pockets, and the defiant look of a naughty child on his face. Detaining him in the porch, his wife clung to his arm and began a whispered entreaty.

''Tis a terrible bad job to be comin' into a district, strangers from ten miles away as we are, and quarrellin' with our next o' neighbours within the year. Indeed, and I dare say as there wasn't no truth in what you was bein' told agin Mr Lloyd, and you havin' had a drop o' drink...'

'I've heard enough about that from you already,' he answered, jerking his arm away from her.

She bit her lip, and tears, ever ready to overflow, came into her eyes. 'Oh dear!' she thought, 'I do allus seem to be sayin' the wrong thing when I'm just beginnin' to win him round.'

She drooped against the wall of the porch, and her husband stood before her, while gossiping groups of neighbours passed with inquisitive glances, and,

22

sauntering out of the churchyard, mixed with the larger crowd from chapel.

The last to appear from under the red-brick archway were the Lloyds. Elias came first with small dark eyes peering out vengefully from the bandages that swathed his face. After him came his wife, with one hand laid on his shoulder, and the other clasping that of a little lad of three or four. She was a tall, gaunt woman, some years older than her husband. Every line of her rigid figure suggested unyielding hostility, for she had been telling the minister what she thought of John Bevan, and had worked herself up into a state of righteous fury. She was followed by her father, spare and stern of countenance as herself, and by Evan Lloyd, whose sallow skin and crafty eyes resembled those of his brother. They were all dressed with neat severity in their Sabbath black, and the three men carried ponderous hymn books in their hands. Mrs Lloyd wore gloves of black kid which were too long at the fingertips and had left a purple stain on the hot little palm of the child. He alone of the party was not engaged in indignant discussion, and he looked up now and then in frightened bewilderment.

Seeing the group pause in the road, Mrs Bevan turned once more to her husband. 'Go you on now whilst there's a chanst o' makin' it up,' she urged, 'or maybe he'll be havin' the law on you for hittin' him.'

'Oh, a' right,' he growled at last. 'I'll go, since you 'on't give over else,' and unwillingly leaving the shelter of the churchyard, he accosted his enemy on neutral ground.

'I 'ould like to be speakin' a word to you in private,' he announced in a surly tone.

Four pairs of eyes, full of astonishment and hostility,

looked him up and down, but no one spoke. The homeward-bound church and chapel-goers stopped and stared, and their presence became a humiliation to John Bevan.

'Can't we be goin' somewhere quiet to have a talk by ourselves?' he asked.

Mrs Lloyd's tongue was loosed. 'Did you ever hear the like o' that?' she cried shrilly, appealing to her husband. 'Havin' the face to ask you to go off alone with him after doin' what he's done. Why, he might be killin' o' you outright this time.'

John Bevan glared at her. It was like a woman's meanness, he reflected, to blame a man after he had become sober for what he had done when he was drunk.

'I am not speakin' to you,' he retorted.

'Nor am I wishful to speak to *you*,' put in Elias Lloyd.

'No, indeed, I should think not,' cried his wife. 'Come away, Elias. Come away, all o' you. He's no fit company for God-fearin' folk.'

She turned on her heel, dragging the child after her, but Annie Bevan interposed.

'Indeed and indeed,' she wailed, 'only anxious to make it up, the boss is. Do you be givin' him a chanst now to ask your pardon.'

'No call for *you* to interfere whatever,' he answered, roughly pushing her out of his way. 'I'm not askin' no man's pardon, and this business is atween Elias Lloyd and myself.'

'That it is; and I'll not be forgettin' of it neither.'

'Call yourself a Christian, do you? Not willin' to forgive nothin'.'

'Spoilin' his face for life, you have been, you brute, you!'

'But I was in drink when I struck him.'

'The more shame to you, then.'

'Aye, aye. 'Tis written as drunkards and them that make a lie shall not enter into the Kingdom of Heaven.'

All their voices rose together in an effort to drown one another. In the background stood Annie Bevan, passing her crumpled handkerchief across her lips. The little boy had begun to cry in anticipation of the blows which usually followed angry words, but no one paid the least heed to him. The bystanders had edged themselves closer, and were grinning. Their mirth stung John Bevan to fury.

'Well, if I do go to hell for bein' a drunkard, you'll go there for bein' a liar – a liar and a thief too,' he shouted.

Elias Lloyd turned his back on him. 'I'm not stayin' to listen to no more o' this low talk,' he explained to those about him.

'You'll stay and hear the truth whatever,' his neighbour yelled. 'You and your bloody hypocrite of a brother, as do set up to be so religious, have been stealin' the sheep off of his old master's place. Robbin' the dyin' – that's a nice thing for a deacon to be doin'.'

Evan Lloyd moved away hastily, making signs to the others to follow him, but Elias turned round.

'I'll have the law on you for callin' me a thief,' he declared. 'The neighbours here 'ull be bearin' witness to it.'

'I'll have the law on you for stealin' my sheep, then.'

'You'll have to prove as I did do it first.'

'That I will, you...'

'Shame on you, man,' cried one of the bystanders, cutting short a string of foul names. 'There's language to be usin' on the Lord's Day. Can't you wait till Monday mornin'?'

The young men and boys broke into a titter; and in haughty silence the Lloyds moved off, the child with his big dark eyes full of tears and his little mouth trembling.

John Bevan, aware that he had made a fool of himself, stood in the road, shouting after their retreating figures. His florid face was sweating, and he pushed back his hat. The day was still and sultry. The sun shone dimly through luminous clouds. The glare of the road was hurtful; the air oppressive as if before a storm. All the birds were hushed, and the monotonous sound of the river arose loud and persistent.

Gradually the crowd dispersed amid a subdued hum of excited conversation. 'Now there'll be a time on us,' was the general opinion, and instinctively, not knowing the rights of the case, the church folk began to decry Elias Lloyd for a dishonest humbug, and the chapel-goers to denounce John Bevan for his blasphemous violence.

Annie Bevan, left alone with her husband, presented a pathetic figure in an ill-fitting black dress that emphasised rather than concealed her condition. Thinking of little Esther whom she had left sleeping in her cradle, she was filled with a sense of dread.

'Oh, boss, boss,' she lamented, 'why was you bein' so rash? This is only the beginning o' worse troubles. Who do know where it may all end, for us and our children as is yet to come?'

BOOK I

CHAPTER 1

Originally the roof of Ocean View had been slated, but layer upon layer of plaster and whitewash had softened the contours until they resembled those of a thatched cottage. The walls of the little house were tinted pink, and from a distance it looked like a button mushroom with snowy top and flesh-coloured stem. A white wall enclosed the trim garden. From the front door to the garden gate was a double row of large pebbles, polished by the scouring of waves. The owner of the place had expressed her love of decoration by ornamenting them with spots and flourishes of white paint. All the diminutive panes of the four front windows were freshly cleaned, and twinkled in the evening sunshine; and the rim of brass that adorned the doorstep glittered like gold.

Esther came out of the house, singing softly to herself, and wandered down the path of crushed cockleshells. She was dressed in the plain black frock in which she went to church, to funerals, and to fairs. Her abundant mass of coarse brown hair, shot with threads of copper, was coiled up beneath a black straw hat, the brim of which turned down demurely and shaded a face neither dainty enough to be described as 'pretty' nor classical enough to deserve the word 'beautiful'. At the end of the small garden she turned and surveyed her aunt's home with profound approval.

''Tis like a doll's house as I was seein' in the toyshop at Swansea,' she reflected. 'I do wish if I was havin' one like it for Gladys and myself.'

She had been staying with her aunt for three weeks now, and already she had begun to blossom like a flower that is transplanted into congenial soil. The spare outlines of her girlish figure were becoming more rounded, her movements less shrinking, her carriage self-confident, and her whole air healthier and happier than it had been under her parents' roof.

''Tis good,' she murmured, stroking the garden wall, '*all* good – and Aunt Polly is bein' the best o' the lot.'

Aunt Polly kept a shop as well as a cottage and a garden full of flowers. Esther could see the large glass bottles, gay with sweets, the picture postcards, the tins of cocoa and packets of cigarettes ranged in an attractive pattern within the window on the left of the front door. In the midst of cooking her midday dinner, Aunt Polly was ever ready to serve a customer in the leisurely gossiping fashion in which business was transacted in Aberdulas. Her niece had often marvelled at her, leaning with plump arms folded upon the counter, as though she were deaf to the sounds of frizzling bacon which issued from the

30

kitchen adjoining the shop, and had nothing to do in the world but to entertain her visitor. Yet the meals were never burnt, nor the crockery smeary from careless washing, and there were always fresh flowers upon the table. Esther and Gladys had delighted in flowers when they were little, but it had never occurred to them that grown-up people could care for such things, unless, of course, they were the 'quality' who had plenty of time to waste. Aunt Polly was not one of the 'quality', but her quiet days contained leisure as well as work. Night after night she would sit in the snug little parlour, playing hymn tunes upon the piano, and Esther, curled up in a deep wicker armchair, such as she had never sat in before, would let her eyes wander over the flamboyant wallpaper, sprawling with pink roses, and wonder why her own parents could not lead such a life as this in so ideally lovely a home.

'If only Gladys could share it with me,' she thought as she waited for her aunt in the garden. 'But maybe as we can both o' us be goin' out into service together when she do come a bit stronger, and then we'll be savin' up enough to buy a small little shop of our own some day. Father and mother 'ull be mad if we do leave 'em, but I do mean to be happy if I can, whatever they do say. Ever since I've comed to know Aunt Polly I've believed as 'tis right to be happy same as what she is.'

Turning her back on the house, she rested her elbows on the garden wall and gazed out to sea. Ocean View was the last of a straggling line of cottages which began halfway up a steep hillside behind the village and ended at the brink of a semicircular cove. Here the road lost itself in the shore within a few yards of Esther. The low cliff fell sheer at the place where she was standing so that, by leaning over the wall, she could have dropped a stone into the lapping froth beneath her. The sea was unusually calm – green inshore, and further out a deep blue, slashed by a golden pathway towards the setting sun.

'Now I am ready,' Mrs Jones announced, coming out of the house in her unhurrying way.

Her ample person, clothed in a voluminous black silk pelisse, seemed to fill up the whole of the garden, and her smile was wide as the ocean. She carefully locked the door, hid the key under the mat, where everyone in Aberdulas knew that it was to be found, and clasping an umbrella, a huge hymn book, a folded handkerchief, and a paper bag full of peppermints, led the way up the road through the village.

'We are bein' a bit late,' she observed, without appearing to be in the least distressed by the fact, and nodding right and left to the neighbours who stood at their cottage doors enjoying the close of a working day.

'Goin' to the singin' practice up yonder?' one of them called out.

'Yes, yes, wantin' my niece to hear how good we are singin' in these parts, I am.'

'You'll have to look sharp, then,' the neighbour shouted after her; but she continued at her own steady pace, like a broad-beamed ship in full sail.

'I never did see no use in rushin',' she informed Esther. 'Allus managin' to be there somehow, I am, but never afore time, lookin' all of a hurry and over-anxious, like what some folks is doin'.'

She chuckled at the thought. 'I'll tell you the way to catch a sweetheart, my gal. Don't you be too oncomin' at the start, it do put 'em shy, same as a customer will get with a shopkeeper as is in too much of a hurry to sell his goods. Not as I do fancy you are one to err on *that* side. Don't you be leavin' it too long neither. 'Tis a good job to be punctual in everything, I do say; in courtin' same as in everythin' else, you did ought to be there on the nick o' time.'

Esther gave one of her quiet throaty laughs.

''Tis the serious truth I'm tellin' of you,' her aunt protested. 'That's how I was gettin' holt o' your poor uncle. Very shy at the start he was, so I took him easy; but when I seed as he'd let the business stay there for years if nothin' happened to sharpen it up, well, I gave it a bit of a turn myself. Allus meanin' to marry him I was, long afore he did ever fancy me.'

'Oh, Aunty!'

Mrs Jones gave her niece a look of sly amusement. 'And why shouldn't an 'oman be havin' her fancy same as a man?'

Esther could not say. She only knew that it was contrary to the vague notions of modesty she had acquired from her Sunday-school teacher. But this disconcerting aunt of hers had a gift for making prejudices seem absurd.

'I don't believe you do mean half you say.' Esther tried to find excuses for her as she looked at the round roguish face, embedded, with scarcely any indication of a neck, in the fat shoulders. Certainly her aunt was not beautiful; but who could help loving every bit of her, vast as she was, from the rakish tuft of jet bugles in her bonnet, that leapt to and fro with every emphatic nod of her head, to her feet which bulged over the top of her shoes, and turned out ridiculously as she walked?

She paused and studied her niece with a twinkle in her blue eyes. 'Didn't you never want to sleep with no one?'

Esther flushed. 'What a thing to say,' she cried.

'Oh, a' right, a' right. I did only mean 'ouldn't you like to marry someone? – all quite respectable.'

'*No*,' Esther affirmed with decision. 'I do never mean to marry no one. I'm not likin' men.' She had scarcely spoken to any but her father. 'A drunken, swearin' lot they mostly are, and I do see a house like yours without no man in it a deal tidier and nicer.'

'Well, well, well.' Mrs Jones laughed outright. 'You do talk about men as if they was a lot of mangy old dogs – better poisoned and out o' the way. There's men to be found as do like things as nice about a place as what you are doin'.'

'Well, *I* haven't been meetin' 'em whatever. And Gladys and I do allus mean to keep single, as long as we do live, and to stay together. I've been promisin' her that faithful.'

'How old are you?'

The tone in which the question was delivered startled Esther, and she glanced at the speaker self-consciously, wondering whether she had said anything very callow and foolish.

'Eighteen,' she murmured apologetically; 'nineteen come the autumn.'

'Ah well, time 'ull show.'

By now they had left the village behind them, and had reached a high, undulating plateau. The open country ahead, its outlines unbroken by trees or houses, was still

34

and restful as the sea. There were farms and hamlets dotted about on it, Esther knew, but they kept out of sight, sheltering in hollows from the winter gales, and nothing spoiled the illusion of profound peace and solitude.

In silence she walked on, and presently they reached their destination, a large wayside chapel that served the surrounding district. Dusk had fallen. The tombstones rose like watchful ghosts out of the rank grass, and the whispering groups of young men who hung about the door, too shy to enter until the singing should begin, had the guilty, mysterious air of conspirators.

Into the lighted building rustled Aunt Polly, the jet sequins on her pelisse making a faint jingling sound suggestive of wealth. She wedged herself into a narrow, uncomfortable pew on the ground floor, and deposited in an orderly manner on the book-rest in front of her, her umbrella, her folded handkerchief, her hymn book and her screw of peppermints. The sweets she began to suck audibly while she settled down to heavy enjoyment of what was to her a social function rather than an act of worship. Without appearing to stare indecorously, she looked about her, smiling and nodding at her acquaintances as she observed who they were with and what they were wearing.

Esther also stole a glance at the people who were near her, and was struck by something earnestly expectant in their faces. There were among them men bent double with rheumatism and manual labour, and women who had lost all beauty but that of a kindly expression; old toothless bodies wrapped in threadbare shawls, and young mothers with tired eyes, who incessantly rocked the babies they carried in their arms. There were neatly dressed farmers with the grim look of men who have had a hard struggle in business, and labourers dulled by routine, enduring and resigned. All these people had work-coarsened hands, rough and red, clasped between their knees or folded in their laps in an attitude of devotion. Yet they were not praying. They were waiting eagerly for something to happen for which they had been longing throughout the working hours of the week. Even Aunt Polly ceased after a while to signal her greetings, and fell into the prevailing mood of hushed expectancy.

Most of the younger folk had congregated in the gallery that ran round three sides of the building. Raising her eyes in their direction, Esther encountered those of a tall youth who had come into the shop one day and stared at her so intently that she had retreated in confusion into the kitchen. He was looking at her now with the same fixity, and she turned away her head.

'I'm sure I don't know what's amiss with me for a stranger to stare so,' she thought. 'He was lookin' at me just as hard when I passed him in the road the other night. It can't be along o' my bein' good lookin', nor I don't fancy as I'm all that ill-favoured neither. I can't make him out,' and she glanced up at the gallery once more.

The bright golden-brown eyes of the strange lad were still upon her.

'I do wish if he'd find summat else to look at,' she thought indignantly. ''Tis terrible rude o' him to keep starin' at me; it do make me that uneasy.'

But the conductor had taken his place, the singing began, and instantly she forgot all else.

36

The whole assembly had risen to its feet and was singing as only in Wales can an untrained crowd be found to sing, with a natural sweetness, a fervour, an innate gift of expression that more than atoned for any fault in technique. Hymn after hymn they sang in Welsh, set to tunes that, though modernised and re-named, were ancient as the race itself, wild as the hills from which it sprang. Sometimes soft and plaintive like the sighing of wind in a forest, sometimes loud and passionate as the shouting of a gale at sea, they were all in the minor key, and sad as the Celtic soul. Slowly tears gathered in Esther's eyes and brimmed over unchecked. After each hymn she brushed them away with the back of her hand, and waited in an ecstasy of melancholy for the thrilling bass voices of the men and the clear sweet sopranos and trebles of the women and boys to blend together once more in some mournful refrain. The cause of her sadness, as of their love of singing, lay deeper than reason. She was aware only of a sense of grief, tender, tragic and fearful, as the melody changed.

While she listened and wept, the young man in the gallery above leaned on the rail, watching her.

'Is her own life bein' very sad,' he wondered, 'that the tears is comin' into her eyes like that? Or is it only that the big heart of her is aching for all the sorrows of the world? Kind eyes they are; and a kind and generous mouth. She's one to be more hurt by the troubles o' others nor by her own, I do reckon. If ever I seed the face of a good 'oman, there it is, with all in it as I 'ould like to have seen in my mother's, and all as ever I dreamed of in a sweetheart's.' A wave of joy swept over him and his heart

37

was filled with a song of thanksgiving. 'I'm not in no mood for dirges tonight,' he thought. 'I'm feelin' the same as the man in the Bible that rejoiced for he had found an exceeding great treasure.'

He tried to reason himself into a critical state of mind. He had never spoken to this girl or heard the sound of her voice. He could not possibly know anything about her until he had made her acquaintance.

'Well,' he decided, 'I'll be talkin' to her tonight, so soon as ever the singin' is over. I do wish it 'ould last longer as a rule, but tonight I 'ould have it end now – *now*!'

His lean hands moved impatiently upon the rail. It seemed to him that he was suffering an interminable delay.

For Esther, time had ceased to exist. All the visible world was withdrawn beyond the magic circle of sound which, for the instant, was her whole life. Suddenly the singing stopped. Someone was praying aloud, and she awoke bewildered to see bowed heads. Immediately afterwards there broke out around her whispering and movement, and the shuffling of feet. She became aware of people pushing against her, of the varnished pinewood pews, of the bare walls of the chapel, and of unshaded oil lamps with a hurtful glare. She raised her hand to shelter her eyes, and, finding them wet with tears, was self-conscious and ashamed. Hurriedly she dried them, and, keeping her head bent so that no one might see she had been crying, followed her aunt out of the building.

'Bide you here a bit, there's some neighbours wantin' to speak to me,' came the command, and Esther was left alone leaning against the wall of the porch.

Night had stolen over the deserted countryside while

its inhabitants were gathered together within doors. Overhead bright stars glittered in the sky and on the horizon hung a luminous haze as though the air itself were full of powdered silver. From the narrow windows of the chapel came shafts of reddish light, bright and hot as that of a fire. To Esther they seemed to fight with the cold light of the rising moon.

'What we do see, and touch and taste everyday is like the lamp light,' she told herself; 'but the moonlight is like what I was feelin' now just. 'Tis every bit as real; maybe 'tis even more real nor the other, but 'tis not to be proved so easy. Some folks is afeared o' it, and some is laughin' so as to show they aren't afeared, for the seen and the unseen is strivin' together allus.'

A voice disturbed her.

'You are the very same as me. Those old hymns is wakin' something in you most folks have forgotten nowadays.'

She looked up, startled to find the bright eyes that had so disconcerted her once more fixed on her face. She shrank away.

'I am knowin' Mrs Jones the sweets,' the speaker added reassuringly, 'so I didn't see no harm in comin' to talk to you.'

Still Esther eyed him apprehensively.

'Are you waitin' for her?' he enquired.

'Yes, thank you,' she murmured in a tone which implied that she sought no other company.

There followed a moment's silence in which she looked about her uneasily. Most of the dark figures with their weird shadows had passed out of the graveyard, and Aunt Polly was nowhere to be seen.

39

'You are stayin' with her, aren't you?' the young man resumed. 'I've been seein' you about the place.'

'Yes.'

'Related to her, maybe?'

'Yes; she's my uncle's widow.'

'Are you on a visit, or come to live with her?'

'Oh, only on a visit.' And she added to herself: 'I'm sure I don't know what business it is of his.'

'What do you think of Aberdulas?'

'I do like it grand.' She found it impossible to be curt with anyone so persistently pleasant, and she went on: 'The sea is bein' wonderful.'

'Ah!' he spoke with enthusiasm, 'that it is! Wide and big! It do do me good to look at it.... You ought to be walkin' along the cliffs to the Gaer – that's my uncle's place.... What are you doin' with yourself all day?'

'Nothin'. I'm on a holiday.' The finality of her answers made him laugh.

'Are you workin' so terrible hard at home, then?'

'We're all havin' to work, I suppose.'

'Ah, I suppose. But there's some work I could fancy better nor others. Readin', now – that's my delight.'

It was her turn to laugh. 'Readin'! You don't call that work, do you?'

'Oh I don't mean only novels and the like. History, that's my line. I'd be readin' for a scholarship at Aberystwyth if I was only havin' the time; but I'm havin' to work on the farm all day, worse luck.... Mind you, I'm not dislikin' to use my hands, neither.'

He held them out, palms upwards, for her inspection. They bore the corns of manual labour, but were too slim and sensitive to be by nature those of a labourer. She found herself looking at them with interest, and from his hands her glance travelled upwards to his face. It was keen and wide-awake as no other face she had known. There was less in it of the healthy animal contentment or dulled resignation that mark the countryman. The nose was sharp, the eyes deep set, and the lips thin. In the moonlight it showed pale and haggard as the face of a man starved, but the strong voice, and the quick restless movements were those of a youth brimming over with vitality. She had never before met anyone with whom the mind was a flame to consume the body. She looked up at him attentive and puzzled.

'Life's that short,' he was complaining. 'There isn't time for near everything. It do make me mad sometimes when I've to keep on late out o' doors, knowin' as there's a new book waitin' for me up in my room – pages uncut and all. That's a job I do love, now – cuttin' the pages of a book. 'Tis like what an explorer must feel in an uncharted country – all manner o' good things before him, he do scarcely know what.... A new book in the house when I'm out workin' 'ull give me the itch; and sometimes, at harvest, days and weeks 'ull go by before I can get at it. Uncle, he isn't keepin' no more labour than his place 'ull carry, I can tell you.'

Esther was becoming interested. 'Whenever are you findin' time to read, then?' she enquired.

'Oh, at night mostly. I've a room to myself up under the roof where no one can't see my light burnin'. Uncle and Aunt 'ould raise a terrible outcry about the danger o' burnin' down the old place if they was to guess as I do

41

read in bed. But I do keep a store o' candles hid away, so they aren't none the wiser.'

'I wonder you can keep awake though, after workin' out all day. My brothers and father is asleep as soon as ever they do sit down in front o' the fire after supper.'

'I don't blame 'em. 'Tisn't easy to keep your mind on a book when you're as tired as a dog. But we've all of us the strength to do what we do most want to, and books is meat and drink to me.'

'Fancy your cravin' for book learnin' like that,' Esther murmured. She had forgotten her embarrassment, but it was revived by his next remark.

'I don't see no signs o' Mrs Jones nowhere. May I be walkin' home with you?'

In an instant she was on the defensive.

'No, no, indeed, thank you. I must be lookin' for her. I couldn't think o' startin' home without her.'

''A' right,' he agreed good-naturedly, 'let's see if we can find her, then.'

They searched the deserted graveyard in vain, and made enquiries of the last group of loiterers on the high road.

'I do believe as I seed Mrs Jones the sweets gettin' into cross-eyed Evans Ty-Gwyn's trap,' one of them said. 'She do mostly have a lift home with him. They're all gone back now as do come from Aberdulas.'

Esther stood clasping and unclasping her hands, and looked up in distress at her companion.

'It's a' right,' he smiled down at her. 'I'll see you home safe.'

'But I don't never go walkin' with boys.'

42

No sooner had she spoken than she could have bitten out her tongue with vexation. Whatever had made her put such a complexion on the matter?

'No more do I go walkin' with gals,' he laughed. 'But we've both of us got to go back along the same road some time this night. We may as well walk side by side as one after the other.'

She too was forced to laugh, and they set out together.

'I don't know how 'tis,' he began after a while, 'in these parts a man can't say two civil words to a gal without folks beginnin' to gossip and giggle – not as I do want to talk to none of our neighbours' daughters. I'd rather a deal read o' the great women of olden times nor waste my breath on them. Fairings, and tellin' fortunes by the tea leaves in their cups, and how much they'll make by the poultry – that's all they do care for.'

There was a brief silence, and suddenly Esther nerved herself to ask: 'Why were you wantin' so much to talk to a gal like me, then?'

The unexpected boldness of the question arrested him as though she had struck him a blow. He stopped in the middle of the road and looked down into her eyes. She felt the colour mounting to her cheeks, but she did not turn away.

'Did you know I'd been watchin' you for days?' he demanded abruptly.

She nodded her head, too shy to reply, now that the conversation had taken so personal a turn.

'And you wondered why?'

Again she nodded.

'Well, I've been wonderin' too. 'Tisn't because you're all that pretty.'

'Well, I never! Isn't that what the boys do go for?'

'Some, maybe but prettiness alone 'ouldn't be fetchin' me.'

'I'm not bein' nothin' to look at, I know.'

'Oh yes, you are – but there's something else about you – something –' he spread out his hands as though seeking for it. 'I can't put it into words, not exactly; but it's a sort o' dignity, for all you're young and shy, as puts me in mind of the women I read of in history, brave and strong women with a mind above any I've ever met.'

They had been standing staring like old friends long parted who had encountered each other upon the highway. All at once Esther began to walk on rapidly, and when he overtook her she exclaimed with apparent irrelevance, 'I'm not even knowin' your name.'

'Rhys. That's my Christian name. And yours?'

'Esther.'

'A grand old name. I do like the sound of it. Esther!' He repeated it softly. 'She was a fine woman, the one of that name in the Bible. It do suit you.'

'Tell me about them women in days gone by as you was speakin' of.'

He flashed a grateful glance at her. 'Oh, I'll be talkin' all night if you'll be listenin' to me. Shall I tell you about the legends and the history o' Wales, about the saints and the princesses as you are puttin' me in mind of?'

'Yes, if you 'ould be so kind.'

The night wind, soft and westerly, stirred the hedgerows to mysterious rustlings. The tang of the sea and the sweetness of the countryside were blended in it. The moon, hanging low on the horizon, cast long, sharp-

44

cut shadows before the two walkers, larger than any other moving thing within their view. If their footsteps were muffled by a patch of grass, the wind's quiet sighing brought with it the far-off sound of waves, and they would pause to listen to it and their gaze would become fixed upon the wide landscape. The detail of noontide was no longer visible, but the obscurity of small things gave strength to the greater outlines, and the undulating country swept out skyward with a naked vigour.

Esther, listening to the talk of the strange youth beside her, wondered whether she were awake or dreaming, so unreal did everything appear. He talked of the 'golden age' of Wales, of poetry and harp playing, royal hospitality, and chivalrous love. From a smattering of historical knowledge he drew large deductions, ignoring what did not appeal to him in his country's story, and enlarging on what was best, making the past appear as he would have the future be. In all good faith he fancied himself looking back, when in reality he was straining forward. But to his silent listener his talk was one with the magic of the night. Strange memories, not of her own, but of her race's past, began to stir in her. A thousand starlit love-makings that had gone to her creation haunted her as had the sweet sadness of the singing an hour ago.

As they descended the steep hillside behind Aberdulas she ceased even to hear what her companion was saying, so conscious was she of his near presence. As though aware of her mood he also became silent. The smell of seaweed came up to them, and the sound of the sea, grown louder now and more triumphant. Esther could feel the quickened beating of her heart, and noticed, with an odd

45

pleasure, that the hand she laid upon the garden gate was trembling. Rhys had come close to her. She was aware of his almost touching her shoulder as she turned away from him with a murmured 'Goodnight'. He stood motionless behind her as she fumbled with the latch. Would he suddenly take her in his arms and kiss her, she wondered, afraid, but unable to move beyond his reach. Did she desire him to kiss her or would she try to escape? Was this the excitement of longing or of dread? He was so close to her that she could not think. Suddenly she found herself on the far side of the gate. He moved away abruptly as though awaking from a trance, muttered something about lending her a book, and straightway was gone.

Esther crept into the house. She was vaguely disappointed, for it seemed that a kiss, intended and desired, had gone to waste in the cold night air.

CHAPTER 2

When Esther stole downstairs the following morning she found her aunt busy cooking breakfast.

Since five o'clock she had been awake in her little white room that was filled like a shell with the sound of the sea; but the longer she had thought of her new friend the less had she been able to make up her mind about him. The recollection of their walk aroused a sensation that was both pleasant and akin to fear. She wanted to see him again, but shrank from the thought of meeting him in daylight.

Mrs Jones dexterously cracked a couple of eggs on the edge of the pan, and, watching them fry, commented with mischief: 'You were not down as soon as usual this mornin'.'

'Indeed and I'm sorry, Aunty.'

'Oh, you're bein' early enough whatever... tired, no doubt, after last night?'

'Well, it was a goodish long walk.'

'Go you on! You're a capital walker. 'Twasn't that as did tire you!'

Esther coloured; and Mrs Jones, glancing over her shoulder, began to chuckle.

'I thought as how you didn't like men.'

'I don't – not most of 'em whatever.'

'But you've found one to your taste at last, after so many years of life, is that it?'

Esther had been asking herself the same question for the last three hours. She evaded it now by hurriedly asking another.

'There wasn't no harm in my walking home along of a boy, was there?'

'Duwch, gal, there's simple you are! Harm, indeed! There's a deal more sense in your practice nor what there is in your talk. And you've picked up a very likely lad too.'

'Why, however did you come to know who I was with?'

'Oh, I'm not gone so blind yet but what I can use my eyes a bit. Young Rhys Lloyd, Pritchard the Gaer's nephew, was lookin' at you all through the singin' practice as if he'd a mind to eat you. I knowed he'd be tryin' to give you the wink on comin' out – that's why I was slippin' away, so as to give him a fair chanst.'

'You did it on purpose? Oh, Aunty, you are a wicked 'un, and me lookin' for you everywhere, and in a terrible way about goin' home without you.'

'Go on! You'd come by no harm with Rhys. He's a sober, tidy boy or I shouldn't have been leavin' you together.'

'Well, he's not like no other young man,' Esther

admitted. 'Oh, you may laugh so much as you like, Aunty, but indeed he is different. He do talk so strange. Is he bein' reckoned terrible clever?'

'He do read some old books whatever. His uncle's allus on at him for wastin' time on 'em, I do hear say. But for all that the boy's likely to come into the place when the old 'uns do die. Not havin' no children of his own Pritchard the Gaer isn't – pity on him. That's why he's been adoptin' his wife's nephew.... Well, well, you're a sharp 'un at pickin' up a bargain! They do say as there's a good few gals about here do fancy Rhys, but he's too took up with them old books o' his to notice 'em.'

This was not the sort of information which Esther desired, and as Mrs Jones enlarged upon the wealth and respectability of the Pritchards, her attention wandered.

Throughout the morning her thoughts were busy with Rhys. She pictured him alone in his raftered attic, poring at midnight over his books. Wondering what could be the subject of so many volumes, she sighed to think how many matters there were of which she knew nothing in the world. For the first time in her life she was acutely conscious of her own ignorance, and ashamed of it.

The day wore away quietly, but her thoughts would give her no rest. As the drowsy afternoon gave place to evening she said to herself: 'I've been asleep and dreamed a dream.... There's no such person to be found in this 'orld as a young man with eyes like fire, set in a face pale and thin as a corpse's – nor, if there were such a one, 'ould he be walkin' home at night with an ignorant gal like what I am, and comparin' her to the great ladies o' bygone days.'

Her thoughts wandered away to the fairy tales of which

49

her sister Gladys was so fond. 'Ah, well,' she sighed, 'I suppose he *is* a real human bein' and not some make-believe spirit; but 'tisn't likely as he'll come to look for the likes o' me no more, for he can't have been meanin' all he was sayin' to me last night.'

At that moment Rhys came into the little shop. It was just before closing time, and Esther was behind the counter with her aunt, putting away the stock. She felt the colour rush into her face, and was angry with herself for having blushed. Giving him a distant nod, she retired behind a stand full of picture postcards. Mrs Jones, on the contrary, leant over the counter with her most expansive smile and her china-blue eyes bland as a baby's.

'Well, well, fancy *you* calling in at my small little shop,' she sing-songed. 'Comin' to buy summat, are you?'

He looked embarrassed, but laughed. 'No, indeed, I don't want to buy nothin'.'

'Go you on! What are you comin' here for, then?'

'I've brought your niece a book as I did promise to lend her.'

He dived into a pocket as he spoke and produced a history of the locality. Mrs Jones picked it up and glanced at it mockingly.

'Well, well, there's a dull old thing to be givin' a gal! When the boys was courtin' *me*...'

'Aunty, don't talk so foolish,' Esther expostulated from her hiding place.

'When they was courtin' me,' Mrs Jones continued unperturbed, 'they was givin' me ribbons and sweets and all sorts. But duwch, times is changed, and you are too clever by far to be knowin' how to please a gal. A schoolmaster, that's what you did ought to be, so as you could be keepin' company with your blackboard close at hand. You'd be givin' your sweetheart a lesson on it most like, when any sensible fellow 'ould be kissin' her.'

'Aunty!'

'A' right my gal, Rhys don't mind what I'm sayin'. Maybe, before long, you'll be wishin' as he'd come to me for advice.... Well, I'd best be gettin' my spectacles, or else you'll be tellin' me as I can't make no shape o' the dull old books you young 'uns is readin' – you and your education!'

She disappeared into the kitchen, chuckling to herself. Rhys flung back his head and laughed. 'Your aunt's a good 'un! I wish if all the old folks was bein' like her.'

Esther joined in the laugh a little shamefacedly, and peeped out from behind her shelter. He looked browner and more robust in the warm evening sunshine than he had by moonlight, and more rugged in his earth-stained corduroys than in his best black suit. He was without a collar, and his bronzed face contrasted sharply with the whiteness of his neck. His hands were caked with mud, and he brought with him the familiar smell of the stables. Altogether, he was more homely and less alarmingly unusual than he had appeared the night before, and she ventured out to talk to him. Picking up the book which lay on the counter, she thanked him for bringing it to her.

'I'll lend you any o' my books as you do fancy. I'd like you to be readin' the ones I do enjoy most myself,' he told her eagerly, and began to show her the illustrations in the one which he had brought.

Their hands met in turning over the pages, and he leant across the counter, his head close to hers, but he went on

51

talking, evidently anxious to capture her interest. According to her cousin Megan, any man would take hold of a girl and kiss her roughly if she were left unprotected in his company. Men, she had decided, were inconsiderate, and did not care what a woman's wishes might be. Her unmarried aunts declared even that the majority of them would deliberately ruin and desert any girl who gave them encouragement. Megan ridiculed their solemn warnings against 'keepin' company', but Megan herself was a 'come-by-chanst' whose mother had brought disgrace upon the Bevan family, and her confidences had increased rather than lessened Esther's suspicions. Her reserved manner had driven away the few young men she had met. While her cousin, no better looking, and jealously guarded by two old maids, had contrived a series of secret affairs, Esther had never had a flirtation even at a fair or a shearing.

But with this unusual youth, who seemed to have no intention of taking a kiss by force, she gradually became at her ease, and when Mrs Jones at length returned it was to find them talking away without constraint.

'Best stay for a bit o' supper,' she suggested.

Rhys flashed a grateful look at her. 'I've to see to the horses,' he answered regretfully, 'but I'll come tomorrow after puttin' 'em right, if uncle's willin'... might I be doin' that?'

'You might, indeed. I do fancy a bit o' young company. It do give me summat to laugh at, though you may be thinkin' as the laugh is all on your side – bein' so terrible clever as you are.'

'I don't know how you can be makin' fun o' his learnin',' Esther protested as soon as he had gone. 'It do fair frighten me to hear a boy o' his age talk so grand.'

But her awe was not such as to prevent a flutter of pleasure when he arrived on the following evening, bringing her another of his books. This one was about the legends of Wales, and was full of what she considered gorgeously beautiful pictures. She looked at them entranced, murmuring to herself: 'There's bright colours! There's pretty!' And throughout supper, encouraged by her rapt attention, Rhys held forth on Celtic folklore. It was, for the moment, his favourite theme, and, pushing aside his plate, he talked away, his bright eyes fixed on her face, his elbows resting on the table, and his long-fingered hands gesticulating freely.

Everything in the kitchen was clean and tidy. Along the mantelshelf shone a row of highly polished brass candlesticks, and complacent china dogs smirked above the fireplace. On the walls hung pictures out of Christmas magazine supplements, and the white window curtains were tied up with pink satin ribbons. Esther admired them afresh every time she entered the room, but now she was not conscious of her surroundings, for the magic world of Fair Olwen and Kilhwch, and of all those whose adventure is recorded in the Mabinogion, had taken her to itself.

'I must be rememberin' these tales to tell Gladys,' she murmured, 'all her delight is in summat strange.'

Somehow the thought of her sister brought a pang of self-reproach, as though her own enjoyment were the betrayal of a trust.

Aunt Polly leaned back comfortably in her chair and chuckled between large mouthfuls.

'Some old tales,' she scoffed, no longer able to contain

53

her derision. 'There's nothin' new in what you are findin' out, my boy. I heard it all from my grandmother when I wasn't so high as this table, and 'twas reckoned nonsense in my time. But there, each generation do think itself wonderful sharp to find out what the one before has forgotten. Solomon was sayin' summat about it too – or was it Isaiah, now?'

At length she called his attention to the fact that it was growing late and he had not finished his meal.

'Likin' the sound o' your own voice better nor your food, you are,' she exclaimed, 'the very same as some old preacher as 'ull let his Sunday dinner go cold rather nor give over addressin' the poor Lord – as must be terrible tired o' listenin' to his foolishness.'

'You're right,' Rhys laughed. 'I'm a terror to talk if I've got the company I do like. Mind you, I don't scarcely open my mouth at home, and that's how it do all get bottled up and do come out with a rush like when I'm with someone as I do feel I can tell everything to.'

He smiled at Esther as he spoke, and she smiled back. After which he gulped down the remains of his food, pushed back his chair, and stretched himself so that his shadow showed like a crucifix upon the wall behind him.

'Can I talk a bit more now, Mrs Jones?' he enquired.

'Better let off your love o' sound in singin',' she answered, and led the way into the rose-decked parlour. There she sat down to play her favourite hymn tunes, and the boy and girl seated themselves side by side upon the horsehair couch.

'Are you both o' you gone too shy to sing?' Mrs Jones enquired over her shoulder, and, very much embarrassed, they rose and came to stand behind her.

Rhys had a rough bass voice, untrained but pleasing. He sang lustily, for the most part in Welsh, his rugged head with its unruly mop of black hair thrown back, and his golden-brown eyes growing each moment more radiant and alive. Esther had never seen eyes so brilliant. She watched them covertly, and kept silence, except when her aunt announced that they would sing a hymn in English for her benefit. Then she was forced to join them in her soft contralto, small in volume, but sweet in tone. When she sang, Rhys, in his turn, became silent, and watched her so intently that at the end of each verse she turned away flushed and self-conscious.

'I am not singin' very good,' she murmured for lack of something better to say.

'You are singin' same as an angel,' he cried impetuously, and Mrs Jones chuckled.

The evening passed by all too soon for Esther, and when it was over she sat on the lace-flounced bed in her tiny room wondering why she felt so wide awake, so excited, so happy. She had brushed out her hair, so that it spread like a cape about her white-robed shoulders. Sitting thus in the twilight with devoutly clasped hands, and eyes raised to the starlit square of window, she might have been a saint in contemplation, so tranquil and virginal did she look. Presently she slid down from the edge of the bed, and knelt to say her prayers. But those she had been taught in childhood no longer seemed adequate and she was not certain what it was for which she now desired to ask.

'Make me happy,' she prayed, and paused to wonder whether such a prayer were wrong. 'Make me able to give others happiness,' she substituted. 'Indeed, I do believe as I could find happiness – more'n ever I've dreamed of, in the giving of it.' Her thoughts wandered away perilously. '*If*,' she thought, 'but I daren't hardly hope for that,' and her prayers resolved themselves into a vague and voiceless act of worship. Presently she climbed into bed and fell asleep smiling.

The whole of the next day she spent poring over the books which Rhys had brought her, and hoping that he would come again. On the following morning he burst into the shop, bringing with him a great gust of wind and the salt taste of the sea. White clouds were racing across the deep blue of the sky, and boisterous waves dashing in sheets of spray against the sides of the cove. Rhys was in his workaday clothes, and the horse he was taking to the blacksmith's stood hitched to the garden gate. He was hatless, and the wind had blown his hair into a ripple of unruly waves. As he came in he shouted joyfully 'Mornin' all! I've had an idea!'

'You do seem to have a good many,' Mrs Jones chuckled. 'I wonder is there any sense in *this* one.'

Disregarding her, he enquired of Esther: 'Have you heard tell of the movin' pictures? They've opened a picture-house at Carnau; I've been to see it onst. It's somethin' quite new, and all the talk o' the countryside.'

'You don't say! Our Vicar's daughter was tellin' me summat about pictures as could move; but I didn't rightly understand her...'

''Ould you like to see 'em for, yourself?'

She flushed with pleasure and looked at her aunt.

'I was thinkin',' Rhys continued, 'to beg a horse and

trap off o' my uncle on Saturday night, and drive you into Carnau.' He paused and looked at her anxiously. ''Ould you come?'

She was too taken aback to make any reply. This bold offer, made in the presence of Aunt Polly, was entirely contrary to her notions of the way in which young men 'carried on'. In her own district love-making was done for the most part stealthily at night, and Megan often told her how the various youths who kissed her on the way home from church deserted her hastily and leapt over the nearest hedge at the sound of approaching footsteps.

Since her niece seemed to be incapable of utterance, Aunt Polly took it upon herself to reply.

'O' course she'll be willin' to go. There's a lovely treat it 'ull be for her! Indeed and I 'ould like to be comin' myself,' she added mischievously, and was quick to note the change in his expression.

'You'd best be comin' along too, then,' he said, trying not to show his disappointment at not having Esther to himself.

For answer the old dame shook her head and cackled with laughter.

Accordingly, Rhys and Esther set out together on the following Saturday evening on their seven-mile drive to the county town. Esther, who had only of late emerged from the stage at which clothes are regarded as mere necessary coverings, had been painfully conscious, on going over her wardrobe that morning, of being shabbily dressed. Mrs Jones, however, took the matter in hand, and spent the day in trimming her mushroom-shaped hat with blue and grey shot ribbon 'to go with the solemn colour o'

57

your eyes,' as she explained. She also insisted upon taking her to the village draper in order to buy her a present of grey cotton gloves and stockings to match. Esther was overwhelmed by these preparations which put her in mind of a bridal.

'Well, indeed,' cried Mrs Jones, surveying her handiwork with pride, 'there's a regular picture o' modesty you are! I don't believe as no man could keep his hands off o' you!' With which alarming statement she bundled the girl into the old-fashioned gig that stood waiting for her at the garden gate.

Rhys, all impatience to be off, picked up the reins, cracked the whip and shouted 'Goodbye'. They rattled away up the hill with the smiling neighbours looking out of their cottage doors to watch their departure.

Beyond the village, at the top of the ascent, the road curved to the right, and thenceforward ran parallel with the coast all the way to Carnau.

Esther, with her hands to her hat, looked up at a host of seagulls, white as snowflakes, that swirled above them. The fantastic grace of their flight delighted her. She touched Rhys' arm and pointed up at them without speaking. Silently he followed the direction of her glance, and smiled with her. Somehow this pleasure shared between them broke down the constraint of the first few minutes, and Rhys began to talk of his home life, and his failure to win his uncle's sympathy for any of his ambitions and interests.

'He and my aunt do think as anything only chapel-goin' and money-makin' is a waste o' time,' he complained. 'But I do want to learn all about everything' – and he made a comprehensive gesture with his arm, as though he would have embraced the universe. 'Mind you,' he added, 'I do want to make money too – not as I do want a lot for myself, but I 'ould like to master the makin' of it.' As he spoke he flicked his whip restlessly to and fro over the head of the old horse that jogged along between the shafts. 'The farmers round about here do nothin' only talk about money-makin', but they don't even study the best way to do that. They 'on't move with the times. They're terrible afeared o' education and up-to-date methods. They 'on't have it as a trained mind is better nor an untrained one, if it's only to learn the best way o' hoein' turnips.'

'Maybe they're afeared as the one with a trained mind, as you do call it, 'ouldn't want to go hoein' turnips all his life,' Esther suggested. 'Father he took us away from school so soon as ever he durst, fearin' as we'd go too sharp to be workin' at home for him without no wages.'

'Ah!' cried Rhys, 'that's just what they're up to, the old 'uns! I wish,' he added with regret, 'if I had gone to Aberystwyth College, same as I was beggin' on uncle to let me do.'

'Is your parents dead, then?' Esther asked softly.

'Dead? No; they're livin' up in the same parts as you do come from,' he answered, pointing with his whip in the direction of the distant mountains. 'But they're not doin' nothin' for me. Havin' a lot more children nor they can rear – no sense in it; so they was bein' glad enough to let Aunt Liza adopt me. I've lived here since I was a small little lump of a boy. No, I don't owe my parents nothin', only for bringin' me into the 'orld, and I do reckon as they did do that to please theirselves, and not along o' my sake.'

59

Esther laughed at this unorthodox view. 'You do say some things.'

'Are you terrible fond o' your parents, then?' he enquired, and saw the light of amusement die out of her eyes.

'I'm fond o' my poor mother,' she sighed, turning her head away. And little by little she confided in him the troubles of her home life, embittered by her father's drunkenness and the ruinous feud he maintained with his neighbour on the mountain.

'Allus coursin' one another's sheep, they are, and goin' to law over a right o'way, or the repairin' o' a boundary hedge between them, or summat; and whenever father do lose his case – he's been losin' several as I can remember – he'll go on the drink for days after, and be abusin' o' us at home somethin' cruel. Afraid o' him in my heart, I was, till a year or two ago. He's given over hittin' me now, but he's knockin' Gladys about sometimes yet. She's got a sharp tongue on her, has my sister, and do answer him back when he's in drink; and indeed it do make me go fair mad to see anyone lay a hand on her. 'Tis on her account as I've been sufferin' most.'

'It's a damned shame,' Rhys cried, 'as everyone isn't kind to you allus!'

She laughed a little and shook her head. 'I don't know as they did ought to be kind to *me* in partic'lar, but I 'ould like if everyone was to be kind to everyone else.'

'Ah,' he agreed, 'that's how I do feel.'

Thus they came to Carnau in high spirits, and put up at the Green Dragon Hotel, where Pritchard the Gaer stabled his horse on a market day. When Rhys had given old Bowler a feed, he turned to Esther, who was waiting patiently in the yard, and asked her whether she would like something to eat. She looked up at him wide-eyed, for she was accustomed, when she went into Llangantyn with her father, to stand about for hours at the street corners, tired and hungry, while he refreshed himself at the inns into which a respectable girl might not enter.

'I don't know as I do want nothin',' she murmured.

'Better see how you do feel when it's set before you,' he decided, and piloted her to a small eating-house, the like of which she had never seen before.

There, with a bewildering selection of fancy cakes from which to choose, she discovered that the drive had given her an appetite, and she ate away contentedly, while Rhys, with his elbows on the marble-topped table, and his chin in his hands, watched her, smiling. He did not appear to want anything to eat himself, which, she thought, made his solicitude for her the more surprising. She had ceased to be embarrassed by his looking at her, and smiled back at him, trustful and happy, whenever their eyes met.

The meal over, it was time to go to the cinema, and the large crowded hall, the brilliant lights, the laughing, animated audience, the gilt and red-plush splendour of the place, sent Esther's spirits soaring still higher.

'This is as good as a fair,' she whispered to Rhys, who was absorbed in the new and joyful sensation of having stood her tea and bought her a ticket for the entertainment with his own money, part of his small and precious savings.

When the lights went down, and the moving pictures appeared upon the screen, Esther held her breath with excitement. 'Don't you go to spoil it now,' she adjured Rhys, who had begun to explain to her how films were produced. 'I 'ould rather believe as they're real people as I'm watchin' through a window.'

'A' right,' he laughed, delighted by her childishness, and watched her sitting with tightly clasped hands and round eyes.

The film was an early specimen of what has developed into the grand tradition. Esther was appalled by the scenes at a West End restaurant, in which a millionaire's decadent son sought to seduce the innocent sister of his father's poor clerk.

'Do they really carry on like that, wearin' next to no clothes, and drinkin' and smokin' so shameful?' she asked Rhys.

'Well, I don't fancy as *all* you do see on the pictures is quite true,' he answered, smiling, and offering her a paper bag full of pear drops which had become very sticky in his hot hands.

But she was far too absorbed in the drama to suck sweets, and surprised that Rhys should treat it with so much levity. 'But then,' she reflected, 'he is readin' and knowin' such a wonderful lot, a play isn't nothin' only make-believe to him.'

But in the scenes of tender sentiment between the self-made hero and the millionaire's daughter even Rhys seemed to be affected, and during the duel scene Esther's right hand crept into his left. She was scarcely conscious of having placed it there until the blood-curdling episode was over. Then she found her hand held fast. Rhys, far more absorbed in the possession of it than in anything which was taking place upon the screen, tightened his clasp for fear she should withdraw it; and when the young woman at the piano thumped out 'God Save the King', he rose and drew it securely through his arm.

Linked like lovers, they passed out into the dimly lit street, fragrant with a salt wind from the sea and a tang of tar. Esther was full of reflections on the drama she had just seen, and began to state them on the way out.

'I don't think she did ought to have married him, do you? I'm sure as he 'ouldn't really live respectable, not after bein' so loose all those years. Pity as she didn't take up with a tidy young farmer, or someone as 'ouldn't have minded so much as the quality do do about her havin' made a mistake when she was a gal.'

But Rhys had only smiled at her as though he were thinking of something else; and once out in the open under the stars, amidst so many actual lovers, she found that the story of the play paled in interest before the youth at her side. At first he had alarmed her; afterwards he had excited her admiration and absorbed her thoughts; but now she found her heart beating faster, and a delicious warmth stealing over her at his touch. She was bewildered but not frightened by this change in her feelings, and stood watching him as he harnessed up in the yard of the Green Dragon. It was dark by this time, and the swinging lantern which the ostler carried cast weird lights and flickering shadows on the surrounding buildings, on the old horse standing patiently with hanging head, and on Rhys moving swiftly to and fro buckling the harness. The whole scene filled Esther with a sense of unreality. That she should find herself at night in this strange place, in company with a youth whom she scarcely knew, was enough, she told herself, to frighten any honest girl. But she was not frightened. She was glad; and when he jumped into the trap, and swung her up beside him, she gave a little laugh of happiness.

'I do love to hear your laugh,' he whispered, as he tucked the rug round her.

'Why?' she whispered back, while the sleepy ostler, heavy-eyed and indifferent, stood waiting for them to depart.

''Deed, I dunno. 'Tis deep and soft, like no other girl's ever I heard.'

'Go you on,' she answered, laughing once more; and they rattled out of the yard, and over the cobblestoned streets of the town.

In its deserted by-ways and afterwards on the white road they passed many shadowy figures, always a man and a girl strolling together with arms entwined. The wind had dropped with the turning tide, and only a quiet breeze sighed over the fields, wan beneath the stars and a slowly rising moon. In silence Rhys studied the pleasant rugged lines of Esther's profile, the thoughtful forehead, the short blunt nose, the generous mouth, the strong, almost masculine chin. The moonlight shone on her rounded cheek and full throat, softening them with delicate shadow. She sat gazing straight ahead of her with that expression of steady contemplation and latent strength which had at first attracted his attention. Her hands were folded in her lap, but, though she was still, nothing in her pose suggested indolence. Rhys thought her the incarnation of all that was patient and wise and enduring in womanhood. He did not profess to understand her, as he fancied that he understood most things. Many of her ways were childlike, and she was ignorant of many subjects upon which he could talk glibly; yet, he thought, there was an instinctive wisdom in her which gave interest to all she said and an unconscious dignity to her every movement. Thinking over what she had told him about her home, he marvelled that she could have become what she was.

'Do you know,' he said at last, 'as you are lookin' beautiful tonight.'

Slowly she turned her moonlit face to his. He had never looked down into eyes so soft or been so moved by feminine encounter.

'I never heard tell,' she murmured with a faint smile, 'as I were anything partic'lar to look at.'

'You are to *me* whatever. You are the most beautiful, the most precious thing in the whole 'orld.'

He tried to say more, but his throat seemed to have contracted. His mouth was dry and his eyes smarted. Not until he had sought to put his emotion for her into words did he realise how great it was, and he became then helplessly tongue-tied. But the spell of peaceful silence between them had been shattered, and they sat staring at each other, startled and fascinated by the swift beating of their own hearts. Esther was the first to speak.

'Say that onst again,' she whispered, unable to believe her ears on this night of wonders.

He gave a nervous laugh and shook his head.

'Did you mean it?' she whispered still more faintly. 'Did you mean as I was seemin' beautiful and precious to you?'

65

He nodded.

'To *you*?'

'To me.'

The old horse jogged on quietly, and the night wind pursued its monotonous way over the deserted country; but to Esther its low murmur seemed to have turned into a song of gladness. The multitude of stars overhead appeared to have grown unaccountably bright, and to be laughing down at her. To someone in this lonely world, about which she had gone hitherto often bewildered and almost always weary, she was precious, 'precious and beautiful!' She repeated the words to herself, entranced by the sound of them. So great was her ecstasy that she almost forgot his presence, and the sound of his voice startled her.

'May I be kissin' you?' he was whispering, leaning towards her with eyes that had grown brighter than ever.

She was too much moved to make any answer.

'O' course if you don't want me to...' he cried sharply, and drew himself up.

'But I do,' she said, and raised her face.

When at length he released her, she was trembling, and her breath came in short sobs. She felt more weak and incapable of exercising her own will than she had ever done before, but deliriously happy. Rhys passed his hand across his eyes and looked down at her like one dazed. She no longer seemed to him the remote and mysterious embodiment of all that he most admired in womanhood, but a soft warm creature, very young and confiding, of whom he must take care. He gathered up the fallen reins, and, taking them in his right hand, put his left arm around her protectively. She nestled up close to him and hid her face on his shoulder. The old horse, which had dropped into a walking pace, resumed its leisurely jogging.

'It's strange,' Rhys said at last, as if speaking to himself.

'We don't hardly know each other,' Esther murmured, guessing at his thought.

The pressure of his arm increased. 'The time we've known one another don't count. We're sweethearts from now on *always*,' he said. 'So soon as ever I set eyes on you I knowed as you were different from any other girl.'

She shook her head. '*You* are bein' different from anyone else,' she protested, 'not me.'

They argued in whispers.

'You're a wonderful one to talk to.'

'I can listen, whatever.'

'No, no. You can *understand*. You've more sense nor any 'oman ever I met.'

'That's only bein' your fancy.'

''Tis the truth.'

'No, indeed it isn't. Don't you go to think me what I'm not, else you might change your mind when you did find me out, and not want to see me no more.'

'Don't you talk so dull now,' and with that he sealed her lips with a kiss.

After that they spoke little on the homeward journey, for he found that it was impossible to put his tenderness for her into words; and he became as silent as any other lover. It angered him that his gift of easy speech, of which he had been not a little proud, should have deserted him when he most desired to use it, but he could only whisper

67

from time to time, 'You *do* know how much I am lovin' you, don't you, bach?'

She did not know – how could she? – what was in his mind, but, judging by her own emotions, she answered him each time with a smile that seemed full of understanding. It was not until long after that she realised how isolated, how lonely her soul had been, even at that moment when it seemed to have drawn closest to another.

When they came to the steep hill leading down to Aberdulas, they encountered a couple clasped in each other's arms, who separated quickly and shrank into the shadow of the hedge as the trap came abreast of them. Megan's stories of promiscuous love-making crossed Esther's mind, and, feeling uneasy, she sought for words in which to define the difference between such affairs of the senses and the exaltation of her love for Rhys. She stroked his hand timidly.

'You were kissin' me so sudden like,' she began, and hesitated.

'You aren't angry with me for that, are you, bach?'

'No, no, only' – her caressing fingertips seemed to beg his forgiveness – 'you are not thinkin' as I 'ould go with any boy like that?'

He laughed and pressed her closer to him. 'I 'ouldn't take you for a bold sort o' piece,' he assured her, 'but even if other boys *had* kissed you...'

'No one never kissed me like that before,' she told him solemnly, 'and no one shan't kiss me again.'

'They 'on't get no chanst to,' he laughed. 'From now on I am goin' to keep company with you too close for no one else to slip in.'

68

'But this is like a dream,' she sighed. 'I can't believe as it 'ull last.'

'I'll *make* it last,' he cried, challenging the listening night.

The stars glittered coldly overhead, and the sea moaned in the cove beneath. The lights were extinguished in the windows of the cottages. Esther shivered.

'We can't be sure o' nothin',' she said.

'O' course we can,' Rhys contradicted her, 'for man is man and master o' his fate. That's my creed, whatever.'

'Well, it don't say nothin' about 'oman,' Esther answered.

He set her down reluctantly at the gate of the mushroom-like cottage, and leaned over the splashboard to kiss her goodnight.

'I'll be comin' to keep you company tomorrow evenin',' he told her, and added as an afterthought, 'if you are willing.'

She nodded her assent, marvelling that he should have needed to ask it, and lingered to watch him drive away. He turned to wave to her every few yards. Old Bowler climbed the hill slowly, and it was long before Esther tiptoed into the cottage.

'I 'ould cry if anyone was to ask me questions now,' she thought as she stole upstairs, 'and yet I've never been so happy in all my life.'

'Is that you, gal?' murmured a drowsy voice as she crept past her aunt's door.

'Yes, Aunt Polly.'

'Enjoyed yourself?'

The only answer was a low laugh.

'Well, well,' thought Mrs Jones. ''Tis like that, is it!' and she turned over her comfortable bulk in bed, and went to sleep once more.

CHAPTER 3

With her back to the white-roofed cottage Esther looked down into the sunlit waters of the cove. It was Sunday, and the noises of a working day were stilled, but the waves and the wind and the wild birds filled the air with sound, and the mood of the day was one of joyful activity.

She had a sense of being about to take the most important step in her life. She was flushed with excitement, and moved about the small garden restlessly. Aunt Polly had already driven off to the Gaer with a preacher who was going in that direction. Esther was left alone with her hopes and her anxieties until Rhys should come and fetch her.

'I wonder 'ull his relatives be likin' me,' she thought. They 'on't see me good enough for the likes o' him, of course, but at least I do hope as they 'on't take bitter against me,' and she clasped her hands together. 'I don't know *what* I 'ould do if summat was to come atween us now.'

Her troubled thoughts were interrupted by the arrival of Rhys. Instantly she forgot her cares. She flung open the garden gate, and ran to meet him on the beach.

'There's grand you are!' she cried from a distance, catching sight of his socks as gay as lilac bushes in bloom.

He glanced down at them with an expression of mingled embarrassment and complacency.

'I'm glad you are likin' them, whatever. They was bought to pleasure you. I don't care nothin' for such finery myself.'

They had reached each other by now, and he took her hands in his. They were neither small, smooth nor white, but the capable rough hands of a worker, and he loved them for what they were, as he loved her honest face, and the direct gaze of her grey eyes. He loved, too, the sprinkling of golden freckles about the bridge of her nose, and the way in which her hair grew in a wave over each ear, the coarse abundance of it, and the coppery gleams that lurked amid its darknesses.

'I've been runnin' the whole way along the cliffs from home,' he told her, 'so as to get here in good time. You never seed such an age as they took over their Sunday dinner.'

She laughed at his impatience. 'You are bein' here too soon as it is,' she told him.

'But you were waitin' for me,' he objected. 'I was seein' you from the cliff.'

For answer, she laughed again and hung her head. This time he laughed with her.

'There's no one about,' he whispered, trying to draw her closer, but she evaded him.

'Not here,' she protested, 'someone might be seein' us.'

'Well, what if they was to? I'm not carin' who do see me kissin' you.'

She shook her head, unable to express the sense of exaltation, almost of religious ecstasy, with which his kisses filled her. Others should not witness them. 'They might be laughin',' she said.

Smiling, he released her hands.

'Won't you be feelin' shy then when everyone do know as we are man and wife?'

She coloured under his scrutiny, but did not turn away her eyes.

'I'll be too proud and too happy to care for nothing nor nobody then.'

He gave her a caressing look, and in silence they climbed the steep path which led up the cliff side. When they reached the top, the wind buffeted them roughly, but it was warm and westerly and scented with gorse blossom. The furze bushes that covered the headland were a blaze of gold, the sea beneath them sapphire blue, and the country that stretched away inland rich in the tawny shades of early autumn.

''Tis a beautiful 'orld,' Esther murmured, looking round her.

'And you are bein' the most beautiful thing in it,' Rhys cried, taking her in his arms.

Often, before he met her, he had been deeply lonely. But to her it seemed that his mind could be unfolded as to no other, and he held her to him silently, crushing her body in wild gratitude for the joy and peace which she had brought him. She no longer tried to escape, for they were out of sight of the village, surrounded by empty sky and sea, and a countryside heavy with Sabbath slumber.

'You are lovely,' he murmured, '*lovely*. Your cheeks are all pink and cold with the wind, and your forehead when I do push back the hair is as white as snow, and as soft to touch as curds…. And sometimes,' the words were muffled by her hair, 'I am guessin' at all your beauty by the little I do know, and it is settin' me on fire.'

Trembling, she closed her eyes and lifted her face to his.

When they continued their walk his arm was round her, and her head rested against his shoulder.

'I am wantin' you to share everything with me,' he told her. 'Not my money only, whatever I do make, but my thoughts as well.'

'Yes, yes, Rhys bach, if I am bein' able to share your thoughts. You are terrible clever, though, and I'm not bein' much class, and havin' no education.'

'You're wise for all that,' he answered, pressing her to him. 'This last fortnight, since we was comin' home from Carnau together, has been wonderful.'

'Wonderful,' she echoed, touching his shoulder.

'I've been talkin' to you every night till Mrs Jones the sweets do turn me out o' the house. I've never been able to tell no one before all as I've told you, and you aren't never callin' none o' my notions foolish.'

The idea of anything which he said being foolish struck her as funny, and she gave the soft laugh he loved to hear. Stopping impetuously, he seized her face between his hands, and raising it to his, kissed her again and again.

'They do think me terrible dull at home for readin' so

many books,' he said as they went forward once more, 'and the boys about the place do call me not near square. I never did take no delight in drinkin' and hangin' around the roads on a Saturday night to try and pick up any gal as happened to come along. To get outside o' the small little circle as I've been livin' in, that's been my ambition always.' He made one of his sweeping gestures with his disengaged arm.

'Till I was meetin' you, bach,' he went on, looking down at her tenderly, 'I was only havin' two friends as 'ould talk about the things as I do care for, Owen Pugh, son o' the Neuadd, and Mr Evans, the curate o' Cwmbach. Owen has been to Aberystwyth College, but I don't see as he made so much use o' it as what I'd have done if only I'd had his chanst; and Mr Evans has not been near so friendly with me of late as what he did use to be.'

'However is that bein'? I 'ould have thought as anyone as knowed you 'ould be thinkin' more o' you every day.'

'Go you on! I'll tell you how 'tis. Mr Evans he's a man as is readin' a lot, and he's been wonderful kind to me, fair play on him, though he is a clergyman of the old church. Lendin' me books on geology, and takin' me to see fossils as he'd found here and there about the cliffs, he was. Well, that set me to thinkin' as the Bible account o' creation couldn't be true, though he seemed not to doubt it.'

'You didn't never go to argue with a parson on matters o' religion?' Esther cried aghast.

'Why not? He's bein' paid to preach a certain thing, but I'm a free man. I can look for the truth wherever 'tis to be found.' But though he spoke thus lightly, Rhys felt a thrill of daring. He had been taught to believe that mankind was divided into four main groups, Heathen,

74

Papists, Church folk and True Believers. Of these, only one could be sure of entering heaven. It was not, therefore, presumptuous for a plough-boy from among the enlightened to confute a priest of Baal. But having summoned courage to do so, he had gone further, and begun to criticise the teachings of his own ministers. Now he was coming to regard himself as a very advanced freethinker, and, looking down at his flaunting violet socks, he thought how bold a fellow he was. ''Twas endin' in my gettin' all the books on Bible criticism as was to be had from the free library at Carnau,' he told Esther, 'and poor Evans the parson was warnin' me against my ways the very same as if I'd took to drink.'

Esther, to whom this talk of Bible criticism and geology conveyed nothing, looked up at him with puckered brows. He tried to explain to her the evolutionary theories contained in the books he had read, but the idea that her Bible had not been inspired, word for word, by the Creator, was altogether foreign to her.

'That's a strange way to speak o' the Book,' she protested at length. 'How 'ould we be knowin' what was good and what was wicked if the Bible wasn't tellin' us right?'

'We don't know,' he cried vehemently. 'We are only findin' out little by little, age by age. One prophet is seein' one truth, and one another, and someday maybe we'll come to the whole. That's how we do grow from ape to savage, and from savage to civilised man, gettin' a bit kinder to each other, a bit less fierce and cruel like, and more able to think before we do act, instead o' actin' on instinct no matter how we are goin' to harm others by doin' so.'

He had forgotten his lightly held belief in the past Golden Age of Wales.

'Actin' tidy by others,' Esther said. 'Yes, yes, that's what I do think is the meanin' o' bein' religious. I'm not quite likin' your talk about the Bible, bach, for all you are knowin' more nor I am; but maybe 'tis all the same in the end.... Helpin' the weak, that's what I do believe is our duty here below.'

She had put her whole creed into a phrase. After a pause she added: ''Tis strange, though, as you should be followin' the teachin' o' the Saviour, if you aren't believin' in His Holy Word.'

'But His teachin' is the teachin' o' all the religions ever I comed across. I'm believin' in them all – in that side o' them, whatever – "love thy neighbour as thyself!"'

'I wish if everyone was believin' that too,' she sighed. 'I wish if father was believin' it.'

As she spoke, an unreasoning terror of leaving Rhys and returning to her own home seized her. She looked up at him anxiously, and struggled to put from her a host of vague fears.

'There is a deal o' sadness in the 'orld,' she murmured, 'but it 'on't do no manner o' good for us to think of it now, when we are bein' together, and might be so wonderful happy.'

He looked down at her with one of his character-istically rapid changes of expression, and smiled.

'You are right, sweetheart. I am talkin' a lot o' rubbish, but 'tis you, as do talk so little, as are allus the one to say something wise.'

When they came to the Gaer she was overcome by her old shyness.

''Tis like one o' the gentry's mansions,' she said, lingering at the gate leading into the fold.

'That's what it was onst,' Rhys answered. 'But the country gentries is mostly ruined here. Move with the times or go under, I do say, and move they 'ouldn't.'

He led the way under a porch, supported by squat Doric columns, into a bleak hall. There, having knocked upon a door of yellow-grained wood, they entered the parlour. Esther found herself in a large gloomy room, heavy with the smells of furniture polish and of stagnant air. She knew at once that Rhys' aunt was on the defensive. When a bony hand, with no warmth of greeting, was thrust into hers, she murmured an incoherent word and took shelter behind Aunt Polly. That cheerful woman reassured her, and, though she did not venture to share in the conversation, she began to take stock of her hostess and her surroundings.

Mrs Pritchard was a small, sallow woman, with lank black hair turning a streaky grey, and eyes as sharp and bright as bits of jet. She was precise in her dress, which smelt of camphor, and proud of her wasp-like waist. Rigid on the edge of a horsehair chair dressed in black satin, and wearing a massive gold chain around her neck, she seemed to match the room. This, Esther found even more melancholy than her own squalid home; compared with Aunt Polly's diminutive parlour, gay with pink roses, it seemed like a vault. The vast Victorian furniture was a mass of gleaming bevels and fringed mats. The anaemic geraniums in pots upon the windowsill wilted for lack of light and air. Esther wondered that anything so untidy as a growing plant should be allowed to exist in a room where

77

all the chairs were arranged stiffly round the walls, and looked as upright and uncomfortable as soldiers on parade.

Mrs Pritchard, while making polite conversation in a hard, rasping voice, guardedly looked her up and down.

'She do *seem* a modest, quiet gal, whatever,' was her thought, 'but the boss and I 'ull have to be watchin' her a bit afore we can be makin' sure.'

''Tis a pleasure to see a gal dressed so quiet in black and grey as your niece is bein',' she said with condescension to Mrs Jones, and Esther drew a breath of relief.

Aunt Polly, whose rotund figure overflowed upon all sides the chair on which she was sitting, nodded complacently.

'Indeed,' Mrs Pritchard continued, 'I don't know what's comin' to the gals these days. They are gone that flighty! Short skirts and silk stockin's. The very same as play actresses and others we 'on't name. 'Tis enough to turn religious folk from their prayers in chapel. We was allus taught to wear nothin' only black on the Lord's Day.'

Aunt Polly smiled. 'Yes, indeed,' she agreed, 'and I was allus fancyin' bright cheerful colours all my life. When I was a gal at home, father he 'ouldn't allow me to wear 'em; and when I married my poor husband, he wasn't willin' neither. I wonder am I bein' too old to begin now?'

Mrs Pritchard looked at her askance. ''T'ouldn't hardly be becomin' in a widow,' she observed, and changed the conversation. 'Rhys do tell me as your niece is fond o' singin'.'

'She do sing grand,' Rhys broke in.

The sound of his voice was a blessed relief to Esther, for he had scarcely spoken since he came into the room.

His aunt looked at him reprovingly, as if to say, 'Who

asked for *your* opinion,' but to the girl she gave her first frigid smile. 'We'll be havin' a few hymns after tea.'

It was a solemn meal, served on the long table in the dining room, which was used only when there was 'company', and Esther was thankful when she was back in the parlour and singing hymns with Rhys. Aunt Polly at the harmonium considerately drowned her first quavering notes. Gradually she gained courage, and her deep soft voice filled the room. Mrs Pritchard nodded approval.

'Pity as the boss were called away this afternoon,' she said. ''Twas to see a relation as is dyin'; indeed, and he 'ouldn't be goin' from home on a Sunday for no other reason whatever.'

He came in shortly afterwards, in the middle of a hymn, and stood in the doorway listening until it was finished. Esther's singing pleased him, and her grave young face, seen in profile, was enough to disarm the criticism of any man. He looked enquiringly at his wife. She signalled back a nod that implied, 'Not near so bad as we feared she might be,' and his features relaxed a little.

'If the missus 'ull pass her, she'll do,' he reflected, studying the simple face with renewed satisfaction.

There was no denying that Rhys was a sober, hard-working lad, and very useful about the farm. True, he had strange tastes, and a will of his own, of which Thomas Pritchard did not approve in young people; but there was something appealing about him standing there in the freshness of his youth beside his sweetheart, and the elder man's heart softened towards them both.

'If her father is tidy and they do shape well, I'll see what I can do to'ards settin' of 'em up in a small little byetack o' mine in a few years' time,' he decided in an unusual outburst of generosity. 'But I'll be havin' to find out summat about her father first.'

The singing ceased, and he came forward and shook Esther by the hand. She was much too much overcome by the searching stare of another pair of strange eyes to take in what he said: something complimentary about her singing; but she was aware that, though he looked better tempered than his wife, he would be equally formidable as an enemy. He was not of Mrs Pritchard's type, but round-headed and grey-eyed, with heavy lids under massive projecting brows, and a clumsy, obstinate chin. Short, thick-set and deliberate in his movements, he gave the impression of being slow to anger, as she was swift, but as sullen and enduring in resentment as she might be vindictive in rage.

Esther did not like either of them; but for her lover's sake she was trembling with anxiety to make a favourable impression, and the mute appeal of her eyes completely won over Thomas Pritchard. He drew up a chair, and, sitting down beside her, began to talk. He asked, first, to what denomination she belonged. Church of England? He exchanged a dubious glance with his wife. Aunt Polly intervened. Her niece had been with her to chapel since she came to stay in Aberdulas, and had assured her that she much preferred the singing there to that in her own church at home. Well, well, he was very pleased to hear it; and looked at his wife triumphantly, as if to say, 'We may be winnin' her over to Methodism.' He next asked her whether she could speak Welsh. No? That was a pity, but then the missus couldn't neither when first he married her; and she would soon pick it up. He then questioned her about the work she was accustomed to do, while Rhys, made angry by her being subjected to such an inquisition, glared at him from the other side of the room. In spite of her nervousness she acquitted herself well, and, seeing that both of the Pritchards were satisfied, she began to take courage.

When her aunt got up to go, Rhys came across to her and whispered in her ear: 'I never seed the old 'un so taken with no one before. If ever a young person is venturin' into this house, he and aunty are bein' terrible sharp with 'em.'

'Oh, Rhys bach,' she whispered back, 'I'm so glad, oh dear, so glad! And you don't think, if they are likin' me, as they'll be makin' no objection to our gettin' married some day?'

'Some day? Now just, I am thinkin'.'

She was so relieved, so happy, so full of hope for the moment, that her eyes filled with tears. He squeezed her hand, and in silence they rejoined the others.

On the front doorstep Thomas Pritchard turned to her. 'You are havin' to go home tomorrow?' he asked.

She nodded.

'They did send for me to go back at onst, as they are busy with the harvest. But Aunt Polly has promised to ask me down here again if I shall come.'

He smiled at her.

'Maybe as I'll spare Rhys after the corn's in, to go up and see for his parents; you are livin' in their parts, I do believe. What's your market town?'

'Llangantyn.'

Mrs Pritchard threw up her hands in surprise. 'Well, well,' she cried, 'and 'tis bein' theirs too! I was livin' near

81

there afore I comed to get married. Maybe as you do know my brother?'

'A very religious man,' put in her husband, 'and one as is held in great respect in the district. You're sure to have heard tell o' him, whatever.'

'What's his name?' Esther asked.

'Elias Lloyd the Henallt,' came the answer.

Fear gripped her heart. She looked at the speaker blankly and the colour died out of her face. Afterwards she never knew what she had said nor how she had taken her leave. No one had noticed her agitation, yet she remembered that her knees had weakened under her, and that she had been hardly able to cross the fold.

At first she had been stunned, seeing only that trouble was upon her like the sudden jaws of a trap. It was in her way of life as she knew it. She did not question it. She suffered none of the vain rebellion that asks: Why has it come to me? Why now, when I was so happy? A bleak acceptance of the strokes of chance was a part of the nature she inherited from her long line of hillmen. Stricken in her turn, she looked into God's face and was not surprised by the sternness she found there.

It was not until a later period of her grief that, having a faith which attributed all things to God with primitive directness, she perceived how vast had been the stretch of the Eternal Arms in her case, and how precise the finger which had chosen Elias Lloyd's son as her lover. Tears came to her then, and hysterical laughter with them. She sobbed and laughed into the night, twining her fingers round her bedrails for the coolness of their metal. A little calmness came as she began to imagine her lover, to see him before her in scene after scene which, even while they lasted, some instinct had urged her, for Fate's sake, to remember. At last she fell asleep. She awoke with full command of her courage, but with that impress upon her which gives to country folk their air of having lived in slow intimacy with a god of many moods.

CHAPTER 4

The river was in flood, and raced, discoloured and angry, beside the railway line. Mist hid the hills on both sides of the valley; and Esther, looking out of the window as her train slowed down, could have believed herself in a country as flat as the riverside meadows, which alone were visible.

She left her compartment reluctantly, and an aged porter, bent with rheumatism, and looking as if he had been weary and wet since the beginning of time, banged down her small tin trunk, which he had hauled out of the luggage van, and hobbled away. Tightly clutching the wilting bunch of flowers she had brought with her from Aberdulas, she cast a forlorn look over the familiar scene. The rain dripped from the roofs of the station buildings – a persistent, penetrating rain. Having no umbrella because they 'cost a deal o' money', she was wondering how she could preserve the cherished new ribbon in her hat, when a whirlwind of flying arms and legs swept down the platform towards her; and in a moment, Gladys, with skirts and sleeves too short for her long limbs, was hugging her rapturously.

'Indeed 'tis good to see you again! Well I never, how well you are lookin'! You've growed fatter. And you're sunburnt. Was you out o' doors all the time? Did you have a good journey? You'll be gettin' starved here. I've brought a sack to put round you. I drove the gambo in myself and I've made you Welsh cakes for tea…. No, no, *I'll* manage your box – why, you've got a coloured ribbon in your hat – a lovely silk one, and grey stockings too – well, well.'

She was overwhelmed by chatter as Gladys carried the trunk out of the station. A farm cart stood waiting for them, with a patient horse, sleek with rain, asleep between its shafts. Gladys led it through the narrow streets of the town, but, once out on the country road, she jumped up beside her sister.

'Take your hat off and put it under here,' she commanded. 'That's right. Are you cold, Essy? Give me your hands to rub. Now then, draw up close and tell me all about everything as has happened to you.'

Esther tried to gain time. 'Let's hear about things at home first.'

'Oh, there's nothin' to tell, only as I've missed you something dreadful.'

Then, after a pause, she added: 'Oh, o' course, I was forgettin'. There's been a reg'lar to-do. John and Idris was out shepherdin' the other day, and they seed the eldest Lloyd boy coursin' our sheep. So they up after him, and

85

gave him a terrible hidin'. Father he were that pleased when he comed back home after market.' She laughed... 'Why, you're shiverin', Essy. Are you cold?'

Esther shook her head for answer, and Gladys, having rearranged the sacking, continued: 'There wasn't no bones broke – not like the time when you was a baby, when Father spoiled old Lloyd's face for him – so all old Lloyd could do was to write and threaten Father sayin' he'd not rest till he'd got his sons in gaol for attackin' a poor innocent little lumper as was mindin' his father's sheep, and on his own side o' the boundary too – those was his very words – the villain – when 'twas on *our* side o' the boundary as our boys did catch his son. Indeed we've had many a laugh over his letter.'

But Esther only sighed and stared ahead of her through the drizzle. 'One or other of us is to blame all the while,' she murmured.

Gladys tossed her head.

''Deed I don't think as *we* are. I'm none too fond o' Father, as you do know, but I do think as them Lloyds has been actin' shameful by him. Aunt Lily were over at our place yesterday, and she said as the Lord were on our side for sure, and He'd be helpin' us if we was only keepin' on fightin' long enough. Seein' how religious she is, she did ought to know.'

Esther said nothing, and Gladys looked up at her searchingly.

'You do seem like as if you'd summat on your mind.'

'No, no, bach; tell me some more news.'

'Let's see, now. Oh! A fox took two of our ducks; someone went and loosed 'em out o' the coop at night.

Done on purpose, it must have been, seein' as I'd shut 'em in safe. Them Lloyds, sure to be.' She stopped abruptly. 'You're not listenin'. What's on you? You're gone so quiet. Is there anything the matter?'

'No, no, there isn't nothin' the matter.' Esther tried to smile, but Gladys insisted.

'It's no manner o' use tryin' to deceive *me*. I am knowin' you like no one else isn't. You're not the same with me as you did use to be.' Her large, greenish-blue eyes dilated, and her sensitive little mouth began to quiver. 'Summat's come atween us,' she cried.

Once more Esther put her arm around the slim shoulders, and laid her healthily browned cheek against the pale one. She had more than the average mother's love for this slip of a girl, who, for all her vivacity of speech and manner, looked as if she might fade out of life as her younger sister Lily had done. Esther, the first-born, and John and Idris who had followed her, were robust as the Bevan family in general, but Gladys, who came within a year of the brother next to her, bore unmistakable signs of her mother's failing health, and the four later children had died in infancy.

'Nothin' is changed atween us, little 'un,' Esther said. 'You and I 'ull allus care for each other the same – only...'

'Only?' repeated Gladys suspiciously.

Esther hung her head.

'I've got a young man.'

Gladys freed herself with a violent movement from her sister's embrace.

'You did use to say as you did never want one.'

'Well, I found out my mistake.'

87

'Are you carin' for him a lot?'

Esther nodded.

'More nor what you do care for me?'

''Tis different.'

'You are carin' for him enough to marry him, whatever?'

'Why, yes, bach, o' course.'

'And you do tell me as nothin' isn't changed atween us! What 'ull *I* do if you do marry and go away from here?'

'Maybe as you could come along o' us.'

'Oh, don't talk so dull! When a gal's married she don't want her sister no more. You 'on't never want me now. I might as well be dead for all you'll care.' She burst into ungovernable weeping.

'Gladys, Gladys bach, don't take on so,' Esther begged. But the child sobbed the more, one thin arm flung up over her face, about which dishevelled hair hung in damp wisps.

'You promised me – as you 'ould be – standin' by me – allus,' she gulped. 'You said – small little shop – together, you said....'

'Yes, yes, bach. I do know. But I was fallin' in love. It do happen. Indeed it can't be helped.'

Gladys wept with fresh violence.

It all seemed to Esther so childish and pitiful, and she herself was so tired that she also began to cry. She had taken off her hat, and her wet hair clung to her forehead like seaweed. Her head drooped, and tears rolled unchecked down her cheeks. After a while Gladys gave her a hostile glance, and found her so unlike the strong protecting sister who had been wont to comfort and

88

soothe her, that her jealous resentment fell suddenly away.

'What's on you, Essy? *You* didn't ought to cry whatever.'

'D'you think as I don't mind hurtin' you, little 'un?' Esther answered, ruthlessly scouring the tears from her face with a corner of the rough sack that covered her shoulders. 'It do make me terrible wretched to see you so grieved, and indeed I'm unhappy enough as 'tis.'

'Unhappy! Why?'

Esther told her who her sweetheart was.

'Well I never,' Gladys cried. 'What a terrible business this 'ull be! Oh, my poor Essy, what a time you 'ull be havin' of it at home.'

They had reached the foot of the hill on which Pengarreg stood. They dismounted from the cart, turned off the main road, and began the steep ascent of a mile or more into an impenetrable curtain of mist. It grew darker and colder as they climbed, walking silently with their hands joined as they had often done in childhood. Nothing was visible but the stony track a few yards before them, and the old horse labouring slowly upwards in a cloud of steam that mingled with the mist.

''Tis all dark and lonesome ahead o' us,' Esther whispered.

After a long uphill struggle, made the harder by the clinging of their wet skirts, they came at last to a gate which loomed up suddenly across their path. Opening it, they were in the deep slush of Pengarreg fold. There, with the feeling of unwelcome familiarity which had chilled her on Llangantyn station, Esther found herself greeted by the barking of many dogs that appeared, vanished and reappeared. Around her, as she approached the house, she

89

heard the suck and patter of their paws in the mud. When she came into the kitchen she was struck anew by its unspeakable meanness. Long ago the walls had received a coat of drab paint, and were now mottled with sickly patches of mildew. The ceiling, once white, was discoloured with smoke, two of the window panes had been broken and covered with brown paper, the cloth on the table was tea-stained, and the wooden chair with its broken back – which she remembered from earliest childhood propped against the wall – remained unmended. There were no books, no flowers, no comfortable seats; only a deal table, a horsehair couch with the stuffing coming out of it, and a dozen wooden chairs that screamed like pencils drawn along a slate when they were moved over the stone-flagged floor.

'I wish I could walk out o' my home today, and never set eyes on it no more,' she was thinking, when her mother trailed into the room.

Incessant drudgery, poor health, poorer spirits, and overmuch childbearing had reduced Annie Bevan to a wraith so colourless and thin that it seemed strange she should not be transparent as a pane of glass. Her once abundant yellow hair had turned to the nameless shade of dust. She had lost nearly all her teeth, and her shrunken mouth intensified the peevishness of her expression. On seeing Esther, however, her faded eyes lighted. She clung to the girl with one of her limp embraces, pressing her pale lips to the warm young cheek. To Esther, it seemed that her mother's spirit hung upon hers like a dead weight. Now it was almost more than she could endure, and she felt herself flag beneath it as Mrs Bevan poured forth questions in her toneless voice.

'How is poor Tom's widow? Jolly as ever? You don't say! Not showin' her age? And a lovely little house, and everything in it done up like a reg'lar palace? Well, well, she's one o' the lucky ones, that's sure – allus was lucky, poor Tom bein' so kind to her. She had a tidy husband, and he's left her with plenty o' money, and her health, no wonder she's allus been so cheerful. Nothin' only luck.'

Mrs Bevan was still envying her sister-in-law's good fortune when her husband and her two sons clattered in to their tea.

John Bevan, slouching in first, paused on the threshold for Esther to come and kiss him as a daughter should.

'Time you comed back and did a bit o' work. Your poor mother's fair done. Look how weak she's gone.'

'You didn't do nothin' to lighten her jobs whilst Essy was from home,' snapped Gladys.

He glared at her and dropped into the nearest chair.

'Work indoors is 'oman's work. D'you expect me to do that as well as my own?'

''Tisn't 'oman's work to sit up half the night waiting to take off your boots when you come home drunk.'

'You keep your mouth shut, or I'll be teachin' you a lesson – speakin' to your father like that…. Now then, missus, come on with my tea, I can't wait here for it all day.'

Mrs Bevan had risen on his entrance, and now, looking imploringly at Gladys, she began to wait upon him. John and Idris came in as he was pouring his tea into his saucer, and, shaking the wet from their clothes, greeted Esther with a brother's hasty and embarrassed kiss. She sat down between them, and looked from one face to

91

another around her. For John, who was burly and sullen as his father, she could never feel anything but an irrepressible dislike, but for Idris, who took after his mother's side of the family, and had tow-coloured hair and innocent blue eyes, she possessed the protective maternal feeling she had experienced for all the other children. He was easily led and completely under the influence of John, of whom he was almost as much afraid as his mother was of their father. Coming back to them after her first visit from home, Esther was aware of being utterly isolated in the midst of her own folk. She believed it her duty to love them, yet, when she dared to be candid with herself, she had to confess that for two of them she had nothing but aversion, and for two, little more than half-contemptuous pity. For Gladys alone had she any real affection, and it was the little sister whom her own happiness and her departure from home would most wound.

'I must make shift to take her with me somehow, if only Rhys and I can come by the money,' she thought. 'I can't be leavin' her alone. She do depend on me so.'

The meal was not, as Gladys had intended it to be, an hilarious one. Not until John Bevan had finished, and had stuck his teaspoon upright in his cup as an indication that he wanted no more, did his wife venture to sit down and sip tea that had grown black and lukewarm, and to nibble a piece of bread and butter. Gladys would not come to the table at all. She complained of being 'fair starved' and, turning her back on the others, crouched over the fire with defiance and misery in every line of her body.

That night she and Esther went upstairs together to their raftered room in unusual silence. They undressed by the flickering light of a tallowed candle that guttered in the draught between an ill-fitting door and a broken window. Each got into her own bed, separated from the other by the width of the dim room. When the light was out, the moaning of the wind seemed to grow sadder. The roof leaked, and the monotonous splashing of a drop of water falling every few seconds into a basin placed on the floor to catch it was startlingly loud. Esther lay awake listening to it, and presently from the other bed came the faint noise of stifled sobbing. She rose, and feeling her way over to where Gladys lay, put an arm round the heaving shoulders. She raised the hot, wet face from the pillow, smoothed away the strands of hair that covered it, and kissed it gently. In an instant two thin hands clutched at her desperately.

'Essy,' Gladys gasped as soon as she could control her voice, 'I can't bear it. Promise me as you 'on't never go from here.'

'I can't promise that, dear.... Don't fling away from me like that now. Listen, I'll be tryin' to take you with me.'

'You 'on't have the money.'

'Maybe not at first.'

'Promise me as you 'on't marry, then, not till you can be takin' me too.'

Esther dared not answer. 'Maybe I'd be wrongin' Rhys if I was to do so,' she thought 'but indeed he's strong and full of hope and courage; and she's a poor little bit of a thing, and I'm wantin' to go to him too.'

Somehow the fact that her own happiness was bound up with that of her lover made their marriage seem a selfish thing. Rhys made no appeal to that weakness for

93

the weak, wherein lay the penalty of her own strength. He represented all that was bright and glad in life, and instinctively she turned, half ashamed, from her own happy thoughts of him, to the grief and helplessness that clung to her for support. Thus for a moment she wavered, until her love for Rhys reasserted itself in all its wholesome force, and she whispered: 'I can't promise you nothin', little 'un, but allus and allus to be doin' my best for you. Tryin' to do what's right, I'll be, so long as I do have strength.'

With fingers that sought to console, she stroked the tousled hair, but Gladys, hanging about her neck, continued to cry inconsolably in the darkness.

CHAPTER 5

Though many days passed, Esther heard nothing from Rhys, nor did she dare to speak of him to her parents. Then one afternoon, when the family was sitting at tea, the dogs in the fold began to bark, and Mrs Bevan went to the door to see who was there.

'Well, well,' they heard her saying, 'you are not often comin' our way, Mr Price.'

'Price the post, is it?' demanded her husband, turning round in his chair. 'Come on in, man, and take a cup o' tea. Here, one o' you idle gals, lay another plate, quick.'

Dripping like some small animal that had been half drowned, the postman entered the room. He was flat-chested, more like a collier than a countryman, and the motion with which he flicked the raindrops from his coat sleeves was that of a cat shaking its paws.

'What have you got for me there?' enquired his host.

'Nothin'.'

John Bevan stared, and the postman winked at Esther.

'I've a letter here for your eldest daughter.'

The colour rushed into Esther's face, and she leant across the table to seize the envelope he held up. Chuckling, he placed it in her hand, and she thrust it into her apron pocket.

'From her young man, no doubt,' he observed to the assembly at large.

John and Idris sniggered.

'I was hearin' tell as she was stayin' down at Aberdulas these last few weeks,' the postman resumed knowingly. 'Them seaside resorts is the place to pick up a boy. They're as thick there as shells on the beach. And mind you, a gal isn't bein' so shy there as what some o' them are at home, eh, Esther?'

There was no reply, but Mrs Bevan smiled vaguely for politeness' sake, and her husband stared at Esther across the table. Now and then she had shown quiet obstinacy in taking Gladys' part against him, but ordinarily she was hard-working, silent and submissive – so much, indeed, of what a daughter should be that he had seldom noticed her. Gladys had been a troublesome child whom he had had frequent cause to beat. Now that he considered the possibility of some man's desiring either of his daughters he wished it had been she. Esther would be a loss to the household. 'But the missus 'ull have to put up with that,' he decided. ''Twould be a good job to have one of 'em at least provided for.' His expression was complacent as he looked his eldest daughter up and down. It was strange, he reflected, that he had never noticed her good looks. 'A fine, upstanding gal, that's what

96

she is.' She took after his mother, who had been the only person able to 'make him mind'.

'Did you take up with a boy down at your aunty's?' he enquired good-humouredly.

For answer she hung her head.

'Speak up, gal,' he cried.

'Maybe as I did,' she faltered, and no longer able to endure the mocking scrutiny of so many pairs of eyes, rose abruptly and went over to the fireplace.

Her father struck the table with his fist and gave vent to a shout of laughter. She heard the crockery rattle and her brothers break into a titter.

'Ah, I do wish they'd give over,' she thought, as the postman fired the first shot of a volley of banter. 'They 'ouldn't have the heart if only they knowed what Rhys' love do mean to me,' and she pressed her hot forehead against the cold stone of the mantelpiece.

'Let's have a look at your face, gal. 'Tis the colour of a picklin' cabbage, I do believe.'

'*You're* a sly one, pretendin' as you was goin' to be an old maid.'

'What's he like, Essy? Come on, don't be so close about it.'

'Gone dumb with love, she has. I've heard tell o' love turnin' folks blind, but our Essy's lost her tongue as well as her eyes.'

Presently Gladys came and crouched down at her feet.

The sisters pressed close to each other. It seemed to them an age before the others abandoned their sport.

'There's no fun to be had out o' someone as 'on't say a word,' John Bevan grumbled. 'Any news hereabouts? 'Tis

97

your job to pick up what is goin', bein' a postman.'

'Ah, there's not much as I don't come to know of, what with postcards, telegrams, postmarks and handwritin'. I'll tell you what's the talk today. They do say old Mrs Lloyd the Henallt is likely to die.'

John Bevan spat past his daughters into the fire.

'Good job,' he commented, 'if there's one less o' that brood o' vipers alive.'

'Oh, John,' said his wife, 'you don't really mean that now. She's only a poor old 'oman as never did you no harm like what her sons have done.'

'She did suckle the evil litter, whatever. Bad stock don't come out o' good. Them Lloyds is rough-woolled 'uns – man, 'oman, and child.'

Esther's shoulders moved as though she had shuddered with cold.

'Well,' said the postman, drawing the back of his hand across his mouth, 'I'm much obliged for a cup o' tea. I 'on't see it so hard goin' over the hill to the Henallt now I've a good bellyful. Well, well, I was earnin' the run o' my teeth, eh, Esther?'

No sooner had the door closed than Esther felt the weight of her father's huge hand on her shoulder. She would have liked to throw it off, but with an effort stood still, trying to nerve herself for the inevitable conflict. It began pleasantly enough.

'Now then, gal, tell us all about it. There's many parents 'ould take on terrible at a bit of a gal o' your age keepin' company along of a boy they'd never so much as set eyes on. Still, if he's a tidy fellow with a bit o' money, I'll say nothin' against it.'

98

His wife did not speak, but she began to twist and untwist her apron round her thin wrists.

'Aunt Polly 'ull tell you as he's a tidy fellow a' right,' Esther assured her father.

'Ah! And what prospec's is he havin'?'

'He's been adopted by an uncle, a wonderful well-to-do farmer as hasn't got no children of his own.'

'Well, well, there's more sense in you nor I gave you credit for.'

John and Idris had risen and come nearer. Their faces expressed surprise and admiration. Only Mrs Bevan continued to wring her hands, and Gladys, with her back turned on them all, to stare gloomily into the fire.

'Well,' her father demanded, surveying Esther with satisfaction, 'and what's his name?'

She looked down at Gladys for support, but on the forlorn face that was raised to hers for an instant she saw only the expression of jealous misery that had disfigured it for the last five days. 'I'll have to go through this alone,' she thought. 'Oh, if only mother 'ull help me.' Slowly she turned towards the four expectant listeners, and in a low voice said: 'His name's Rhys Lloyd, but I wasn't never thinkin' to meet one o' the Henallt lot down there – I took up with him afore ever I thought o' such a thing – and I only comed to find out the day afore I was leavin' as he was a son to Elias Lloyd here.'

There was a moment's silence. Then her elder brother swore under his breath. Her mother stared at her, bewildered, with stupidly open mouth.

'*Who* did you say he was?' she asked, scarcely above a whisper.

John Bevan turned on her, red as a turkey-cock.

'Are you gone deaf, 'oman, as well as dull? Didn't you hear what she said?' He swung round on Esther, leaving his wife shrinking against the wall. 'You went and took up with a son o' that bloody rascal, Elias Lloyd? You let one o' that low thievin' lot go courtin' you? If you wanted a boy that bad, you slut, you, wasn't there nothin' else in trousers as 'ould look at you?'

'I didn't know who he was.'

'Well, you do know now,' he said more calmly, though his face was still flushed with anger. 'That do put an end to it, and don't you come talkin' to me about it no more. I'd break the neck o' any damned son o' Lloyd's as did set foot inside my house.'

'None o' them as is at the Henallt now 'ould dare do it,' said John, grinning.

'But my Rhys hasn't had nothin' to do with his folks' quarrels,' Esther protested. 'He's not seen them hardly since he were a small little lump o' a boy.'

'Shut your mouth, will you?' cried her father. 'I don't care if he's *never* seen 'em. *Your* Rhys, you...'

His wife interrupted tearfully.

'Don't say no more, boss, I do beseech you. 'Tis over and done with now. We don't want to lose her. Indeed and I couldn't spare her. I'm glad 'tis come to nothin'.'

Esther looked at her aghast.

'A' right,' John Bevan grumbled, 'that do put an end to the matter; only don't let me never hear the name o' Lloyd again.'

One by one Esther studied the faces confronting her. To Idris, whom she had so often sheltered in trouble, she

100

looked for sympathy, but she realised now that he was still too much of a child to understand what she was suffering. 'If father had broken my arm,' she thought, 'the boy 'ould be terrible sorry; but he'll stand by and watch the heart torn out o' me and never know I'm hurted.' All the figures by whom she was surrounded seemed to grow smaller and to recede. She felt as though the kitchen were an immense vault, in which she would have to shout her loudest in order to make herself heard.

'This is not the end o' the matter,' she found herself saying with surprising calm. 'Rhys is innocent o' wrong, and you didn't ought to take against him along o' his father and his uncle's sins.'

John Bevan had turned away. He came back and stood towering over her.

'Are you mad, gal? Do you want your own father to be the laughin' stock o' the countryside? A fine joke it 'ould be if my daughter was to go out walkin' with a boy whose relations has been fightin' me and mine in and out o' court these eighteen years. Why, the whole district is in it, and the very children is throwin' stones at one another on the way to school.'

He raised his fist, but before it fell the dogs in the fold raised an uproar, and Mrs Bevan had cried out shrilly:

'Boss, boss, mind what you are doin'. There's someone comin'.'

The door opened, and John Bevan's sister Martha thrust in her head. 'Whatever's up?' she enquired in a harsh voice akin to that of her brother.

'Come on in,' he shouted, 'and do you be listenin' to this, now.'

She took a stride over the threshold, and began without wasting time to unpin her skirt which had been tucked up over a black-and-red striped petticoat. She was followed by her sister Lily, who surveyed with disapproval the troubled faces of her relatives, and by their niece Megan, on whose full red lips the smile of greeting was frozen by lack of response.

'Come on in, the whole damned lot o' you,' shouted John Bevan; 'the more o' you the better, to witness as this gal o' mine did ought to be locked up.'

Martha Bevan drew herself up to her full height. She and Lily were alike gaunt and tall, though her sister's face was uniformly pale as parchment, and hers mottled like her brother's by a network of purple veins. They were both clad in the black cloth of respectability, and each grasped an umbrella.

Megan presented a striking contrast to her aunts, from behind whose backs she was now making signals of encouragement to Esther. Hers was a youthfully rounded figure, its contours emphasised by her efforts to obtain a small waist. Under a rusty black overcoat, which she had thrown open on entering the room, she wore a working pinafore of blue print, that lent to her robust beauty a touch of the picturesque.

'After all as has taken place,' John Bevan announced, 'this daughter o' mine is wantin' to marry a son o' that hypocrite, that lyin' thief of a chapel-goer, Elias Lloyd.'

The steely grey eyes of her two aunts were fixed upon Esther.

'But there isn't a young Lloyd of an age to marry,' objected Martha Bevan.

102

'Not none o' the lumpers here, but some bastard or other livin' down near Aberdulas.'

'He's no such thing,' Esther interrupted. 'He's the eldest son as you've seen about the Henallt when he were a small little lumper.'

'Well,' said Aunt Lily, 'I couldn't never have believed it of you, after all as your poor dear father have gone through along o' them wicked folk.'

Aunt Martha's comment was more pertinent.

'You're a fool, Esther. What good did you think could come o' your takin' up with a young man against his relations' will and yours?'

Esther repeated her explanation.

'Well, 'twas a pity you didn't find out at the start who he was. Now you *do* know, there's no more to be said.'

'There's this to be said: I am lovin' him, and he is lovin' me. We've neither of us done no wrong, so why shouldn't we be bein' happy?'

She had taken courage now. Her head was thrown back, her cheeks flushed. Aunt Lily looked at her sourly.

'You are doin' wrong to disobey your dear father.'

'Yes, indeed,' Mrs Bevan whimpered. 'Don't you go against him, Esther. 'T'ould be undutiful.'

The raised voices made Esther's head ache. She yearned for peace and solitude. How hot the room had grown! How her eyes smarted! Gulping down the tears she could no longer control, she pushed her way past her brothers who stood at the foot of the stairs, and stumbled up to her room.

The hubbub by which she had been pursued died away as she closed the door behind her. The familiar room soothed her. She knelt down beside her bed where night and morning as long as she could remember, she had said the Lord's Prayer and made such personal petitions as occurred to her.

'O Lord,' she prayed now, 'I do want to be happy; O, I do so want to be happy. I wasn't knowin' what happiness was like till I did meet Rhys, and I can't never bear to be kept from him now. Please let me go to him, Lord, whatever my relations do say.' The words of the fifth commandment crossed her mind, and she hesitated. 'I wonder is it right to go against my father?' she thought. Then once more she buried her face in her hands. 'Guide me, O Lord, to do what is right,' she prayed, and added after a while, 'but please make it right for me to marry Rhys.'

CHAPTER 6

A few days later the ancient porter at Llangantyn railway station was surprised to see three strangers alight when it was neither market day nor holiday time. They stood grouped beside a box which they evidently shared, whilst old Evans hobbled slowly towards them, eyeing them inquisitively from under his shaggy brows. They were dressed 'respectable' in his opinion; he judged the thick-set man to be a well-to-do farmer, and the small sallow woman with black eyes, bright as a rat's, to be his wife. Their son, if he were so, who resembled neither of them, was more difficult to place. He had an air at once alert and thoughtful, unusual in a countryman, yet he was too healthily suntanned to be a collier or a shop assistant; and something free and careless about his bearing and rakish in the angle at which his hat was worn made it improbable that he was either a schoolteacher or studying to be a minister. With other types of humanity the porter was unfamiliar.

Before he had reached the strangers he saw the trap from the Greyhound drive up to the station gate, and, altering his course, hissed a whispered enquiry over the railings at the driver.

'Are you come to fetch *them*?' He jerked his thumb in the direction of the strangers. 'Who are they bein'? Relations o' the Henallt? Ah, to be sure, the old 'oman is dead. Are you knowin' what she cut up worth? Well, indeed! As much as that! Then her children 'ull give her a stylish funeral, no doubt. Fancy their hirin' a trap for these here. What 'ull that cost 'em? Seven-and-six. You don't say! Ah, they are goin' to do the thing proper, and not have the mourners ridin' on a farm cart, and all shook up inside till they can't be enjoyin' the bakemeats.'

Having satisfied his curiosity, he helped the strangers to squeeze themselves and their luggage into the trap.

As they rattled through the narrow streets and across the bridge spanning the river, Rhys, perched on the back seat, looked about him eagerly. This was the place to which Esther came on a market day, and he pictured her trudging along, patient and sturdy, with a basket on either arm, down the straight road on to which they had now turned. It must be from those steep hills rising above them on the left that she descended. What a long tramp it was for her, poor child! When they were married he would buy her a pony and trap so that she might drive about in comfort. He was confident of his own ability to make money, and rejoiced to think of all the things he would get for her which she had never before enjoyed. When and how he was to have a start in life was still uncertain, and he realised that it was of no use trying to hurry his uncle. For the present he must exercise patience. When the funeral was over he would broach the subject once more, and point out that, in fairness, he should be given a chance to earn a living wage.

How sweet the air smelt after the smoke and stuffiness of the train! How exquisitely blue was the sky that showed in fragments through the parting clouds! How good it was to be alive and full of health and hope!

As they drove out of the town, Mrs Pritchard asked the driver what he knew about her mother's death, and, while hearing his account, made the pious ejaculations and heaved the sighs that seemed proper. After that she fell into the general silence which went unbroken until, at some distance from Llangantyn, they came to the cart track leading up towards Pengarreg. Here Rhys suddenly leant forward and gave the driver a prod in the back.

'What place do that go to?' he demanded.

'To a farm on the mountain. Pengarreg they do call it.'

'Holt then,' Rhys cried impetuously, and had leapt out on to the road before his relatives could protest. 'Go you on,' he commanded, 'and I'll be walkin' across the hilltop to the Henallt.' He turned to the astonished youth who had let the reins slip through his fingers. 'I can be gettin' across to our place that way, can't I? By what I do remember 'tis only another half-mile or so along this road, and then up another track the same as this one.'

Speechless with surprise, the driver nodded.

'Then 'tis no distance from the one farm to the other?' Rhys asked brightly.

'They are next to one another, but indeed...'

'Well?'

'I suppose you do know your own business best.'

Mrs Pritchard interposed.

'I don't see it at all decent, Rhys, for you to be goin' courtin' on your way to the house where your poor granny is lyin' a cold corpse,' and she dabbed her dry eyes with a black-bordered handkerchief.

'No, indeed,' added her husband, "tisn't showin' due respect to the dead.'

Rhys, full of joyful anticipation, only smiled at them good-naturedly.

'Come you, nothin' as I can do 'ull be harmin' poor old granny now; and seein' as I can hardly remember her, you can't expect me to be terrible sad. 'Twill be all the better for you, Aunty, to go by yourself, and have a talk with Mother and Father. You was all knowin' the corpse well, and I wasn't, so you can't want me there like some stranger in your midst.'

'Your duty,' she answered sourly, 'is to be along o' your poor, grief-stricken parents, and comfortin' them.'

But Rhys, who knew as well as she did how relieved they must be to escape the burden of a bedridden and querulous invalid, shook his head and strode away up the track.

Once out on the open hillside he flung off his hat, and, swinging his arms round like the sails of a windmill in a gale, began to run and at the same time to try and whistle a lively tune. Thomas Pritchard and his wife, jogging sedately along the road below, heard him, and exchanged a disapproving glance.

Having run himself to a standstill, Rhys stood panting,

108

and flicked the sweat from his forehead with a flourish.

'Drat this old black-bordered handkerchief!' he exclaimed aloud. 'I 'ould like a fancy one, all bright red and yellow.'

After many days of rain the valley below glistened with moisture. The new grass was vividly green bordering the brown and swollen river, on the further side of which the hills showed so distinct that he felt he could have jumped across to them. About him stretched the open mountain, scarred by outcrops of grey rock, shining like the slates of a house after a downpour, and the bracken, now waist-high, shone as if it had been varnished. The air was full of pleasant smells, called forth by dampness, of moss, and mushrooms and decaying wood; and the mingled tinkle and deep gurgle of running water sounded from every gully.

''Tis a good world when we are knowin' how to enjoy ourselves in it,' he thought as he went forward. 'I 'ould like, if I was to have children now, to give them a chanst o' bein' happy, happy all the while from when they was born healthy, and not taught to be afeard.'

Thus he reached Pengarreg. The muck in the fold was so deep that it made him think of the earth in its earliest stages, when Megatherium and Diplodocus ploughed through the warm slime. Steam, invisible to the eye, but detected by the nostril, arose from the huge manure stack that encroached upon the house. The slates of the roof were mottled with patches of lichen, green like the mould on a Stilton cheese. The whole place reeked of moisture and decay. There was no one about but a blue-eyed lad who ceased his chopping to stare timidly at the stranger. Rhys smiled his most ingratiating smile; but the boy's mouth and eyes opened wider than before. He had let the axe drop, and his large red hands hung down limply at his sides. Thinking him half-witted, Rhys went past him to the door, on which he knocked loudly. Whilst he waited for an answer he was in danger of being bitten by the dogs, which barked furiously and snapped at his heels.

'Can't you call off the dogs?' he shouted to the lad but he received no reply. At length the door was opened by a thin little woman with a lined and faded face, whose dirty apron was torn, and whose bodice was pinned together untidily over a meagre bosom. It was inconceivable that this draggled creature should be the mother of his bonny Esther, but in case, by some miracle, she should be, he made an effort to smile at her as he had done at the boy who was obviously her son.

'Good day,' he began civilly, though the atmosphere of the place had already chilled him. 'Is this Pengarreg, where Mr Bevan do live?'

Mrs Bevan stared as Idris had done, and slowly nodded her head.

'You are not guessin' who I am?' His smile was becoming somewhat forced, and it flashed through his mind that thus he must have looked when having his photograph taken that he might send it to Esther on a postcard.

She retreated a step as if she feared he might be a madman.

'Maybe Esther's said nothin' about me to you, then?'

Her terror seemed to increase. The dogs were no longer barking, but snarled at him from a distance, and the tongue-tied youth had approached him cautiously from the rear. Neither he nor the woman showed any inclination to speak.

After a pause Rhys began again: 'I had best be explainin' who I am,' but he wondered whether it was of any use to do so to beings so devoid of intelligence. 'I was gettin' to know Miss Esther Bevan when she was stayin' down with her aunty at Aberdulas. That's where I do live.'

The woman gave a low sound like one mesmerised.

'And seein' as I did happen to be comin' up into these parts, I thought as I'd make bold to come and see her – and to have the pleasure o' gettin' acquainted with her folk,' he added hastily, his desire to propitiate them proving stronger than his love of truth.

'Duwch! That's what I did fear from the first moment I set eyes on him,' exclaimed the lad.

The woman's behaviour was equally unexpected. She made a nervous movement with her hands as though warding off a blow, and retreated into the house.

'Boss, boss,' she called, 'whatever am I to do?'

There followed a muttered conference of which he could not catch the drift, and a man's voice raised in anger.

'Has there been any accident or trouble in the house of late?' Rhys demanded of the boy whose sole reply was to gape as before.

'Is there any reason why I should not be seein' Esther Bevan?' he shouted, hoping that the apparent stupidity of these people might be accounted for by deafness, but the boy stepped backwards, startled. Rhys turned away from him in despair and as he did so was confronted by a burly man, whose face was purple and distorted with fury.

'What the hell is your name?'

Rhys stared at him in astonishment. 'I hope as you've no objection to my callin' friendly like...'

111

'What's your name? Are you dull or drunk, that you can't answer a straight question?'

'Excuse me, Mr Bevan, but I am knowin' a relation o' yours, Mrs Jones of Aberdulas, and I thought as you'd be glad to have news of her.'

'What's your name, damn you?'

'Rhys Lloyd. There's no call to be so uncivil.' His own temper was rising at this extraordinary treatment.

'A son o' that bloody fox at the Henallt?'

'A son o' Elias Lloyd, if that's who you're speakin' of.'

'Then get out o' my place quick, afore I make a mess o' you.'

'But, Mr Bevan...'

'Get out! D'you hear me? You'll be glad to go alive if I do catch holt o' you.'

Rhys saw his huge fists swing up, and sprang nimbly beyond their reach.

'Whatever is the meanin' o' this? You might be givin' me some explanation, whatever.'

'I'll give you summat in a minute as you'll remember better. Here, missus, get me out my gun,' he roared over his shoulder.

'No, no,' she whimpered, 'don't you go shootin' no one, or maybe 'twill be found murder.'

'Get out o' the way then, you fool. Here, John, come on out with them sticks.'

A loutish youth, of big build and lowering countenance like his father, came striding out of the house, in either hand a stick. His elder snatched one of them from him and together they made a rush at Rhys, shouting to the boy with the axe to join them. Through mud and water

112

Rhys fled to the gate and vaulted over it. From the far side he faced the three of them.

'Are you all mad here?'

He was answered by a volley of incoherent abuse and threats, and by John Bevan setting the dogs at him. Amidst their furious barking he retired up the hillside, warding off attacks on the calves of his legs by sideways kicks, but before he had gone many paces he was arrested by a woman's scream rising shrilly above the uproar. Swinging round, he saw Esther on the threshold of the house below. Her father caught sight of her at the same moment, and, abandoning the chase, turned back, splashed across the fold, and, catching her roughly by the arm, dragged her into the house. She struggled like some frantic fly caught in a web by a spider twice its size.

Rhys turned hot and sick with anger at the sight.

For a while he hesitated whether to return and fight 'the whole pack o' them bullyin' brutes' as he designated Esther's relations – but, realising that a man without weapons can do nothing in a combat against three armed men, he decided to go on instead to his parents' house and to ask their advice.

While this tumult had been taking place at Pengarreg, all was quiet at the neighbouring farm. The blinds were decorously lowered. They were the colour of brown paper, and the light shining through them filled the rooms with the sickly yellow of a London fog. In the small unaired parlour sat Elias Lloyd, clothed in his Sabbath black which he had put on to show his respect for his visitors. Beside him was his wife, also in black and holding a white handkerchief with a mourning border in the hands with which she continually

113

smoothed out the stiff silk in her lap. Husband and wife sat erect on chairs that were not of a pattern to encourage lolling. Opposite them and equally upright were Thomas and Mrs Pritchard, seated upon the shiny horsehair sofa which was so slippery that they had to brace themselves against a tendency to slide on to the floor. Between them was the parlour table covered with a cloth the colour of dried blood, upon which lay a ponderous Bible and a photograph album. At the far end of this table sat Evan Lloyd, and behind him stood his nephew Dan, the second son of Elias.

Dan was a lanky lad of fifteen who fidgeted uneasily in the presence of his elders, shuffling his feet on the linoleum-covered floor, and craning his neck in slow spasms to relieve the discomfort of a high starched collar that was too small for him.

The family likeness between Elias Lloyd, his brother, his sister, and his son, was remarkable. Four lean, sallow faces confronted one another in the unflattering light, and four pairs of slightly oblique black eyes shifted in their owners' embarrassment at this forced solemnity and unwelcome crowding together. Dan was secretly wishing that he could escape into the fold to play football with his younger brothers. His father was thinking gloomily of the expenses of the funeral, and his uncle of the dangers of leaving his smallholding for a day.

'No doubt them Bevans is havin' a grand time coursin' our sheep whilst we are wastin' ours in buryin' Mother,' he sighed inwardly.

Mrs Pritchard was equally anxious about her household concerns.

'I didn't ought to have come here,' she reflected,

tightening her thin lips. 'That servant gal is sure to be havin' a young man in the house when I'm from home. Maybe sleepin' in our own lawful bed. I do know what she is – the hussy.'

'Poor Mother,' she sighed audibly.

'Aye,' echoed Elias Lloyd, 'poor Mother,' and he resumed his calculation. 'There's the coffin and the tombstone, and the expense o' feedin' all the neighbours as 'ull come to show their respects, and the hire o' that trap to bring my sister and brother-in-law up here. 'Tis a terrible lot to expend on an old 'oman as was costin' me more nor enough in doctor's bills whilst she was livin'.'

He heaved a deep sigh, and the others sighed in chorus to show their sympathy with his grief.

'But I'll not have it said as I were too poor to bury my own mother stylish,' he thought. 'The way down to Lewisbridge from here bein' that steep, the coffin 'ull have to be carried, so the neighbours 'ull have a good chanst to see what an expensive one I've stood her. Yes, indeed, the talk 'ull be goin' out, and 'twill come to John Bevan's ears no doubt, and vex him proper to hear me praised for so good a son.'

The silence having lasted a long time, Mrs Lloyd felt it her duty as hostess to say something.

'She did die a Christian death, penitent and tearful,' she announced with pride.

'Ah, poor Mother,' exclaimed her sister-in-law, startled out of her thoughts on the iniquity of servant girls. 'I'm sure you were allus a good daughter-in-law to her, Sarah.'

'Well, it was a burden, Minnie, I can tell you. I did see it hard at times as the old lady's own daughter didn't take her.'

'I'm sure it was allus my wish to do so; only Thomas here...'

'It wasn't none o' my doin' as you didn't,' interrupted her husband. 'You settled that between yourselves.'

'Well,' snapped Mrs Pritchard to the Lloyds, 'I'm sure as we've been a great help to you in takin' your eldest boy off your hands.'

'Yes, yes,' Elias hastened to reply. 'We are tremendous grateful, I can tell you.' There was a brief pause, then he added: 'Rhys must be comin' pretty handy on the farm by now.'

'Oh, I don't know. He do eat a lot, whatever, and give a terrible deal o' trouble in the house with his muddy boots and his careless, untidy ways.'

'Oh, come you,' put in Thomas Pritchard, 'he 'ull shape well, I do believe. A bit too headstrong, that's what's the matter with him, but I do hope to break him o' that. He doesn't answer back nor talk in the presence o' his betters near so much as he did use to.'

Since the lad no longer expressed his unorthodox views, his uncle was convinced that disapproval had quenched them. That they were held in secret with all the greater tenacity did not occur to him. Rhys obeyed him, and obedience was what he most desired. It was more flattering, however, to assume that it was rendered willingly, in thought as well as in deed.

Elias Lloyd turned to his second son, glad of so good an opportunity of reading him a lesson.

'Are you hearin' what your kind uncle is sayin', boy? If your elder brother is doin' all as he do wish, and if you are doin' the same by me, you 'on't neither o' you be left so

116

bad off. That's the truth, isn't it, Thomas?'

Thomas Pritchard nodded. 'I don't believe in promisin' young folk nothin'; but what I do say to Rhys is – "Allus respect your elders, and you'll have your reward both here and hereafter."'

'Very true, Thomas. Are you layin' that to heart, boy?'

The lad coloured and hung his head as all five of his elders looked at him admonishingly. He was glad that there was not a funeral in the house every day, for he had been forced to stand in the parlour for nearly an hour listening to talk which bored him, to wear his detested Sabbath raiment, to wash his face and hands, and to refrain from whistling.

'Why can't we be enjoyin' ourselves in our own way when we're young?' he asked in inward rebellion. 'Well, never mind, *I'll* take it out o' someone when I'm old enough not to be answered back.'

'Boys and gals are all thinkin' theirselves a deal older and wiser for their age nor what they are,' Mrs Pritchard said. 'What d'you think Rhys is up to now? Keepin' company, if you please, with some strange gal he do tell us he is goin' to marry.'

Dan grinned, but his mother's lantern-jawed face became sterner than ever.

'Well, I never heard such a thing,' she cried, flinging up her hands, and letting fall the black-edged handkerchief.

Thomas answered with contemptuous toleration. 'No need to vex. 'Twill blow over like as not. Rhys he's given to first one fancy and then another. He was for ever botherin' me some years ago to send him to the county school to try for a scholarship for Aberystwyth College.

We don't hear nothin' of it now. He's settled down to farmin'.'

'But to talk o' gettin' married at his age,' his mother persisted.

'Oh, well, 'tis some years now since you seed him. He's growed quite a young man.'

'Is she a tidy gal?'

Thomas Pritchard pursed up his lips.

'She do *look* quiet enough.'

'But she's a stranger to us,' put in his wife suspiciously. 'Maybe as you are knowin' her parents, though. They do come from these parts. Bevan their name is.'

'*Bevan!*' exclaimed Elias Lloyd and his wife simultaneously. 'There's only one lot o' Bevans in this parish and they're low, drinkin', irreligious folk, the very worst o' the church people.'

'Our Rhys could never be so wicked and undutiful as to take up with a daughter o' theirs,' cried his mother, aghast.

'But he weren't knowin' nothin' about 'em,' Thomas Pritchard objected.

'I wonder, now, could it be?'

They looked at one another in dismay. Along the flagstoned passage outside came the clatter of nailed boots. The swarthy face of one of the younger children was thrust into the room.

'Brother Rhys is here,' she announced in an awestruck whisper.

The clatter increased, and Rhys, followed by two open-mouthed younger brothers, burst into the room. The frigidity of its atmosphere held him arrested on the threshold.

118

'Well,' he began, and stood unable to frame any other greeting to his five elders, who sat still as stones about the central slab of the table. It flashed through his mind that they resembled the monoliths of Stonehenge, of which he had seen a picture. He was flushed and excited, but their appearance chilled him like a plunge into cold water. Slowly his mother rose and came towards him.

'Is this my boy Rhys?'

My boy! The words had an ironic sound as he surveyed the gaunt grey-haired woman on whose harsh features he could never remember to have seen a look of tenderness. He looked swiftly from one of his parents to the other. He had come to them burning with indignation at the treatment he had received from the Bevans, thinking of them as his own people from whom he might expect sympathy and help, but he found them strangers who looked him up and down with narrowly observant eyes.

'Wherever have you been all this while?' his mother demanded. 'Your uncle here said as you were walkin' up after the trap.'

'Yes,' Thomas Pritchard interposed, 'I didn't like to tell them the truth; but 'tis all out now.'

'Where have I been? In a madhouse, I should think. I don't hardly know whether I'm standin' on my head or my heels.'

They stared at him in amazement, and the three children in the doorway crept into the room.

'What is the meanin' o' this trouble with your neighbour, Father?' he continued.

'My neighbour?'

'Aye. Bevan, Pengarreg.'

At the hated name Elias Lloyd's little eyes contracted, and his head moved from side to side like that of a snake about to strike.

'Have you been to Pengarreg courtin' a gal o' Bevan's?' he demanded.

'Yes, Father.'

'How dared you do such a thing?'

'Listen, Father...'

'A son o' mine!'

'I wasn't knowin' nothin'...'

'Not knowin' – all o' you here present – *look*.'

They had risen to their feet, and the younger ones tiptoed and craned forward to get a view of the strange brother who had come among them.

'Are you seein' my face?' cried Elias Lloyd. 'Spoiled for life it has been by that ruffian John Bevan.'

'Yes, yes,' his wife chimed in, 'if ever there was a smart-lookin' young fellow, it was my man before his nose was broke, as you can remember, Minnie, bein' his sister.'

Mrs Pritchard remembered no such thing, but since the honour of her family was at stake she was ready for once to agree with her sister-in-law.

'You are right, Sarah. And is this Bevan the wicked fellow as was doin' our poor Elias such an injury?'

'He's done more nor that. I'll tell you just a few o' the ill trickses he's played me.'

Elias Lloyd addressed himself to Rhys, who, angry as he was with the common enemy, shrank from the sight of the venomous hatred in his father's eyes.

'What is a hill farmer carin' for most? What is he gainin' his livin' by? Sheep. Well, since first he struck me that blow, the mark o' which you do all see, John Bevan has not let a day go by in all these years but he's been coursin' my sheep and those o' my brother Evan here, away from our boundary, and drivin' his own sheep up to it, aye, and over it, so as they shall graze the grass that is ours, and our sheep shall go poor.'

Evan Lloyd nodded his confirmation of this statement, and the suppressed Dan piped up, knowing that on this topic alone he was sure of a hearing from his elders.

'Yes, and so soon as ever I comed of an age to help father shepherdin', what did them two Bevan boys do but lie in wait to catch me unawares; and the other day they was settin' on me afore I'd time to run off, and very near breakin' every bone in my body they was. Look, I'll show you some o' the bruises as is to be seen.'

He stripped off his coat and pulled up his shirt. His aunt inspected his shoulders and uttered clicking sounds of commiseration; but her husband shrugged impatiently. The blows a boy had received were of no importance in his opinion, but he was distressed to hear of this coursing of sheep, for that meant a loss of money.

'Can't you and Evan between you put a stop to such goin's-on?' he demanded with a hint of contempt. 'I'd learn a neighbour o' mine as comed trespassin' a lesson as he 'ouldn't forget.'

Evan Lloyd grinned cunningly.

'Bevan he's too powerful of a fighter for us to be meetin' in the open; but there's many ways o' gettin' even with him after dark, and by day too: when one o' us is keepin' a watch on him the other 'ull be coursin' his sheep.'

'There's time wasted over a business like that,' said Thomas Pritchard. ''Tis doin' a farmer no good to be quarrellin' over his boundary.'

'You are right,' Elias agreed. 'This place is gone to ruin just, hedges down and fields overgrown with thistles along o' my havin' to spend the greater part o' my days on the hill. Aye,' he continued, glaring at Rhys, 'and 'tis that man, a drunkard, a blasphemer, a lyin', brawlin', wicked fellow as has done me all this harm, my own son do fancy for a father-in-law.'

The whole tribe turned angry eyes upon the offender.

'I'm not wantin' nothin' to do with John Bevan.' Rhys spoke resolutely, though he was conscious of intense excitement and of a nervous quivering of the lips which he tried to repress. 'I was callin' friendly like at his house now just, a stranger as had never done him no harm, and he set on me, he and his sons and his dogs, same as if I'd been a thief in the night.'

The heads of all the Lloyds were nodded in assent.

'That's the manner o' man he is,' Elias said. 'One as the Lord Himself 'ull surely punish, if we do fail to do so for Him.'

'May He be deliverin' the job into our hands, though,' murmured Evan piously.

'I thought as he were mad,' resumed Rhys, 'but now you have told me how matters is between you and him I do understand why he was goin' so violent at sight o' me come courtin' his daughter; and maybe he is treatin' her cruel even now on my account – 'tis more nor I can bear to think on...' His voice became husky, and he turned away from the unsympathetic scrutiny of all those dark

122

eyes. 'She's been sufferin' a sad childhood along o' that brute her father,' he exclaimed as he regained his self-control. 'I must be gettin' her away from him – *quick*. Will you be helpin' me, all of you, to do so?'

There was no sound in the darkened room when he ceased speaking, and awaited an answer with trembling eagerness. Nobody moved or spoke, until at length Elias Lloyd cleared his throat and spat into the fireplace.

'I 'ould sooner see you in your coffin,' he announced deliberately, 'nor raise a finger to help you marry the child o' my lifelong enemy.'

'And I too,' added his wife in the tone of pious finality with which she was accustomed to utter 'Amen' when in chapel.

'But *Esther* has done nothin' to harm you,' cried Rhys in dismay.

'She's Bevan's daughter none the less – may all his children live to beg their bread.'

'But, Father, if I do take Esther away without her parents' consent they'll not be comin' near us. She'll be free of them then, and one of ourselves.'

'You dare call a Bevan born and bred one of ourselves?' Elias Lloyd's eyes flashed like jet held close to a fire.

'Why should you blame her, as is innocent of all evil? 'Tis her misfortune, not her fault, to have been born his child. She is hatin' his bloodthirsty ways. She has told me so herself.'

'I don't care what she's told you. No one o' that breed ever yet spoke the truth. And is it not written in the Book as the Lord shall visit the sins o' the fathers upon the children unto the third and fourth generation?'

Rhys turned away in despair. He knew from experience that if any isolated text could be made to support a contention of his elders' it was of no use for him to argue.

'You are no Christian, Father, showin' so unforgivin' a spirit.'

'Is that the way to speak to him whom it is your duty to honour?'

'Shame on you, boy.'

A storm of anger and reproach broke about him. After the babel of voices had lasted for some time, Thomas Pritchard interposed: 'I am knowin' Rhys' hasty ways better nor any o' you here. By tomorrow he'll be sorry as he spoke so disrespectful.... Go you on out, Rhys, and take a walk to cool yourself. You have said enough. We don't want to hear no more about the matter.'

'But 'tis life and death to me, Uncle. How can I be keepin' calm about it?'

'Don't talk so wild, boy. Life and death, indeed.' He laughed.

'Uncle, will you be helpin' me, since Father's heart is hardened by rage? *You* do know how good Esther is.'

'I don't know nothin' about the gal.'

'But you have seen her. To have looked at her onst, isn't that enough to prove it to you?'

'Go on! I've no patience with the way you do talk. Even if it weren't for this quarrel between your families, 't'ould be a bad job for you to take a gal without her father's consent. She'll be havin' no money after him.'

'D'you think I want her for her money?'

'Oh, do talk reasonable, boy! You can't live in this world without.'

'But you could be settin' us up first for a start, Uncle.'

'Well I never! If you're not behavin' more respectful to your elders nor what you've done today, I 'on't be doin' nothin' for you.'

Stunned by this last disappointment, Rhys turned away. His mother's harsh voice pursued him.

'I'm surprised at you takin' on so about this foolishness, when your poor granny is lyin' dead upstairs.'

Foolishness! His love for Esther, which seemed to him the most sacred and beautiful thing in the world! He flung round and faced the whole tribe.

'You do think only o' the dead, never o' the livin' as is needin' your help,' he cried. His face was working, and his fists were clenched. 'Old folks as is dead, old wrongs, old sufferin', that is all as is in your minds, rottin' there like every lifeless thing do rot, and poisonin' you. Love may starve, so hatred be fed, the young grow grey in their sorrow, so their elders are havin' their spite and pride satisfied. Here is your chanst to make two young folks happy, and to be blessed by them for your kindness throughout the years to come. Now at last you could let old evil bygones be forgotten. You could make a fresh start in charity and kindness. But no – all you do talk of is the respect I did ought to pay to a spiritless corpse – a carcass, that's all it is, no more nor the carcass of a beast, now that the soul is gone out of it. I 'ould have treated the old 'oman kinder nor what you did while she was alive, but what is her cold clay to me now? What does it matter to anyone, since it can't feel nothin' no more, and since the livin' is able to suffer such agony?'

He strode back into the room and violently pulled up

125

the blind. To the consternation of those upon whose faces it fell, the serene light of evening flooded the little parlour.

CHAPTER 7

During the day on which old Mrs Lloyd was buried no word was spoken of her grandson's love affair. The united family and their friends followed her coffin from the house on the hilltop to the chapel graveyard in the valley below. In the greyness of an autumn afternoon that veiled the rich colours of the landscape in a universal monotone the little procession of black-clad men and women, solemn but without grief, their hats adorned with crepe, their stout boots scrupulously polished, wound their way down the bleak hillside. Over the open grave his relations eyed Rhys with covert hostility, but they said nothing to him either on the homeward way or during the dreary evening when they sat once more, rigid as stones, ranged along the parlour wall.

'What is the good of all this gloom?' thought Rhys. 'If the dead are goin' to heaven like what they do believe, why are they not rejoicin'?' He threw himself back in his chair, and all the eyes in the room were fixed on him reproachfully. 'They are sad and sour,' he thought, 'because they are worshippin' an old God – the God of Abraham, of Isaac, and of Jacob – a jealous and revengeful tribal deity. But I am glad in my heart, for I am worshippin' the new God of Evolution as is makin' my love for Esther and my hope of our children part of His service. That's a good idea,' he thought – pleased with himself and wishing that Esther were present so that he might explain it to her whilst she looked up at him attentive and puzzled. 'The God o' Evolution, or the Goddess maybe – I wonder now was those wise old Greeks I was readin' of symbolisin' her in Aphrodite?'

On either side of him sat his relatives, content to let their hands lie idle in their laps. For them, this was as a Sabbath day, a day of silence and inaction. They had put on their best clothes and eaten their fill, and, little as Rhys suspected it, they were enjoying their holiday.

The following morning at breakfast Thomas Pritchard announced his intention of returning home that day. 'I'll be comin' along of you,' said his wife. Her brother demurred half-heartedly. 'You'd best be stayin' on here a while, hadn't she, Sarah?'

'Aye,' Mrs Lloyd agreed sourly, 'I'm bein' only too glad o' the trouble visitors is givin' me if they are relations of yours, boss. 'Tis my duty.'

'Very kind of you, I'm sure,' her sister-in-law sniffed, 'but 'tis my duty to look after my own home, so I'll be gettin' back along o' Thomas – sorry as I'll be to go.'

They consulted a timetable three years old and

128

decided that they had better start for Llangantyn in half an hour's time.

'We 'on't miss to catch a train in the course o' the day, then,' Thomas Pritchard remarked. Then, slowly turning his head, he addressed Rhys, who had risen and was restlessly stirring the fire with the toe of his boot.

'Go you and get together your things, boy, and say goodbye to your brothers and sisters.'

'I'll be glad of a few days longer here. Could you be sparin' me till Saturday, say?' Rhys spoke hastily and kept his eyes fixed upon the hearth.

Thomas Pritchard looked an enquiry at his wife's relations. Simultaneously they shook their heads, and made warning signs behind their son's back.

''T'would be very awk'ard to spare you now just,' he said when he saw what was required of him.

'But the harvest's all in, Uncle.'

'Aye, but there's plenty o' jobs for you to do.'

'There's allus plenty o' jobs on a farm, but now is the slackest time o' year – if I do miss to stay now you 'on't be able to spare me later on, and there'd be the expense o' the railway journey. 'Twould be a pity not to let me be now I *am* here. I haven't been at home not for years and years.'

His words tumbled over each other in his eagerness.

'I'm not wantin' to keep no one from his relations.' Thomas Pritchard spoke slowly, trying to gain time. 'But...'

'Best go along o' your uncle, boy,' Elias Lloyd hastened to interpose. 'We don't want you here just now. You can be comin' again, no doubt, later on.'

'Yes! Yes! Later on,' Mrs Lloyd echoed.

129

Rhys faced them.

'Let me stay a day just, I do beg of you.'

'No! No! 'Tisn't convenient just at present.'

'Well, I'll tell you what it is,' he cried. 'I'll not go from here, not till I've seen Esther, not if I do have to sleep out under a hedge.'

His four elders looked at each other in consternation.

'You wicked, undutiful lad,' began Elias Lloyd, but Thomas Pritchard cut him short.

'I am not wishful to have no high words,' he announced, raising himself deliberately by the pressure of his hands upon the table. 'Rhys and I'll be talkin' reasonable,' and he moved heavily towards the door. 'Come into the parlour, boy. No need for temper. I can keep mine, so do you be behavin' quiet and tidy too.'

In silence Rhys followed him out, angrily aware that he was being made to feel in the wrong. With studied calm his uncle closed the parlour door behind them and seated himself upon the horsehair sofa, his feet apart, a massive red fist reposing upon either knee.

The blind was no longer lowered, but the room, lit by one small window, was still dark and its unventilated atmosphere oppressive. Rhys, standing like a naughty child with his back against the door, stared resentfully at the black marble clock under a glass shade on the mantelpiece.

'It don't never go,' he thought with irritation. 'Ugly, useless, expensive thing as they are bein' so proud of. I would like to kick it to pieces.'

'Now, boy,' Thomas Pritchard said with ponderous emphasis, 'I am goin' to be patient with you, knowin' as you are young and of a hissy temper. 'Tis time you were learnin' to curb it, but I 'on't say nothin' about that now. I'll tell you what did ought to make you grateful, if there's any gratitude to be found in this generation. I do mean to act generous by you.' He cleared his throat and squared his shoulders. 'Your parents is not bein' well off. They are havin' a large family. 'Twas a tremenjous piece of luck for you to be taken off their hands by your kind aunt and myself. You've been havin' a good home, plenty to eat – tidy clothes to wear...' He eyed Rhys narrowly for signs of appreciation. 'But that is not the end o' it. Now I'll tell you what not one man in a hundred 'ould do – I'll tell you summat about the way my will is made. After my death 'tis all for your aunt, as is only right and proper, seein' as she's been a good wife to me. But she shan't have the leavin' of it away, for fear she should be tempted to marry again. No. No. What's mine I'm keepin' hold of to the end, and seein' as there's no children to be for me, when your aunt do die my money is all for you.'

He leant back against the wall and watched for the effect of his announcement. Far from the grovelling gratitude he had expected, his nephew's face still wore a look of dogged resistance.

'After my death all my money is for you – only if you are pleasin' me to the end of my life,' Thomas Pritchard reiterated. 'Are you understandin' that?'

'I'm understandin' it very good – and what am I to do now to be pleasin' you?'

Thomas Pritchard puffed out his cheeks and let his breath escape slowly with a hissing sound.

'Well, havin' acted so generous up to now, I 'on't be

131

hard on you. If your heart is set on sayin' goodbye to this gal I'll shut my eyes to it – but, mind you, there's to be no more courtin' her after this. You must be tellin' her plain as 'tis all off. I'll give you until the end of the week here, and then mind as you do come back to Aberdulas. I'm wishin' you well. There's many as 'ould have acted very different by you, seein' how headstrong you were the day before your poor granny's funeral. I'm a kind man and a patient man, but a firm one too, mind you. What I do say, I do mean.'

He raised one of his huge hands, on the back of which grew coarse black hairs, and brought it down with a resounding slap on his knee.

'If you'll take up with a respectable well-to-do farmer's daughter as I'm knowin' all about and approvin' of, I 'on't say a word against your gettin' married – there now. But if you are persistin' in this nonsense about a penniless gal whose folk is bein' good-for-nothin' and bitter enemies of your good parents too, I'll' – his heavy eyebrows contracted so that they met – 'I'll go straight to the l'yer in Carnau so soon as I do get home, and alter my will. Not a penny o' mine shall you touch unless you are obeyin' me now.'

Rhys' bright eyes flashed.

'You are wantin' me to throw over the gal I do love for the sake o' your bit o' money?'

'I am wantin' you to act as any but a madman 'ould act.'

'What have you got against her as you do want me to treat her so shabby?'

'She do come of bad stock – that is bein' enough for me. I 'on't argue with you about it. 'Tis for you to make your choice.'

132

'I'll not give her up. She's more to me nor all your money – more...'

Words failed Rhys, and he felt his eyes fill with tears. Turning away with a violent gesture, he brushed the back of his hand across his face.

Thomas Pritchard rose to his feet and went slowly towards the door.

'I dare say as you are a bit unwillin' to part with the gal, and upset-like for the moment. But you'll be thinkin' better of it when you've cooled down. If you're stayin' stubborn you'll be a beggar no better nor any old tramp on the road. You'll never be such a fool for the sake of an 'oman as is almost a stranger to you.'

'She's no such thing!'

'Oh well, if she isn't, there's plenty more of her like to be had, and come of a better breed.'

His hand was on the doorknob. Rhys turned towards him in a desperate attempt to make him understand.

'Uncle, look you here. I'm the nearest you have to a son and you aren't a cruel man neither, if only...'

Mollified by his tone of entreaty, Thomas Pritchard paused.

'Cruel? No indeed, I should think not! You do talk odd on times.'

'But Uncle, can't you understand as she's everything to me? Oh duwch, I don't know how to put it to you if you don't know the meanin' of love.'

'Haven't I lived with your aunt tidy and respectable for twenty years?'

Rhys looked into the unmoved face that confronted him.

'Yes, you've lived respectable for twenty years, but have you ever loved? If you had, you'd know that if you can't get the woman you love no other don't matter. Esther is being all I do want in the world.'

'Don't talk so dull! You did ought to be ashamed o' yourself, a growed man carryin' on like a child after a toy. Food you do want, and shelter, and clothes to your back. That's what a man is needin' first of all, and after that a tidy position and a bit o' money to turn to in the bank, and land. All that you'll have after me if you do give over this foolishness, but not otherwise. When a man's got them things as is necessary he can think about a wife, but she isn't bein' all he do want in life, and I've no patience with you sayin' such a thing.'

'I'm wantin' the other things only for her sake to share with her.'

'Then I'm sorry ever I reared you. Thinkin' to have a tidy sensible lad as 'ould be a comfort to me in my old age and take a pride in the place as I've laboured in all my days.... Well, I do hope as you'll be in a better mind by the time as you do come home, or else you may go from there again, for you 'on't be no use to me. Three days I do give you.' And Rhys was left alone, staring at the marble clock that had ceased to record the passing of time.

All the following day he hung about the Henallt with his hands thrust deep into his pockets, indignantly wondering how he could get into communication with Esther. In the evening he strayed across the fold towards the plantation of fir trees that sheltered the buildings from the prevailing west wind.

A prolonged 'Hist' coming from behind one of the trees

134

attracted his attention, and he caught sight of a girl in a blue print pinafore retreating into the thicket. Because she was of the same height as Esther, his heart began to beat wildly. He crossed the fold, swung himself over the fence, and was in the wood in a moment. He found the girl hiding behind a tree. She was a stranger to him. But while they stared at each other, he noticed that she bore a slight resemblance to Esther.

'Are you bein' her sister?'

She shook her head and smiled, displaying a row of large even teeth, very white and strong.

'I am a relation whatever,' she told him, and added mischievously: ''Tis Esther Bevan as you are thinkin' of?'

'Who else should it be?'

'Well,' she said, 'I am wishful to help her,' and she continued to study him with a bold enquiring gaze.

'How can I get word with her?' he asked.

She drew her eyebrows together in a frown. They were dark, straight and thick, and seemed to contradict the smiling good temper of her lips.

''Tis difficult,' she said. 'They 'on't let her out of their sight so long as you are here. I've been hangin' about whenever I could slip away from home these three days to try and get holt o' you.'

'Will you take her a message?'

'That's what I comed for.'

He gave her a look full of gratitude.

'Wait you here and I'll be slippin' indoors to write a letter.'

She nodded, and when he returned with a hastily pencilled note full of assurances of his love, she greeted him with an encouraging smile.

'I've been thinkin' as I could fix for the both of you to meet tomorrow night.'

'How? When? Where?'

'You're a proper sweetheart,' she laughed, looking him up and down with a frank air of approval.

'Tell me quick,' he entreated, and she laughed again.

'Well now. They are lettin' their nasty old dogs loose at night so as you shan't come to the house without they'll get to hear of it.'

'Yes! Yes!'

'Well, the dogs are knowin' me. I do think I could 'tice 'em with a bit of meat, and get 'em into the buildings without no noise. I'll try, whatever. But I dursn't do it tonight – my aunts'll be that angry with me for bein' gone so long from the house as 'tis. I'll be workin' hard to please 'em all day tomorrow, and slippin' out after goin' to bed. Do you be waitin' in the rocks by Pengarreg at eleven o'clock. I'll whistle for you going home after shutting the dogs up, and I'll go now and tell Esther to be down and waitin' for you with the door unlocked.'

'There's sharp you are!' he cried. 'You're wonderful good under the hat.' And he had it in his heart to kiss her.

'I'll be off now with the letter for her,' she said, and added over her shoulder: 'Mind you not to make no noise tomorrow night – or you'll have the lot of 'em down on you.'

'I'll mind.'

'I thought maybe as you weren't used to courtin',' she mocked, and disappeared into the wood.

The adventure of the following night excited and pleased her. She crept out of her aunt's house as soon as she had heard the regular breathing of sleep come from their two rooms. She scrambled over the dark hillside to Pengarreg, and stealthily approached the fold.

Here, though a single bark filled her with momentary alarm, the dogs were silenced when they recognised her voice and were easily enough beguiled into the cowhouse by the food she had stolen from her aunts' larder. She then returned homewards swiftly lest she should be missed, pausing only to whistle for Rhys at the foot of the rocks overhanging Esther's home and to hear his answering whistle close to her in the darkness. She was glad that she had played the part of go-between, but was a little envious of the lovers' good fortune. 'No one 'on't be keeping company with me tonight,' she thought. 'But I'm glad someone is being happy, whatever.'

She waited until Rhys' tall figure loomed out of the surrounding night and whispered to him: 'When'll you be comin' to see her again?'

He had been reviewing the situation all day long. 'I'll be going back to my uncle's tomorrow,' he muttered despondently. 'I 'on't be able to see her again – not until I've fixed up something about gettin' married.'

She made a clicking sound with her tongue.

'So 'tis a serious business?'

'Of course 'tis serious,' he retorted. 'I'd be takin' her off to get married tonight if only I'd a bit o' money.'

'If you are havin' no money, you'll be havin' to wait for her a long while, maybe.'

'Aye,' he agreed.

'Maybe as they'll keep your letters from her.'

He had not thought of such a possibility, and it angered him.

'They 'ouldn't dare.'

She made no reply, but continued in a matter-of-fact tone: 'If she do miss to answer your letters, or ever you do want to hear how she is lookin', you can be writin' to me. There's my name and address,' and she thrust a slip of paper into his hand.

They could scarcely see each other, but before they parted their hands met in a firm clasp and Rhys muttered thickly: 'I'll be bein' your friend allus for this.'

Then he was gone, and Megan with a sigh went on her solitary way.

In answer to a subdued tapping Esther cautiously opened the back door and in the glimmer of light from the fire which she had kept up saw Rhys standing on the threshold.

'Oh, my darlin', you are come at last. Thank God! Thank God!'

His heart gave a throb of joy and he took her in his arms. For a long while he did not kiss her, but stood looking down anxiously into her upturned face.

'Are you a' right, bach?'

'Yes! Yes, since I was havin' your letter. Indeed, but I was breakin' my heart just afore that.'

He pressed her to him tenderly.

'You didn't never think as I 'ould desert you, whatever your father and brothers was doin' to me?' he asked with a hint of reproach.

'I was never doubtin' you, but I was afeard of what life 'ould do for the both of us.'

'Don't you fret. I'll make it all come right in the end.' But his confidence in himself as the vanquisher of Fate had been shaken, and he had to repeat his bold assurances many times before he had quite convinced himself of their truth. She drew him into the room and softly shut the door. They sat down side by side, their heads close together and the fingers of their hands interlocked. The hot embers of the peat upon the hearth threw a rosy glow on to their faces. The room behind them was dark and profoundly still.

'I wish if this night could last for ever and ever,' Esther murmured.

'Come you, we'll be together like this allus now just.'

'How?' she asked, nestling up to him.

He knitted his brows.

'I am goin' home tomorrow, and then I shall see if nothin' 'on't move my uncle. I'll work for him under any conditions as he do fix. I'll go on my knees to him if need be, so long as he'll set me up in a small little cottage and let me fetch you out o' this damned place where folks is tormentin' one another like so many mad devils in hell. I'll never rest,' he added fiercely, 'until you're out of it.'

She drew a deep sigh.

'And what'll you do, bach, if your relations 'on't help you?'

'Go straight off to Canada,' he answered without a moment's hesitation.

She gave a low startled cry and instantly he lifted her off her chair on to his knee.

'Don't, my sweetheart, don't, 'twill be a'right. 'T'on't be for long – leastways, not without your comin' out to join me. I've been thinkin' it all out, if only you'll trust me.'

For answer she clung to him desperately.

''Ould you be afeard to come out there to me?'

139

'No! No! I 'ouldn't be afeard so long as nothin' do take you from me.'

'Nothin' can do that, bach.'

'At least, I'll never be lovin' no one else,' she said, not daring to share his faith.

Then he fell to making plans for their future. He had a friend who was doing well in Canada, and would help him if he worked his passage over. Travel and the adventure of seeking employment in a new country were just to his taste. Money could be earned with surprising rapidity out there, and he would soon be able to make a home for her. He would build it with his own hands as he had heard of men doing in that country, and there should be nothing in it to remind her of the life she had left. He would get jolly pictures out of the Christmas annuals of dogs and children romping – that was the sort he liked – and books, all those he loved best, and she should read with him. Women had a better time of it over there, he'd heard tell. They had to work, of course, but they weren't expected to make an endless drudgery of life as the 'tidy 'oman' did at home. People were more friendly there, too, and would ride or drive miles in order to attend a party.

'I don't care nothin' for that so long as I can be with you,' Esther told him, and he stopped in his eager plan-making to kiss her gratefully. Then he went on with fresh enthusiasm and, as he talked, his caressing hands loosened her hair about her shoulders. It framed her pale attentive face in a dark cloud and added so strangely to her attraction that after a while he ceased to talk and sat entranced, winding her long curls round his fingers, smoothing them out, ruffling them up again, and burying

140

his face in them from time to time.

'I could be playin' with your hair for ever,' he whispered. There's a scent of new-mown hay in it, and 'tis soft to touch like yourself.'

'If only we were being able to hold this minute fast,' she sighed.

They had sat silently for a long while, her head pressed against his breast, when the small square of the window became faintly discernible in the surrounding darkness of the room. The fire had gone out, the place was cold, and as the light grew by imperceptible degrees a shiver passed through them both. At first they tried to disregard the coming of dawn, but presently the face of the clock came out of the shadows.

Esther jumped down off Rhys' knee, and impulsively stopped the massive pendulum that had swung to and fro inexorably all night. When she turned with a little rueful smile, she found Rhys already on his feet. He held out his arms to her with a well-remembered gesture of farewell.

'Don't you say it now,' she implored, 'same as you did use to at Aberdulas. "'Tis long past the time as I ought to have gone," you did use to say, but then you was allus adding, "But I'll come again tomorrow night," and now,' she cried brokenly, 'there 'on't be no tomorrow.'

'I'll manage to come round Uncle some shape,' he said, 'and then maybe you'll be seein' me again in a few days.'

She raised her head and looked up at him, returning the longing but not the hope in his eyes.

'I'll write you at once when things is settled,' he promised.

At length he let her go and, turning abruptly on his

heel, strode out of the house across the fold. At the gate he looked round, and seeing her standing just as he had left her in the doorway, hastened back to kiss her once more. She clung to him passionately this time, and her breath came in sobs, but her eyes were dry, her grief at losing him was too great for tears. When he left her the second time he did not dare to look behind him, but swung off at a great pace over the dim hillside, drenched in dew and wreathed in the grey mist of an autumn dawn.

It was a faint, fantastic world in which he found himself. At first he was so dazed by his parting from Esther that he scarcely knew where he was going, but, as the little lake on the hilltop shimmered out of the mist at his feet, his mind cleared and hope revived within him. Full of his determination to win over his uncle, he set off at a run towards the Henallt. He was wild with impatience to pack his clothes and leave the hated place immediately.

Esther, meanwhile, had gone back into the kitchen. She dropped into one of the two chairs set close together by the hearth, and there, with her hands clasped in her lap as if in prayer, she sat staring at the lifeless clock.

A week later the postman called once more at Pengarreg with a letter for Esther bearing the Aberdulas postmark. He came as before at tea-time, but he was not asked to stay and share the meal, nor did he make any facetious remark as he handed the letter to her. The intended pleasantry died on his lips as he saw her look of agonised anxiety and the glaring eyes of her father fixed upon her.

No sooner had the door closed than John Bevan demanded: 'Well, who's writin' to you now?'

Esther did not reply. She tore open the letter and read

142

its contents with trembling haste.

'If it's from that damned young scoundrel Rhys Lloyd, you'll put it in the fire and think no more about it,' shouted John Bevan, and made a grab at her across the table.

She stepped out of his reach and stood looking at him without fear.

'Show me that blasted letter,' he thundered.

'Show it to you I 'ull,' she answered in a low voice that quivered with passion. 'Enjoy you it if you can. You are bein' wicked and cruel enough to do so.' And flinging down the letter on the table, she turned and went out of the room.

'Sailing for Canada at once.'

He picked up the slip of paper and spelled out its meaning slowly to himself. So the lad was going and there was the end of it; perhaps he'd been hard – anyway, 'twas done with now. Sullen and a little shamefaced, he folded the letter again and replaced it where he had found it.

CHAPTER 8

On a hot afternoon in the following summer, the whitewashed buildings of Tyncoed shimmered in a blaze of sunshine. The valley beneath and the hills on the opposite side of it quivered in the haze. The grassy slopes of the hill on which Tyncoed stood were beginning to turn brown, and the air above them was filled with a hot, drowsy scent. In the fold, flies buzzed over the midden heap with a low continuous murmur.

Even the indefatigable Martha Bevan was overcome, and, though she still sat bolt upright on a high-backed wooden chair, she had fallen asleep with her cavernous mouth open and her chin sunk on her flat breast. Lily had gone to her room to lie down. The hired labouring man whom the sisters employed was in the fields, sleeping under a hedge; and Megan seized the opportunity to steal out of the house.

Softly she slipped across the sun-baked fold into the cool twilight of the cowhouse. Half a dozen white-faced Herefordshire calves stared at her stupidly as she climbed the rickety ladder into the loft. Once there, she let down the trapdoor after her, and flung herself with a sigh of contentment on to the nearest pile of hay.

Rays of bright sunlight, thick with golden dust, pierced the darkness around her. The air was comparatively cool and the hay soft to lie upon. The querulous voices of her aunts, which were almost continuously raised within the house, could not penetrate to this, her special retreat. Here she could enjoy her own company undisturbed. No one was likely to suspect that she used such a place in which to hide her secret store of treasure. If they were to catch her descending from it, she could always pretend to have been fetching fodder for the cattle or searching for hens that had 'stolen their nests'. Sometimes there were actually eggs to be found up here, and she could then enjoy the pleasure of sucking one, without being told by Aunt Lily that she ought to resist the sin of gluttony, or scolded by Aunt Martha for treating herself to a luxury which would have 'fetched good money at market'.

She was supremely happy in her hiding place and could have dreamed away the afternoon, with hands clasped behind her head, staring up at the cobweb-draped rafters above her. But she had work to do which must be done whenever she had the opportunity of escaping her aunts' vigilance.

She produced a workbox and a bundle wrapped in newspaper from beneath a heap of hay. Smiling in anticipation, she unfastened it and spread out its contents

145

on her lap – a pink silk blouse and a set of lace-trimmed underclothes with ribbons threaded through them.

'Like those of a real lady,' she reflected proudly, bringing out from the depths of her workbox a handkerchief adorned with roses to match her ribbons. She smoothed it out and held it up at arm's length in order to admire it the better.

''Twill look fine just peepin' out o' the pocket o' my best black coat,' she assured herself. ''Tis no good whatever to be blowin' my nose in, but I must be managin' without that day, same as the quality is bound to do if they aren't carryin' handkerchiefs no bigger nor that. Aunt Lily do fancy as I'm goin' to Llangantyn fair dressed all in black. Not lettin' me have a coloured dress like what other gals is doin' nowadays. But she 'on't spoil my day's pleasure – not this time. Black and pink is very smart, I do reckon, and quite out o' the common. I'll dress up in the nasty old clothes she's bought me, and then I'll go up to Esther's with these stylish things hid in my pocket, and I'll change into 'em there and tie a pink ribbon to match them round my hat and put on my pearls as big as peas, and then away to go as smart as any gal in the fair.'

She clapped her hands at the thought, and searched again in her workbox for a string of sham pearls which she fastened lovingly round her full throat. They were a present from a lad to whom she had once been engaged. Her aunts had disapproved of the match, and had caused it to be broken off, and Megan was determined to find a new sweetheart in order to show the faint-hearted one that she could console herself for his desertion. Moreover, a girl who wished to be thought well of by her fellows

146

must be known to have a suitor. Megan was acutely susceptible to public opinion, for she loved to be in a crowd and to attract favourable attention. Fairs, markets and Sunday school treats were a source of delirious delight to her, and even the decorously disguised enjoyment of a funeral was a welcome change in the lonely monotony of her daily life.

Now, as she sewed, her buoyant thoughts returned to the only day's outing she had enjoyed for the last few months.

It had been the wedding of a neighbour. Her colour heightened at the recollection – the service in chapel, the ponderous breakfast of roast beef and goose at which the older men had made facetious speeches on the pleasures of matrimony, and the younger ones had nudged the giggling girls who sat next to them. The departure of the bride amidst tears, good advice and chaff had been pleasant enough. But the best part of the day had been reached at a late hour when all the elderly and married people sat within doors drinking innumerable cups of tea, and the boys and girls played games in the meadow in front of the house. Megan's needle travelled faster to the tune of 'Nuts and May' and 'Bobby Bingo', which she hummed to herself reminiscently. It was 'Bobby Bingo' that had started her affair with Tom Pugh. She had been the first to stand alone in the ring of dancers who capered around her singing:

'A farmer had a little dog,
His name was Bobby Bingo;
B-I-N-G-O,

147

> B-I-N-G-O,
> B-I-N-G-O,
> His name was Bobby Bingo.'

Then it had been time for her to decide by whom she would be kissed, and she had surveyed youth after youth as they circled past her. But she had not made up her mind which she preferred when they reached the final

> 'Tra-la-la,
> Tra-la-la.'

A shout of laughter had gone up on all sides, accompanied by cries of 'Hurry up or you'll be left single!' 'Come on, gal, choose your mate!' Laughing, flushed, bright-eyed and excited, she had turned at last and slipped her hand into the crook of Tom Pugh's arm. She had not meant to do so, for everyone knew that he was a good-for-nothing with whom no respectable girl would 'take up', but he had contrived somehow to be always the one before her, whichever way she turned, and the bold, alluring stare of his blue eyes had drawn her to him in spite of herself.

Sitting alone in the hayloft, she reconstructed the scene – the sunlit field, gay with the new grass that had sprung up since the hay was carried, the white farmhouse in the background where her aunts were kept safely out of sight, the happy faces of a host of holiday makers, all young and merry like herself, the dances with Tom Pugh many times repeated.

''Twas lovely,' she sighed. 'I do wish as there was a weddin' every day o' the year – but there, it'll soon be time for the pleasure fair, and then I'll be havin' some fun, sure to be.' She paused to look in approval at her work. 'If Tom Pugh was fancyin' me all in black, he'd be mad for me when I'm dressed up in these,' she thought with a little thrill of excitement. 'But I 'on't be takin' up with the likes o' him. I'll be lookin' out for a respectable chap, one as a gal can trust,' and she continued her sewing with a demure expression, which, however, she maintained with difficulty. To quiet her thoughts, she began to sing the hymn which of all those she knew pleased her best.

'Ten thousand times ten thousand,
In sparkling raiment bright,
The armies of the ransom'd Saints
Throng up the steeps of light.'

What a gorgeous picture it conjured up! It would be better even than the crowd which poured into Llangantyn on the yearly fair day.

'What rush of Alleluias
Fills all the earth and sky!
What ringing of a thousand harps
Bespeaks the triumph nigh!'

A thousand harps! That would be even finer than the noise of three steam organs, she thought, and went on singing with gradually rising voice. Her exaltation grew until she forgot that her whereabouts must be kept concealed, and she finished the last verse with a loud, triumphant 'Amen'. In the succeeding silence she held her

149

breath in horror. The trapdoor rose and the pale, resentful face of Aunt Lily appeared in the opening. Megan had no time in which to hide the lace and ribbons in her hands or the string of pearls round her neck. She sat petrified, staring into the indignant eyes.

'What are you doin' hidin' up here?' Lily demanded. Stalking across to where her niece sat speechless, she snatched the underclothes out of her lap. 'Whatever are these things you are makin' on the sly?' As she realised what they were, her disapproval turned to disgust. 'Shame on you, you brazen piece, you! You aren't never goin' to wear them things instead of decent calico and flannel?'

'No one 'on't be seein' them if I do,' Megan began faintly.

'Then what are you wantin' 'em for? What is an honest gal wantin' with such trash, tell me that?'

Megan held up her blouse and tried to explain that the ribbons on the chemise would be visible at the shoulder, but her aunt cut her short.

'First you do say as they 'on't show, and then you say as they will. I don't believe a word you do say, you wicked, deceitful piece, stealin' away up here to make things as you 'ould be ashamed for your Aunt Martha and me to see. And where have you had the money from to buy such stuff with, I 'ould like to know?'

'A little bit as I saved from the fairin' you was givin' me last year.'

'That wasn't enough to pay for them beads round your neck, nasty worldly things, just such as your poor mother as brought disgrace on us all 'ould have fancied. Come you on down at once and give an account of yourself to your Aunt Martha.'

Megan followed her down the ladder, across the fold and into the kitchen, where Martha, who had awakened stiff and unrefreshed from her sleep, was vigorously sweeping the floor and grumbling to herself at the heat.

'Where have you been all the while?' she asked. 'You're never to be found when there's work to be done.'

The accusation was unjust and Megan threw back her head defiantly, but before she had time to reply Lily had poured forth an account of her doings which proved her to be not only lazy, but deceitful, vain and of doubtful respectability. It was this latter charge on which the white-faced Lily laid the heaviest stress, but Martha, florid and stern, with the sullen, bloodshot eyes and heavy jowl of her brother, was more concerned with the waste of time which the making of finery implied. She had dropped her broom and stood with her arms akimbo studying her niece with disfavour. The girl's handsome and becomingly flushed face and the defiance in her bright eyes were provoking.

'What have you to say for yourself now?' she demanded.

Megan had a great deal to say, but she found it impossible to put it into words which would not further enrage the two soured spinsters. Her whole nature cried out for what she called 'happy' colours, for gaiety and congenial companionship, and none of Aunt Lily's sermons could induce her to believe that these things were wrong in themselves. She knew that the making of pretty things with her hands gave her pleasure, and that such pleasure seemed to her harmless.

'I do believe as 'tis more wicked to hold the angry

thoughts and say the spiteful things they are doin', nor to enjoy nice clothes and goin' to parties like what I 'ould do,' she thought. 'I 'ould like to make everyone around me pleased, but they are makin' everyone miserable.'

Martha took her silence to imply stubborn indifference.

'A' right,' she announced. 'You shan't go to the fair this year.'

'No,' chimed in Aunt Lily. 'Many's the gal as has come to trouble that way.'

'Not go to the fair!' Megan could hardly believe her ears. 'Oh, Aunty Martha,' she cried in an agonised voice, 'you 'ouldn't never stop me to go? Why, there's not a servant gal in the countryside as doesn't have that day off.'

'Well, you 'on't, whatever,' came the reply, delivered with grim determination. 'Lily or I has had to do the milkin' for you that night these good few years, and since you've been deceivin' of us, and wastin' our time like what you have been, you can stay home and do it yourself now.'

With that, Martha Bevan recommenced her sweeping. Lily stalked over to the hearth and picked up the bellows. When she had rekindled the fire which had been allowed to languish, she cast her niece's trumpery little trimmings into its midst.

'There's a waste o' good material,' Martha exclaimed, glancing up from her sweeping. ''T 'ould have come in handy for polishin' the furniture.'

''Twas accursed finery. 'Tis better cast into the flames,' Lily answered.

Megan burst into a violent fit of weeping.

'Oh, you're hard and cruel, you are,' she sobbed, 'spoilin' my chances o' gettin' a boy, the one day o' twelve months as I've looked forward to – you don't know what it is to be young – you – you..'

But her rising sobs choked the end of the sentence. The tears streamed unchecked down her face. It grew red and blotchy and her swollen eyes lost their beauty.

Lily Bevan watched her with covert satisfaction and Martha turned her back on her.

'Time to feed the pigs,' she announced over her shoulder. 'Go you out and see to it.'

Megan went, still crying loudly, her full bosom rising and falling in great sobs. For all her finely-developed physique she was no more than a child at heart, and inconsolable in the grief of the moment.

As she leaned over the pigsty wall she heard the postman's whistle behind her, and, ashamed of her tear-stained face, would have hurried into the house unobserved; but he shouted to her, and she went reluctantly to meet him at the fold gate, drying her eyes on a corner of her blue cotton pinafore.

He looked at her with compassion and handed her a letter.

'For you from foreign parts. Maybe you're havin' a sweetheart out there?'

'I've no sweetheart,' she sighed.

'Then what have you been cryin' about?'

'My aunts 'on't let me go to the fair.'

'Well, indeed, that's too bad.' He lingered at the gate, shuffling his feet. 'Strange as a pretty one like you shouldn't be havin' no sweetheart.'

She knew that note in a man's voice and looked him up and down. He was short, dark and sallow, and had decayed, discoloured teeth. She was not tempted to

153

encourage his advances. Still he persisted.

'Since I 'on't be able to treat you at the fair, maybe I'll bring you a small little fairin' one evening.'

Men were invariably kinder than women, she reflected, and gave him a dim smile of gratitude.

''Ould you be comin' down one night if I was to throw a pebble at your window?' he enquired, fumbling with his post-bag.

She studied him again dispassionately. He was known for an honest, steady fellow. It was a pity that he did not possess Tom Pugh's good looks.

'I'll be lettin' you know again.'

'All right,' he answered, apparently not greatly concerned, and slouched off on his rounds.

''Tis no use a man bein' tidy and respectable,' she thought, 'if he isn't havin' good looks nor a way o' handlin' a gal. Now that wicked 'un, Tom Pugh...' But she checked the thought that it might be pleasant to sit up with him at night. It was not wise to think of that.

When the postman was out of sight she tore open her letter. It contained one for Esther and a few lines for herself from Rhys Lloyd. He complained of having heard only once from Esther, and feared that his letters to her might have been intercepted. Megan spelt out his note, which was too much that of a fluent writer for her to read with ease, and when she had at length grasped its import, clapped her hands with joy and instantly forgot her own troubles in the prospective delight of bearing good tidings to her cousin.

She hid the letter in the bodice of her dress and hurried into the house.

'Since I'm not to go to the fair, Aunt Martha, may I be

154

slippin' over to let Esther know tonight, after my work's done? Else she'll be countin' on me goin' with her.'

Martha was beginning to be ashamed of herself, and annoyed with Lily, whom she loved even less than she did her niece. Accordingly, she answered with a curt 'A' right.'

When Megan set out, the sun was dipping behind the distant mountains and a faint breeze had sprung up to cool the parched earth. A few hundred yards from Tyncoed, sheltering it from the prevailing westerly winds, was a plantation of funereal spruce fenced in from the surrounding hillside. Megan's path, wandering away small and lonely as a sheep track across a ridge to Pengarreg, passed close to these trees and led beyond them to a desolate little lake on the very summit of the ridge. From there the two homesteads could be seen, divided by a mile of open hill-land, each looking down on to the rich river valley below. But from the side of the plantation farthest from Tyncoed neither house was visible.

Megan was hurrying along joyfully with her news, when she saw the tall figure of a man at the edge of the wood, and with a flutter of fear and excitement recognised it for that of Tom Pugh. She paused, undecided what to do. He looked about him cautiously to see that he was not observed and came out towards her.

'What are you doin' there?' she asked.

'Hangin' about to get a word with you, same as I've been doin' for weeks now.'

'You haven't?'

'Ever since Maggie Williams' wedding I've been doin' nothin' only tryin' to see you. You're the prettiest gal I've ever set eyes on.'

155

'Go on!'

'Who's dared to make you cry?' he demanded, noticing that her eyelids were red.

'No one,' she answered, unwilling to make a confidant of him, but, as he kept pace beside her and looked down at her, she was moved to confide in him all that had taken place that afternoon. He did not take the matter calmly as the postman had done. On the contrary, he was very angry, and called her Aunt Martha 'an old bitch'. She professed to be shocked, but was in reality amused.

'I'll tell you what,' he cried. 'If you shan't go to the fair, I'll come and keep you company whilst the old 'uns is out o' the house.'

She stopped and stared at him incredulously. 'You 'ouldn't go to miss the fair on my account?'

'I'd rather you nor a hundred fairs.'

This was real love-making. It set her pulses throbbing. Something of the elation that swept over her for an instant must have appeared in the look she gave him, for before she knew what had happened he had snatched her up in his arms, and was covering her face with kisses. For a moment she abandoned herself to physical enjoyment, then her reason returned and she struggled violently to free herself.

'Don't you dare do that,' she cried. 'I'm an honest gal – I don't want none o' the likes o' you.'

He had released her and she felt suddenly small and weak standing beside him.

'Why d'you go to say that?' he demanded, his eyes dark with resentment.

For the moment he reminded her of her Uncle John

156

Bevan. 'I wonder,' she thought, 'if he was bein' handsome afore he took to drink?' And the thought steeled her against Tom Pugh.

'You do know very well what the countryside is sayin' about you,' she answered, tossing her head.

'As 'twas I got old Prosser's gal in the way? A likely one for me to pick! I can have better gals nor her for the askin'.'

''Tisn't only that. You aren't never keepin' no job. What are you doin' at home now?'

'Helpin' the boss,' he grinned. ''Tis true indeed,' he added as she walked on with an indignant shrug of her shoulders. 'I'm helpin' him over the summer, and then goin' to take work reg'lar in this district. I may have been a bit wild onst, but...'

'Well, 'tisn't nothin' to do with me whatever,' Megan answered, all the more firmly because she was conscious of wanting to stay and hear more of his compliments. 'I've business at Pengarreg. Good day, now.'

He laid his hand on her arm. His touch sent a quiver through her whole body.

'I 'on't be comin' no further or they'll be seein' me from Pengarreg; but I'll wait for you by comin' back in the 'ood near your home. Don't you be cruel now,' he implored, as she shook her head and turned away her eyes so that she might not see how good he was to look upon. 'I've been waitin' and waitin' my chance to have a talk with you, and now it's come at last you might be sparin' me just a minute or two.' Again she shook her head, but less positively than before. 'You could be makin' o' me so happy,' he urged. 'Don't you go to send me away wretched.'

The sense of having his happiness in her hand flattered her, and she paused for an instant, undecided.

'You'll come and talk to me in the 'ood?' he murmured, running his fingertips up and down her arm.

She snatched it away.

'Maybe as I will, maybe as I 'on't,' was all she allowed herself to say, and hastened on without venturing to look back.

Her heart was beating fast when she came to the gate that opened into her uncle's fold. She paused to draw breath and leant her arms upon the topmost bar. No one was to be seen and not even a dog was about to bark at her approach. Only from one of the sheds forming three sides of a square came the monotonous muffled sound made by steadily repeated blows of an axe upon wood. She opened the gate, crossed the fold in which lay stagnant pools of dark liquid never wholly dried up even in summer time, and paused before the woodshed. It was unenclosed, and the golden light of evening that follows a burning day fell upon Esther as she swung an axe and split adroitly the small log she had placed on the block. Megan watched her lift another log from the pile and split it as neatly as the last, throwing the two halves into a basket at her side. With untiring regularity she went through the same movements again and again, only varying them when a stubborn log required to be raised with the axe embedded deep in it, and to be knocked against the block until at the second or third blow it split. The sleeves of her black bodice, rusty with age, were rolled up, and showed her white arms, muscular as those of a man but more rounded. Her figure had developed in the last year

158

from girlish strength, spare and angular, to the fullness of womanhood. Her dress, that had survived from days of immaturity, fitted her too tightly across the broad shoulders and hips, and Megan, watching her, saw the firm curves of her body displayed by every movement.

'Well, indeed,' she thought, 'she isn't lookin' like one as is frettin' for her lover. How steady she is bein' in everything she is doin'! Allus the same, keepin' on reg'lar as clockwork ever since I knowed her, only this last year she has growed more calm and better lookin' nor ever she was before. I don't believe she do care for him – not as I could be carin' for a man o' his looks, whatever. Why, I'd be mad just, if I'd a fancy sweetheart out in foreign parts and all the gals there after him. I couldn't be eatin' nor sleepin' for botherin' about what he was up to o' nights.... Esther!'

The axe was laid down and Esther turned, unstartled.

Her broad face, becomingly flushed with exertion, broke into a smile that showed her large even teeth. 'Why, Megan, I *am* glad.'

'You'll be more nor glad when you do see what I've brought you.'

'Summat from Rhys?'

Megan stared.

'Whatever made you guess 'twas from him?'

'I'm allus thinkin' of him, I suppose.'

A shy smile lurked at the corners of her mouth, but her grey eyes looked steadily into her cousin's.

'Well, there's odd you are! I can't make you out.'

'Why ever not? Isn't it bein' natural for a gal to think o' her young man?'

'He's been gone close on a year now.'

159

'Oh, Megan, Megan!'

'Oh, I don't say as I 'ouldn't be keepin' constant for a year – even if I wasn't never settin' eyes on my young man, but you don't seem to fret, somehow.'

'I'm trustin' him.'

'Well, and if you are trustin' him, don't you see the time go terrible slow without no one to kiss you?'

'I am livin' in the future,' Esther answered softly. After a long pause she returned slowly from some unfathomable depth of contemplation and asked: 'What's your good news bein'?'

With a shrug Megan pulled at her pocket. 'Here you are, though it don't seem to matter much to you whether your sweetheart's holdin' you in his arms or livin' the other side o' the 'orld.'

Esther took the letter and stood with it in her clasped hands.

'Well, is it too much trouble to read it?' Megan enquired sarcastically.

'I've not been hearin' from him for months.'

'One 'ould think that 'ould make you in a hurry to see what he's got to say for hisself.'

'I'm bein' too happy,' and she turned away, her eyes full of tears.

Megan picked up the axe and began vigorously to chop wood. Tom Pugh would he waiting for her on the way home. The cheek of it – covering her face with kisses! The good-for-nothing! No knowing what he'd try to do next. Why wasn't she having a young man whom she could trust? What had Esther done to deserve such unusual good fortune?

'Megan! Megan! He's taken a piece o' land from the

Government. He's started farmin' on his own. He do want
me to go out as soon as I can. He's sendin' me the money
for my passage.'

Esther had turned towards her, flushed and breathless
as a happy child, her eyes bright with unshed tears, the
hand that held the sheet of paper trembling, the other
raised to her face with fingers that tried to conceal the
quivering of her lips.

This was a mood within Megan's comprehension. Her
anger abated. Flinging away the axe, she took Esther into
her arms.

'Oh, I'm so glad, Essy! Someone 'ull be happy at least,
and since it can't be me, I'm glad as 'tis you, dear.'

They sat down on the wood block and began to talk in
eager undertones.

'D'you know why you've not heard from him for so
long?'

'His letters have been goin' astray, bound to be.'

'Go on! They've been taken by someone here.'

'No! No! 'Tisn't possible. Father'd do it in a minute,
and the boys is bein' none too good neither, I know, but if
ever I haven't been about to catch the postman myself
Mother's taken the letters from him. She 'ouldn't never act
so cruel by me as to be keepin' 'em from me.'

'Well, well! You *are* dull! Not act cruel by you? Why,
she'd act cruel by anyone if uncle was orderin' her to.
Besides, she's afeard in her heart o' losin' you!'

Esther straightened herself and a flush of anger
overspread her face.

'D'ye believe she'd be so wicked?'

'O' course she 'ould, you stupid.'

For an instant Esther sat frowning, then she laughed, flinging wide her arms and letting them come together again about Megan's neck.

'Oh well, we needn't fret about that now. All my troubles is over. I've only to wait for the money for my passage.'

They had sat making plans for half an hour, when the clatter of a horse's hooves in the fold made them both start up guiltily. Esther thrust her letter into the bodice of her dress, and they strolled out into the open with assumed nonchalance to confront Gladys.

She was astride a small black pony that champed at the bit and shied away nervously from them as they approached.

'Isn't he lovely, the little wild beauty?' she shouted to them.

Her pale hair that had been newly done up was half-tumbled about her shoulders, and there was a patch of colour, bright as the tint of a dogrose bud, in either cheek.

'He was that wild the boys couldn't make nothin' of him, throwin' all the while like a mad thing. *I* did know how to come round him, though. I'd been making friends with him in the fields and givin' him a bit to eat now and again. He'll come to kindness. Look at him now. I can be doin' anything with him just.'

She pressed her knees against his lathered flanks. He started forward with his nostrils distended, and his frightened eyes rolled in the direction of the dogs that followed at his heels.

''Tisn't a very safe job for a gal, tamin' horses,' Esther murmured.

'Go on!' Gladys had made the round of the fold, and, reining in her mount beside the others, had slipped to the ground and was proudly surveying him. 'Look how he's lettin' me touch him now. D'ye think either o' the boys shall do that? Why aren't you lookin', Essy? Now then... oh! You aren't takin' no interest in nothin' I'm tellin' you.'

She paused, her hand on the pony's mane, and looked at her sister with suspicion.

'What were the both o' you so busy talkin' about in the 'oodshed when I comed up?'

There was no answer, but Megan grinned.

'Why don't you tell me?' Gladys cried sharply. 'Why am I to be kept in the dark as do share everything with you, Essy?'

'I wasn't meanin' to keep you in the dark, bach. I'll be tellin' you tonight.'

'Why shouldn't you be tellin' me till tonight if you've been tellin' Megan now? I'm comin' first, aren't I?' Her voice rose high with jealous anger.

''Twas Megan as did bring the news to me,' Esther answered with a hint of weariness in her tone.

'What news?'

'News o' Rhys.'

'Oh, that Rhys again, is it?'

Gladys flung away, her eyes full of tears. She had heard no mention of Rhys for months, and had secretly hoped that Esther would forget him as she herself strove to do, not daring to enquire after him lest she should hear what she most dreaded.

'How's he gettin' on?' she asked in a husky voice, her face hidden in the pony's mane.

163

'Very good. He's set up in a farm on his own.'

'Then you'll be goin' out to join him now just?' There was no answer, and presently she turned with an effort and faced Esther once more. 'Is that it?'

Esther nodded, and Megan, looking from one girl to the other, saw with surprise how much of Gladys' suffering was reflected in her sister's face.

'I shan't see you no more after.' The colour had gone from Gladys' cheeks.

Esther made a movement of protest, but was stopped by an abrupt gesture that made the pony back away startled.

'Oh, it's no use to say no other. D'you think you shall set foot in this place again after goin' against Father? When you're gone from here you'll be dead to us all. *Dead.*'

She flung her arms up over her face and began to sob. Esther took a step towards her, but, still sobbing and stumbling as she went, she turned and led away the pony.

When Megan set out on her return journey there was bitter rebellion in her heart.

''Tisn't right,' she muttered, swinging along at a great pace in the cool of the evening. ''Tisn't fair the way the old 'uns is treatin' all of us as is bein' young.'

She thought of Rhys, who had been driven from home; of Esther, who would have to escape secretly like a criminal in order to attain her happiness: of her own lover who had been persuaded to give her up.

'Selfish – that's what age is,' she muttered.

A little further along her path she added: 'I'm not carin' for what one of 'em do say. I'll be doin' what I like. I 'on't be listenin' to 'em no more.'

164

She was now approaching the plantation near to her aunts' house. The air was heavy with the smell of resin. Here it was that Tom Pugh had kissed her and it was this smell which had reached her from his hands when she had struggled with him. She must be on her guard with Tom Pugh, of course, but there was no harm in his kissing her once again. As like as not, his evil reputation had been invented by older men who were jealous of his strength, his good looks and his youth.

There he was waiting for her in the shadow. It was flattering to have a man wait for her all these hours. How he must be fancying her! And he was young. She would have no one of her own age with whom to talk when she returned to the gloom of Tyncoed. There would be no sound of laughter, not even her own. She looked at the waiting figure, tall and clean-limbed, and hesitated between following the path straight home and turning aside towards the plantation. She could see his face now. It was ruddy, and the look on it was eager as that of a boy awaiting a treat – a childish, greedy face which made her smile indulgently. His fair hair also was like a child's. A thrill passed through her that, for an instant, left her dizzy. How young he was! she thought, as she went towards the wood.

CHAPTER 9

'Is there no more o' them pancakes to be had?' asked John, helping himself to the last on a plate which had been set in the centre of the table.

Esther, busy at the fireplace with the bellows, shook her head. From the opposite side of the table Idris, who had watched with apprehension his brother's large red hand, chapped at the knuckles, reach across the table, raised his thin voice in protest.

'I'm not havin' near my share. John do eat so terrible quick.'

'There's not much to choose between you, whatever,' Gladys said. 'It's hard on a gal only havin' the scraps as is left over.'

'Go on! You're allus gettin' the dainty bits, bein' so nice about your food,' John retorted, his voice muffled by a mouthful of pancake. 'I'm havin' an honest hunger on me after doin' a man's work – 'tis you as is greedy, fancyin' this and that...'

'Greedy, is it? Venturin' to eat a quarter o' your share. You're like father, you are – the very spit o' him, grudgin'...'

'Come you,' Esther interposed, 'there's no sense quarrellin', seein' as I've been givin' you all a treat for tea.'

'A treat, are you callin' it?' John grumbled. 'No more nor a lick, it wasn't.' And with the back of his hand he wiped the grease from his upper lip, on which a few coarse hairs were beginning to grow.

'There's some folks as is never satisfied,' Esther answered and, as he pushed back his chair angrily: 'No! No! John, don't you take it like that. You should be havin' your fill o' pancakes if we was able to afford it.'

Having made the fire blaze up, she set down the bellows, patted her elder brother on the shoulder, and began clearing away the tea things.

'Come on, Gladys,' she called, determined to avoid further disagreement, 'do you be washin' up and I'll dry.'

Without a word, John slouched out into the fold; Idris followed at his heels as usual.

'Are you goin' round the sheep?' Esther called after them through the open doorway.

'Aye.'

'Then I'll have to be fetchin' the cows in myself.'

She returned to the sink in the back kitchen where Gladys was making an alarming clatter with the crockery. Esther had been churning all the morning. As often happened in thundery weather, the butter had not come until an aching arm had turned the churn for hours. She could still feel the strain of her tired muscles, but she was eager for yet more manual labour to calm the growing excitement of her thoughts. She had been long enough in planning the decisive step she was to take, and now that her mind was resolved, she felt more than ever kindly disposed towards those around her.

'Allus takin' the easy jobs for theirselves, the boys is,' Gladys burst out. 'I could be sendin' the dogs up after the sheep as good as them.'

She straightened herself and wiped the soap suds from her thin wrists.

'I 'ould be happy if I was workin' out o' doors. But the men is knowin' well enough what is the dull jobs, and those is the ones they are leavin' to us.'

'But we're not havin' the strength for all as they do do,' Esther expostulated as she dried a cup with a deft turn of the cloth in her hand.

Gladys answered with an impatient shrug. 'We're havin' the strength to keep on at the haymakin' all day, though we shan't drive the machine as is the lightest job of the lot; and we're having the strength to break our backs just plantin' potatoes, and pickin' stones and doin' anythin' as it don't take the men's fancy to do theirselves. Look at these old stone floors now. 'Tis a hard day's work to be scrubbin' the lot in a house this size, but after doin' it we must be on our feet to wait on the men when they do come back from leanin' up against the walls o' the pubs on market day. I've no patience with 'em. There's Father today, ridin' off to Llangantyn as soon as he's had his breakfast – like a king just, after me puttin' a polish on his boots – and poor Mother walkin' all the way to town when she's done her morning's work, carryin' two

168

great big old baskets full o' butter and eggs. Is that along o' her not havin' the strength to do his job? Go on!'

Her complaining voice rose higher and higher, but Esther scarcely noticed it. Her mind was busy forming plans.

She had been to Llangantyn last market day, and there, with a sense of adventure that had made her redden and stammer as she thrust a long-hoarded half-crown over the counter, had bought a pad of violet notepaper with a picture on its cover of a simpering young woman with a kitten in her arms. She had chosen envelopes to match, and had bought also a penholder and a bottle of ink with which to write undisturbed in her own room, and a stamp that had needed a special journey to the post office. That stamp, stuck on crookedly with deliberate care, now adorned one of the gay envelopes which had been taken from its hiding place at the bottom of her clothes chest, and looked at many times during the week. There was no address on the envelope as yet, but in her fancy it had been written. So had the letter which was to go inside it, for the planning of love-letters to be written to Rhys was as great a delight to her as the actual writing was a labour. This was to be the happiest of all letters, and therefore she could not hurry over its composition. She had often sat down to write it, but always some duty had called her away. She was determined to slip down tonight and to write it in the deserted kitchen where she had once sat with Rhys. ''Twill be like keepin' company with him again,' she thought with a smile as she hung up the last of the gold-and-white cups on the kitchen dresser.

'Well, well,' she said aloud to Gladys, whose complaints

had never ceased, 'we must be takin' the 'orld as we do find it.... There now, that is bein' done.'

Gladys, looking at her suspiciously, asked in her sharp voice: 'What are you lookin' so pleased about all of a sudden?'

Poor little Gladys! How lonely she would be! The smile died on Esther's lips. She turned away, crossed the fold to the woodshed and gathered together an armful of dried branches with which to re-kindle the kitchen fire that night. Heaping her store on one side of the open hearth, she went out again to fetch in the cattle.

'Angry weather,' she thought as she looked at the sky. 'The beasts is bein' restless, and everyone is gettin' sharp-tempered at home, only I am bein' too happy for nothin' to touch me.'

She stretched out her arms and looked a challenge at the sombre heavens.

'Nothin' can't stop me to go to Rhys now. Tonight I'll be writin' to him to send the money to Llangantyn post office for my passage, and so soon as ever it do come I'll be slippin' away on a market day, and takin' the train to Liverpool, and then off to go.'

A low growl of thunder startled her, long expected as it had been. With hurried footsteps she reached the gate of the field, and opening it called: 'Ho-i, ho-i, ho-i... come on, Maggie bach; come on, Daisy; ho-i...'

Slowly from the far side of the enclosure, where they had stood all the afternoon switching their tails to keep off the flies, five cows moved in single file towards her. They presented the staring white faces and uniform rust-red backs and flanks of Herefordshire cattle. A stranger could

170

not have told them apart, but to Esther each had a name and a distinct personality.

'I'll be sorry in my heart to say goodbye to 'em,' she sighed as they trooped through the gate, breathing at her their pleasant hay-scented breath. They wandered up the hillside in their invariable formation, and, on reaching the fold, each entered her stall and stood there stolidly. Esther fastened the chains round their necks and set to work milking Maggie. The same routine was followed night and morning.

Esther had on the faded blue print sunbonnet that had hung on the cowshed door since she first took over from her mother the business of milking. She fetched the three-legged stool from the corner, and seating herself upon it, nestled her head into Maggie's warm flank, and murmuring 'Whoa there – whoa there,' passed her hands gently over each of the four teats in turn, and began to tug at them with calm regularity. The rustle of litter and the clank of chains as the cows moved in their stalls, the monotonous munching noise made by their slow-working jaws, and the sharp hiss of two jets of milk spurting into a tin pail filled the drowsy twilight of the shed. Maggie was inclined to hold her milk, and in accordance with custom Esther began reassuringly to talk to her.

'Don't you be doin' that now, there's a good gal. There! There! That's better. Allus the same, day after day, year after year, your lives are, and nothin' new 'on't happen to none o' you. Bein' reared on the land and skippin' about when you was little, you were, same as all the other calves as ever was here before you, and comin' quieter as you growed older, more slow and patient all the while. Goin' to

171

the bull at Tynpant some time in late summer or autumn, and calvin' down in spring every year the same, frettin' after your calves when they're tooked from you, just like an 'oman after a child, restless for a while and then goin' back to your old patient ways. There! There! There! Give me down your milk easy, bach.'

As she talked on in a level murmur she was aware of no great gulf dividing her being from that of the large, quietly breathing creature against whom she leaned. Mankind, she had been taught to believe, had a moral sense with which the other animals were not endowed. Yet it was her habit always to speak of a 'kind dog' or a 'wicked horse', and the distinction between man and beast was never very powerfully marked in her mind.

'There,' she announced as she rose from milking the last of her charges, 'I 'on't be milkin' none o' you so very much longer, and you'll be missin' me same as I'll be missin' you. You 'on't take to a new hand at first. Gladys 'ull be milkin' you, and you're a bit afeard o' her quick, noisy ways. But you'll come. We're comin' used to anything strange in time.'

She raised a heavy pail in either hand, and walking with steady deliberation to avoid spilling a drop, made her way towards the house.

'Strange,' she repeated to herself. 'I'm fancyin' the sound o' that word now.... Strange. 'Twill be all strange for me from now on.'

The back door was open and from it issued the sound of her mother's thin voice. Mrs Bevan had returned from market, and, trailing her skirt through the liquid mud of the fold, had entered the house and dropped down on to the nearest chair. There she sat, limp and crumpled as a rag doll from which half the stuffing had gone. Her hands had fallen from her lap and dangled at her sides. Her head drooped like the wisp of ostrich feather which, having adorned the bonnet she wore on her wedding day, now straggled mournfully over the brim of a black hat. Beside her Gladys stood, arms akimbo, and pale lips tightly compressed. Every line of her figure bespoke defiance, and she greeted Esther in a tone shrill with anger.

'He's on the booze again. He 'ouldn't come home along o' poor Mother. He was swearin' at her in the street in front o' all the neighbours. What d'ye think o' that?'

Esther put down her pails.

'I'm sorry,' she sighed.

'*Sorry!* Can't you *do* nothin'?' Gladys flung up her hands in a gesture of impotent anger. 'What's the law for, I do say, if a man may be ill-usin' of an 'oman and robbin' of the children as is dependin' on him, and shoutin' and swearin' about the place like what he'll be doin' when he do come back tonight? Why, they'd run him in for breaking the peace if he was to carry on anywhere else like what he do do in his own home. Is it bein' fair as all of us should be made to suffer by him? 'Tis a wicked thing, tyin' folks up in families so as the innocent shall be punished along o' the guilty.'

''Tis how the world is bein' made,' murmured Mrs Bevan, a tear trickling down her cheek towards the drooping corner of her mouth.

Gladys turned away impatiently.

'Why can't you be leavin' him? Why can't we all be leavin' him to do for hisself?'

173

'Oh, Gladys dear, whoever heard o' such a thing? No! No! I'll be havin' to bear it, however hard it is goin'. There's no way out since I married him. I'll be havin' to keep on somehow till it is killin' me.'

Esther looked down at her, bowed by the burden of her resignation, without the courage either of rebellion or of endurance, tearful in her self-pity, weak and afraid. It was she who had stolen and destroyed Rhys' letters. She had confessed as much when taxed with it. Esther had been hotly angry when she thought of what those precious letters meant to herself, and of the disaster their disappearance might have caused. She had scarcely spoken to her mother for the last few days, but suddenly she was sorry for her. She crossed the kitchen and laid her hand gently on the bowed shoulder. The only result of her sympathy was an uncontrolled outburst of weeping.

'Oh, Esther – dear – you are – bein' good – to me. Don't you be leavin' me alone with him when he do come home,' sobbed Mrs Bevan.

Esther answered quietly, 'A' right, I'll be standin' by you.' Looking down at her mother, she contrasted the tenderness of Rhys' protecting love with the brutal lust of which this helpless creature had been a victim.

'Poor little Mother,' she murmured, stroking her arm, and to herself she added: 'How she'll be missin' me.'

When she had gone to her work in the dairy, Mrs Bevan still sat inert, and Gladys moved irritably about the kitchen.

Out in the fold the ducks and hens had gathered for their dole of Indian corn. After a while the hum of the separator and the splash of running water ceased and

Esther came out to them. A fluttering of white, speckled, brown and grey wings rose about her feet and the pigs in their sty began to squeal. They and the calves were fed, and finally she set aside the skim milk and meal that was the sheepdogs' portion when they returned from the hill. The beasts had no fear of her quiet, unhurrying movements. The calves sucked at her fingers, mistaking them for teats, and the old sow and her farrow of little pigs snouted about between her feet. She paused for a minute to scratch their backs, and, leisurely swinging her empty buckets, turned towards the house.

Aunt Lily had arrived during her absence. She was seated on the edge of a chair, her feet pressed close together, and her thin hands joined in her lap. A hat like a pork pie was tilted far forward on her forehead, and beneath it her lank grey hair was tightly screwed up. Esther's glance rested upon her from the doorway.

'Poor Aunt Lily,' she thought in the mood of good-humoured compassion that had led her to pardon every injury during the last few days. 'No one's never been lovin' her, no wonder she was bein' so sharp with us as children.'

Then she became aware that her gaze was returned by the flinty grey eyes, and that a chill silence had fallen upon the company.

'You may well stand there lookin' ashamed o' yourself.'

'I don't know as I've nothin' partic'lar to be ashamed on,' Esther smiled.

'*Not* ashamed? Then you did ought to be, whatever.'

'Maybe you'll be tellin' me what's the trouble?'

She leant against the doorpost, strong, sunburnt and

175

smiling. Her red hands rested on her hips and her head was thrown back, displaying the short full throat of a singer. Her aunt looked at her long in envious silence and hated her.

She herself had been pale and ailing as a girl. The laughter and romping of her fellows had been a cause of distress. From any merrymaking she had shrunk instinctively, conscious that her combined shyness and lack of good looks would prevent her ever being a favourite. Vague longings and unrests had oppressed her, but what she could not attain she had taught herself to despise, and as the years went by she had reversed the order in which religion and misanthropy had come upon her and now regarded both gaiety and love-making as things primarily displeasing to her God and hence to herself. When she met a pair of lovers strolling arm-in-arm, she told herself that 'gals as was courtin' too free was comin' to no good'. A wedding was a source of discomfort to her, unless there was reason to suppose, as she frequently hinted, that it had been hastened by necessity. Sex was, to her, a thing unclean, and since she knew that in this matter the feeling of the simple, healthy-minded community in which she lived was not with her, she was forced to seek for instances in which its manifestation was forbidden, in order to have popular opinion on her side. No scandalous rumour escaped her, and there was no harmless piece of gossip relating to any neighbour's courtship to which she did not try to give a discreditable turn. Today she was burning with angry satisfaction. She had discovered that both Esther and Megan were 'courtin'', and she had ample grounds for objecting to both their lovers. All their relations would agree with her, and she would not, as had

176

sometimes happened, have to stand alone, nursing in secret beneath the shield of a sour smile her resentment of another's happiness.

'You are bein' found out,' she announced.

Esther's reply was to raise her eyebrows.

Aunt Lily's voice was also raised.

'You've been caught receivin' letters from that Lloyd – Rhys, or whatever he do call hisself.'

'Mother and Gladys have been knowin' that this long while.'

The words, quietly spoken, caused Lily Bevan to rise from her chair, glaring at her sister-in-law.

'You've been knowin' as this was goin' on? You've been allowin' of it?'

Annie Bevan began to cry.

Esther, without altering her position, resumed: 'Mother has been destroyin' Rhys' letters to me whenever she was able to lay hands on 'em. Actin' on Father's orders, she was.'

Gladys, upright behind her mother's chair, looked from one to another of them, white-faced, angry and helpless.

'That's a shame, I do say,' she burst out. 'Though I'm the last as is wantin' Esther to leave home.'

'You holt your tongue, will you,' her aunt retorted. 'I'll get your father to take a stick to you if you are interferin'.'

She turned to Mrs Bevan, who was dabbing her eyes with the back of her hand. She had not yet taken off her marketing clothes or put on the apron which usually served her as a handkerchief.

'Well, I'm glad to hear as you were tryin' to do summat to stop this business.... So that's the reason why this fellow Lloyd was sendin' his letter to Megan?'

177

'How was you gettin' to know of it?' Esther asked.

'Ah, there's not much as I 'on't be gettin' to know. Wickedness is not to be hid. I've been tellin' Megan that many a time. She thought to deceive me, but the whole story is out now.' Aunt Lily rubbed her bony fingers together. 'Price the post has been courtin' her. Many's the time I've been forbiddin' her to sit up at night along o' no man livin'. "They're not to be trusted," I've said to her, and I've told her of all the gals ever I knowed as comed to trouble that way – and her poor mother among 'em. But 'twas to no purpose. It seems she was promisin' the postman to come down and let him in some night when we was in bed – the wicked, ungrateful gal after all as we've done for her! But as if that wasn't wickedness enough, she was takin' up with that good-for-nothin' fellow, Tom Pugh, as is drinkin' and swearin' something terrible, and runnin' after the gals, and all sorts. I 'ouldn't have believed it of a gal as Martha and I'd been rearin'. But there, a bastard child born in sin is allus going back to the devil, like a dog to his vomit, as the Bible do say.' She took breath. 'Well, that's how Megan comed to quarrel with the postman, and the postman comed to tell me about her havin' a letter from Canada as she was askin' him partic'lar not to mention to no one. I thought as there was summat wrong goin' on, and I had it all out o' him over a cup o' tea, now just.'

'What are you goin' to do?' Esther asked.

'Tell your father.'

Esther and Gladys exchanged a swift glance of fear. Mrs Bevan began to cry afresh.

'Best not do that, Lily. Indeed, he'll be goin' terrible violent if he's in drink.'

From the fold came the sound of a horse's hooves on the cobblestones.

'There he is.'

The four women looked at one another in silence. The threatened thunderstorm had not broken. It was an oppressively still evening, and the noises in the stable were distinctly audible. There was a clatter as though an empty bucket had been overturned, the sound of a pony's frightened plunging and a string of oaths from the rider.

'He's angry drunk,' whimpered Mrs Bevan.

'*Again*,' commented Gladys in a fierce whisper.

No other word was spoken. Esther was physically afraid, but she did not stir. Something proud and stubborn in her nature kept her with folded arms awaiting whatever should follow. She saw her father, flushed and with bloodshot eyes, come out of the stable, walking unsteadily. She moved aside to let him pass. He clutched the edge of the table and swayed as he stood.

'Halloo, Lily, you here? What d'ye want?'

For a moment there was no reply. Aunt Lily was afraid of the look on his face. She glanced at Esther and saw her standing as she had stood throughout the interview, self-possessed and unyielding.

'I've come to warn you as that fine daughter o' yours is still carryin' on with one o' them Lloyds the Henallt.'

The name brought a deeper flush to her brother's face, but he stared at her stupidly.

'No! No! He's gone to Canada, damn his eyes, darin' to come courtin' a gal o' mine.'

'He's gone to Canada, right enough, and she'll be out there after him if you don't look sharp.'

179

'The devil she will!' He struck the table with his huge fist, on the back of which the hairs grew thick and red. 'I'll be lockin' her up in the beast-house first.'

'Well, I've warned you, John. They're writin' to one another yet.'

She rose, feeling it wise, having shot her bolt, to depart, but he made a grab at her across the table.

'Holt – I do mean to have this matter out. Here, missus, wasn't I tellin' you to throw on the fire any letters as comed here from that bloody young fool?'

'Yes, yes, boss, and indeed I was doin' it, indeed I was!'

'Then how the devil...?' He stared, bewildered and furious, from one to another.

His sister, edging away from him, furnished the explanation. He was some time in grasping the meaning of what had happened, and all the while Esther stood, her back turned to him, staring up through the open doorway at the dark clouds that covered the sky, and Gladys, quivering like a frightened filly, bit her fingernails with sharp little pointed teeth.

'Now,' thundered John Bevan, when his fuddled brain had at last taken in the situation, 'where's that gal, Esther?'

'Here, Father,' she answered in a low voice from behind him.

He swung round. 'You write another word to one o' them blasted Lloyds and I'll – I'll break every bone in your body – d'ye hear me?'

'Yes, Father.'

'Now you mind what I say.'

'Yes, Father.'

'She's been deceivin' o' you,' put in Lily.

180

'Aye, I've a good mind to learn her now.'

He took a step forward, and Gladys darted in the same direction.

'You shan't touch her, you brute,' she screamed. 'You shan't lay hands on her – you shan't – you shan't!'

'Don't, Gladys,' cried Esther sharply, suddenly shaken out of her immobility, but Gladys was already between them, and had aroused her father to fury.

'Get out o' the way, you bitch – you...' He had flung her aside with a sweep of his arm. 'I'll learn my daughters to go makin' a mock o' me. I'll be master in my own house, d'ye hear? I'll give Esther the hidin' she do deserve if I choose to, and you too, you spitfire, after I've done with her.'

They had both retreated beyond his reach, and he stood with feet planted wide apart, uncertain upon which to turn first.

'Get out the front way, *quick*,' Esther cried but Gladys did not move.

'What right have you to lay a finger on her?' she cried. 'What have you ever done for your daughters as they should be heedin' you? You're good for nothin' only to drink and ill-use some poor creatures as isn't strong enough to defend theirselves from you, you beast.'

He spun round on his heel and strode to the table, shouting curses at her. She darted away to the door, but, finding her mother had inadvertently got in her way, she altered her course and made for the staircase.

'Now I'll have you! Now I'll learn you a lesson as you 'on't be forgettin' in a hurry.'

She fled upstairs, but tripped over her torn apron as she reached the top step. Her father was close behind her

181

and grabbed her by the shoulder. She shrieked with terror like a trapped animal as he swung her round and shook her. Esther rushed to the foot of the stairs.

'Stop, Father, for God's sake, stop!' she cried, looking about her desperately for some weapon with which to attack him. 'Stop! Stop! Or you'll be killin' her!'

But before she had time to mount the stairs he lost his footing on the landing and shot out a hand with which to steady himself. Gladys, suddenly released, tottered backwards, caught at the banister, missed it, and fell head first down the steep flight of uncarpeted stairs.

For an instant there was silence. Gladys lay on her back, so white that Esther thought she was already dead and fell upon her knees beside her.

'Lord have mercy upon us,' she heard Aunt Lily whisper; and from above her father's voice: 'That'll learn her, that will.'

As he came downstairs, Esther raised her eyes to him.

'You've killed her,' she said in a cold, low tone.

He gaped at her and stooped clumsily over Gladys' body.

'Killed her,' she repeated, and rising – 'Get out of the way.'

He moved away into the kitchen, his hand to his head.

'Is she really hurted?' he asked, staring at his sister.

Aunt Lily stared back as if she had not heard or had failed to understand his question. Suddenly she moved from the fireplace and walked stiffly across the room.

'This is my doin',' she thought, and repeated aloud: 'My doin', O God!'

At the door she passed Mrs Bevan and met her eyes. They exchanged their terror but no words.

Esther had carried Gladys into the kitchen. Her mother came and went, now crouching beside her, now wandering aimlessly about the room, sobbing and wringing her hands. Her father, sobered by fear, leant over her.

'No need to fret. 'Tis only bein' a bit of a fall – only a bit of a fall.'

The boys returned, clattered in noisily, checked, and stood open-mouthed.

'Go quick and fetch the doctor,' Esther said over her shoulder to Idris.

'Duwch, whatever's the matter?'

'Don't stop to talk. Go, d'ye hear, at onst.'

She heard him go out. She heard her mother's wailing renewed, and her father muttering to himself. John she felt standing close beside her, breathing heavily, but she did not lift her gaze from the waxen face in her lap. Gladys was not dead. From a wound on her head, slowly oozing blood darkened and matted her hair. Esther gave an order for water and someone brought it to her. She bathed and bound up the cut, which was not deep.

The main injury she knew was not here. Perhaps Gladys was not seriously hurt, after all – who could tell until the doctor came? It would take long to find and bring him, but until his coming she dared not move. A dog slunk in at the open door and the touch of its hot tongue upon her cheek brought the first tears to her eyes. It began then to lick Gladys gently, and she did not prevent it.

CHAPTER 10

The silence of a sunny afternoon brooded over Pengarreg, and a thick scent of dry rot, stored grain and wool came from the loft.

When the doctor came out of the room in which Gladys lay, his brows were contracted into a scowl above his sunken eyes. He had been a good-looking man once, but the sickness, poverty and suffering with which he had struggled daily for forty years on the farms about Llangantyn had left their mark upon him. His mind had grown rough with his body. He had acquired a reputation for being at once kindly and callous, and his attitude of dogged devotion to what he believed to be a duty, but could no longer find a source of sympathy or inspiration, showed itself in his whole bearing. 'No good to worry oneself to death over the poor devil,' he was wont to say of the saddest case, but today he found no solace in that practical reflection. He *was* worried, moved, in spite of himself, to pity and rebellion of spirit.

The sound of his step on the landing brought Mrs Bevan to the foot of the stairs. She had been crying not so much from sorrow as from fear, for Esther, on whom she had learned to lean more and more during the past two weeks, had gone to market.

'Was you tellin' her?' she asked the doctor.

He descended slowly into the kitchen before answering 'Yes.'

Mrs Bevan burst out crying afresh. 'Oh dear, oh dear! Is there nothing whatever to be done? 'On't nothin' as you can do to save her? Is she to lie on her back – allus a burden to herself and to us all?'

He turned and regarded her with severity. Her weak complaining and her easy flow of tears clashed with the agonised silence in which the girl upstairs had received the news.

'Can't you do nothin' to cure her?' Mrs Bevan repeated, laying one of her frail hands on his arm.

He shook it off impatiently.

'Good God, woman! D'you think I'd have left anything undone after seeing the child's face when I told her she'd never walk again? D'you think I wouldn't get a specialist down from town – if I had to pay his fees myself?' He broke off, irrationally angry with her. 'There's nothing *to* do. I've told you that a hundred times. Her spine is fatally injured. That's the end of it.' And he walked out of the house.

'I'm sure he needn't be so sharp with me,' Mrs Bevan thought as she stood alone in the desolate room, leaning against the table for support and crying from mere force of habit.

Then in one of her ill-timed efforts at conciliation, she hurried out of the house and encountered the doctor as he was in the act of mounting his cob.

'I'm afeard as I was makin' you angry now just, doctor,' she whined, detaining him with that limp hand, the touch of which upon his arm he had grown to detest. 'I'm sure I didn't mean to say nothin' to put you out, but I've been that vexed – and indeed I don't feel near well myself, so you must please...'

He cut her short with a hasty assurance that he bore her no ill-will, and swinging himself into the saddle, rode out of the fold.

As his cob jogged down the track leading to the main road he stared about him gloomily as if the familiar landscape had acquired a new and sombre significance. Far below him lay the river, serene and silvery in the mellow sunlight of late afternoon. Somewhere out of sight larks were singing their rapturous song.

'Nature's callous,' he muttered, 'callous.' It was a word that had often been applied to himself.

Mrs Bevan did not go up to her daughter. She was afraid and hung about the kitchen, full of dread and self-pity, longing for the sound of crying to break the fearful stillness which brooded in that upper room.

Gladys lay rigid as when the doctor had closed the door upon her. She did not know how long it was since she had been left alone. The silence seemed to have endured from everlasting, and to be going on for all time to come. She might have been dead and lying in her grave, so quiet it was, and so motionless her body. All sensation had left her. She could not feel the bed on which she lay, nor the clothes that covered her. Only when at length she closed her eyes, did she become aware of the cold tears entangled in her lashes. Those tears had filled her eyes a long age ago, it seemed, but they had never overflowed. She might not die for years to come, but she would lie here dying slowly, oh! so slowly. Would she know the moment when she ceased to live, if death stole upon her so stealthily? Was she not already almost dead? She seemed to float in space, and darkness began to revolve about her. She was fainting – that was all – but she tried, even as consciousness slipped from her, to pray that it might never return. But it returned by imperceptible degrees, dragging her, with a painful sense of disappointment, out of a merciful oblivion. With it came a renewed craving for life, abundant and healthful, and tormenting images of the things she most loved.

She closed her aching eyes and fancied that it was early morning, four or five o'clock in the chill of autumn, and that she had awakened with a sense of adventure, and started up out of her bed. *Mushrooms!* She had laid plans to gather them before the rest of the world was astir. All the secrets of the countryside were known to her – where the best nuts could be found in a disused lane with hazel trees meeting overhead; where the blackberries were juiciest beside a stream overgrown with brambles; what was the best place for sloes and crab apples; which grasses were sweet to nibble and from what flowers honey could be sucked. As she thought of all the fruits, the good tastes and smells of autumn, her imagining took the firm shape of reality.

She seemed to feel the touch of the floor beneath her bare feet and the tingling of her hands as she plunged them into cold water. She saw herself slide quickly into her clothes and tiptoe downstairs. The opening of the door let in a wisp of mist, and she stole out into a world hushed and white. The buildings rose dim before her, and, beyond them, the trees were the ghosts of giants. Nothing kept her company but the swish of her feet through the wet grass, until, as she plunged down into yet denser, chillier opaqueness, the muffled sound of the river reached her ears. Now the road was hard beneath her feet. She could see it indistinctly, light between the dark masses of hedge on either side. Over one of these she scrambled, hearing the dead wood snap beneath her, and laughing to think that the mist hid her from the farmer's eyes. At last she was in the level fields, close to the unseen river, hurrying to and fro, peering this way and that for a gleam of whiteness at her feet. When the mist lifted and the mushrooms were easy to find, there would be others out in search of them, the owners of these fields; but she, a night marauder, would have been there before them and would be hurrying back to her hill-fastness laden with spoil! Oh! it was fun! What was that? Her heart gave a terrifying leap, for a huge ungainly shape had suddenly risen out of the earth before her. She started back trembling. What could it be? It had enormous horns.... Why, she was laughing now, but still trembling a little. A *cow*! How monstrous ordinary shapes could look when seen through the mist. How queer it all was, how exciting! But she would never see it thus again. This was a memory. Adventure had gone from her life for all time.

She lay for a little while in blank despondency, but soon her indomitable spirit snatched her up again and set her riding across the hills on an April day. She was out of sight of the house, with no one to call after her, 'Don't you be sweatin' the pony, gal!' She was on a young horse. The close-cropped turf was springy under its hooves. It sidled and curveted as she reined it in. The strength and vitality of this big creature under her control filled her with a triumphant sense of mastery. It should go then, since they were both in the same mood. She leaned forward suddenly, her hands low on its neck, and urged it into a gallop.... Away they went, the wind blowing through her clothes, so that she felt it cold and stinging on her body as if she had been naked. Water splashed up about them. Sheep scurried to right and left. Rocks and trees seemed to fly past. They were racing the purple cloud shadows that swept across the hills. They were a part of the boisterous vigour of the wind, the youth of the spring, the strength of all nature bursting into leaf and bud and flower. Oh! the delight of motion! She shouted aloud in the joy of such reckless speed.... Gone! She would never move again. The room was oppressively still. She drew in her breath with a sob, and the sound of it frightened her.

While she lay with closed eyes, pictures of what she had lost came thronging upon her again with maddening insistence and clarity. She remembered wading up a stream, her skirt tucked up, her shoes and stockings thrown on the bank; the exhilarating coldness of the water on a hot summer's day, the gurgling, tinkling sound of it, the scent of the meadowsweet along the brink. She recalled the excitement with which she had seen a silver

189

streak flash into the still brown pool before her, and the ultimate delight of catching a fat, red-spotted trout in her hands, and flinging it out to be carried home in triumph.

'Oh God!' she cried out suddenly: 'Why wasn't he killin' me outright? Why was he leavin' me like a poor mangled rabbit caught in a trap?' A wave of fury swept over her. 'Damn him,' she screamed, so that her mother in the kitchen below heard her and trembled. 'Damn him! The brute! The devil! I 'ould like to make him suffer as he has made me. I 'ould like to see him lyin' bleedin' and broken and weak. I'll be lyin' here, thinkin' o' the 'orld I do love, and he, as has brought me to this, 'ull be goin' about with the trees and the birds and the wind around him, all glad and free.'

A soft evening breeze had arisen. It stole through the open window and fanned her face with a gentle caress that made tears of passionate longing and regret start into her eyes. The slanting sun threw shadows of the ash leaves outside on to the whitewashed wall. They began to dance and sway as she watched them. Colourless shadows cast by the sun she never could see again – that was all that was left to her of the glorious, growing, stirring world that held all her heart. The tears overflowed and fierce sobs shook and choked her. Her hands tore at the patchwork coverlet and ripped a piece of it to shreds. In the doorway she saw, through a blinding mist, her mother's frightened face.

'Go away. Get out. Leave me be,' she shrieked. And then she was alone once more – beating with clenched fists upon the bed.

The shadows were lengthening when Esther, having sold the butter and bought the groceries in Llangantyn, started on her homeward way. Her laden basket was heavy. She moved it from one arm to the other and trudged on steadily. She was tired before she came to the track that led up to Pengarreg, and the ascent made her aching limbs feel as heavy as lead. Halfway up to the farm she stopped. 'Indeed,' she thought, 'I did ought to hurry on back to see how Gladys is keepin', but I'm that tired today I feel as if my back 'ould break in two, just.'

She set down her burden and seated herself on the grass beside the path. 'I'll be givin' myself a minute or two to catch my breath,' she thought, and, wiping the sweat from her forehead, let her hands fall heavily into her lap and closed her eyes. The sun poured down and innumerable gnats hovered about her. Presently the first faint breeze of evening, that had set the shadows dancing upon the wall of Gladys' room, fanned her burning face, and with a sigh of relief she let her head drop and all her muscles relax. She had aged more than a year in a couple of weeks, for new suffering and responsibility had come into her life, and her heart was sick with hope deferred.

But with the silence of the hillside around her and the soft touch of the breeze, her spirits began to revive. It was good to be at rest and alone. Love, which had been driven from her thoughts by care, stole back. No personal pain and weariness, no pity for another, or toil or anxiety could rob her of Rhys' love. It was an abiding miracle that he should have given it to her. She was blessed among women in that he had chosen her out, he who was clever and handsome and self-confident, who cared nothing for his uncle's bribes or threats, who had left home and forgone his inheritance for her sake – 'As though,' she told herself, 'I was bein' queen o' the world.'

'No matter what is happenin' here,' she murmured, 'I am bein' lucky – the luckiest 'oman on earth, I do believe.' Her throat contracted and there was the smart of tears in her eyes; but she smiled, feeling that all things could be borne by one possessed of her treasure. In the peace of that thought, she rose and struggled on her way.

When she came into the fold, no one was astir. The dogs lay stretched out like dead beasts in the shade of the buildings. With a sense of reluctance she raised the latch and stepped into the kitchen. It seemed to her cold and dark as a dungeon, and silent as the grave. What had happened? Where was everyone? Suddenly she saw them standing motionless and close together, like sheep, at the foot of the staircase. Her mother shrank against the wall, her hands pressed to her face. Her father stood irresolute, as though arrested in an attempt to turn away, and her two brothers craned forward, open-mouthed. They were all listening to some sound from the room above.

'What is it?' she asked, her eyes wide with apprehension. 'Is Gladys...?'

They turned troubled faces to her and her mother began to sob.

'What is it?' she asked again quickly, setting down her basket on the table.

She could feel her heart beating faster, and a wave of heat surge over her. Something horrible had taken place. Her father lowered his sullen eyes. His underlip, purplish and full, protruded beneath his ragged moustache, and his bushy red eyebrows were drawn together. Esther was pushing her way past him when her mother's clinging hands laid hold on her.

'Don't you go up, or maybe she'll be doin' you a mischief.'

'*Gladys?*'

'Yes, yes. She's like a mad 'oman. She's tearin' everything to pieces and screechin' and callin' on God – oh dear! oh dear! 'tis terrible. Don't you be goin' up now. Maybe she'll rise from her bed – I have heard of such things – they are goin' terrible strong – them as isn't right in their minds.'

'Loose me go.'

'Oh, Esther, Esther, what are you doin', gal?'

'I am goin' up to her.'

Brushing aside the weak arm that tried to bar her way, she went swiftly up the stairs and across the threshold of her room. She had supposed Gladys to be suffering physically, but saw at once that she was now in the grip of some force fiercer than any bodily pain. With an effort that demanded all her courage, she walked to the bedside. Her broad, sun-browned hands closed gently over Gladys'. The muscles of the taut arms slackened, a quiver passed through the stiff body, and at length Gladys spoke in a whisper.

'Oh, Essy, I am *hatin'* him... you don't know... 'tis tearin' me, here.'

Esther winced. She sought for something to say that would bring healing. There were verses from the Bible, if she could but remember them, which would draw the poison of hatred out of her sister's wounds, but all she could recollect was the prayer she offered up night and morning, '...and forgive us our trespasses, as we forgive them that trespass against us...' It was of no use to repeat

193

them to the sufferer just now, to say that all hatred was wrong; that she, who had never willingly hurt a living thing, must strive to forgive the man who had inflicted on her such agony of body and soul that he was her father, whom it was her duty to honour, or that God would be angry with her unless she forgave him.

'O Lord,' Esther prayed silently, 'do You be teachin' me what to say. Do You be puttin' words not o' reproof but o' comfort into my mouth.' But none came. She remembered with a pang of misgiving that Rhys had doubted the truth of the Bible, her Bible to which she turned for guidance in any trouble. Was there no Divine help to be had, then? Her eyes filled with tears but she blinked them back. She dared not give way. Now, more than ever in her life, she must be strong, for, though her God had failed her, yet she must never fail Gladys. She forced herself to speak, steadying her voice with an effort at every word.

'Listen, little 'un. You mustn't be lettin' hatred get a holt on you.'

'Don't you dare to preach at me,' Gladys flashed, snatching away her hand. 'You haven't suffered like what I have.'

Esther gently regained the hand.

'I am not venturin' to preach, bach.'

'You'd best not. I don't care for God, nor man, nor devil now.'

'You did use to care for everything as was beautiful, whatever.'

Slowly the resentful green eyes were turned upon Esther's face.

'What is that havin' to do with it?'

194

'Only this. Hatred is bein' an ugly thing, withered and black like the old tree as was struck by lightnin' you did use to be afeard of. It don't *grow* nothin'. Love is bringin' new things into the 'orld. Hatred is turnin' back all the while to what is dead and rotten. Can't you see that, bach, you as are lovin' the spring and all the fresh growin' things, and the birds matin' and the little young creatures?'

The bloodless lips quivered.

'I'll never be seein' them no more.'

'But you'll be lovin' them so long as you do remember.'

'Don't, Essy, don't. I can't bear it!'

Her voice was softer now. The frozen tears had begun to flow. Still Esther persisted urgently in a low tone.

'Tell me, little 'un, was you ever seein' anything beautiful in the looks as passed atween our folk and any o' the Lloyds when they was meetin'? Think o' Aunt Lily's face, all sour and pinched, or Aunt Martha's, red as a turkey-cock, when the name o' Lloyd was bein' mentioned. 'Tisn't as they are uncommon ill-favoured. 'Tis the spirit o' hatred within them as do make them look old and ugly afore their time. And Father...'

'Don't speak to me o' him.'

'Ah! But 'tis wantin' you never to be like him, I am. 'Tis hatred as has broken your poor body. *Don't* let it break your spirit, *don't* let it master you.... Come you, there's a fight to be fought as is worth the winnin', not like most fights as is fought in the flesh.'

There followed a long stillness, during which Esther softly slipped an arm under her sister's shoulders.

'Maybe I'll try,' Gladys said at last.

195

'God 'ull be helpin' of you,' Esther murmured, holding her close.

'I don't believe in Him no more. Why should He let me suffer so, if He's carin' for me?'

'I don't know, bach. I'm thinkin' sometimes as He can't help bodily sufferin' Hisself – as He isn't bein' almighty, only as it were in the spirit. Oh! I dare say I'm wrong, and the parson 'ouldn't holt with me talkin' like that, but that's how I'm tryin' to account for a lot as we can't rightly understand. There 'on't be no miracle in these days to raise you up out o' bed again, but if your spirit is seekin' after comfort you'll be findin' it – I do believe.' After another silence she resumed: '"The souls of the righteous are in the hand o' God, and there shall no torment touch them." It isn't sayin' nothin' about their bodies. Maybe God can't save the body, but 'tis your *soul* I do want to see safe in His hand.'

Suddenly the girl in her arms was shaken with sobs.

'Oh, Essy!' The words came brokenly. 'You – have – been – makin' me want to live brave and fine – not to give way like what I've done today. Oh! But I'm so weak, unless you are bein' with me. Keep you close to give me your strength. Essy, *don't* you never leave me, not till I do die. It 'on't be long.... Promise me, Essy, *promise*.'

The words which the doctor had spoken returned to Esther's mind. 'She may live a few months; she may live a few years, or it may be only a matter of weeks.' Nothing was certain but that she could not live long and that, while she lived, none but Esther could calm and comfort her. In a low voice, shaken by inward conflict, Esther promised.

'So long as you are livin' I'll never be leavin' you.'

After a while the sound of crying ceased. The sun had dropped behind the western hills, and no shadows moved upon the wall. All was quiet and still. Gladys lay sleeping, a dead weight on the shoulder that supported her. The burden of the faith-healer was heavy upon Esther's heart. She was conscious of being utterly exhausted, too tired even to sleep. She tried to recall the thoughts of Rhys which had renewed her strength earlier in the day, but then she had been suffering only from physical weariness. Now she was worn out in mind. Virtue had gone out of her. She was empty even of faith. The thought of Rhys was a reproach, for her pity had been greater than her love. She stiffened as she knelt and her knees were hurt by the uncarpeted floor, but she made no attempt to move. With her wide eyes empty of hope – filled only by resignation to the strongest instinct within her – she watched the day turn to twilight and darkness come into the room.

CHAPTER 11

Before long, John Bevan took to his old ways again. One evening Esther was called suddenly from Gladys' bedside to the kitchen. The light of the candle she carried shone on her frowning brows and tightly compressed lips.

'Is he dangerous drunk?'

For answer her mother began to cry. 'I'm – terrible – afraid. My heart – the palpitations is chokin' me.'

Esther held the candle close to her face and saw that there was a bluish hue about the sunken lips. 'One o' these nights she'll be dyin' o' fright,' she thought, hot with anger against her father. From the fold came the sound of his incoherent shouting and swearing as he stumbled towards the house.

'Lock the door – *quick*, Mother.'

Mrs Bevan stared at her daughter as if paralysed.

'Quick!' Esther moved towards her with rapid decision.

'No, no, gal. I dursn't turn the key on the boss. 'Tis his house.'

''Tis your life, maybe.'

Her hand was on the door when it was burst open from without, forcing her back a step. On the threshold stood her father, in his raised hand a lantern that lit up vacant bloodshot eyes. Esther spread out her arms, resting a hand on either doorpost, and barred his way. Acting upon the impulse of the moment, she found herself face to face with him in the conflict which she realised had been long preparing. Now it must be fought to a finish. At first he did not attempt to thrust her aside, but stared at her stupidly. Then he spoke in an angry growl.

'What in the name o' hell are you standin' there for? Get out o' my way, can't you?'

With difficulty she found her voice. The sound of it, so low and steady, surprised her.

'Mother is took ill. You can't be comin' in and frightenin' her tonight.'

'*Can't* be comin' in? What 'ould you have me do, then?'

'Go and sleep on the hay.'

It was strange, she thought, how quietly she said it. There seemed to be one Esther speaking and another who had shrunk from this man all her life, listening in astonishment.

'Are you gone mad, gal?' he shouted. 'Here, get out o' my way, or it 'ull be the worse for you. Sleep in the hay, indeed!'

Still she stood her ground. He seized her by the arm with his disengaged hand, but she clung with all her force to the doorpost.

199

'You'll fight me, 'ull you?' roared her father, unable, with one hand, to dislodge her. 'A' right, then. I'll show you!' He let go her arm and set down the lanthorn. 'Now then – 'ull you go quiet, or shall I be makin' a mess o' you?'

'If you do touch me,' she said quietly, 'I'll tell the doctor and the parson and the police, I'll tell the whole countryside as it was you as injured Gladys.'

He gaped at her open-mouthed.

'Oh yes,' she went on quickly, 'you do know well enough, drunk as you are, what a business we've had keepin' it quiet, and how it was only along o' my beggin' her so, as Gladys was holdin' her tongue. But you ever raise a hand to Mother or I from now on, and I'll be fetchin' the police to you.'

'You 'ouldn't dare. I'd – I'd be killin' you just,' he stammered with rage.

'No fear o' that. You've killed one daughter already. You'd swing for the second.... Are you wantin' a rope round your neck?'

He retreated and broke into a storm of oaths. She heard him to the end, standing stolidly planted in the doorway. When at length he paused in his abuse, she answered him calmly.

'No use to talk. If you are comin' into this house tonight, I am goin' straight down to the magistrates in Llangantyn to tell them the whole story.'

'You 'on't never get out o' the place alive – damn you,' he shouted, coming close to her again, his right fist clenched and drawn back as if to strike her.

'A' right,' she cried unflinching, 'do your worst, then. 'Tis you as 'ull have to pay for it. The worse you are usin'

200

me, the harder it 'ull be goin' against you. Dead or alive, I'll be bringin' you to justice for what you've done to *her*.'

His arm dropped to his side. 'I do believe as you are tellin' the truth, you vixen,' he muttered. He picked up the lantern and raised it so that her features were sharply lit. Perhaps through the effect of drink upon his vision, perhaps because the harsh light, held close, threw unsoftened shadows upon her face, he saw a different Esther. She was the spit, he told himself, of his dead mother. Long ago that other woman, with grey eyes set far apart, had faced him with her level gaze, until he hung his head ashamed. He had angered her often, and, though he had loved her too, after a fashion, her death had been a relief. Now she had returned in the likeness of her granddaughter to be a reproach to him. He was afraid.

When he had turned on his heel and stumbled off into the darkness, swearing under his breath, Esther swiftly entered the kitchen and locked the door.

'Oh, Esther,' wailed her mother, 'however was you able to act so brave?'

'Deed, I don't know.'

She passed her hand across her eyes. Was she, she wondered, like some timid animal that will suddenly grow valiant in the defence of its young? Was her courage dependent upon the weakness of those she sought to protect?

'I don't know,' she repeated, 'I can't tell how nor why I did do it, but 'tis done.'

The feeding of the stock, the milking and the separating had been done, and a bright fire was crackling on the kitchen hearth. Esther had lifted down a flitch of bacon that had been suspended on hooks from the ceiling, and, resting it upon the table, held it pressed to her side as she cut slices from it. When her father slouched into the house, she looked up for a moment only. His shoulders were hunched, his hands thrust deep into his pockets. On his rumpled clothes were fragments of hay. With a surly look round the room he dropped into a chair. John and Idris, behind his back, nudged one another and grinned. Mrs Bevan, turning pale, hurried from the room. Esther, unmoved, continued to cut the bacon for breakfast.

'Hurry up there, can't you?' growled her father. 'I do want to get out after the sheep, so look sharp.'

He intended to resume the old tyranny. She studied him thoughtfully, with that direct gaze he could not endure, and laid down her knife.

'Tell Mother to come on in here a minute,' she said, turning to John, 'and do you and Idris be steppin' out into the fold till I call you for breakfast, there's good boys.'

Although they considered her, as a girl, their inferior, her quiet tone of authority impressed them. They obeyed, and she was left facing her father, with her mother upon the threshold, hesitating whether to enter or retreat.

'Now, Father, we'll have this out, onst and for all. If you do want me to stay at home and nurse poor Gladys day and night, and to do all the work o' the place for Mother, as is gone too weak to be doin' much herself, you'll have to be payin' me wages.'

He sat amazed at her insolence, but unable to free his mind from the impression which her likeness to his mother had produced upon him.

202

'Whoever heard of a man payin' his own daughter wages?' he growled at last.

'Whoever heard of a father injurin' his own child, like what you've done poor Gladys?'

He coloured. 'So you're goin' to fling that in my teeth again?'

'No. I'm not goin' to say no more about it. Only I am goin' to have the wages as a servant gal is havin'; so as I can be gettin' some small little comforts for her and for Mother, as you're grudgin' even the poultry money to.... Mother is bein' witness. If you 'on't pay me reg'lar, I'll be goin' off. I've a home of my own waitin' for me.'

Mrs Bevan threw up her hands. 'Oh, Esther! You 'ouldn't never go to leave your poor mother and your dyin' sister?'

'She's without no pity for her own flesh and blood,' her father averred solemnly.

She could have laughed at the irony of such a speech from him. Her mother, believing that she really intended to desert them, pleaded with her tearfully to stay. Her father rose, shouting that she might go to hell for all he cared, but, seeing her invincible, dropped once more into his chair. He was growing hungry. He needed the presence of a capable woman in his house. Esther was indispensable and his wounded pride exhausted itself in a final outpouring of abuse. In the end he promised to pay her a monthly wage, and swearing at her for an unnatural daughter, demanded his breakfast.

Having won her point, she set to work again, laid the table, went to the door and called to her brothers. They came in obediently, seated themselves in silence, and ate what she placed before them, watching her from time to time out of the corners of their eyes. Her mother's trembling fingers caught at her apron whenever she came within reach, and timidly caressed her.

'Thank you, dear, you are bein' terrible good to me,' she murmured, when Esther filled her teacup. Her father, with a surly attempt at civility, asked her to clean his boots. He had been in the habit of kicking them off on her newly washed floor, and leaving them without comment for her to pick up. She noted the change in him with a certain grim amusement, but there was little laughter in her heart. Upstairs, amongst her hidden treasures, was a gaily coloured envelope on which some weeks ago she had written the name 'Rhys Lloyd'. Since then the unwritten letter which it was to contain had changed its character in her mind. All that it now seemed necessary to write was the bare statement, 'Gladys is hurted. The doctor do say as she 'on't live long. She and poor Mother is needin' me.' Rhys surely would understand the rest.

'I am bein' boss here from now on,' she thought, surveying her mother and thinking of the cripple upstairs. 'Boss, along o' their weakness. But 'tis that same weakness as is keepin' me here, like what no power on earth couldn't be doin'...' and at the moment of her triumph her eyes filled with tears.

CHAPTER 12

'Think o'summat more to tell me.'

On the windowsill where Megan was perched a handful of orange, flame and tortoiseshell nasturtiums stood in a cracked and handleless jug.

'Tell me more,' Gladys insisted. ''Tis seldom as I do see anyone from outside, and Essy's goin' so little from home, she isn't bein' much of a newspaper.'

'No,' Esther said with a look of apology, 'I'm a poor one to pick up gossip.'

'I do go from home terrible seldom myself,' Megan complained, pulling at the petals of a flower.

'But someone is tellin' you tales, or tryin' to kiss you whenever you do,' Gladys protested. 'You're a wonder for gettin' to know about other folks' courtin', and for bein' courted yourself. Tell me about love, now.'

Megan began to laugh. Her warmly sun-browned face

and rosy cheeks grew redder.

'When there's no news to be had, I'm havin' to go back to the stories in the Bible,' Gladys said. ''Tis odd, what a lot o' sorts o' love is bein' written of in the Book. I, as am not knowin' nothin' about it myself, am not rightly understandin' how such different things is comin' to be called by the same name.'

Megan turned on her the puzzled stare of her brown eyes, which, like her hair, had a glint of red in them.

'What I do mean,' Gladys went on, 'is the kind and constant thing, and the cruel one too – all called by that one word Love. There's Jacob now, servin' seven whole years for Rachel, as the story do say, "and they seemed unto him but a few days, for the love he had to her".'

For an instant Esther's hands lay still in her lap, and a faint smile spread over her face. Then she bent her head again and went on with her work.

'And then there's the story o' Amnon. Are you rememberin' the verse, after he'd acted so wicked by the poor gal, "then Amnon hated her exceedingly, so that the hatred wherewith he hated her was greater than the love wherewith he had loved her". What are you thinkin' o' that now? ''Tis hardly seemin' possible to me.'

'Oh, 'tis bein' true enough,' cried Megan. 'There's plenty o' men like that to be had today. I am knowin' summat about men. There's Tom Pugh and the postman, both after me. I 'ouldn't trust neither o' 'em.'

'I wonder,' Gladys murmured, watching her with solemn eyes, 'as you are wantin' the company o' folks you can't be trustin'.'

'Oh, you don't understand. Courtin' isn't a thing you do

want, no more nor you are carin' *that*' – she snapped her fingers and laughed again – 'for the men themselves. Courtin's a thing as you *must* have, after the manner of all the earth! Look at the folks as is tryin' to live without it – how sour they do get. Did you ever see such dry faces as my aunts have got on' em? Never havin' no man near 'em just. And men too, as isn't takin' no notice o' the gals, they is goin' long-faced and bitter as sloes. No, no, 'tis right and natural to be courtin', only if you can't marry 'tis playin' with fire, I do grant you.'

She had taken up another flower, and was pulling it to pieces with restless fingers.

'Mind you, I do know well enough what I'm up to with Tom. When I do let him into the house at night, he's got to behave hisself, or I'd call on my aunts and wake the household and there'd be a time on him! He's allus threatenin' to go off down to the works, but he 'on't get over me that way. I do tell him to go if he's a mind to, but back he do come.' She sighed again, but her laughter sounded uneasy. 'I'd be missin' him if ever he was to go.'

Esther looked up with a pucker between her brows. 'You aren't goin' to marry him, are you?'

Megan turned away and stared out through the open window. 'He hasn't asked me – yet.'

After a while she swung round with a resumption of her usual confident manner.

'Oh, he'll be askin' me a' right, never fear. I am knowin' how to play a man, the very same as a fish on a line. I don't know shall I have him if he *do* ask me, a bit too wild he is for a husband, but he's a rare one to love. I'm safe enough – no need to worry about me.'

She boasted a good deal of her safety before she rose to go, for in her heart she was afraid. Standing by the window, she looked round the colourless room in which there was never any noise but that of murmured conversations, and no movement save Esther's quiet coming and going. She looked at Gladys with her innocent eyes cold as water, who lay there motionless, listening, wondering, far from the stir of life; at Esther, watching over her, calm with a steadfast faith unknown to Megan, and she turned away envious.

When she had gone, Gladys said, 'She isn't findin' love the same thing as you are, Essy.'

'"In my Father's house are many mansions",' Esther murmured, her eyes on her work.

Megan swung along with her rapid, bouncing walk. The dead bracken that covered the hillside was a deep auburn like her hair; the sunshine was warm on her shoulders, and the autumn wind sharp in her face. Up over the mountain path she went, her blue apron fluttering, her skirt swept back. The springy turf under her feet and the smell of moist earth were a source almost of ecstasy.

But when she came to the crest of the hill she was suddenly afraid. On the edge of the dark plantation that sheltered Tyncoed from the mountain winds, she had seen the figure of a man, and guessed it to be that of Tom Pugh. For a moment she thought of turning back in order to avoid him; but she decided that there was no knowing how long he would wait for her, and she dared not leave her return till very late because of her aunts' anger. Then she wondered whether she could make a wide circle round the hillside, and reach Tyncoed without his having seen her. But already he had descried her figure on the skyline and was waving to her from the shelter of the plantation.

'I must go down and speak to him, but I 'on't be-stayin' long with him in that 'ood,' she determined, and down the grass-grown track she went with swiftly beating heart.

Having made sure that she had seen his signal and was coming, Tom Pugh took cover under the spruce trees, whose branches made a roof overhead, and whose red trunks formed aisles of rounded columns. No wind could penetrate into this temple of trees, which was carpeted with dry, dead pine needles, and no birds sang or nested there.

Megan, entering it from the sunny wind-swept hilltop, was dazed by the sudden transition to twilight and profound silence. Before she had recovered herself she was fast in Tom Pugh's arms, and his hot kisses were making her face burn. Breathless and bewildered, she abandoned herself to his caresses, and felt a drowsy glow steal over her. It was not until his kisses became so rough, and the warmth of her response so great as to frighten her, that she made a violent effort to regain self-control, and tore herself away.

'Leave me be,' she cried, angry with him because she was angry with herself, 'you didn't ought to be kissin' a respectable gal like that!'

'I'm kissin' o' you like that because I do love you so. I can't live without you no longer; havin' you I must be,' and he took a step towards her.

She retreated, though her instincts urged her to throw herself into his arms once more. 'No, no,' she cried, her eyes filling with tears, 'go away. Don't you be 'ticing o'me like that.'

She stepped backwards, but he followed her and seized her by the shoulder. Quick to anger as she had been to passion, she struck him in the face. A blow from her was no light matter, as it might have been from a town-bred girl, who could not wield an axe or a spade as she did. He put his hand up, laughing, half angry.

'Duwch, but you're a spitfire!' And before she could escape him he caught her, pinioning her arms behind her so that she could not move them. Angry as she was, his over-mastering strength gave her a thrill of pleasure. She ceased to struggle and looked up at him, dishevelled, defiant, yet admiring.

'Now,' he cried, crushing her to him, ''ull you be listenin' to what I have to say? I do want to *marry* you and have you for allus.'

Her body relaxed, the colour rushed into her cheeks, and she hid her face on his shoulder.

'Indeed, and I'm ashamed o' myself,' she whispered. I didn't ought to have struck you. Was I hurtin' you, dear?' She peeped up at him.

'Indeed, and you're a reg'lar vixen,' he told her, 'but there's never been no gal as I loved like I am lovin' you. You're just everything to me. I'll never be happy without you now,' and for the moment he believed what he said. 'I don't know how I can bear to be leavin' you, even for a bit.'

'Leavin'...?' She looked up at him again, startled. 'Why must you be leavin' me at all?'

His face clouded. 'Oh, that's what I came to tell you about. I've had a row with the boss. He's turned me out, the old devil.'

'Oh, Tom! What was you doin' to deserve o' that?'

'''Twasn't my fault,' he protested sulkily.

But she guessed that he had been drinking once more. 'You'd be a fool to marry him,' her reason insisted; nevertheless she laid her head on his shoulder.

'What 'ull you be doin' now?' she asked, the spirit gone out of her.

'Goin' down to the works. There's good money to be had there.'

'They're a rough lot,' she sighed. 'Fightin' and drinkin' and playin' cards and all sorts.'

'Don't you believe it. There's good company to be had there as well as bad.'

'Ah, but Tom, 'ull you ever be takin' up with the good 'uns?'

He frowned. 'Are you goin' to nag at me, same as the old 'uns at home do do? Or are you goin' to trust me to keep tidy and make a home for you?'

She looked up at him imploringly. 'I 'ould like to be trustin' you, whatever. If only I was bein' able to.'

'I 'ull be keepin' straight from now on. I 'ull be makin' a fresh start for your sake,' and as he declared over and over again that she might trust him, she let herself be beguiled into believing him.

Her instincts demanded that she should give herself to him freely, unconditionally, as the wild creatures mated; but her reason told her that she must deliberately choose and lawfully marry a man able to hold his own in a hard-working community and provide a home for her and the children she might bear.

'Come you, and sit down, and we'll be talkin' over our plans,' he urged.

'No, no indeed. I must be goin' now,' she answered, in a last attempt to act prudently; but she let him half drag, half carry her to the darkest part of the wood, where he flung himself down full length at her feet. For a full minute she hesitated, standing above him, looking down at his handsome face and blue eyes, raised pleadingly to hers. He was only a boy, after all, and he was unhappy because he was about to leave her. Big and strong as he was, he awoke pity in her. He loved her better than she had guessed. He had offered to marry her. She seated herself beside him and he placed his head in her lap. Softly she ran her fingers through his thick wavy hair. He shivered with pleasure at her touch, and, raising himself on his elbow, adroitly pulled her down beside him.

'Let me go,' she entreated, but in spite of herself her arms stole round him, as his had done round her. And then she became conscious only of his flushed face close above hers, and his hot lips seeking her own. She surrendered herself to a long and passionate kiss, in which the remnants of her self-control melted away like vapour before the heat of a fire. It left her trembling, sobbing for breath, quivering with a strange delight; she ceased to struggle or to think, and instinct had its way with her.

When at length she stole out of the wood, she was unwontedly pale, and the hands she raised to her dishevelled hair were unsteady. Exhausted and frightened, she made her way to Tyncoed, and the sound of her lover whistling blithely as he descended the opposite side of the hill brought no joy to her heart.

CHAPTER 13

The dancing shadows of summer had passed. Through the autumn the ash leaves had whirled across Gladys' window like flights of birds going southward, and now, if ever a gleam of watery sunshine lit her room, only the bare branches of the tree outside were shadowed on the wall. She lay still and wove her fancies. Reading was a labour to her; writing an art hardly acquired and seldom practised. She had rarely been outside the parish in which she was born, and her vivid imagination had been fed solely upon scraps of gossip, legend and folklore. But as her strength and her longing for the joys of running wild about the countryside waned, her interest in humanity and her thirst for fiction quickened. She seized upon any modern story books that Esther was able to bring her, and spelled her way through them laboriously. But she never enjoyed them as she enjoyed the simpler stories of the Testaments.

Always, on her patchwork coverlet, lay an open Bible, the old volume, thumb-marked and greasy, to which Esther turned day by day for spiritual guidance. Gladys cared nothing for the teaching it contained. To her it was just a book full of adventures, battles and love-making, of the journeys, the business and pleasures of a pastoral people who were nearer to her than more sophisticated heroes and heroines whose psychological intricacies bewildered her. Not only were the characters in the Bible more comprehensible, but their stories were told with a simplicity that left her free to fill in the details to her own satisfaction. She did not want to stumble with difficulty through descriptions of dress and appearance. The one word 'comely', or the brief phrase 'fair to look upon', were sufficient to set her mind at work. The line, 'Solomon in all his glory', would conjure up visions that far surpassed any newspaper account of a court function that she spelled out letter by letter. Esther had brought her an illustrated Bible, with coloured photographs of the Holy Land, and pictures of present-day Jews and Arabs, in robes such as their forefathers had worn since the time of Abraham. But, though she was proud of showing it to her occasional visitors, Gladys preferred the old volume with its faded print, between the lines of which she could in fancy paint her own scenes – David, clothed in red velvet and ermine, as she had seen King Edward represented on a biscuit tin, and the Virgin Mary, with Esther's grave, calm face, and the old black dress covered by a blue print pinafore which Esther wore. Like a Renaissance artist, she clothed her biblical figures in the dress of her own day, and set them in a landscape with which she was familiar.

214

Today the sky seen through the window was dark, and the fire of peat burned low. Winter twilight was in the room; but Gladys was too absorbed in a story suggested to her by the often-read Book to notice the passing hours. Esther, coming softly into the room with her tea on a tray, found her staring straight before her.

'Well, bach, you've not done none o' the sewin' I set you. Been readin', have you?'

'Aye. The story o' Dinah. I've read it many times before, mind you, but today, 'twere comin' before me, like as if I seed it all acted in the room here.'

'Tell me.' Esther seated herself upon the bed, and from time to time handed her food as she talked.

''Ould you be carin' to hear, *really*, what I am thinkin' in my head?' Gladys asked.

'Why, yes. You are thinkin' such wonderful things – like a writer o' books just. I do wish if I had your gift.'

Gladys flushed with pleasure. Her face had grown whiter of late and her skin was transparent as alabaster, but her sunken eyes that looked unreally large shone as she began: 'Well then, in years gone by, ever so long ago, afore even Father's grandfather came to Pengarreg, Jacob went wanderin' about the countryside with his horses and his caravans and his small little light carts and his lurcher dogs, same as the gypsies do do to this day. And he came to the land o' Canaan, and bein' richer and more respected nor what the gypsies are now, he bought hisself a field for an hundred pieces o' money, and he and his sons kept cattle there. I am not rightly knowin' what the land o' Canaan were like, but maybe it was a land o' green hills with small little fields and a stream runnin' down the

215

middle o' every valley; and I do fancy it was beside one o' these streams as Jacob spread his tents on a bit o' common, same as gypsies do do at Llangantyn fair. It must have been a wonderful grand sight to see old Jacob sittin' upon the box o' his caravan as was painted so gay, and drivin' his fine horses. Havin' a tremenjous long white beard, Jacob was, and lookin' old and wise and solemn-like. I have been seein' his picture in the church window at Llangantyn, and I 'ould be afeard to meet him, for all he was a man o' God. But Dinah, his daughter, she weren't afeard o' him, for he was lovin' her and givin' her all as ever she asked him for. Drivin' ahead o' the caravan, she was, in a light little cart with pink and red flowers painted on it and a piebald pony between the shafts, the very same as they do have at circuses, wonderful pretty, and Dinah herself the prettiest thing o' the lot. Big plaits o' hair she was havin', twisted round the back o' her head, as black as coal and as glossy as silk, and she wasn't wearin' no hat but a bright-coloured shawl, and great, large gold earrings and beads and all sorts hung round her. She wasn't never wearin' no collar, but her tight-fittin' bodice were cut a bit low, and for all she were dark and sunburnt, her neck rose up so small and round and soft, a man could hardly keep his hands off of it. Singin' in a sweet low voice, she was, by drivin' along, and smilin' and noddin' to the little brown children as was runnin' alongside her cart. That is how she did come to Shalem, where was the property o' Hamor, who was ownin' all the farms in that district, and puttin' his sons into them. One o' these sons, Shechem by name, was standin' by the roadside when Jacob and his folk passed by, and he was

216

hearin' Dinah sing and seein' her teeth so even and white, and catchin' a glance o' her bright dark eyes, and he was fancyin' her somethin' odd. There is 'omen, by what I do hear tell, as men is thinkin' wonderful pretty so long as they do see them, but they are no sooner out o' sight nor they are forgotten. But there is others, and maybe not so good-lookin', as has summat about 'em as do haunt a man for all the 'orld like the ghost o' a body as is gone. Dinah, she were like that, and havin' onst set eyes on her, Shechem couldn't never get her shape out o' his head. Thinkin' o' her for days after, he were, but never gettin' no sight o' her until Jacob had bought his field off o' Hamor, and settled down to live like a respectable man in Shalem parish. Then Dinah went out to see the daughters o' the land, carryin' a basket full o' bootlaces and clothes pegs and ribbons, and walkin' so dainty, swayin' a bit from the hips. When Shechem set eyes on her the second time he was thinkin' her even prettier nor he had done the first.

'"What have you got to sell, gal?" says he. But he wasn't lookin' at the basket but into her eyes.

'"Beautiful laces and ribbons goin' cheap," says she, smilin' up at him.

'Shechem were a great swampin' fellow, with fine broad shoulders on him and blue eyes, and she was likin' the looks o' him.

'"Come you on up to my house," says he, "and show me all you've got."

'Now Dinah was that innocent she went along with him same as a child might be doin'. Shechem was livin' in a cottage o' his own, on a byetack o' old Hamor's, and bein' as they was rich folk he had done it up terrible smart. There was a harmonium in the parlour, and a real silver teapot and sugar basin in the corner cupboard, and lace curtains tied up with pink ribbons, and photos of Shechem's family and friends framed in red plush. Grand it must have seemed to Dinah as was used to livin' in a caravan. Forgettin' all about her business, she was, and lookin' at this and that, and givin' little cries o' pleasure, and Shechem was watchin' her and takin' more and more delight in her all the while. Makin' a cup o' tea for her, he was, and pressin' her to stay, and so the evenin' was goin' and at last it comed late. Then Dinah got up and said as she must be goin'.

'"Not until you've given me a kiss," says Shechem, and he comes up close to her.

'She hung her head and was blushin' very pretty, and with that Shechem takes her in his arms and starts kissin' her on the mouth. Meanin' to act honest by her, he was – comin' of decent people; but onst he got her in his arms he couldn't let her go. Holdin' her closer and kissin' her more lovin' he was all the time, and Dinah, as had never been kissed like that before, were half-afeard but wonderful happy. Forgettin' everything, she was, and just lettin' him do as he liked with her, till all o' a sudden it came on her as she didn't ought to let a strange man carry on with her like that. Then she tore herself away from him and runned to the door and out down the garden path. Maybe, if she'd spoken to him nasty and gone away quiet like, he'd have let her be, but by runnin' after her and catchin' holt o' her, just as she were off into the road, he got that excited he didn't hardly know what he were doin'. Pickin' her up in his arms, he was, and she beggin' on him to let her go free, but clinging to him all the while because he was so big and strong, and she was that frightened. So he carried her into the house and up into his room.'

'Oh, Gladys! You didn't ought to tell such stories.'

'Why,' Gladys returned, opening her eyes very wide, 'the Bible do tell it. Only,' she added thoughtfully, 'the Bible do say as Shechem saw Dinah and took her and lay with her, but seein' as it do go on to say as he loved her and spake kindly unto her he can't have been a cruel, wicked man, so I'm thinkin' as he was over hasty and was havin' his weakness for the ladies. There's a good few as was like that in the Bible. Shechem were sorry for what he'd done after, seein' poor Dinah with all her great shinin' plaits o' hair lyin' loose about her, and her big, dark eyes lookin' up at him all wet and frightened-like, and tears in her lashes as were wonderful long and thick.

'"Don't you be afeard, bach," he was whisperin' to her, "I 'on't never leave you now, and I'll make an honest 'oman o' you so soon as ever I can."

'And he kept on kissin' her and tellin' her how much he was lovin' her, till at last she gave over cryin'. As soon as it were light in the mornin' he were goin' to his father and tellin' him all as had happened.

'"I do want to marry the gal," says he, "and no other 'oman 'on't do for me."

'Hamor he were terrible angry, and blamin' his son for actin' so wicked but blamin' him still more for wantin' to marry a gal as he'd led astray. I've noticed as respectable folk is allus like that when 'tis a question o' one o' their own sons. Well, at last he were goin' over to Shechem's cottage, as he said, "to turn the whore out o' it," but when he was seein' Dinah, so pretty and so modest, and busy settin' the breakfast for Shechem all neat and nice, he comed to change his mind.

'"'Twouldn't do to have no scandal in the parish," says he, and he was goin' with his son to visit old Jacob as had been frettin' all night and sendin' his servin' men to look here and there for his daughter.

'Now Dinah's brothers, Simeon and Levi, were in the field lookin' to the cattle when Hamor and Shechem comed into their father's camp, and the talk was goin' out about what had happened, and they were comin' to hear o' it whilst Jacob was still listenin' to his visitors, and bein' too vexed at the news they had brought him o' Dinah to give them no answer whatever. Simeon and Levi they were havin' a terrible lot o' pride on them, and when they heard as a stranger had treated their sister as if she had been no better nor what she should be, they was goin' just mad with anger. Thinkin' a lot o' Dinah they were, seein' as she were so pretty and had allus been a credit to the family, but not thinkin' nothing o' her happiness, nor what she might be likely to want in this matter. Actin' the very same as John and Idris did with you when they set on Rhys Lloyd. So they made a plan to take their vengeance on Shechem and all his relations; and they comed up to their father's camp, where the old man was still sittin' with his head bowed, and his long white beard restin' on his breast, because o' the shame that had come upon his daughter. And seein' as Jacob 'ouldn't take no notice o' them, Hamor made a speech to all Jacob's people, invitin' them very friendly like to settle in Shalem parish, and rent farms and marry amongst his own folk. When he had finished, Shechem, as was terrible red and nervous, made a speech too, but he was only thinkin' o' Dinah, and beggin' Jacob and his sons to let him marry her and offerin' to give them whatever they should ask o' him. Very rash he was, bein' so much in love. Then Simeon and Levi answered as all the sons o' Jacob were circumcised, and 't'ould be a shame on them to marry those as weren't. I don't rightly know what circumcised do mean, but the Sunday-school teacher said as 'twere a mark o' some sort, and I've noticed as the gypsy men do wear gold rings in their ears, so maybe it is that.

'"Havin' to have your ears pierced, same as us,' Simeon and Levi was sayin', "and to wear rings as we'll give you afore we can marry your gals or let our gals marry your sons."

'And Shechem was ready to have his cars pierced, or to do anything else at onst, because all his delight was in Dinah; and Hamor, bein' a peaceful man, was glad to come to some agreement. So he and his son went back to Shalem village, where most o' the folks were relations to him, and told them the news, and they were bein' ready to welcome the strangers, and no doubt hoping to gain summat by rich folk comin' to settle amongst them, and they agreed to be circumcised. You have been hearin' tales o' the gypsies' poison and the gypsies' medicine, and how they are bein' wonderful wise in the use o' plants? Well, Simeon and Levi, they was givin' the people o' Shalem rings to put in their ears as had been rubbed with summat poisonous, and on the third day the men in the village were taken sick and havin' to stay in their beds. Then these two wicked men took swords and went into the village and killed all the relations o' Hamor, and poor old Hamor hisself as hadn't done them no manner o' harm, all along o' their family pride. There were a fearful slaughter, and blood runnin' same as if they'd been killin' a pig in every house; and last o' all they came to Shechem's cottage, and burst into the kitchen. Shechem were sittin' at the table havin' his tea and talkin' to Dinah o' how they 'ould soon be married, and she were standin' by the fire lookin' down into it and not answerin' him nothin'.

"'Dinah, bach," says he at last, very sorrowful, "I'm afraid in my heart as I did do you a wrong, and as you don't love me, nor 'on't never do so."

'At that she turned round and comed towards him, smilin' very shy-like and blushin', and, never sayin' no word, she stoops down and kisses him all o' a sudden. 'Twas the first time ever she kissed him o' her own accord, and he were took so by surprise and delight, he couldn't do nothin' but look up at her, and tears in his eyes for a while. Then he pulled her down on to his knee and whispered: "Dinah bach, Dinah bach, do you love me?"

'And puttin' her arms round his neck and hidin' her head on his shoulder, she whispers back: "Yes, indeed, it do frighten me to think how much."

''Twas then as her brothers broke in on them. Simeon seized her by the arm and dragged her away from Shechem, and Levi, with his dark wicked little eyes flashin' like fire, rushes at him with his sword. Almost afore Dinah had begun to scream Shechem were lyin' dead with the blood from his wound pouring out on to the floor, and the screams were bein' froze on her lips, and she were goin' as white as a sheet. Draggin' her out o' the cottage,

222

they was, and back to her father's camp, but 'twasn't a
live 'oman they brought him, 'twere a livin' corpse, for she
wasn't singin' nor smilin', nor drivin' her little cart never
no more. She were sittin' with her hands lyin' listless like
in her lap, and starin' and starin' in front o' her as though
she were lookin' at summat terrible all the while – enough
to frighten you to look at her, with her poor face growin'
more thin, and her eyes bigger every day. Not sayin'
nothin' to no one when they spoke to her, she wasn't, only
shrinkin' away and cryin' out if either o' her brothers
comed near her, and after a while she comed to die, and
they was havin' her death at their door, along o' all the
others. Not gainin' nothin' by their wickedness they
weren't, for old Jacob were very angry with them for
makin' him hated by all the folk in that district, and havin'
to flee for his life from Shalem, where he had bought land,
he was. But afore they went away his sons stole all as they
could lay hands on, the horses and the cattle and the
poultry and the little children even from Shechem's
village, and the gypsies have done so ever since, and they
are travellin' from place to place, not livin' respectable in
houses, and no honest folks 'on't marry them nor have
nothin' to do with them to this day. And that,' Gladys
concluded, 'is what do come o' pride and hard-heartedness
same as Father's family is havin'.'

''Tis a wonderful story,' Esther murmured, 'but Jacob's
children were bein' the Jews as settled in Palestine, and
not the gypsies.'

'The Jews,' retorted Gladys, 'were springin' from the
two tribes o' Judah, but what has become o' the lost ten
tribes o' Israel? Gypsies, I do say.'

A sharp ping sounded on the window pane, as though a small pebble had struck it.

'Boys,' said Gladys.

Esther moved uneasily.

'There's no boys courtin' me. They do know 't'ould be no use.'

In silence they waited, and presently another pebble struck the glass.

'Don't have nothin' to do with him, whoever he is,' snapped Gladys.

'But what if it should be someone as do want me?'

'Want you? You do know very well what they do want you for. 'Tis I as do want you honest, Essy dear.'

A third and a fourth time the signal sounded, and at last Esther rose.

'If 'tis some silly lad come courtin' me, I'll tell him not to be wastin' his time.'

She opened the window, and, peering out, felt the night swoop down like a huge black bird, whose wings fanned her face, hiding the universe from her.

'Who is there? What do you want?'

A woman's voice reached her, mingled with the whistling of the gale. 'Come on down quick.'

'Megan! Whatever...'

'Come down. Come down. I do want you,' cried the voice in agonised entreaty.

Esther shut the window and with trembling fingers struck a light and set the candle at her sister's bedside.

'I must be leavin' you alone, bach. 'Tis Megan. She do seem to be in trouble or grief.'

'What's she come takin' you out o' doors on such a

night as this for?'

'I dunno, but I must go quick. She do need my help.'

She went downstairs into the kitchen. Her mother sat knitting by the fire, her father and the boys were out in the buildings foddering the cattle.

'Goin' to fetch more peat?' asked Mrs Bevan without looking round.

'Aye. I'll be back now just.'

She opened the door and was lost in the darkness. The wind howled mournfully, and drove against her face solitary raindrops cold as tears long shed. With her hand on the wall of the house, she felt her way round to the railed-in space on the far side of it, where grew the single ash tree, the creaking of whose branches made a dismal noise overhead, and rank grass that was wet about her ankles. She could see nothing, but as she groped for the gate she fancied she heard someone sobbing above the sad voices of the night.

'Megan,' she said, 'is that bein' you? Whatever's the matter, gal? Where are you?'

There was no answer, but the sound of crying guided her to where her cousin crouched beside the dripping wall. She was just visible, a patch of blacker shadow in the darkness of the night.

Esther laid a hand on the rain-soaked dress. 'Why, gal, you've come out without no coat on, and on a night like this! You'll be catchin' your death o' cold.'

'And a good job if I do.'

'Megan! Megan! Don't you go to talk so wicked. You've been in trouble with them over there before now. 'Twill all come right again, I've no doubt.'

225

'There's never been trouble like this before. It can't never come right – never.'

She was so shaken by sobs that Esther knelt down beside her, and put comforting arms about her.

'What is it, then, dear?'

'I'm in the way.'

Esther's arms relaxed. 'Oh, Duwch!'

'Now I suppose you'll be turnin' your back on me too.' The voice in the darkness beside her was bitter.

'No, no, dear, o' course not – but oh dear! What's to be done?'

She leant against the house, feeling cold and helpless in the face of this fresh calamity. A chill from the sodden earth struck up through her whole being. She was not shocked or angered by her cousin's confession, and wondered vaguely whether – as an honest girl – it was her duty to be so. She was merely puzzled and distressed.

'What's there to be done?' came in a sullen whisper. 'Nothin' but for me to bear it.' Suddenly Megan's voice rose almost to a scream. 'But I *can't* bear it! I can't! Oh, Esther, since ever they comed to know, they've been on at me all the while. They're killin' my baby, Esther, killin' it along o' me... I 'ouldn't mind for myself; he's deserted me when I was believin' in his promises – Oh! I've been a fool! I could be killin' myself, but the child...'

She hid her face on Esther's shoulder and wept. 'Life,' Esther caught the words... 'Life is bein' so strong within you when you are bearin' another beside your own.'

'Yes, yes,' Esther whispered, pressing Megan closer to her. 'I am understandin' that.'

'You *do* understand? Oh! Thank God as someone is

understandin'! Them two old maids is thinkin' as I did ought to hate my child, but I am lovin' it from the roots o' me, too deep to be touched by no shame. I'm terrible alone, Esther, Tom havin' left me. I'm worse off nor if I was alone. I've my child to fight for.' She drew her breath in a long, quivering sigh. 'I'm better now, havin' told you,' she said after a silence, in which Esther gently stroked the rough, rain-sodden hair that hung about her forehead. 'I'll be goin' back home.'

She spoke the word bitterly.

'Not all cold and wet like what you are. Come on in first and warm yourself.'

'No, no. I 'ouldn't bear for the others to see me. 'Twas you as I did want. You are bein' strong and kind.'

She stood up, but Esther, rising with her, kept hold of her hands.

'What are you goin' to do, dear?'

'Keep on somehow here, I suppose, till the child do come. Then I'll be havin' to leave it to them old cats, and goin' out into service. 'Deed, I'd be goin' now, 't 'ould be better for the child if I was away from their cruel, spiteful tongues, and Maggie Cwmddu's daughter, as is married down in the works, 'ould take me and give me my keep for the work I'd be doin' till I was near my time; only I'm not havin' the money to go to her, and my aunts 'on't give me none. They are thinkin' as I'd be after Tom,' she added bitterly. 'I'm bein' ashamed to tell 'em as he's gone from the address he did give me, and no one do know where he is.'

She was standing with bowed head. The wind had fallen and the rain had begun to beat down straight and steady as if the heavens meant to crush the earth.

227

'I am havin' a small little bit o' money. Maybe 'twill be enough to take you to Maggie's.'

'Oh! Esther!'

'Wait you here till I do fetch it you.'

It was all that she had saved out of her meagre wages, the greater part of which went to buy Gladys the small comforts she would otherwise have been without. The coppers that remained when her purchases had been made she put by in a stocking. They now amounted to a few shillings, with which she had long intended to pay for a photograph of herself to be sent to Rhys.

''Tis allus he as do have to go without,' she thought.

CHAPTER 14

Esther noticed that as time passed and her sister grew frailer she brooded more in silence over her own imaginings, withdrawn into herself, motionless, wrapt and unapproachable. Fits of fierce rebellion at her captivity no longer tormented her.

'Is it only two years as I have laid here?' she murmured. 'Two years? Yes, yes, for I do remember to have seen the leaves go flyin' past my window twice. And now the spring is come again, when I did use to look to see new shadows, growin' bigger day by day. Sometimes they was puttin' me in mind o' the young lambs as 'ould be playin' out in the fields I 'ould never look on no more – and sometimes o' children runnin' out o' school, as I did use to do. I've told myself many a tale o' sons and daughters gone forth from the old folks' homes, many a strange tale of adventure, and all put into my head by the shadow of a leaf... but that wasn't bein' all.' Her voice sank lower still. 'Not the stories they was settin' me to tell, but the hope they was somehow puttin' into my heart... are you rememberin' how we did use to believe when we was little as an odd-numbered ash leaf was bringin' luck to the one as did find it? I can't see the leaves o' that tree out there, from where I do lie, but amongst the shadows as is never still, I was sometimes catchin' sight – just for a minute like – of a lucky leaf.'

Blinded by tears, Esther turned away her head.

'But I was lovin' to see that shadow, the lucky one as I could never hold,' the low murmur at her side went on. 'And now the roses as you was puttin' on the wall is spoilin' shadows – I can't see them plain no more. I do miss lookin' for the one as do bring good fortune.'

In the dark days of winter Esther had returned heavy laden from market with rolls of gaily coloured wallpaper that had at first sight delighted Gladys. A barely perceptible flush had come into the ivory face, and the listless hands had been raised in a gesture of surprise.

'Oh! Essy, what beautiful flowers! Like the ones in your Aunt Polly's parlour at Aberdulas you was tellin' me of. 'Twill be summer all the year round with me now,' she had exclaimed. But of these unchanging blossoms within her room she had soon grown tired.

'I'll be paintin' over the roses for you,' Esther said now, her voice steadied with difficulty. 'What colour 'ould you be fancyin'?'

'No colour as is havin' a name to it. Empty I 'ould like the walls to be... empty,' and after a silence enduring for many minutes, the lifeless voice whispered, 'empty as air.'

230

'Look, Gladys,' Esther said a few days later, 'I've brought you a light kind o' green, almost white it is, to paint your room with. Look, bach, you'll be seein' the shadows fine on this.'

There was no movement of the partly opened lips, no interest in the vacantly staring eyes; and Esther turned away sorrowfully to her task. Mounting upon a chair, she slapped a brushful of the pale colourwash on to the wall, and spreading it downwards with a ruthless stroke effaced a broad strip of the gaudy pink roses she thought so lovely. Roses, gay and flaunting, were associated in her mind with happiness. In that little parlour at Aberdulas, where they had sprawled over the walls, she had spent the most radiant hours of her life. There was nothing at Pengarreg to bring back thoughts of that bygone time but these painted flowers that she was blotting out. Aunt Polly had died in her sleep. She did not know who owned that dear cottage now, nor whether it was altered beyond recognition. She, at any rate, would never see it again. The roses were blurred. They swam before her eyes, but she laboured on. When her task was at an end she waited, but the sunshine did not come to make the shades flicker upon the patternless expanse of wall.

Day after day her father and the young men slouched into the kitchen for their meals, bringing with them the musty smell of wet corduroys, and leaving the track of muddy boots upon the floor. When, at length, the rain ceased, the mist hung thick upon the sodden hills. Esther, sitting with tired, watchful eyes beside the bed on which her sister had lain for days with scarcely a sign of being alive, saw a pale glimmer of sunlight steal into the room.

It threw the pallid shadows of the ash tree outside upon the wall at the foot of the bed.

'*Look*, Gladys, *look!*'

Slowly the waxen lids were raised, and the big eyes stared straight before them. For a time they appeared to see nothing; then recognition crept back into the long-expressionless face. The hands, lying limp upon the coverlet, stirred feebly. It seemed she wanted to point with one of them.

'There it is,' she whispered, trying vainly to lift her hands and grasp the shadow towards which she strained, 'there it is – the lucky one.'

CHAPTER 15

It was night time and the noises of the house and farmyard had ceased when Esther stole downstairs into the kitchen. On the hearth glowed a few embers, and from the pale square of the window came a wan gleam of starlight. The silence was profound, but it did not oppress her as did the silence of the room upstairs from which at last the coffin was gone. Beside that coffin, it seemed to her, she had watched throughout a lifetime, and now the work of a lifetime was over. Somewhere far removed from her tired body her own voice seemed to be calling, 'I am free! I am free! I have kept my word, and now I am free to go.'

Drawing herself up by the table at which she had seated herself, she moved like one in a dream across the room. In a drawer of the dresser she found ink and paper, and brought them to the table. The candlelight shone on the empty sheet. Presently she would write on it the words that were ringing in her heart. 'I am free! I am free!' That sheet of paper would cross the world, and Rhys receiving it would be made glad – oh! how glad. The paper became blurred and the flame of the candle prismatic. She passed her hand over her eyes and laughed unsteadily. Then, with trembling hand, she began to write. Writing was at all times a labour, and now her thronging emotions seemed to strangle all thought. Words halted and were set down with difficulty; but as she wrote laboriously, her head on one side and her right foot twisted round the leg of her chair in an attitude of nervous tension, her spirits rose until, tired as she was, she could have sung with joy. When it was finished she read the letter through and was disappointed in it.

'Dear Rhys,' it ran, 'poor Gladys is passed away. i was with her to the last, and closed her eyes. She made a lovely corpse. We had a poor little funeral. Father is gone so low, only very few neighbours was showing their respects to our poor Gladys. i am free now, Rhys. Do you know what that is meaning to me? So please write soon and tell me what i am to do, please.

'Hoping this finds you as it do leave me.
'i am your loving
'ESTHER.'

It was the best of which she felt capable, and for lack of words she added by way of postscript a row of crosses. Then she addressed the envelope, sealed and kissed it, and sitting motionless with it clasped in her hands gave herself up to glad pictures of its arrival.

There was a sound of shuffling feet. She started, and turning, saw her mother's shrinking figure at the foot of the stairs. Mrs Bevan wore a dun-coloured shawl huddled over her nightdress; her feet were bare and her wisp of pale hair hung in a tiny pigtail down her back. She looked strangely young in the dim light, with a starved pitiful youth, having neither beauty nor vitality. Esther's heart went out to her as it did to a draggled chicken that was dying of the gapes, or a tottering, straggly legged lamb that had been born in the snow.

'Why, Mother,' she cried, going to her, 'whatever's brought you down?'

Mrs Bevan did not answer, but clutched at her with trembling fingers.

'You're tired – reg'lar wore out,' Esther went on. 'That's what it is. Wait till I've made you a nice hot cup o' tea. Then you'll feel better.'

'I 'on't never feel no better; I'm not long for this 'orld, Esther. That's what's the matter.'

In an instant Esther was down on her knees beside her, and hugging her in strong comforting arms.

'Now, Mother, don't you talk so foolish. When you've had your tea, I'll take you back up to bed, and tuck you up warm.'

'No, no,' she answered shuddering, 'not up there. Not near him. I'm afraid in my heart o' him. He's been killin' his own child, and maybe he'll kill me too.'

'Now, Mother, you know as that were an accident. He was in drink at the time.'

'And isn't he often enough in drink now? But 'tis when he's in a good temper I do fear him most o' all. His comin' close to me, catchin' holt o' me, and I not able to get away from him, not havin' strength to struggle even – not darin' to neither. My heart 'on't stand it. Do you know what the doctor was sayin' to me?' An outburst of crying choked her. 'He did say as my heart were terrible weak.'

'Worse nor it's been before?'

'Yes, yes. So weak as it might stop any time.'

'Oh, Mother, you never told me!'

'No need to tell no one. You'll be findin' me dead in my bed some mornin', or maybe I'll drop down sudden when the boss has come in drunk and struck me.'

'The doctor did say as 'twas as bad as all that?'

'He did indeed. And I've a feelin' as I 'on't last out this winter. Yes, yes, 'tis true. You might be stayin' with me till I am took. Oh, Esther! 'Tisn't askin' much o' you – it 'on't be for long – maybe I'll die in a month or too, and you just gone from home that very day. Oh, yes' – her thin voice rose to a wail – 'I know very well what you've come down here tonight for. You've been writin' to your young man to tell him as you'll go out to Canada so soon as he do send the money for your passage. You'll be stealin' out o' the house, and your father 'ull be half-killin' o' me when he do find as you're gone; and indeed, I don't mind if he do kill me. My life here without you 'on't be worth nothin' to me. You are the only one o' my children ever I loved; I was tryin' to love the others, but I did dread their comin' so – I was ailin' and cryin' all the while afore they was born, and I wasn't able to suckle 'em neither – that do make a terrible difference. Like strangers to me they was, but you was havin' all my love afore I did go too weak to care for nothin'. And you've allus been my help and comfort. There never was a better daughter, nor one as was more needed. Don't leave me now, Essy – if you've any pity in your heart, if you're wantin' God to bless you – *don't* leave me....'

The kettle had begun to boil. Esther was suddenly aware of its bubbling and of the steam that poured into the room. All other perception was numbed by a great dread that had descended upon her. She disengaged herself almost roughly, and rose. Mrs Bevan sobbed afresh, but with her back turned towards her resolutely Esther made the tea. When it was ready she brought her mother a cupful, and shook her by the shoulder to attract her attention.

'I couldn't touch it, not with the thought o' you goin' away and leavin' me here to die,' she whined.

'You'll drink it up at onst, and you'll come upstairs to bed with me,' Esther answered. Her voice, usually a soft sing-song, was harsh, and she spoke on one even note.

Mrs Bevan looked up at her nervously.

'I'll be keepin' you awake with my cryin'.'

'No need to cry.'

'Oh, Essy – you don't mean... you 'on't be stayin' with me, will you?'

For a moment hope shone in her pale eyes that were still brimming with tears.

'I'll be seein' the doctor tomorrow.'

Mrs Bevan's face fell.

'He can't tell you no more nor he's told me already. Maybe I'll live a month or two, maybe a year or two.'

'Maybe a month or two, maybe a year or two,' Esther repeated. Her hand sought the letter that lay concealed

237

near her heart. Scarcely conscious of what she was doing, she walked across the room and dropped it into the fire. Bright tongues of flame licked at it, leaving it charred and blackened, fluttering in the draught from the chimney. 'That letter 'ould have made two folks happy as 'ull be miserable now,' she thought, 'and I've only to write it again to give to the one as I do love best on earth what he do want most, and what I and no one else livin' can be givin' him... but I mustn't be writin' it – for he's strong and can do without me, and she's weak, poor soul, weak as water.' How her heart ached again now, and how unutterably weary she was. With an effort that was both physical and mental torture she straightened herself and turned towards the huddled figure on the chair. Resentment was mingled with her pity as she noticed that Mrs Bevan's outstretched hands were clutching at her like those of a greedy child.

'Now then, Mother, come along. That's done with, and we 'on't never say no more about it.' Her lips quivered as she spoke, but she managed to smile, and taking her mother round the waist she lifted her to her feet.

Three years passed before Esther wrote to tell her sweetheart of her release. In the small hours of a summer's morning she entered her bedroom and softly closed the door behind her. She felt stunned and stared in the twilight at dim familiar objects as though she saw in them something new and strange. Incessant toil had numbed her pain, and so remote from her daily routine had grown the thought of her love that Rhys' rare letters had been received with something of a shock. She had scarcely noticed how long it

238

was since he had written last. He was there in her life always, the only glad thing in it, but his picture had become overlaid with cares and responsibilities. Now she could sweep them away and find her dear picture untarnished as when she had looked at it first.

The stars were gone, and the sky had faded to a pale grey. A pearly light was flooding the room as she began to search in the old oak chest, where she kept her best clothes, for her cherished bundle of letters. There they were, hidden away with the presents Rhys had sent her from time to time and the photographs which did not do him justice, but which were none the less her dearest possession. She carried the letters to the window and looked through them – would it be for the last time? Here was the last one. It had followed the others after a considerable interval, and was already three months old. She drew it out from the rest with a stab of pain, remembering how it had hurt her when she had received it. She sighed, wishing that her release had come before that letter was written.

'Are you never coming to me?' it ran. 'Am I to wait all my life while you nurse one after another of your sick relations, all of whom you seem to put before me?' Then it had broken off abruptly, and she could almost hear him talking, as he used to talk with rapid movements and transitions of expression. 'I'm sorry. I don't mean to be unkind; and I can't blame you, for you are a saint; but that is where the trouble lies. Child, I don't think you can ever have loved me as I did you, or you would understand something of my longing for you. I believe you fancy that it is enough for us to love each other from opposite sides of the earth. It's no good. I'm a man, and I can't stand much more of it. It's damnable.... And then you don't know the awful loneliness of this place. Not a soul to speak to, never the sound of a human voice for weeks at a time, and the prairie flat as your hand stretching away on all sides. The hideous monotony of it! Day after day I do the same jobs and see the same dreary waste. I work like a nigger. There's nothing else to do. If I wasn't sweating from dawn till nightfall I'd go mad with the silence, and my longing for human companionship and for you. I'm coining money, but what's the good of it all? I want someone to share it with. I want a wife and children to make all this labour worth while, and all I get is a cold little note now and again telling me you are "terrible busy with the hay", or that your mother is no worse.'

Her cold little notes! She had not meant them to be cold. Those crosses she had added to them were not to her an empty formality. Each one of them signified a kiss, such as she would have put up her lips to receive had Rhys been with her, and with each one that her pen had traced awkwardly upon the paper, she had thought, 'Oh, if only it was given atween us now, how happy I 'ould be!' But he had not understood, he had thought her cold and indifferent. It was hard to be so poor a scholar.

Well, it did not matter now. He would understand and forgive her when he looked into her eyes and read there everything she had been unable to put into words. She leant heavily against the window frame and drew in long breaths of the cold moist air. It was like drinking the pure icy water from a mountain spring. She felt refreshed, but the luxury of being weak was too sweet to be forgone. With her tired muscles relaxed and her hands hanging idly at her sides, she allowed the tears to trickle down her cheeks.

'I wish if Rhys were here to take me in his arms, like a child as is tired and fretful,' she thought, 'I 'ould like to cry on his shoulder till I could cry no more, with them great strong arms o' his around me, holdin' me safe.' Now that the strain of her labours was over she seemed to stand apart from herself and to see the dogged enduring Esther, on whose strength and goodwill the entire household had depended, as a poor, tired girl who wanted to be comforted, sheltered and loved. 'Come you,' she smiled through her tears, 'heaviness may endure for a night, but joy cometh in the morning.'

About Pengarreg the mist was dissolving. A pale flicker of sunshine shone into the room, and the dew-soaked leaves of the ash tree outside began to glitter. The first sparrow had given a wakening twitter and the birds were now in full chorus. The singing of larks flooded down from overhead. A cock crowed cheerily in the yard, and the sheep upon the glistening hillside were astir and bleating.

Esther raised a corner of her apron, and, wiping her eyes on it, leaned out of the window. The valley beneath was still hidden in mist, white and soft as lamb's wool, but all about her the sunlight, growing every moment in strength, made the wet hilltop sparkle. Never, she thought, had a day broken so brilliantly, with promise of such fair weather to come. So still and keen was the air that from far below, deep in the valley's dense whiteness, she could hear the roar and rattle of the mail train that passed through Llangantyn on its way to the coast. One day, not far distant now, she herself would be speeding towards the sea. How she had loved the vast expanse of waters across which she had gazed at Aberdulas! How much more would she love it when crossing it on her way to the new country where an ideal life awaited her!

'Rhys,' she cried, holding out her arms, 'Rhys bach – *at last!*'

'Dear Esther,' he wrote in the letter she received a few weeks later, 'your note came too late and I cannot in loyalty to my wife tell you what I felt when I found it here on my return after a short absence. I had been to Edmonton to escape the solitude of this place, which was driving me mad; and I was married there.'

There was more writing on the sheet of paper, but she could not read it.

For a long while she sat motionless, her head thrown back, her mouth dropped open. Then, slowly, she closed her eyes and shuddered. Even the relief of tears was denied to her, but she began to laugh shrilly. Not the deep laugh, she thought suddenly, that Rhys had loved.

BOOK II

CHAPTER 1

On a Sunday afternoon, eight years later, Esther came into the kitchen at Pengarreg. Her brother John was in the fold foddering the cattle.

''Tis as though a movement or a sound 'ould be spoilin' something,' she thought, and allowed her eyes to travel round the place which held so many memories. The room seemed to contain more light than in bygone years, for the walls were newly colourwashed and the unvarnished table scoured milk-white.

''Tis the spring sunshine,' she mused, 'as do lighten up a dark place and cause the hidden colours to show. Why, 'tis almost cheerful today – a deal better, whatever, nor when I did set to work on it in the autumn.'

She moved towards the hearth, where a fire that was slowly dying sent up a few flames, clear and steady as those of candles. Thoughtfully she stared down at them.

'That fire is bein' like my life. All smoke and blackness and crackle when 'twas new, but now it has settled down like, more calm, and again after a while 'twill be only grey ashes.'

She seated herself on a wooden chair, arranging carefully the folds of her best dress. She had made it recently from a store of mourning bands accumulated by her grandmother in the days of splendid funerals. The stiff silk, that had draped the chimney-pot hats of mourners long since gone the way of those they followed to the grave, was pleasantly substantial to touch. She smoothed it out in her lap.

'Seven years I was gone from this place,' she thought, 'and 'tis not yet seven months since I did come back. But the seven years is gone by like as if they'd never been; and 'tis here, where I was born, as I do seem always to have lived. 'Tis like the lean kine in the dream of Pharaoh as did swallow up the fat kine. And yet I don't know neither; comin' back here I do see it less like a place o' famine nor when I did go away. This sad old house full o' ghostses is still the same; only I am changed. I am no longer so sad, nor quite without hope o' the future as I was bein' then.'

Eight years ago her dream of marriage with Rhys had been shattered. She could no longer recall distinctly what she had suffered then. All she remembered was that there had followed a period of misery and sleeplessness in which she had turned desperately to incessant and exhausting labour. Her tired body had clung to a life her spirit no longer desired to preserve. A girl, spiritless, hopeless, numbed by grief, whose white face had startled her mirror, had gone about her work like an automaton.

246

And now once more those same labours were being performed in the same surroundings by a woman into whose life the hope, at least, of new contentment was beginning to steal.

''Tis a long while ago, that sorrow,' she reflected. ''Tis not to be quite forgotten, o' course, but 'tis not to be dwelt on for ever neither. The very sharpness o' my pain did serve to kill the memory of it. They do say 'tis like that with the pains o' childbirth, so terrible that they are soon forgot.'

The only vivid picture of the past that she could now conjure up was of her father's death. One stormy evening he had been seen by some neighbours galloping home from market, as usual the worse for drink. Seeing him on a young horse they had shouted to him to be careful going up the precipitous track to Pengarreg; but he had sworn at them for a set of fools, and thrashed the terrified pony into a more furious pace. Half an hour later it had clattered into the fold, riderless and lathered white about the chest. She remembered waking from her gloomy lethargy, and hurrying out with her brothers to search the windswept hillside. At length, at the bottom of the deep dingle below the house, they had stumbled upon their father's dead body, soaked with rain and with blood. He must have been flung down the precipice bordering the track, and, cut by the sharp edges of rocks as he fell, have bled to death before help could reach him. Esther had stared long at his disfigured corpse, all her resentment turned to pity. Idris, frightened by the horrible sight, had broken into loud sobs; but John, who most resembled his father, had spoken resolutely, though his lips were drawn

247

inwards with a strangely wooden effect: 'Well, well, 'tis only to be expected with him goin' on so wild.' And he had added, as they stooped shudderingly to raise what they shrank from touching: 'Keepin' off the drink I'll be from now on, so long as I do live.'

He had kept his word, and was a sober, hard-working fellow. In spite of that she had been glad to escape from his company when, after a quarrel, the two brothers had parted and Idris had taken the post of shepherd on another farm. Without hesitation she had chosen to go with Idris to his cottage on the sheep walk, remote from road, railway or neighbour, within ten miles of their old home, but in new surroundings that helped her to make a fresh start in life. Here they had lived while four generations of sheep, with whose fortunes their own were bound up, were born, weaned, sheared, mated, sold and slaughtered. Rumours of war across the seas then reached their lonely hillside. As a result of distant happenings the price of food rose, but they, who were almost self-supporting, were little affected. Orders to plough land that had been laid down to grass since the exodus of young men to the collieries in their grandfather's time caused consternation in the district. Government interference with the farmer's right to do as he pleased, the threat of conscription, and the increase in wages were added to the usual complaints. But although they appeared unwillingly before the tribunals, the men who laboured on the land were not sent to join the army. Nominally better paid, the hirelings struck bargains with their employers of which the Agricultural Wages Board knew nothing. The unfertile soil, on which for a year or two thin crops were induced to grow, once more went out of cultivation.

Sometimes a newspaper found its way to the shepherd's cottage; more often a book of travel borrowed by Esther from the Vicarage. Her neighbours wondered at her strange taste in reading. She was one of them, yet in some ways apart. Long ago, in a time that seemed to her of legendary happiness, she had learned to take an interest in the world beyond her own parish; for she had seen life, though but for an instant, with Rhys' eyes, and like one who has strayed into fairyland, was for ever after subtly changed. She had repulsed the tentative advances of young men of her own class, who had occasionally 'called in by passin',' to fumble with their caps and eye her covertly for any sign of encouragement. It was not until her recent return to Pengarreg that she had met any man whose conversation aroused her from her half-forgotten grief. Now that Idris was married and she once more dependent upon the society and goodwill of the brother she did not love, a newly formed friendship with the Vicar of Lewisbridge was her only solace.

''T'ould be too much of an honour, his marryin' me,' she told herself. 'And besides, I'm not bein' sure – not quite sure whatever – as he do want to do so.' A sigh escaped her and she looked down at her left hand, trying to picture the magnificence that would be imparted to it by a massive gold wedding ring. 'Mrs Jones, the parson's wife,' she murmured, 'how grand it 'ould sound!'

As she sat, this Sunday afternoon, meditating upon past and future, John entered from the fold. His shoulders brushed the doorposts. His head almost reached the lintel. Esther noted afresh the bulk and strength of her brother

249

which moved her sometimes to admiration, but never to fondness. He had, however, been in a good humour of late and his likeness to their father was less pronounced than when he was sullen.

'Well,' he exclaimed, cocking his head on one side, 'so you're a'ready dressed up for church, are you?'

She smiled, and he continued with ponderous joviality, 'You're impatient to be there, no doubt? You're terrible partic'lar about your prayers these days, eh? The women in a parish is all bein' the same when the parson's a single man.'

'Go on!'

'Oh, you can't deceive me. I wasn't born blind like a puppy.'

He lumbered off into the back kitchen, whence the sound of his whistling reached her ears as he washed his hands under the tap.

'I'm ready now,' he announced, re-entering with his bowler hat on and a lock of red hair elaborately arranged to show beneath it on his forehead. 'Come on, my dear.'

She had never heard him address her thus before; the prospect of a creditable marriage makes a difference, she reflected, to the way in which her relations treat a woman. But her thoughts were without bitterness, for she had come to accept life placidly, and they set out together. John took the longer strides, and Esther, carefully holding up her skirt in both hands, hurried after him, always a pace behind.

Suddenly he said over his shoulder: 'I've been thinkin' about this marriage...'

'So have I.'

He scowled at the interruption.

'Now just you listen to me. I'm not likin' to talk about the time poor Father did come to die.'

'No, no, o' course not. 'Twas terrible.'

'Oh, 'tisn't his death I'm thinkin' of now; 'tis my havin' had to sell the farm along o' his debts.'

''Twas hard, no doubt, but Lord Glanwye did let you stay on in the old place as tenant.'

He spat to signify his disgust.

'*Tenant* – when I did ought to have been the landlord.' He strode on in sullen silence for a while, and at last recommenced: 'That was nigh on eight years ago. I 'on't say nothin' about your takin' my brother's part against me when he 'ouldn't stay on here to work.'

'You 'ouldn't give him no wages.'

'He did ought to have been willin' to serve me without; and you didn't better yourself neither, leavin' me for him, seein' as he's married and showed you the door. I do think as I've acted uncommon generous by you, takin' you back.'

'You was wantin' a housekeeper.'

'Keep your mouth shut, can't you? If you'd been stickin' by me as 'twas your duty to do, you'd know how I've worked and saved to buy back the land. If it hadn't been for the trickses o' them cunnin' Lloyds, I'd have had enough to do it by now. As it is, when the place is put up for sale this autumn, I'll be havin' to borrow very near all the money for it.'

'Are you wise to do that, John? The new landlord might be lettin' you stay on, same as this one has done.'

He shook his head gloomily.

''Tisn't likely. Property is mostly bein' bought by farmers

251

as do want it for their own use these days. And even if a landowner was to buy up our place and the Henallt together, same as his lordship did do, I'd out him if I could.'

'Why?'

'*Why*?' he repeated angrily, turning round on her. 'Haven't you got no pride on you? Don't you want to see your own brother a man o' property, and them Lloyds still payin' rent and havin' to touch their hats to a squire? They shouldn't be stayin' at the Henallt as tenants even, if I could have them from there, and now is my chanst to do it.'

'Supposin' as they are biddin' for their place same as you do mean to do for ours?'

'I've thought o' that. But they 'on't be havin' money enough when their time do come.'

'But John, how do you know that?'

'Don't you be askin' no questions yet. I am havin' my plans right enough. You was interruptin' summat I did wish to say.'

'I'm sorry.'

'When Parson Jones do marry you…'

'Don't talk so foolish.'

'When he do marry you, I say, he'd best be comin' to live at Pengarreg.'

Esther started. 'Oh, I don't know about that.'

'But I do. We could do very well with his money, and what's the use o' his settin' up a house in Lewisbridge, and me havin' to pay the wages of a housekeeper? She might be wantin' me to marry her, or she might be robbin' me. No, no, Mr Jones is lodgin' in a farmhouse now, and he can come to us as our lodger then. You can be doin' for the both of us.'

Esther smiled and raised her eyebrows. 'We'll see.'

They had reached the level road on either side of which stood the rival places of worship. During the last thirty years the red-brick chapel had lost the aggressive crudeness of its youth, but the church, ivy-covered and with its roof mottled by lichen, remained as on the day when John and Annie Bevan had issued from its porch. 'I am bein' proud o' that small little steadfast church,' Esther thought, 'and 't'ould be an honour to marry its minister.'

He was stationed at the door, clothed in the priestly cassock that had amazed his congregation when first he came amongst them, for they had been accustomed to see the trousered legs of the ordinary man protruding from below the surplice of the officiating priest.

As she approached him, Esther was aware of the envious glances of a group of girls. 'They aren't seein' me good enough for him,' she reflected. Though her manner was composed, her heart beat a little faster than usual when she held out her hand to him, and felt the lingering pressure of his fingers.

'Well, Mr Bevan, I'm glad to see you here. You don't always favour us with your presence, but your sister is most regular.'

He smiled down at her graciously. His was a handsome face, she decided, studying it dispassionately. She found his near presence agreeable, but it did not in the least excite her. The habitually phlegmatic John writhed with appreciation.

''Tis terrible kind o' you, I'm sure, Mr Jones, sir, to praise my sister. Yes, she's a great one for 'tendin' church. We did allus tell her as she was cut out for a parson's wife, eh, Essy?'

He dug her in the ribs, and she retreated beyond his reach. Standing aside, she watched the rest of the congregation arrive, while the verger tugged patiently at the rope that kept the bell tolling. Family by family the church-goers of Lewisbridge walked sedately up the path. The children's faces shone with Saturday night's soap, like the polished apples in a fruiterer's window. The small boys, enduring the discomfort of newly starched collars, came to church less readily than they went to school. They might run and shout, chase butterflies and pick flowers on their way to lessons; but they must walk in full view of their parents and 'mind' their Sunday suits on their way to prayers.

Now they were looking enviously at a child who played with a heap of bricks lying near the graveyard wall. He was unknown to Esther, dark as a gypsy, alert as a robin. For some time she watched him, amused by the dexterity of his little hands, and his intense absorption in the building of a miniature house. Then her brother followed the direction of her gaze.

'What's that lumper there doin', playin' in the churchyard on a Sunday?'

'I dunno. Poor little fellow. He's all alone.'

'Well, he didn't ought to be there, whatever. He's not dressed in a Sunday suit, neither. Some good-for-nothing tramp's child, sure to be.'

'Oh, no, John, he's dressed tidy enough, only for weekdays like.'

'There's a strange man stoppin' at the inn,' chimed in one of the neighbours. 'I did see him last night walkin' hand in hand with that there child.'

'A towny on a holiday, I dare say,' growled John.

'They're an irreligious lot, bringin' up their children to break the Lord's Day.'

Esther too was a trifle shocked; but, as she passed under the gloomy doorway into the church where the air was acrid with dry rot, she looked back and smiled at the little boy who built his play house out in the sunshine. As if aware that she was looking at him, he raised his eyes. They were not so dark as she had expected them to be, but a bright golden brown, the colour of certain agates. His lips were parted and his whole face was more eager than that of any child she remembered having seen. He spared her a grave little smile in response to hers, and again bent himself over his work.

She remembered that smile now and then during the service and looked for the child again when, the weekly act of devotion being done, the congregation streamed out into the graveyard. Everyone was cheerful in anticipation of Sunday night's supper. Friendly greetings were exchanged and shouts of 'Good night, now,' and 'See you at market,' rang out in the crisp air. Groups of women lingered to gossip, their nodding heads close together. Children, forgetting the oppression of the day, began to romp with one another round the tombstones, and blackbirds, dislodged from their roosting places, flew scolding overhead. While Esther was waving salutes to her friends, her Aunt Lily seized her by the arm, and the bony fingers seemed to have a less hard touch than usual.

'Parson do want to see you in the vestry,' the envious whisper sounded in her ear. 'Some business about the parish tea. Indeed, he don't seem able to do nothin' without you. There's lucky you are!'

She found herself flushing with pleasure. Then she turned round, and her glance, travelling over the bystanders, fell on a man who was without the churchyard, leaning upon the surrounding wall. Only his head and hunched-up shoulders were visible, and lean hands that were bronzed like his face. He was thin, haggard almost, though even in his lounging pose he gave an impression of great vitality. About his mouth were scored deep lines, and beneath the shade of a wide-brimmed hat his eyes showed sunken. They looked steadfastly into her own, and for a moment she wondered where she had seen those golden-brown eyes before. Then, all at once, she felt as though the heart had dropped out of her body, and the next instant as if the ground on which she stood were rushing up towards her. She had seen Rhys. She caught at the wall of the porch for support.

'I dursn't faint here amongst all these folks,' she thought, and desperately concentrated her attention upon a cushion of moss that grew in the mortared chink between two stones. Against the grey wall it showed emerald green. She touched it with her fingertips, squeezed it, stared at it, and dared not turn away. A wave of heat had spread over her at the first shock of her discovery, her face had flamed. Now all the blood seemed to have left it, and her hands and feet were cold.

'Mr Jones is speakin' to you. Are you gone deaf?'

It was John who spoke, accompanying the loud whisper by a vigorous nudging with his elbow. Stunned into an appearance of calmness, she faced the parson, who had hurried out of church in search of her.

'Those cakes, you know, for the tea – perhaps you've forgotten?'

Without answering, she moved towards the vestry door. He turned towards her brother.

'I won't detain your sister long, Mr Bevan. But if you are in any hurry to get home, don't let us delay you. I'll bring her back myself.'

She did not protest, but stared at the speaker in the bewildered fashion of one just awakened from sleep.

'You are wonderful kind, I'm sure,' she heard John saying. 'I'll be goin' on up home, then; but, mind you, if you are bringin' Esther back, you shan't leave without you've taken supper with us first.'

'Thank you. I shall be delighted.'

'Not near good enough for the likes o' you, sir, it 'on't be. But you are havin' no pride on you, indeed.'

'Nonsense. You have the best of everything in your house.'

Esther was aware that this remark was delivered with a smile intended for herself. A minute later she was sitting on a bench between two neighbours who conducted a heated altercation across her. The words 'a real smart table-centre', 'young folks', and 'goin's on' occurred; but she did not understand what they were disputing about, nor what was the substance of the vicar's soothing interruptions. Once or twice he appealed to her, and she answered at random, 'Yes, yes, to be sure,' or 'You are right, Mr Jones,' and he seemed pleased with her replies.

'You are always so practical and helpful,' he told her as they set out together through the deepening dusk.

The road beneath their feet was white in contrast to the dark hills on either hand. Overhead the sky was still too pale to form a background to the stars, and a honey-coloured radiance lingered in the west.

'You are very quiet tonight,' he said, smiling down at her and drawing nearer so that his arm touched hers.

She shrank away; and chilled by her lack of response he did not speak again for a long while. They turned off the high road, and began to climb up to Pengarreg in the gathering gloom. On the hillside the air was sharper than it had been in the valley, and the icy tinkle of streams suggested the coming of a late frost.

'Are you cold?' he asked.

'No, thank you.'

'But you shivered just now.'

'Did I?'

'You *are* cold. Here, I'm going to make you put on my overcoat.'

'No, no. Indeed...'

He loomed close above her, barring the path, and laid his hand upon her arm. His touch was gentle, yet she resented it passionately, and could scarcely control her impulse to tear herself free and burst into tears.

'Please – don't,' she managed to breathe out.

'Miss Bevan – Esther – don't turn away from me. Listen – for a long time I've wanted...'

'Oh no,' she cried, putting up her hands to her ears; but there was no stopping him now.

The considered dignity of his usual manner was gone. He talked rapidly in short, jerky sentences. She did not follow what he said; her mind was in too great a turmoil. But she knew that he was excited and that the words 'love' and 'marriage' occurred in his speech. Every time he uttered them she winced, and all the while he held her fast.

Gradually he was drawing her closer to him. In another minute both his arms were round her. His presence, which she had found comforting only an hour ago, now filled her with revulsion and terror. She struggled fiercely to escape. Hurt and perplexed, he let her go, and she stepped back quickly beyond his reach, her breath coming in angry sobs.

'Esther dear,' he expostulated, 'I thought – you led me to believe – whatever is the matter?'

He took a pace towards her.

'Don't touch me! Don't come near me,' she cried. 'I can't abide it.'

His outstretched hands dropped to his sides.

'Listen, dear. You must at least try to tell me what is the matter. You have nothing against me?'

'No.'

'Nor anything in your past of which you are afraid to tell me?'

'No.'

'Of course not. I've complete faith in you. Besides, I know all there is to be known about you.'

Something like an hysterical laugh escaped her; but he continued imperturbably: 'Everyone here respects you for the good woman you've always been.'

He was regaining his normal assurance of manner; and for the first time she found his tone of benevolent patronage towards herself offensive.

'You've no objection to being a clergyman's wife, surely? I've a little money of my own, you know.'

Still she remained silent and the darkness hid her face from him.

'What *is* the reason?'

''Tisn't a matter o' reason.'

'But my dear girl...'

'Oh, don't you understand as there's things deeper and stronger nor reason – forces as do drive us as the sheep are bein' driven?'

'But this is absurd – this sudden change...'

''Tisn't my fault,' she cried helplessly. 'You do talk as if I did *want* to refuse you and everything safe and comfortable you have to offer me, as though I did *want* to bring back the past with all its griefs and tears – to let my life be broke to pieces just – again.'

Her voice rose almost to a wail, and she wrung her hands with a gesture of impotence.

'She's overwrought,' he decided, 'it's no use talking to her now.' He made his way past her down the path, and turning round addressed her soothingly as he would have done a frightened child.

'I'm afraid my offer was too sudden. You are rather upset – naturally. I'm very sorry, dear, and we won't say any more about it tonight. Just you go home and have a good cry, and in the morning you'll be able to think the matter over calmly. Tomorrow you'll see things in quite a different light – and I shall be awaiting your answer. You have only to write one word, remember, whenever you wish to do so. There now, I'll go away and leave you.'

'You are wonderful kind,' she murmured.

He hesitated whether to return and try to touch her again but decided that it would be wiser to refrain from doing so.

'Excuse me to your brother,' he said over his shoulder. 'You can tell him I had some church accounts to attend to, which prevented my coming to supper.'

Even in this crisis, she observed, he thought of everything.

When his footsteps were no longer audible, the silence of night returned. The perpetual trickling of water and the occasional barking of a dog at some distant farm further emphasised the quiet.

'Was it only a dream, a nightmare?' Esther asked herself. 'It don't seem hardly possible as all this should have happened.'

From the valley beneath came a faint roar, increasing as the night mail flashed into sight. A cloud of red steam, lit from below, trailed behind it. For the space of a minute it was the only illuminated and moving thing in the landscape. Then it vanished into the unknown from which it had appeared.

Crying inconsolably, she turned her face uphill and stumbled on her dark way alone.

CHAPTER 2

On the hilltop an Atlantic gale swept inland, driving before it sheets of rain. Beside the little lake whose waters, leaden in the twilight, broke into angry waves, a woman crouched. She was dressed in black. The sodden ribbons in her hat hung down limply over the brim, and wisps of wet hair were blown about her face. Her broad shoulders were bowed and shaken with sobs. She did not notice a man who approached her from the direction of Pengarreg, his form dim in the gathering darkness, the squelching sound of his footsteps lost in the howling of the storm. For a long while he stood a few paces from her and gloomily contemplated her misery as though it were in tune with his own mood and with that of the dreary evening. Suddenly she rose, and with hands extended took a rapid step towards the water.

'Stop!' cried a voice behind her. 'What are you up to?'

She spun round, a hand raised to her breast, and he saw that she was a strapping countrywoman, still young and good looking. He came close to her and in silence they stared into each other's faces.

'Who are you?' he demanded.

'Leave me be, can't you?'

'Why did you mean to drown yourself?'

'Oh, *go – do go!* 'Tis nothin' to nobody what I am doin' with my life.'

He took hold of her arm and peered into her face.

'Let me alone,' she cried fiercely.

'I've seen you somewhere before.'

'Let me go! Let me go!'

But still he held her.

'I know who you are now,' he said. 'Your voice was familiar – and by what I can see you haven't changed so very much either.'

'You never set eyes on me before in your life. 'Tisn't the first time I've been told that tale by a man. Get out, can't you?'

He answered calmly, 'You're Megan, who used to live at the farm down there with your two old aunts. Don't you remember me?'

She stared. There was something foreign in his accent, and in the wide-brimmed hat he wore. Beneath it she could just discern the spare lines of a clean-shaven face and the flash of bright eyes. In them at least there was something that awoke memories.

'I'm Rhys Lloyd.'

'Duwch!' she exclaimed under her breath. And for a moment forgetting her own grief – 'Esther's sweetheart.

263

She's unmarried yet. But you've only just come back in time. They do say as the parson's courtin' her; and 't'ould be a terrible good match for her, o' course.'

'I dare say it will be.'

It was her turn to peer at him.

'Do you mean...?' She was at a loss for words.

'Never mind that. What was the matter with you when I found you here?'

Her lips began to tremble again. Reluctantly she told him her story. When she was 'bein' unfortunate', as she put it, Esther had given her money with which to go away to a friend who kept her until the baby was born.

'I was very near dyin' along o' the trouble I'd been through and the low state I was in,' she said. 'But I was havin' the loveliest little gal, for all that. No one do know how I was lovin' her.'

But she had found it impossible to keep the baby with her when she went out into service, and the foster-mother to whom she paid all her wages complained that the money was not enough. At last in despair she had brought the child home to her aunts. They had 'seen it their duty to take it, and bring it up Christian and virtuous,' which in their opinion entailed keeping it from its sinful mother.

'They 'ouldn't let me see her more nor onst a year when I did get a few days' holiday,' she sighed, 'and then they was sayin' things to me in front o' her to poison the poor child's mind against me. And now I shan't be seein' her at all, not even onst a year. They've forbidden me the house. I can't bear it. 'Tis killin' me just.'

She had flung up an arm over her face and begun to cry again.

264

'Why have they refused to let you see the child now?'

The question provoked a fresh outburst.

'Indeed and I'm ashamed to tell you. I've been terrible wicked and foolish, no doubt.'

'You needn't be afraid of shocking *me*.'

She clutched at his arm.

'I wonder now could you be understandin'. No one here don't seem to be able to see but what I'm a common wanton, as 'ould go with any man. But I'm not, indeed and indeed I'm not. I've had a second child, Mr Lloyd, but 'twas by the same father, and I did love him so.' Her head was bowed, and she uttered the last words with difficulty in an agony of grief. 'There now, you are thinkin' me a low, good-for-nothin' hussy.'

'I'm thinking you rather splendid in your way, Megan. You gave yourself to him again without a thought of the consequences to yourself?'

'Oh, he did promise faithful to marry me. Only he'd lost his job and gone poor. Everyone was against him – and,' her voice sank once more, 'he was wantin' me so.'

'Yes, yes, I understand. And since?'

'Oh, I can't bear to talk o' what came after. I wasn't surprised as he played me false a second time, but for all that 'twas very near killin' me. I went back to the farm where I'd been a servant gal, and I kept on working and tryin' to seem cheerful-like till close on my time without no one guessin' as I was in the way. But at last the missus did see how matters was. A terrible strict Methodist, she was, and so she did turn me out o' doors to go back to my aunts without no character. I made up my mind as I'd go to the workhouse rather, and there I was standin' in the

265

road beside my box cryin', when an old farmer as was knowed in the district for a wicked fellow was passin' and seein' me. "What's on you, gal?" says he. So I told him. "Come you," says he, "I do want a housekeeper. I'll take you home along o' me now. You're a fine strong 'oman," says he, "and you'll work up to the last. I don't mind your havin' the bastard in my place neither. Since you 'on't have been with me more nor a month or two, folks can't say as 'tis none o' mine."

'Mr Lloyd, I were gone that low, I'd have taken service with the devil hisself, and old Daniel Jones he hasn't been much better. Oh, he's treated me kind, too kind by half, lettin' me keep the child along o' me, payin' me good wages, and allus givin' me presents and offerin' to take me for treats. Twice I've left him and put the little 'un out to nurse. But he's weakly and went pinin' for me, and the 'oman as took him, knowin' him to be a come-by-chanst, did think 'twas a kindness to me to neglect him so as he'd die. 'Twas breakin' my heart just to be parted from him as well as from his sister; so there was nothin' for me but to be livin' in sin. I had to bring the boy with me when I comed on my holiday this year to look for the little gal, and that's how my aunts did find out about him, and how I made shift to keep him, and they have shut their door on me. Now 'tis all the talk o' the district. Followin' me and cheekin' me', the men are. Oh! But I 'ouldn't mind that so much, if only I wasn't havin' to go back to that dreadful old man, and to lead a life o' shame. What else can I do, Mr Lloyd, with my poor little ailin' lad to keep, what can I do?'

'I'll tell you what you can do – come and keep house for me. I've rented a cottage here. You can help me buy furniture and move in tomorrow.'

She came close and looked up at him to see if he were jesting.

'None will dare to insult you whilst you are under my protection. And you can have *both* your children with you. I've a boy of my own.'

'You 'ouldn't never let him mix with mine?'

'Why not, if you keep them clean and bring them up decently?'

'Think what the neighbours 'ould say.'

'I don't care a damn for that.'

She began to cry softly.

'Oh, you don't mean it. I can't believe 'tis true. To have the both o' them with me – to get away from Daniel Jones...'

She broke off abruptly, and came close to him again, gulping down her tears.

'Mr Lloyd, are you meanin' to act honest by me?'

He gave an impatient laugh.

'Look here, my girl, I've no interest in you or in any other woman, as such, now. This is a straight offer.'

For answer she flung herself on her knees, and seizing his hands, impetuously kissed them.

'Get up, for God's sake, and don't make a fool of yourself. We'll discuss wages and so forth in the morning.'

He dragged her to her feet and they descended the hill together. He was silent, save when she burst forth into some expression of gratitude, when he cut her short. As they skirted the enclosed lands of Pengarreg, she observed: 'My cousins is havin' to go from there this summer.'

'How's that?'

'Why, the talk is goin' out as Lord Glanwye as did buy up the place after Uncle John's death is havin' so many complaints from his tenants there and at the Henallt as he's gone sick o' their quarrels. He don't like to give either o' them notice to quit, for fear he shall have to pay this new compensation for disturbance, or whatever they do call it. So he's sellin' the both places over their heads, and glad to be rid o' them, no doubt.'

Rhys was silent for a while. Then he burst out laughing.

'Will Pengarreg and the Henallt be put up at the same sale?'

'Aye, at the same sale.'

'Good! It will be great fun.'

She stared at him in astonishment.

'But, Mr Lloyd, the Henallt is your own father's. I was forgettin' that. You knowed all about the matter, surely?'

'No. I've not heard from my parents for years, and I've no wish to visit them now that I've returned home. Still, I don't believe in harbouring grudges. I'll meet them if they ask it.'

'Well, there's odd you do talk about your relations!' She tried to scrutinise his features in the deepening gloom. 'Mr Lloyd, might I be makin' so bold as to ask what you are doin' in these parts, if 'tisn't Esther nor your relations as you've come back to see? Why are you stayin' here?'

'To convince myself that I no longer love it – nor anyone living in it.'

'But...'

'I had to return here to make sure. Don't let's discuss the matter.'

He refused to answer any more questions, and in silence they struggled on against the gale, close together, but almost hidden from each other by the darkness.

CHAPTER 3

'I do do a terrible lot o' work these days,' Esther reflected as she stood one afternoon in Pengarreg kitchen. 'Yet 'tis never enough to hinder me from thinkin', and I can't abide now to sit alone here countin' the minutes. They do pass so cruel slow.'

'Oh, will nothin' *never* happen?' she cried aloud. The sound of her own voice startled her, and her next thought was whispered to herself. 'Will he *never* come to me? Will he *never* write? If he don't want nothin' to do with me, why did he come back here? Why is he standin' at his cottage door, and starin' so hard when I do pass by on a Sunday?'

Her head was hot and her eyelids heavy from lack of sleep. In the last two months she had lost the composure that had been the slow growth of years, and her movements had become restless.

'I'll go and dig till 'tis time to get John's tea,' she

decided. 'Maybe as I can be tirin' o' myself out that way.'

She tucked up her skirt over a red petticoat, picked up a spade and made her way to the front of the house. The ash tree, the shadow of whose branches Gladys had loved to watch, was gone, and the railed-in space before the unused door was no longer a wilderness but a well-kept garden. It had not been set, for Easter fell late that year, and the custom of the country decreed that Good Friday should be the gardeners' special day. Esther, however, in her feverish activity, had dug and double dug the larger part of it. Digging tired her more than most forms of exercise, and the smell of wet earth calmed her.

As she paused to lean upon her spade, she heard her name called in a low tone, as though the speaker were afraid to utter it. She turned round and saw Megan at the gate, holding a little boy by the hand. Esther stared at her in surprise, and was struck by her mature good looks, and by an air of matronly importance that underlay her momentary shyness. She was no longer the draggled girl, half defiant and half cringing, who had appeared at Tyncoed from time to time.

'May I be comin' on in?' she asked.

'O' course you may, gal. So it's true as you are back in these parts, keepin' house for him – I do mean for – for...?'

'Mr Lloyd. Yes.'

'I never seed you about when I comed down to Lewisbridge on a Sunday?'

'No. I did keep close. Two months I've been with him. 'Tisn't long, but I do feel a different 'oman.'

She flung her arms round her cousin's neck and kissed her impulsively.

'Oh, I'm so happy! Look, Esther, I've brought my little boy to show you. He's a bit shy with strangers – here, my ducklin', don't you be cryin',' and she dragged him forward, patting him and shaking him as though he were a cushion which had become crumpled.

'He's not the boy he did ought to have been,' she confided to Esther in a loud whisper. 'I do think 'tis along o' my havin' been in such a fret all the while as I was carryin'. Lizzy isn't near strong neither, poor lamb, and I was bein' even more daunted when this one was comin'. Mr Lloyd do say folks as are treatin' a gal as is in the way like what I've been treated, is no better nor murderers – indeed he do. He's a good man if ever there was one, even if he do have some queer notions. Do you know as he saved my life? 'Tis the truth. I'd have ended it but for his kindness – I as was allus lovin' life more nor most folks do do when I was a gal. There, there, my precious, don't you go to cry...' she broke off as the sickly child set up a whimper. 'Mother is bein' safe now.'

Esther led the way into the kitchen and fetched from the parlour the illustrated Bible she had given Gladys.

'*There!*' Megan exclaimed, plumping her boy on to a chair before the table. 'You look at the pretty pictures, and don't you be listenin' to what we are sayin'.'

The effect of this injunction was to rivet his attention to the conversation, but his mother, cheerfully unaware of the fact, talked on without restraint. Esther, seated opposite her, was silent, her hands clasped together in her lap. Through the jumble of information which her cousin poured forth about Rhys, her thoughts threaded their way, returning constantly to the questions which had tormented her for two months. Where was his wife? What had brought him to Lewisbridge?

'He's terrible partic'lar as his boy shan't be "repressed" as he do call it,' Megan chattered on. 'You 'ould think he'd fair spoil the child by the way he do let him do as he likes; but the little 'un don't seem to have taken no harm. He's wonderful sensible for his age, speakin' like an old man just, along o' his father havin' talked to him about all manner o' things. He don't never try to hide nothin'. The other day now, he was breakin' one o' the best plates.

'Now your dad 'ull be angry with you,' says I.

'Oh, no,' says he, so comical-like, 'but I shall have to buy a new one with my pocket money. I shan't have no sweets for a while along o' my bein' so careless,' says he.

'Just fancy, Mr Lloyd do give that child quite a tidy bit o' money at his age, and he's teachin' him to save, and all. Well, I was sorry as he should have to pay for the plate.

'"Shall I say as *I* broke it?" says I.

'"But you didn't," says he, quite surprised. He don't even know the meanin' of a lie, I do believe. Yes, Mr Lloyd is havin' a wonderful way with children.'

'Is his – his *wife* agreein' with him in it?' Esther asked with a catch in her breath.

'His wife? Bless you, she's been dead and buried this long while.'

'Oh!'

Esther felt as though her heart had been wrenched out of its place. The shock left no pain, but faintness and exhaustion.

'There's not many here do know about it,' Megan resumed. 'He don't talk to no one about his affairs. Close he is, and queer on times. There's days as he'll sit readin' in his old books, and not sayin' a word. Fancy, he don't like me to speak to him when he's readin', nor I shan't even dust and put the place straight around him! Have you heard tell o' the free library he do mean to start?'

'The postman was sayin' something.'

'No doubt, for 'tis all the talk. Hundreds and hundreds o' books he's givin' the people o' Lewisbridge, and all for the askin'. Did you ever! Waste o' money I do call it, but 'tis handsome of him, all the same.'

'Megan,' Esther began, and paused, her fingers locked together more tightly than before.

'Well?'

'Is he talkin' to you?'

'Oh, yes. When he's got a talkin' turn on he'll walk up and down and make a reg'lar long speech, the half o' which I'm not payin' no heed to.'

'But...'

'Well?'

'Is he sayin' what brought him back home?'

Esther's cheeks flamed as she spoke, and she turned away her head.

'Oh, now you've asked me summat. I put the very same question to him the first night we met, and he let out some queer talk about havin' come back to make sure as he didn't love the country nor none o' the people in it. I don't know what to make o' him, I'm sure.'

Esther bent forward suddenly and laid a hand that trembled on her cousin's lap.

'Do you think he is angry with me?'

Megan stared.

'Why, he don't never so much as mention your name.'

'Maybe not, for that very reason. Could it be – oh, Megan, suppose if he was here on my account!'

'But all the neighbours has been tellin' him as you and the parson is keepin' company.'

'It isn't true. Tell him it isn't true.' She turned her back on Megan and pressed her hot forehead against the stone of the mantelpiece. ''Tis over, my courtin' with the parson, ever since the first day – oh, don't you understand?'

The sound of whistling, the barking of a dog, and the pattering footfalls of sheep reached their ears from the fold.

'There's John,' she cried. 'We can't be talkin' o' this no more.'

She moved swiftly towards her cousin and put her arms round the short, thick neck.

'Megan dear, will you come again? Will you' – she hesitated – 'be tellin' me all the news?'

'Of Rhys?'

Esther was silent, but Megan smiled at her confusion.

'Yes, I'll be actin' as go-between.'

The door was flung open, and John Bevan came in. With chin thrust forward in a manner that had been characteristic of his father, he surveyed Megan from beneath his lowering brows. She went over to her child who was crying.

'Good evenin', John,' she called over her shoulder as she patted the little cheeks with heavy-handed tenderness. 'Don't you take no heed o' my little lumper. He'll come in a minute.'

'I wasn't takin' no heed o' him,' John answered.

'Oh dear,' Esther thought, 'Megan's comin' here has put him out. I'll be havin' to suffer one o' his tempers as soon as she do go.'

'There, my pet,' Megan crooned, 'don't you go on cryin', or your Cousin John 'on't think you a good boy.'

John scowled at her in silence, and Esther moved to and fro arranging the table.

'You are settin' cups for Megan and that child o' hers, are you?' he enquired suddenly.

'Why, o' course, John. We can't let no one as do come to see us go away without they've taken a cup o' tea.'

'Oh well, you can give her one this onst, since she's here.'

'*John!*' Esther protested.

Megan swung round, nearly knocking the child off his chair.

'If you don't want me here, I'll go.'

He looked her up and down.

'Well, I'd best speak out plain, then we shall all know where we are. We've allus kept ourselves respectable in this house. No child has never been charged on me. I don't bolt with wickedness, and Esther didn't ought to neither, since she's likely to marry one o' the clergy. But I 'on't say no more about what's past and over. If you'd been leavin' your gal along o' our aunts, as 'ould have reared her in the fear o' the Lord, and puttin' that boy there out to nurse or sendin' him to the workhouse, where bastards did ought to be, I 'ouldn't shut my door in your face.'

He leant back in his chair, breathing heavily. So long a speech was an unwonted effort to him.

'Sendin' my boy to the workhouse?' Megan screamed.

'Don't you understand as that's what I've laboured and saved and very near starved for to avoid? Aye, and I've put up with worse nor that.'

''Tis worse nor that as you've come to now.'

'What d'you mean?'

'What I do say. You are livin' with a married man, as is too hardened a sinner to be ashamed o' harbourin' you and your two bastard children along o' his own.'

'How *dare* you?' she cried, striking the table with her clenched fist. The crockery rattled and the child sent up a thin wail of terror. 'Mr Lloyd is a widower, and he's treatin' me the very same as if I was bein' his sister.'

'How are we to know as he *is* bein' a widower? You've only his word for it, I suppose? I knowed a man onst as comed up from the works or some such foreign parts, and gave out as he were single – went courtin' the daughter o' Tynpant, and got her in the way – then one day up turns his wife and calls his sweetheart over like a good 'un – many's the laugh I've had over it.'

'Aye, that's the kind o' story as 'ould make you laugh,' said Esther in a low resentful tone.

He stared at her, but held firmly to his main point.

'Mind you,' he said, 'I don't like no tales told about *my* family, and the neighbours is sayin' as Megan here is this Lloyd's keepmiss.'

''Tis a lie,' she sobbed. 'He don't take no more notice o' me – not in that way – nor if I was bein' the doorpost.'

'Lie or no lie, 'tis all the talk; and any wickedness is to be expected of a man as don't 'tend neither church nor chapel.'

Slowly he rose and, striding over to the door, opened it and held it wide.

'I'm ashamed o' you, Megan, takin' up with one o' that lot – enemies o' your own kith and kin. Out you do go, and don't you be showin' your face inside this house never again.'

'I 'ouldn't set foot in it no more, not if you was to pay me for doin' so,' she stormed, picking up her child and clattering out.

'Megan,' called Esther, but John had slammed the door after her.

He turned and faced Esther angrily.

'You're a nice sister! Haven't I trouble enough without your takin' the part o' them as has compassed my ruin?'

'Trouble, John? What trouble?'

For a while he was too resentful to answer her, but kicked at the cinders on the hearth. Then he began to pace about the room.

'I told you back in the spring as I was havin' my plans to hinder them Lloyds biddin' for their farm at the sale.'

'Yes. I remember.'

'Well, my plans has failed.'

'Oh, never mind. What if the Lloyds *do* buy their farm, it 'on't prevent your buyin' yours too. That's what you do most desire, isn't it?'

'My plans hasn't failed without leavin' me the poorer, you fool.'

She stared at his careworn face.

'John, whatever have you been up to?'

'What's the use o' tellin' you? Women is havin' no sense about business.'

She made no retort, but waited, and presently, unable to contain himself longer, he poured forth the whole story.

It was a long one, comprising the moves and counter-moves of himself and his supporters in a struggle with Evan Lloyd for the possession of a butcher's shop in Llangantyn. Eventually the prize had fallen to the Lloyds, but not before John had driven up its price above its value, and had himself expended both time and money which would have been better employed upon his farm.

Following the sale of the shop had come a further contest over a piece of land on which Evan Lloyd had wished to build a slaughterhouse. Here John had twice thwarted him by bribing those who had land not to sell it. But at last, in spite of all his efforts, a suitable building site had come into the market, and his only remaining chance of ruining his enemy was to run it up above its market value, as he had done the shop. And it had been left on his hands.

'What's the good of it to me?' he demanded. 'There's no one in the countryside as 'ould ever have given me the half o' what I paid for it, but the Lloyds as did want it partic'lar. And even they don't want it now. Evan Lloyd, he is sellin' his shop so as to have the money to help his brother Elias buy the Henallt. They do mean to go shares as owners, whilst I – I as comed o' landownin' stock when they was servants to my great-grandfather, *I* 'ull be set down lower nor them.'

Gradually his anger turned to self-pity. In a husky voice he added: 'We are bein' ruined, Esther. The pride o' the Bevans is humbled in the dust.'

'Ruined,' she murmured, 'after all these years o' fightin', ruined by our quarrel with our next o' neighbours.'

'Aye, if there's keen biddin' on Pengarreg, I'll be havin'

279

to let it go. 'Twill be sold over our heads for the second time, and the new owner 'ull be turnin' us out, sure to be.'

His face worked. She had never seen him so moved before.

'Are you carin' so much for this sad old place, where we've all been so unhappy?' she asked in surprise.

He struck the table with the big red palm of his hand.

''Twas my father's – his own. 'Twas his grandfather's afore him. I was bein' born here. I've worked this land, my sweat is in it, my muscle did grow as a boy by my labour upon it. 'Twas grievin' me summat terrible to have to sell it after Father comed to die. I didn't so much as try to tell you what I was sufferin', for an 'oman whose work is in the house, she don't know what a partic'lar bit o' soil can mean to the man as has tilled it all his life. To buy it back has been my one hope.'

He turned away from her, and she saw him draw the back of his hand across his eyes.

'Poor John,' she sighed. 'He is havin' his love same as anyone else.'

CHAPTER 4

For the third time Esther was an unseen watcher outside Rhys' library. She crouched behind the hedge bordering the road and looked across it longingly at the one window which was still lighted in the village of Lewisbridge. The flowers of the blackthorn, having whitened the hedgerows like a lather, had dropped as swiftly as they had burst into bloom. As yet the swollen buds and unfurled leaves were small, and through the partly bare branches she could see dark shapes flitting across the square of orange light. Scraps of eager conversation reached her ears and the laughter of boys and girls, whose gaiety sharpened her solitude.

'Well, good night all,' came at last.

'Good night. See you here next week?'

'Yes, yes. I 'ouldn't be missin' Lloyd the library's evenin' meetin's not to go to a fair even.'

There was a shuffling of feet on the road as the figures moved away into the darkness.

Lily Bevan was ill, and Esther's frequent visits to Tyncoed after her day's work was done had given her an excuse for slipping down into the valley. Tonight her longing to remain was stronger than the shyness which had previously driven her away after a distant scrutiny. She rose from her hiding place, hesitated for a minute with her hand upon the stile, summoned courage to climb over it, and crossed the road. With quickened pulses she peeped in at the window.

He was seated at a desk with his head, which was seen by her in profile only, bent over a large volume. She watched him for several minutes, afraid of his sternness. How he had aged! Presently he looked up from his reading with a quick toss of the head which she remembered well. His face was turned in her direction, but from his lighted room he could not see her. A fresh idea had come to him; she knew the look – the parted lips, the eyes alight. This was the Rhys of their courtship days. In a moment of reassurance she opened the cottage door, entered and stood waiting. But he had returned to his reading.

'Have you come for a book?' he asked without looking up. 'You're late.'

'Not too late, am I?'

At the sound of her voice he swung round and rose from his chair. His abrupt movement overturned it, but neither of them stooped to pick it up.

'Why have you come?' he asked.

'I – I – was seein' a light in the darkness,' she stammered.

He looked hard at her. Then, picking up the overturned

chair, he pushed it towards her. 'Sit down. Let's have a talk. I've been wondering whether you'd come to see me, but thought it improbable. They told me at the pub you were likely to marry the parson here and I didn't fancy he'd encourage you to visit a man who doesn't attend any place of worship.'

His bantering tone hurt her.

''Tisn't true!' she cried. 'How could you think as I'd marry him after...'

'Oh well,' he said with a shrug as though it were none of his business, 'these little places are always full of gossip. Rural Wales hasn't changed since I left it.'

'What brought you back?' she enquired, thinking miserably, ''Twasn't love o' me, whatever.' And she added aloud: 'There's not many as do come back to these parts onst they do go from them.'

'No, you're right there. I met plenty of Welshmen in Canada making fortunes, but never with the Chinaman's purpose of going home rich. They've more sense than I have. They keep away from Wales – melancholy, wet, depressing place, full of drunkenness, insanity, suicide.'

She stared up at him, puzzled and distressed. 'You are believin' all that, and yet you couldn't keep away?'

Though she guessed now that he felt resentful towards her, hope began timidly to well up in her heart.

'Maybe you do love Wales still in spite o' yourself,' she ventured.

'I *hate* Wales, I tell you – and the Welsh. I hate them more than any other place and people because they are my own whom I have tried to love. What a man has once idealised and has been disappointed by, he grows to despise.'

283

She shrank from the look he gave her and remained silent for a long while.

'Yet you are doin' good here,' she said at length. 'You are bein' generous to the parish same as if you did love the people.'

'I'm trying to make it a bit better for the young folk,' he admitted, 'because I hated my own boyhood in Wales.'

He began to move restlessly about the room, setting a book to rights here and there and talking of his plans to help farm lads to the education which he himself had once so passionately desired. At Aberdulas he was building a village institute. He told her in detail of its architecture, its library, the lectures that were to be given in it but, while she listened, the thought persisted in her mind, 'He is not really wantin' to talk of these things now. He is forcin' hisself to do so for fear we should be speakin' of ourselves.'

This meeting was so unlike the one she had dared, in spite of her fears, to imagine, in which he should take her into his arms and the grief of years be forgotten, that she began to wish she had stayed in the darkness and been content to look at his bright window from afar off.

'You have been here all your life,' she heard him say presently, 'you don't know what it's like to come back to your own country after the war has made it seem a place of peace – a place to be desired – to come back and to be disillusioned about that as about other things.... Did you know I'd been in the army in France and Gallipoli?'

She started. 'No. Was you hurted?'

He smiled again with that wry twist of lips from which she had shrunk before. '"Only in mind," as one of our visitors at hospital said. War's a vile business, Esther, but if you survive it – a man and not a beast – by God, it makes you think.' Still he fidgeted at the bookshelves. 'It's made me cry out for a wider tolerance in the world – tolerance between man and man, nation and nation. But there's little enough I find of it in this place.'

'Not so much as might be,' she agreed in a soothing tone that rekindled his impatience.

'And why? Shall I tell you? Because the church- and chapel-going people of Wales are all obsessed, as you yourself have been, with their family ties – that, and nothing else. They recognise no larger duty. They carry on their petty feuds from generation to generation, and justify them in the name of loyalty.'

'*I* never did take part in the fight between your folk and mine.'

'But you failed me sooner than leave your kindred.'

Her eyes filled with tears.

'You are blamin' me for stayin' along o' poor Gladys and Mother in their sickness?'

He seemed to be struggling to act a part he had set himself to play, for when she thus looked up at him in appeal, her lashes wet, her lips trembling, he abruptly turned his back upon her.

'Blaming you? No! Your sense of right and wrong was not the same as mine – that's all.'

Then, as though this dispassionate aloofness were difficult to maintain, he went to the window and, throwing it open, leaned out into the night. There was a faint sound behind him as of a sob gulped down, and when he spoke again his voice had grown gentler.

'Would you care to come into my cottage and take a cup of tea with your cousin?'

'No, no, indeed, thank you. I must be off home. She do tell me though as you are wonderful kind to her.'

'Well, she'd the courage of her convictions even if they weren't of the best. The man she loved can't complain of her half-heartedness.'

Esther winced at that.

'I rather respect her for her folly,' Rhys went on, still with his back turned towards his listener. 'I'm going to set her up in my village institute at Aberdulas. Her history won't be known down there.'

'You are havin' some odd notions, but you're a good, kind man, Rhys.'

He faced her again.

'Funny that *you* should think so.'

'Why?'

'Because you and I have failed each other, Esther. You were to blame first, and then I – I was so desperately lonely. My God, I've paid for my weakness since! Have you found me very changed – very bitter?' He came suddenly and stood close beside her. 'Doesn't it seem odd that we can still be friends?'

'No. Not to me,' she answered in a low voice.

'Well, to me it does. Perhaps because – spiritually – I've made a worse failure of my life than you have of yours. I've harboured a grievance.' He held out his hand. 'But we *are* friends after all, aren't we?'

She clutched his fingers, released them and turned away swiftly. She dared not trust herself to speak until she had reached the doorway. When her hand was on the latch she longed to turn round and hold out her arms to him, but the shyness of love that felt itself unworthy was upon her.

'Goodnight,' she murmured as she hurried out.

He stared after her, frowning, took a stride towards the door, but turned away from it. From without came the click of the garden gate as it closed behind her. Then, with his old impetuosity, he rushed to the window through which she had looked with longing, and called out into the night that had hidden her from him: 'Esther! Esther! Come again.'

CHAPTER 5

The finest month of a fine summer was come. Every morning Esther was awakened by a shaft of sunshine that struck at her eyes, making of their lids a red transparency. Sleep and vaguely pleasurable dreams had warmed her. She stretched herself luxuriously and lay still a while before rising to begin the day's labours. For many years past she had tumbled out of bed as soon as she awoke. Now, morning by morning, she lingered in the warmth, listening to the cheerful twittering of sparrows under the eaves and wondering when she could next make occasion to visit Rhys. She was puzzled by his alternate friendliness and hostility, by the swift changes of his manner, now so gentle that it seemed almost lover-like, now severe as the manner of a schoolmaster lecturing his pupil. Her secret meetings with him had become at once her greatest pleasure and her keenest disappointment.

This was the season of the year in which the butter was amber-coloured, and cream an inch deep formed upon the milk when it had stood for an hour or two in the old-fashioned leads. It was a pleasure to make cheese in the stone-flagged dairy where the cool air smelled faintly of sour curds. Esther's hands grew soft with dabbling in the whey; her face, which she now took the trouble to wash in buttermilk, resumed much of its girlish bloom. But the greatest change wrought by this Indian Summer of her love was in the expression of her eyes. When she went to church and to market they rested on the landscape with a new delight. The riverside meadows and the railway banks were white with moon-daisies, though the hayfields of the hill farms were still a golden sheet of buttercups. On every piece of pasture land cows lay placidly chewing the cud, and red-and-white calves frisked about on ungainly legs. The late-born lambs of Wales were still but half-grown, and in the evenings, when Esther returned from her marketing, were playing 'king o' the castle' on every eminence in every field. 'All the creatures is havin' their mates and their young to love and cherish,' she would say to herself.

To John's continual lamentations over the approaching sale of Pengarreg she paid little heed, though he and she would be equally affected by it financially.

One evening, when a honey-coloured radiance overspread the fields about them, they leant side by side upon the fold gate.

'I can't come to hear who's likely to buy this place,' he grumbled. 'There's a talk goin' on as that son o' Lloyds as is come home rich 'ull be buyin' the Henallt for his parents.'

She started at the mention of Rhys.

'Yes?'

'And maybe buyin' our place too, so as he can drive us from the district – damn him!'

'I don't think as he'll do that, John.'

'Why not? He's a son o' the Henallt's, isn't he?'

'Aye. But he's not takin' no part in their quarrels. He don't hold as such things are right.'

'How are you comin' to know what he do think?'

She turned away her head.

'One is hearin' a bit o' gossip,' she answered with a vague gesture. And suddenly, 'I'll be goin' to see for Aunt Lily now.'

'No need to go again tonight. She'll mend a' right. She's as tough as an ancient old wether.'

But Esther was quietly obstinate, and after making several objections he shrugged his shoulders and told her to be gone. When she had reached the lower slopes of the hill she sat down upon a boulder and watched the group of boys and girls disperse from the library door. They had come late and were long in going. The sky above her paled while she watched, but though the sun had sunk behind the darkening hills, the earth was warm, and the gorse blossom gave out a heavy scent of ripe apricots. To this was added the sweetness of the honeysuckle that festooned the stunted may trees around her. The sleepy air, saturated with these perfumes, lulled her. She forgot her anxiety about the future which John's words had temporarily aroused, and thought only with shy rapture of her coming encounter with Rhys.

'Tonight, surely, he will tell me as I'm forgiven for treatin' him as I did. Tonight, maybe...'

But she dared not put into words the longing of her heart. No sooner was the road empty than she sprang to her feet and ran down to the village, careless of the stones and rabbit holes in her way, or the brambles that caught at her skirt. When she had pushed open his door and stood before him he saw that her eyes were bright and her cheeks flushed as those of an eager child. She thrust a book towards him across the table.

'How young you look tonight, Esther! How is it you still sometimes have the air of sweet sixteen? I'm demoralising you as they tell me I am half the young folk of the neighbourhood. Haven't you been warned against coming here?'

'Oh, no one don't know as I do ever meet you.'

He frowned. 'Haven't you told your brother even?'

She shook her head and his frown deepened.

'They're bound to find out in time. What will you do then?' Because she did not answer immediately, he went on, 'Be guided by the wishes of your relations, I suppose, as you've always been.'

She bit her lip at the taunt and turned away.

'Will you be lendin' me the second volume o' that book, please?' He found it for her in silence. 'Thank you. Goodnight now.'

'Wait a bit. If you'll stay till I've locked up, I'll see you home.'

'Oh, Rhys dear, and I thought you were angry with me.'

'What did you say?'

He had not caught the murmured words of delight, and only saw her with her back turned to him leaning against the doorpost for support.

291

'Are you tired?' he asked.

'Oh, no. I'm a' right now.'

She straightened herself with an effort and stepped out into the little garden, drowsy with the scent of stocks and evening primroses. Presently he followed her, and his footfalls on the path behind her found an echo in the rapid beating of her heart. The flowers at her feet seemed to swim up and drown her in their sweetness. She was giddy with an excitement unknown until that moment, and when she stumbled against him and her shoulder touched his, she shivered so that he asked if she was cold. She was glad of the twilight that veiled her face, for she felt the blood rush up into it. Ashamed of herself, she went forward into the road without answering him. In silence they crossed it, and began to climb up the slope – a sombre mass sharply outlined against a pale sky tinged with green where the afterglow was fading. The smell of sun-warmed countryside lingered in the mild air. She breathed it in and smiled.

'How good the whole earth is smellin'.'

'Yes.'

'Listen, Rhys. There's a nightjar.' Its burring note thrilled her. 'There was nightjars and corncrakes down in Aberdulas,' she whispered. 'Are you rememberin'?'

But Rhys strode on rapidly. Was he afraid of the memories that were so precious to her? When she overtook him he began to talk of his library, 'same as he might be talkin' to some stranger. Oh, I wish as he 'ould let the evenin' take holt o' him and teach him joy,' she thought.

'Your library is a' right,' she said aloud, 'no need to fret about it now.'

'Oh, but I'm continually being bothered about it. Your parson friend wants me to appoint a committee of all the unread fools in the neighbourhood. I know what that would mean. They'd spend my money on cheap fiction, easy, sugary, untrue to life. Once the young have had their taste vitiated by it, they lose their appetite for anything that demands an effort of their slack minds.'

Esther watched his moving hands.

'If only I was havin' the courage to catch holt o' them,' she sighed inwardly. 'He's not changed since the days when poor Aunt Polly was still laughin' at him for not knowin' how to make love to a gal.'

Still he talked on.

'The majority of those who have power or position want to keep the world as it is,' he was saying, 'rotting for lack of the healthy discontent that might change its worst evils. That's why they hate outspoken books and plays – because the young, who are still imaginative and sympathetic enough to be influenced by them, are set thinking.'

The last word caught her attention. 'Maybe 'tis better for the most of us not to think,' she murmured.

He flung round at her. 'You didn't always say so; but you've been bullied into believing that obedience is the first duty of the human beast of burden.'

She looked up at him, puzzled, conscious that the lingering sweetness of the gorse blossom, the warmth and mysterious beauty of the evening invited them to rest. Why did he argue so? She wanted to remain silent, to absorb the peace that brooded over them, to look up at the first faint stars, to be held in his arms as on that night drive long ago when they had told each other of their love. But he moved on.

'You've got a sound reflective mind,' he said. 'It might go deeper than many a more showy and quicker one.'

'No, no. I'm not bein' clever like what you are. Bein' an 'oman, I am made to feel rather than to think... Rhys...'

'Yes?'

He peered down into her face, but the increasing darkness hid its longing from him.

'Have you lost the thirst for knowledge you seemed to share with me once?' he asked. 'Aren't you interested in yourself any longer?'

'I don't know as I've had much time to think about myself.'

'That's a shame, because you're the most interesting person in the world.'

A tremor ran through her, and she held her breath in expectation. But his next words revived her former bewilderment.

'You are woman personified.'

She did not know what that meant.

'You'd best come no further,' she faltered, 'or maybe you'll be meetin' my brother.'

'D'you think I mind his sour looks?'

'No. But I am havin' to live with them.'

'You chose that.... Well, since you wish me to, I'd better leave you.'

'Oh, no, no! I wasn't meanin' you to go – not yet – not like that. I was only thinkin'...'

'You are always thinking of your relations. If you want to stick by them, I won't cause trouble between you. Goodnight.'

As he strode off down the track she felt suddenly cold.

'Rhys,' she called after him, but he did not return.

When she reached home, she stumbled blindly to her room. The air there stifled her, but the opening of the window let in the languorous scent of tiger lilies, and the calling of blackbirds and thrushes going to roost in the lilac bush. These were a torment to her in her present mood, and she shut the window to exclude them. As she turned towards the bed, she saw her own face reflected in the broken scrap of mirror. Scarcely knowing what she did, she tore off her hat, loosened the braids of her hair so that they fell about her shoulders and rapidly began to undress. When her arms were free of the sleeves in which they had been encased she held them out and stared at their whiteness. A strange fever possessed her. Half-clothed, she paced about the darkening room, now pressing her hot forehead against the window pane, now peering miserably into the looking-glass. 'Such beauty as I did ever have is gone,' she whispered. 'My eyes do look tired along o' all the tears they've shed. There's wrinkles about them, I can see them even in this light, and my mouth has forgotten how to smile.'

Now that she felt it to be too late, she longed desperately to inspire passion. Rhys had turned from her tonight with an indifference more hurtful than anger. Perhaps he would grow once more to like and respect her, would wish to have her with him, would marry her even. But such calm affection was no longer enough. In the moment of their parting a great hunger for his caresses had been awakened in her. She flung herself sobbing on to her knees beside the bed.

'O God, give me back my youth,' she cried. 'Indeed and indeed, I was spendin' it all upon others. I was actin' as the Book do tell us to. Why should I be punished for it? I am not grudgin' the years I did spend accordin' to Thy law. Only I do beg *one* day – one small, little day, dear Lord, of all the weary while I have given Thee. Do Thou be givin' me that much – so as I'll know before I die what 'tis to be young again and well-favoured and married to the man as do love me. Maybe if he could see me the bride I 'ould have made him onst, he 'ouldn't notice so much after as I'd grown old all of a sudden. He 'ould be thinkin' of me still as first he took me. Grant me this, O Lord, of all Thy power and bounty, grant me this.'

The gloom deepened. She could hardly discern her own white arms flung out before her upon the coverlet; only the window showed distinctly like a pitiless grey eye turned upon her distress.

'What is the good o' prayin'?' she thought. 'My youth on't never come back to me, nor the love as I 'ouldn't take when 'twas mine. Megan has been a wicked 'oman, but she has tasted all the glory of love in the days of her youth. I have served God faithful, and now He has deserted me. He is afar off and is not carin' what do happen to us down here.... No, no... 'tis sinful o' me to be thinkin' such things.... Send me some comfort, O Lord, that I may yet believe in Thy mercy.'

But there was no comfort in the knowledge that the past was irretrievable. She became aware of the contrast between herself in her present condition, dishevelled, half-naked and distraught, and the self-possessed woman who had knelt in church a few Sundays ago. Then she had

296

thought of love and marriage as matters to be carefully weighed and considered. Now she, whose life had been blameless, knew what the outcast and the criminal suffer.

In the morning she reappeared and went about her work as usual. She was quiet and self-contained as she had been always. John noticed no change in her but the ordinary marks of a sleepless night. Yet she had passed through a great crisis, and many things were known to her of which until then she had been ignorant.

CHAPTER 6

The sale of the two farms, whose tenants' quarrel had for so long divided the whole population of the neighbourhood, was a matter of intense interest for many miles around Lewisbridge. A rumour spread that Rhys Lloyd had disclaimed any part in his family's affairs. It was instantly contradicted by the elders of the chapel to which Elias belonged. Though Rhys was not, alas! one of the elect, they confidently affirmed that, being the son of so pious a man, he would never act as undutifully as the low-minded church-goers supposed. Reports varied, however, as to what exactly Rhys would do. Some said he intended to buy the Henallt and to make a present of it to his parents. Others, who nodded and winked their listeners into the belief that they had private information on the subject, said that he meant to purchase both the holdings, to turn out the enemy, and to farm Pengarreg himself. Many assumed that it was his intention to become his father's landlord, which they held to be presumptuous in a son. But public opinion in Nonconformist circles was suddenly swayed in his favour by the postman. Having obtained a pledge of secrecy from friends whom he could rely upon not to keep it, he confessed to having steamed open and read a letter in which Rhys promised to advance Elias the money necessary to buy his place, and generously refused to accept any interest on the loan. 'Is Price the post tellin' the truth?' was the question on all lips for days thereafter, 'or is he makin' hisself out to be a villain so as he shall be a hero till he's proved a liar?'

Before noon on the day appointed groups of farmers began to cross the central square of Llangantyn, and to hurry towards the town assembly rooms, The auction of Lord Glanwye's outlying farms was not due to take place until two o'clock in the afternoon, but with their Celtic love of drama the backers of both combatants were more eager to get a front seat at the entertainment than they were to attend to their own business in the smithfield. The first lots to go were one or two small farms to which no particular interest attached. They were knocked down to their tenants amid the mild applause which in Wales always greets the acquisition by the farmer of his own land. As the sound of desultory clapping floated over the now-deserted square, the proprietor of the Greyhound Inn hastened to the door and listened.

'They're not come to Lloyds nor Bevans yet,' he muttered. 'There'll be a shoutin' and a blasphemin' same as if we was on Swansea football ground, when it's their turn.'

His wife interrupted his pleasant anticipations by

coming out of the parlour, breathing hard as though from violent exertion.

'Boss, boss,' she hissed in his ear, 'the quality are wantin' coffee now – at this time o' day – and not a drop o' coffee left in the bottle – and Susan run off to the sale – the flighty piece! Go you on over quick to Mr Hughes grocer...'

'Drat these old foreigners, comin' and spoilin' today's fun for me,' the innkeeper muttered as he went off.

When he had again stationed himself on the threshold of his house there was not a sound from over the way. Then he heard the voice of the auctioneer followed by a buzz of applause. The same voice rose above the others again and again, and was answered each time by an ever-increasing tumult. Finally there was a great outburst of shouting and booing. If his guests had not at that moment called for their reckoning, the publican would have deserted his business and rushed across the square to satisfy his curiosity. As it was, he forgot to charge the 'foreigners' more than the customary local rate for fried ham and eggs, and returned to his doorway in time to hear a second and even louder uproar issuing from the assembly rooms. When the clamour had died down, someone within could be heard making a speech. At first it seemed to command silence, then there were several interruptions, and it came to an end at last amid a hum of what sounded like angry voices, mocking laughter and hissing.

'Now whatever can the meanin' o' that be?' said the innkeeper, scratching his head. As he stood staring he saw Esther Bevan come out alone and walk quickly towards him. 'Here's luck!' he thought, and, as she came close he advanced to meet her, rubbing his hands together. 'Well, Miss Bevan, I do hope as 't has gone in your favour?'

She seemed not to hear, but pushed past him into the house.

'Can I be waitin' my brother in the back parlour?' she asked. 'There's such a press o' people,' and she put her hand to her forehead.

'You're a bit overcome like,' he said, disappointed but forcing himself to be patient. 'I'll be sendin' the missus to you with a drop o' rum.'

'No, no, thank you. I'd rather be.'

'Come you, if you're a teetotaller we'll put it in a cup o' tea for you.... Here, missus...'

He bustled out and whispered to his wife to 'be kind to the poor gal, but to get her news from her as quick as was decent.'

After what seemed to him hours of waiting in the passage, his wife emerged from the back parlour.

'Well?' he cried.

She took up a dramatic attitude with arms folded on her breast in the manner of a bygone school of tragedians.

'The house o' Bevan is fallen – sure to be.'

Esther meanwhile had drunk the tea laced with rum, and dropped on to one of the upright chairs that stood ranged along the wall.

'That drink has been going to my head,' she thought, 'I can't think. I can't make no shape o' what has happened.' She looked about the room, searching for something on which to fix her disorganised thoughts. 'A text 'ould be helpful maybe,' she murmured, 'somethin' about – no, I can't think.'

In the window, supported by a bamboo tripod, a sickly

301

yellow flowerpot held an aspidistra. She noticed the film of dust upon its flat leaves, that looked as if they had been cut out of green glazed cardboard. There was no inspiration to be found there. Her eyes travelled next to the photograph of Aberystwyth parade densely crowded with holiday-makers which hung above the imitation marble mantelpiece. From there they wandered to the two companion portraits in red plush frames that confronted each other from opposite sides of the room. Evan Roberts the revivalist looked sternly at the Prince of Wales. His Royal Highness impenitently returned the fixed gaze with an equally fixed smile. Esther turned away from both of them and hid her face in her hands. She tried to sort her confused memories of the last hour, but could think of little but the smells of beer and damp sawdust that penetrated from the taproom. 'I do hate this place,' she told herself suddenly. 'I don't know why ever I was comin' here – like a sleepwalker just,' and she started up to go. But at that moment there was a clatter of boots in the passage and she heard the raised voice of a neighbour from Lewisbridge whom she dreaded at such a time to meet.

Mrs James was a noted gossip, who ceased to talk only when breath failed her. Esther could hear her now through the closed door, gasping and wheezing in her efforts to speak fast enough, for she had evidently hurried across the square to be first with the news at the inn, and her deep bosom was doubtless heaving and her face florid with exertion.

'Oh, Mr Thomas, Mr Thomas,' she gasped, 'there's a treat you have missed! Well, well, indeed to goodness, there never was nothin' like it heard, not since the buildin' o' the Tower o' Babel, whatever.'

'Whatever has happened? Tell us, quick!' Esther heard the publican exclaim.

'What has happened! Why, what none 'ould ever have guessed. There's some did think the Henallt folk 'ould triumph, and some as set their hopes on Pengarreg...'

'But what *did* happen?'

'Why, what's past belief. I've read all the wickedness reported in *Lloyd's* newspaper every Sunday afternoon o' my life for forty years now, and I've knowed unnatural children in plenty; but I never did hear tell of anything like this...'

'The man is mad, bound to be,' piped a little voice, which Esther knew to be that of Mrs James' husband.

'Who is mad?' demanded the publican.

'Rhys Lloyd, o' course.'

'But what's he done?'

'Made a speech in which he begun nice and civil by sayin' what a grand country Wales might be, and how he 'ould like to see it prosper, and the people too well educated to be drunken no more, and bringin' up their children civil spoken and kind to one another. And we was all clappin' and sayin' 'hear, hear,' except the bitterest o' the Bevanites as was daunted by the way the sale had gone...'

'But, Mrs James, how *had* it gone?'

'Why, hadn't I told you that a'ready?'

'No, no, never a word. Was John Bevan buyin' Pengarreg? The missus here couldn't get no sense out o' his sister, but she did seem terrible low.'

'No. He couldn't rise up as high as Pengarreg did go.'

'Who else was biddin' on it, then?'

'Rhys Lloyd.'

303

'Well, well, I never! The friends o' the Henallt 'ull be rejoicin' tonight.'

'Wait till you do hear the rest.'

But the publican interrupted once more. 'Who was buyin' the Henallt?'

'Rhys Lloyd.'

'Duwch! Was he buyin' the both o' them? Was that the Lloydites cheerin' as I did hear twice?'

'Aye. But they was booin' along o' the Bevanites afore 'twas all over.'

'However was that?'

'If you'll let me finish what I'd begun to tell you, you'll know as much as I do, though indeed 'tis the strangest business ever I heard tell on. There's nothing like it for undutifulness in the Bible, nor in *Lloyd's Weekly* neither, as I was sayin'. Well, so long as he was sayin' what Wales did ought to be like, we was fancyin' it grand, but all of a sudden he was tellin' us what it *was* like – in his opinion, mind you...'

'He's mad,' put in Mr James once more.

'And he is sayin' as his own folk had been as bad as ever the Bevans was, breakin' the peace o' the parish, and as he'd only bought up their place so as he might turn them out of it for ever.'

'*What?*' cried the publican. 'Turn out his aged old father and mother?'

'Now are you agreein' as the man is mad?' piped Mr James.

'"In the name o' justice," says Rhys Lloyd,' his wife cried, raising her voice to silence the others, '"in the name of impartial justice, I 'ull deal with my own kindred same

304

as I do mean to deal with their enemies. They have both been a disgrace to the religion they do profess," says he with his eyes flashin' same as they do say his grandfather the Independent Preacher's did do, "and out they do both go next quarter-day twelvemonth," says he, "and may the neighbourhood be the better for their goin'."'

At this point the voice of Mrs James was drowned by that of many others who began to stream across the square, and when, long after, John came in to find Esther leaning against the mantelshelf with her forehead pressed to the spurious marble, she stared at him as one dazed.

'I've been lookin' for you everywhere,' he grumbled. 'Whatever are you doin' here?'

''Deed, I dunno.'

He returned her stare in anger.

'What are you thinkin' of?'

'I don't know what to think.'

CHAPTER 7

Within the little church the air was stagnant, and the damp-stained walls cold as the grave. The preacher droned on. Children were reprimanded for stirring, and their elders dozed in upright attitudes of attention. But in Esther's mind all was turmoil. Throughout the service she heard only the words of Rhys' strange speech which, though it had alarmed, shocked and bewildered her, had yet compelled her admiration; saw only his eyes lit with a fire of fanaticism which at once fascinated and repelled her. She could not tell whether she admired him more, or loved him less, for the revelation of the day before.

She was now tormented not only by her uncertainty as to his feelings towards herself, but by a new doubt as to her feelings towards him. Struggling with this double dilemma, she came out, when the service was over, into the sunlit bustle and chatter of the churchyard. Vaguely aware that she was an object of curiosity and comment, she lingered in the porch until the gossiping neighbours should be gone. Though commiserating glances were cast in her direction, no one but Aunt Martha ventured to approach her. The large bony hand, the weight of which she had often felt as a child, was laid upon her shoulder.

'Where's John?'

'He didn't care to show himself, not after yesterday. He's terrible daunted.'

'And no wonder; turned out o' the old place where he was born and bred, by a son o' his father's worst enemy. Indeed, I'm glad as my poor brother isn't alive to see it; he was that hasty he'd have done this wicked upstart a mischief, sure to.'

'Sure to,' Esther agreed wearily.

'Yes, yes. But 'tis best left to the judgement o' God that will come on all such – you see if Rhys Lloyd don't die a terrible death, treatin' his own father and mother as he's doin'. There'll be a curse on that man. If it don't fall on him hisself, it 'ull fall on that child o' his. I've heard o' such things happening – unto the third and fourth generation, as it is written.'

'Let me go, Aunt Martha, *please*.'

Esther tore herself free and hurried out of the porch. The superstitious terrors implanted in her mind in childhood had revived.

As she paused by the graveyard wall, trying to overcome her agitation, she saw the last of the chapel-goers emerge from the red-brick building opposite. Elias Lloyd came first, in conversation with the minister. The years had drawn his sallow face to the likeness of creased parchment. Today it seemed more livid than ever. His lips were trembling and his voice sounded cracked and high pitched like that of a very old man. He was scarcely more than sixty years of age, as Esther knew, and she commented to herself, 'Pity on him – he's dunnin' fast.'

His wife hobbled out of the chapel after him. Some years his senior, she was crippled by rheumatism, twisted and gnarled like the branch of an oak tree. In one hand she held a stick upon which she leaned heavily, in the other a handkerchief with a mourning border. Gaunt, infirm, clothed in black, and with bowed shoulders, she was the personification of helpless old age and grief. Esther could see the tears glistening upon her furrowed cheeks, and, ever ready to pity, forgot her fear for Rhys in her compassion for his mother. All the confused and conflicting emotions of the last twenty-four hours were merged in resentment against him.

'Whatever he's doin' to my brother and me, he didn't ought to use the 'oman as bore him so hard,' she thought, 'nor his father neither, if not because they are his own parents, then along o' their bein' aged and at his mercy. I couldn't abear to drive an old dog out o' his kennel, and they ought to be more to him nor some dumb beast is to me. 'Tisn't right. 'Tisn't worthy o' him, with his fine ideas and his high talk.'

She watched the two bent figures make their way painfully down the road until they came to the last two cottages, one Rhys' library, the other his house. For a moment she hoped to see him come out and extend his hand in forgiveness and friendship, but his door remained fast closed, and his parents passed on unheeded. They disappeared round a bend in the road. The last she saw of them was the tiny cloud of dust stirred up by Mrs Lloyd's trailing skirt. It lingered like a puff of smoke after she had gone, and added to Esther's sense of having witnessed a tragedy. Too deeply moved to care whether she were observed or not, she left the churchyard and walked deliberately to Rhys' cottage. She had rapped loudly before her momentary courage, born of an instinct to defend the oppressed, forsook her. The door was opened by Megan, her handsome face flushed by the fire at which she had been cooking. She showed her large even teeth in a smile of welcome.

'Well, I never thought as you'd make bold to call on us. Come on in, Esther. I've a pie in the oven and a lot o' good things as I can't leave, but I can be talkin' to you whilst I'm seein' to them.'

'I can't come in now, but I do want to speak to Rhys – to Mr Lloyd, I do mean – partic'lar. Ask him to step outside a minute, will you?'

'Indeed, but he's not in. He went out a while ago. I'm expectin' him back to dinner, though. Can't you wait for him?'

Esther shook her head.

'I've our own dinner to see to.'

'Well, there's a pity. I 'ould dearly like you to see over this small little place. We've got it to look a treat. I've a fine life, I tell you. Don't I look different now to what I used to do?'

Esther surveyed her with a pang of envy that added bitterness to her anger against Rhys.

'You are growin' stout whatever.'

She was ashamed of the spiteful little thrust as soon as it was made, but Megan only laughed.

'Go on! You're jealous!'

The blood rushed into Esther's cheeks, for she knew the jesting words to be true.

'I can't wait no more,' she announced, turning away abruptly.

'Is there anything I can be doin' for you?' Megan called.

Because she was hurt and envious, it seemed to Esther that the words contained a hint of scornful patronage. Was it in Megan's power to influence Rhys as she could not hope to do? Were the neighbours right when they implied that his relations with his housekeeper were not those of master and maid? If not, why should her cousin have said: '*We* have so and so,' and '*Our* house is this and that?'

'No, you can't do nothin' for me,' she answered. 'I didn't come here on my own account, only to do what I thought right, but maybe I'd best leave it alone. Rhys and his conscience is nothin' to me now.' And she went wearily on her way alone.

Where the green track leading up to Pengarreg branched off from the main road she paused, and, raising her eyes to the hill above her, saw the figure of a man descending the adjoining path from the Henallt. Though he was too far off for his features to be discernible, she knew him for Rhys by his impetuous walk. Grieved and disappointed with him as she was, her first impulse was to hurry away, but after a moment's hesitation she decided to stay and reproach him. She leant against the gate, trying in vain to stifle the doubts as to his character which had been instilled into her mind by others.

310

'I 'ouldn't have believed a word against him, if I hadn't with my own eyes seen him act so cruel,' she told herself. ''Tis that as do force me to think as some o' the other things they are sayin' to his discredit may be true.'

When he came near enough to recognise her, he waved his hand gaily and quickened his pace to a run. There was something singularly boyish about him yet, she reflected. He might not be the hero she had believed, but her love for him, which had brought her little but suffering, had become a part of her. To tear it out of her heart now would be to kill the heart itself. She could never cease to love him, but in this moment she lamented rather than cherished her love. As she waited, watching him come swinging towards her, the sunlight seemed to mock the darkness of her soul.

'This is capital!' he exclaimed. 'You're the very person I wanted to meet. I never thought I should get you alone without endless manoeuvring.'

'I have been to see for you at your house.'

'Well done! In broad daylight too! I admire your pluck.'

He smiled at her grave face. She did not respond and his own expression changed.

'Your relations didn't send you, did they?' he asked suspiciously.

She shook her head.

'You came of your own free will?'

'I did think it my duty to come.'

'Oh, for God's sake, Esther, don't use that word again. It's always on your lips!'

She was so disconcerted that he relented suddenly and took her hand in his.

'I'm sorry, dear, but can't you say you came because you wanted to see me?' There was a moment of embarrassed silence. 'To ask a favour of me, at any rate,' he added in a tone of disappointment.

Reddening, she drew away her hand.

'I didn't come to beg for nothin', Rhys. I 'ouldn't ask you to let us stay on at home – nor nothin' – not for myself nor for none o' my own kin. I was comin' to speak to you straight because I was angry with you.'

He surveyed her in surprise, and finally broke into a laugh, which sounded forced; his eyes held no mirth in them, but a look of pain.

'Well, it suits you to be angry. I never saw you look better. A spice of the devil is what you've always lacked. You've no idea how pretty being in a temper makes you.'

'Have done jokin'. I'm in serious earnest.'

'All right. You can pitch into me, if you like, for giving your brother notice to quit, but you know that it wasn't done out of personal spite. I should think I ought to have made that plain enough by treating both parties in this miserable feud alike.'

''Twasn't about my brother I did come to speak.'

'Who on earth was it, then?'

'Your poor old father and mother.'

He stared at her dumbfounded.

'Did you come to my house, knowing what all your friends and relations would say about your doing so, in order to plead the cause of your enemies?'

'They are not bein' my enemies, Rhys.'

'*Not* your enemies?' He struck the gate with his fist. 'Who induced my uncle to treat me as he did on your account, but my father and mother? If it hadn't been for them and their quarrel with your father, you and I would have been married when we were young, and... have been living happily all these years.'

His voice trembled and his face was twisted with emotion. The change in his tone from light irony to passionate suffering amazed her. Seeing that he could feel thus deeply she forgot her doubts of him, and gently laid her hand on his arm.

'Yes, yes, Rhys, I am not likely to forget what we have suffered. But that is over and done with long ago. They are old, your folks, and in your hands. You could be crushin' the both o' them. No, they are no enemies o' mine now they are gone too weak for that.'

He looked at her long in silence.

You're a great woman, Esther,' he said at last.

'Will you let them stay on then at the Henallt, and end their days in peace?'

Her lips quivered.

'I've tried to act with impartial justice,' he said.

She wrung her hands. 'Other men can be just, Rhys, I am askin' you to be merciful.'

'Why?'

'Why? Oh! how can you ask? Because it do hurt me to see you so bitter and hard!'

'Then you still care what manner of man I am?'

Her eyes filled with tears.

'You have seemed the best man in the world to me, until today. You have been a pattern like, for all others. I couldn't bear to see you fall short...'

Her voice became choked, and, resting her arms on the

313

gate, she hid her face and cried. He slid his arm round her shoulders.

'Listen, Esther bach, and I'll tell you what I've done. I'm glad I did it, since you care for me like that. I have just come from an interview with the old people. I waited for them on the hillside on their way home from chapel. We parted friends; we shook hands. Will that satisfy you?'

She raised her tear-stained face, and gazed at him in bewilderment.

'Why didn't you tell me at onst?'

'How should I know you'd care? I thought you'd come to plead for your own, not for others.' He drew her closer to him. 'Shall I tell you the whole story? I never meant to turn my parents away unprovided for, as you thought. But I was determined to rid the neighbourhood of a pest. You know how strongly I feel about the petty enmities that are the ruination of Wales. Well, Fate put two of the worst offenders into my hands. I had to treat them both alike. To me blood is not thicker than water – not stronger than a principle, at any rate. I stick to every word I said yesterday. But before I decided to make my people leave the Henallt I went down into Herefordshire and bought a little place that will suit them far better. My mother's been a martyr to rheumatism, living in that wretched damp house, but neither she nor my father has had the sense to think of moving. There they'd stay, if I hadn't shifted them, growing poorer and more embittered every year in their lunatic struggle to best your brother; and there they'd have kept my brothers, who'd grow as warped and narrow as themselves. I've seen the boys, and they're thankful to me for giving them a chance to move down country and make money.'

314

He paused and looked into her face, which was close to his own.

'Well?'

'Oh, Rhys, Rhys, how I've misunderstood you.'

Her revulsion of feeling was so great that like a contrite child she hid her face against his shoulder. He did not attempt to raise her head or caress her, but held her gently to him and waited for her to recover her composure.

'Rhys, will you forgive me?' she whispered after a while. 'I've been thinkin' hard things o' you, as are so kind and good.'

'It's I who ought to ask your pardon,' he answered, stooping to catch a glimpse of her face beneath the brim of her hat. 'I've been deliberately hardening my heart against you, Esther bach.'

She trembled with pleasure at the old endearment.

'I know. You were bein' angry with me.'

'Not so much angry as disappointed. I'd grown embittered in all these lonely years.'

'Oh, Rhys bach, and 'twas I, as did love you so, as did make you suffer.'

'As no one else could have done. Well, I wanted to lay the ghost of all that misery – to start life afresh. That's why I came back here.'

'To prove to yourself as you didn't care for me no more?'

'And to find that I cared more than ever.'

Slowly she raised her eyes and looked at him. Through a long silence they stood motionless. Then her hands stole up round his neck. His face drew nearer to hers, and his arms tightened their hold. She threw back her head and closed her eyes.

315

She had ceased to think. The past was blotted out; the future had not begun to present itself. She lived in the ecstasy of the moment, in the happiness that had come to her miraculously when it was least expected. When at length she looked about her once more, the landscape seemed to have changed. Some indefinable addition of beauty had transformed the commonest objects. She glanced down at the topmost bar of the gate on which she had leaned, and noticed the tiny growth of lichen on the decaying wood. So minute a thing would have escaped her observation at any other time, but now a flash of vision revealed to her the detailed loveliness of a thousand diminutive forms. The silvery green branches of the lichen were as intricate as the pattern which frost traces upon a window pane, and as exquisite.

'Look, Rhys,' she murmured with an impulse to share every discovery with him, 'isn't that bein' lovely?'

He glanced at the lichen and laughed a husky laugh that told of a desire to cry.

'Everything's lovely now you and I have made our peace.'

Suddenly Esther became aware that a group of people was coming up the road behind her. She tore herself free from his embrace.

'There's neighbours comin' – Aunt Martha among 'em. I can't face them. I can't speak to no one just now.'

She had opened the gate and was already on the other side of it before he could protest.

'Don't go like that. When shall I see you again, darling? Shall I come to Pengarreg?'

'No – no, not there. Go quick, or folks 'ull see who you are.'

'Damn them! Here – stay a minute...'

'I'll see you the day o' the show in Llangantyn.'

'But that's a long way off, not until the middle of the week – the end of the week almost.'

She laughed with a contentment that found an echo in his heart.

'Next Thursday a long way off! Oh! Rhys, Rhys, after all these years!'

'Mind you come into town early then,' he called after her as she hurried away. 'I shall be on the look-out for you all the morning.'

'And I for you.'

She did not look back, but scrambled upward, her breath coming in sobs,

'It must have been a dream. It can't have been naught but a dream,' she told herself over and over again. 'I did use to dream as he kissed me often enough in years gone by. It can't be true. 'Tis too good to be true! 'Tis a dream – 'tis sure to be a dream, but oh, what a happy, what a wonderful dream!'

CHAPTER 8

On the morning of the Agricultural Show, Esther set out
for Llangantyn with a light heart. As she entered the town
she began to look about her with mingled apprehension
and pleasure. Her lips were parted and her breath came
quickly. For once she was not weighed down by laden
baskets, but was able to walk at a brisk pace, holding up
her skirt with both hands so that its hem should be clear
of the dust. The day was hot, but she wore her best black
overcoat, which gave dignity alike to church- and market-
going whatever the season of the year, and tight-fitting kid
gloves were beginning to stain her palms with purple.
Flushed with excitement and exercise, she looked, in spite
of her elderly attire, young for her years.

Outside the Greyhound was a line of traps and farm
carts. Mrs James and Mrs James' husband, who were
unharnessing their horse, signalled to Esther as she passed,

but she, fearing the habitual readiness of their tongues and remembering their behaviour on the afternoon of the sale, thought it wiser to avoid their questions, and hurried on with a sense of guilt that gave an edge to her adventure. Rhys was nowhere to be seen among the throng between the railway station and the bridge, and she went on towards the river. As she approached it, she became aware that a child had begun to run along at her side.

'Esther, please will you stop?'

Looking down, she saw a small face upturned to hers with an expression of alert enquiry.

'How did you know my name, little Rhys? Your name is Rhys isn't it?'

'Yes, Rhys after Daddy; Llewellyn because he was a brave man and a prince and died fighting for freedom; Samuel after someone called Butler who wrote books, I think Daddy said; and Lloyd – that's my surname because it's his.'

She was astonished by his confiding manner. The neighbours' children whom she had known gaped tongue-tied at strangers or retreated from them giggling. He was so self-possessed that of the two she felt the more shy. It would never do to make such advances to him as she was accustomed to make to those of his age – 'Would you like to ride on a great big gee-gee?' or 'Shall I give you some sweeties?'

'You were bein' wonderful clever to know me in this crowd,' she observed after some consideration as to what she should say.

'Ah, I remember you ever so well.'

'How's that?'

'Because you always smile at me. I know your name's Esther because Daddy told me so. He said you were a great friend of his and I was to keep a look-out for you in case you come into town whilst he was talking to the schoolmaster. I like Daddy's friends – most of them.'

She laughed outright.

'Well, you are a card!'

'What's that?'

But before she could attempt an explanation his bright eyes, that darted glances here and there like those of a bird, were sparkling with a new discovery.

'Oh look at those big horses with their tails plaited up with straws – oh! and coloured ribbons in their manes. Will you lift me up, please, on to the wall? – It's not that I'm afraid,' he hastened to assure her as she stood him upon the parapet of the bridge with her arms round him in protection, 'but they're so terribly, terribly big – and their feet are so clumsy and hairy. They might tread on me, mightn't they? Do you make you feel dreadfully little too?'

'There's a lot of things do make me feel little,' she smiled.

'Are you afraid of the dark?'

'No – not partic'lar...'

'Nor am I, but Lizzy and Tom are.'

'Megan's children?'

'Yes. They believe policemen will come and fetch them and all sorts of silly things. They aren't much fun to play with,' he added. 'I like Mr Jones the plumber better, and I like Daddy best of all. He used to teach me lessons, but now I go to school here and it isn't half so nice. Daddy never caned me.'

'They don't never go to beat you at school, do they?' she asked, drawing him closer.

'Only when I'm *very* naughty. I am sometimes. I've a violent temper, they say, when it's roused.'

'And didn't your dad use to punish you then?'

'No. He just said nobody would like me or have anything to do with me when I grew up, but I could please myself – he's given me a big knife. Would you like to see it?' Fumbling in his pockets, he produced his treasure, at which she looked with some misgiving.

'That's a terrible dangerous thing for you to play with.'

'It's very sharp. There – you feel that blade. But Daddy says if I cut myself it will be my own fault. I'm ever so careful. And I've got a lump of putty and some real tools just like workmen have. Some day I'm going to be a plumber.'

'A plumber! But you'll be growing up to be a gentleman.'

This idea seemed to convey nothing to him.

'Daddy says perhaps I shall change my mind and be an engineer instead. But I like fixing bells and pipes and things, and painting pictures. I'll paint a picture of you when you come to visit us. Shall I? When will you come?'

'Yes, when will you come?' echoed a man's voice behind them.

Esther turned with quickening breath and confronted Rhys.

'You two seem to be getting on pretty well without me,' he observed, smiling. 'D'you want to see the show, old man?'

The small boy scrambled down and clutched at the hand held out to him.

'Oh yes, please. Let's go quickly, now at once.'

321

They moved off together. He had fast hold of his father and presently slid a hot little hand into Esther's. Her fingers closed upon it. But the next moment self-consciousness returned, making her painfully aware of the compromising nature of this walk with Rhys, linked by the child between them. As though divining her thought, Rhys smiled at her.

'You haven't told us when you're coming to see us. After this you can't be shy about it any more.'

She did not answer and tried to disengage her hand, but the little fingers clung tightly, and she could not find it in her heart to shake them off. They had now crossed the river and turned upstream. From this bank the houses retreated and were huddled together upon an eminence some hundred yards away in order to escape the occasional flooding of the flat meadows. A portion of the land thus left open was today shut off by poles and sacking, and within these improvised screens the show was in full swing. Rhys strode on and was purchasing tickets at the turnstile when Esther pulled at his sleeve.

'I can't go in along o' you,' she whispered. 'My brother's down here lookin' at the sheep.'

'He may as well see us together now as later.'

'Oh no, not just yet. I don't want the day's pleasure to be spoiled.'

'Nothing's going to spoil it for me. What are you afraid of? You're your own mistress, aren't you?'

Little Rhys had grown impatient at the delay.

'Aren't we going in?' he asked, standing on tiptoe to peep through the bars of the stile. 'I can see cows, and horses, and oh Daddy, look...'

His exclamations of delight were interrupted by the arrival of a party from Lewisbridge whose children, dressed in their comfortless best, joined him in peering and craning forward while their elders talked to his father. Esther had at once retreated in an attempt to avoid their inquisitive glances, and, when Rhys had waved them a friendly farewell, he found that she was no longer beside him.

'I've put my boy in their charge till dinner-time,' he announced as he came up with her. 'So now you and I can go and walk by the river if you're afraid to be seen here. You odd, shy creature.'

She murmured something about 'fearin' to shame' him and he laughed at her with the tender mockery of the old days.

They entered a path bordered by trees and deserted at this hour. Though elsewhere the air was still, there was a breeze on the river which set the leaves rustling overhead and a pattern of sun and shade dancing at their feet. The glitter of sunlit water drew Esther's thought back to Aberdulas and their far-off walks by the sea. She was both pleased and embarrassed by this lover-like stealing away from the crowd. To be near Rhys was a delight, but she would not look into his face, choosing to walk a pace removed from him, guarding her own memories of the past while he, as usual, talked eagerly of the future.

'You like him, don't you?' he asked, speaking of his child. 'He's as keen as mustard, afraid of nothing, and wants to learn and understand about everything. That's because I never repressed him as Megan's poor little Calvinists have been repressed. It's a terrible thing to plant a morbid conscience in a child.'

323

'But God is givin' each one of us a conscience, surely. There's no makin' or marrin' that, save by our own wickedness.'

'So you've been taught to think, because all the people you live among share the same idea of "wickedness". Have you read any comparative religion?'

She shook her head.

'Or any modern psychology?'

'Any what?' She flushed with shame. 'I'm terrible ignorant for the likes o' you to talk to,' she said sadly.

'No, no, dear, you mustn't get that into your head. You make me feel like an impostor. My talk may sound wise to you. I get carried away by it myself when it's on some subject that's near my heart. I've read and thought a bit. But you must remember I've only a smattering of knowledge, after all. All my views on vast subjects – that are a life study – are founded on a few books only.' This spasm of humility passed, and she saw his face lit once more with impetuous enthusiasm. 'I believe I'm right about one or two principles, though. And they're very different from those I was taught to believe in when I was a boy. For instance, it's part of my creed that pleasure is not an indulgence – not a luxury even – but a necessity to human beings if their minds are to be kept healthy.'

He began to argue that a great part of the 'envy, hatred and malice, and all uncharitableness' which he found poisoning the Welsh countryside was the result of a suppressed craving for gaiety. He spoke of harp-playing and dancing which the early Methodists had forbidden.

'Dancin' is comin' back now, among the church folk whatever,' Esther said when some comment seemed to be

324

required of her. 'I don't see no harm in it, though I never did learn to dance myself along of its bein' thought very worldly in our parents' day.'

'Worldly! and why ever shouldn't we be worldly so long as we live in the world? They don't disapprove of a man for being a good Welshman if he's born in Wales.'

'But aren't we meant to treat this world only as a place o' trainin' like for the next?'

'Possibly. I don't look so far ahead myself. I'm concerned with this life and everything that can be ascertained about it, not with speculations as to the next which can't be proved one way or another. But granted you're right, how would you set about your training here?'

'I dunno,' she faltered, 'I've been tryin', but 'tis hard. Some preachers do say one thing and some another.'

'That's just it,' he cried; 'once you let go of the practical you are lost. The only thing to hold to is successful worldliness. Oh, I don't mean by that just a selfish struggle for money and position – that's not the way to gain and enjoy the best things of this world. I mean learning to make yourself and your children as healthy, happy and useful to the community as may be – learning to handle matter and to master it. Depend upon it, if we haven't learned how to create happiness on this plane, we shall not know how to enjoy it on any other – supposing that we survive as individuals.' He caught her hand suddenly. 'Come, Esther, you've lived in the shadow of Puritanism long enough. Let's learn to be happy together.'

'Ah, if only I was bein' worthy o' such happiness!'

He turned upon her a smiling scrutiny. 'Why d'you wear those black clothes so much too old for you? Look at the day. You ought to be dressed in muslin and ribbons – bright pretty things that would blow about in the breeze and show off your figure.'

'For shame, Rhys! 'T'ouldn't be modest.'

'Don't you want to give me the pleasure of seeing you look your best?'

He pulled off the black kid glove and planted kiss after kiss in her upturned palm.

'Will you come with me now and let me buy you a becoming frock and a hat that doesn't look like the one that Queen Victoria wore?'

His kisses were a delight and she did not resent his laughing at her, but the realisation that he found her dowdy made her sigh.

'I'm gone too old for flighty clothes,' she murmured. 'I've been tryin' to do my duty for many years now, Rhys, and I've had no thought to spare for my looks. 'Tis a young smart gal you do want if that's what you are thinkin' on, one as hasn't tired her eyes with cryin' nor worked her hands all red and rough like mine.'

He drew her into his arms and closed her lips with his own.

'This is our day – our Easter – the resurrection of youth. I must be allowed to commemorate it by making you a present. Are you coming, sweetheart?'

She let him tuck her hand into the crook of his arm, but when they reached the highroad she withdrew it timidly.

Presently they entered the leading draper's shop in Llangantyn.

'I'm never shoppin' here,' she informed Rhys on the threshold. ''Tis too genteel for my class.'

326

But he only laughed at her again.

'I want a light summer dress for this lady.'

Esther shrank from the critical glance of the young woman in black satin who leant over the counter, her white hands and polished pink fingernails displayed upon it.

'Certainly, sir. About what price would you wish to pay?'

'Let's look at the best you've got.'

She hesitated, regarding Esther with thinly veiled disdain. She had decided that the dress was to be a present from her customer to his servant.

'Our best frocks are copied from Paris models. Not very serviceable wear.'

'I don't want anything serviceable. I want the most becoming you have.'

His tone was peremptory and she departed in haste.

'Oh, Rhys, you didn't ought to be so rash,' Esther whispered, and when a number of dresses were held up before her she shook her head. 'No, no, those are a deal too stylish for the likes o' me. Why, they're made of silk.'

'But your dress is of silk – much heavier stuff than these too.'

'Ah, but 'tis black, that do make such a difference, and I made it myself out of old mournin' hatbands o' Granny's.'

This speech caused ill-concealed mirth among three girls, all white-handed and fashionably clothed, who had gathered round the first assistant to enjoy the fun. Esther, acutely conscious of their criticism, felt that she was disgracing Rhys and grew increasingly uncomfortable. But he appeared to be quite unawed by the scrutiny of these stylish beings, and when she came out of the fitting-room in a russet-brown dress that toned with the rich colouring of her sunburnt face and the coppery gleams in her hair, he had a crowd of them about him holding up hats for inspection.

'That's capital!' he exclaimed. 'You're a picture, Esther.'

'It suits Moddam to perfection.'

'It might have been made for her.'

'Get Moddam a glass, Miss Jones, so that she can see how charming it looks.'

They had decided by this time that she was something more than the gentleman's housekeeper, and must not be laughed at in his presence.

The trying on of hats was an even greater ordeal to Esther for she was urged to do her hair a 'little less severely', and Rhys suggested that she should take it down there and then, which deeply shocked her. To her mind such a procedure would have been little less immodest than undressing in public. She was even embarrassed by Rhys' presence while she tried on the new shoes he insisted upon buying at the boot shop, and when he demanded stockings to match, she turned away blushing.

'Rhys,' she protested when the outfit was complete, 'this gown is bein' so low in the neck I'm afeard to take cold.'

'What, on a day like this?'

''Tisn't altogether that,' she admitted, 'but it do hardly seem decent.'

He burst out laughing once more, and she regretted having raised an objection that seemed to him so foolish.

'Never mind if you're decent. You look charming.'

But it was in vain that he admired and praised her. She remained so self-conscious and ill at ease that he was disappointed by her reception of his gifts.

'I don't know what's the matter,' he complained at last.

328

'But nothing I do seems to give you any pleasure today.'

'You have been wonderful kind,' was all she had the heart to reply, and to herself she thought, 'I 'ould give the world just not to hurt him whom I am lovin' so. But I am not crafty enough to make believe as I'm pleased when I do feel so daunted. I've not the looks o' these young gals about us, nor I haven't none o' their wiles and trickses neither.'

Suddenly she drew in her breath in dismay.

'There's Aunt Martha coming. Go, Rhys, quick.'

'All right, if you're ashamed to be seen with me.'

He turned away in momentary annoyance, but, looking back over his shoulder, called out, 'See you later on the show ground.'

When he had disappeared in the throng she faced her aunt.

'Who was that you were with? I couldn't quite see him. No one from these parts, was it?'

Esther professed not to hear.

'Well, Aunt Martha, fancy seein' you down town so early.'

'I brought Lily in. She's not near fit to be here after bein' so ill, but she 'ould come – obstinate always. We seed John lookin' at the sheep and promised to have a cup o' tea with him at the Dot Refreshment here. You'd best come in too.'

Esther followed Martha Bevan into a tea-room over a confectioner's shop close by. It was only when she saw her brother glaring at her that she realised her error. He and Aunt Lily were seated at a marble-topped table and looked her up and down with disapproval.

'Why are you dressed up so grand?'

'Well! Well! Some folks must be havin' a lot to spend on their backs.'

Aunt Martha now joined in the general criticism.

''Tisn't like you, Esther, to be wearin' a hat as 'ould suit an 'oman a deal younger nor you a sight better.'

Esther winced.

'Nor this isn't the time to be buyin' new clothes neither, with your poor brother bein' turned out of his farm,' put in Aunt Lily. 'I'm surprised at you showin' such an unfeelin' and worldly spirit.'

'Unfeelin' and worldly be blowed,' growled John. 'But what d'you want to go wastin' my money for? You take them fancy clothes back to the shop at once.'

'They wasn't bought with your money,' she answered.

'Oh, so you've got some of your own hid, have you? Been makin' more nor you was usin' for the housekeepin' out o' the poultry, have you? You're a nice sister, never tellin' me as you was puttin' by money when you knowed I'd gone so needy.'

'I thought as my poor brother and sister-in-law had brought you up to dress quiet and modest,' said Aunt Lily. 'They'd turn in their graves if they could see you in silk like some rich man's keepmiss.'

Narrowed eyes, like points of steel, regarding Esther from across the table, saw that the shaft had gone home.

'If you think to catch a parson by such flighty ways, you're terrible mistaken. He'd be disgusted by you. 'Tis the sober old-fashioned gals men o' his callin' do fancy.'

John made an impatient movement of his shoulders.

'Oh, she's spoiled her chances with him long ago – put him shy somehow or other. He don't come near our place no more now.'

'Well, there's dull you've been,' cried Aunt Martha.

330

Esther drank her tea in silence and was unable to touch any food. Perhaps they were right, she thought miserably. Rhys, of course, had not dressed her up to make her a figure of fun, but he was blinded temporarily by his fondness for her. Would he not see her after a while as these others saw her now, and be ashamed of his choice?

'I'll be off,' she said suddenly, unable any longer to endure their taunts and her own anxieties.

'I'd go home if I was you, and put on my old clothes, more suitable to my age and station,' said Aunt Lily.

Without replying, Esther went down the stairs into the shop below.

'I hope as you'll come to a wiser frame o' mind,' the acid voice pursued her.

'A wiser frame of mind!'

She was already suffering from that. Her world was grey once more as she walked alone towards the showground. She was so dispirited that the tent containing dairy produce which she had been eager to see did not now tempt her. She passed by the pens around which a crowd of whiskered little men from the mountains were discussing the merits of sheep, and, going up to the ring within which the trotting matches were held, leant with folded arms upon the rail. A class of mountain ponies, mares with their foals, was being exhibited. In the centre of the ring stood the judges. They wore their bowler hats tilted knowingly to one side and assumed an air of profound self-importance as they examined each pony in turn. Friends and supporters of the exhibitors shouted their applause and argued with those around them. The men were all personally interested in one or other of the exhibits, and the women were enjoying the

331

unusual treat of a day's outing. Esther alone in all that crowd was silent and prepossessed. Mrs James and her husband approached her unperceived.

'How is it you're alone, Miss Bevan?' Mrs James asked, elbowing her way to a front place beside the rail.

'Oh, my brother's here somewhere.'

'Go on, you don't want your brother for company always.'

Mrs James' husband, trying to tiptoe into a position in which his view would not be interrupted by his wife's broad shoulders, gave a shrill little chuckle.

'The missus is right there. Where's the parson I heard so much talk of along o' his fancying you?'

'There's a lot of nonsense talked indeed,' Esther returned.

Mrs James shook her head and made a clicking sound with her tongue.

'Lewisbridge is a terrible place for gossip, I do say. The way they do talk about that young Mr Lloyd now – well, you've no idea! Are you ever speakin' to him, Miss Bevan?'

'I have done.'

'I do think Mr Lloyd a religious man, whatever some folk do say,' said Mr James.

Esther remembered how the same piping voice had been raised not many days since to protest that Rhys was mad. Evidently these people suspected her of being in love with him.

'Religious or not, Lloyd is a sharp 'un to make money,' put in the publican from Lewisbridge who had joined the group. 'I tell him he oughtn't to be wastin' his time here amongst us poor folk. He did ought to go and live like a gentleman in some smart place like Cardiff.'

332

'And marry a stylish lady,' added Mrs James, watching Esther's face for any change of expression.

'Yes, yes,' the publican agreed. 'There's no one in these parts likely to take the fancy of such a one as he.'

Mrs James smiled knowingly.

''Deed, I'm not so sure.'

'Duwch no!' the publican returned with contempt. 'Have you heard him talk of all the foreign parts, the cities and people he's seen? Well, if he couldn't pick a gal good enough for him there, where there's the handsomest to be seen, he's not goin' to make shift with some rough farmer's daughter here. No! no! I've seen a bit of the world, too, I have. Cardiff is the place where you'll see pretty gals. 'Tis there he'll be havin' to look for a stylish bride to do his money credit. His first wife were a smart little piece – I've seen her photo. You 'on't make me believe as he'll be foolish enough to marry worse the second time nor he did the first.'

'You're right there; practice did ought to make perfect,' cackled Mrs James' husband.

Esther's face was burning, and with difficulty she kept back her tears. Of course it was plain to everybody that she was no match for Rhys. Though he had been carried away by the tenderness of old memories, she had no business to think of marrying him.

Preparations were being made for the trotting match which was the event of the day, and the neighbours moved off to obtain a better view of the finish. As she watched the throng, Esther saw Rhys striding round the railings in search of her. When at last he saw her, his face lit up with pleasure.

'Oh,' she thought, 'if only I could be sure as he 'ould care for me always same as he is doin' now I 'ouldn't be afeard to marry him. But I do dread his growin' tired o' givin' every-thin' and receivin' nothin' in return – neither money nor position, nor youth nor looks, nor a well-educated 'oman as could take part in his talk. If there was anythin', anythin' at all I could give him, 'twould be different.'

Careless of the inquisitive glances directed towards him, he shouldered his way to her side. There was none of the self-consciousness of a country courtship in his manner, for he was altogether indifferent to local ridicule and curiosity. To her he seemed in consequence a man apart, and her admiration for his boldness further humbled her in her own eyes.

'It's odd,' he announced, 'the feeling aroused by a trotting match. It's of no particular use to any of the farmers who enter their cobs. But the judging of the best bull, which means much more to them financially, doesn't create half as much excitement. It's competition in a dramatic form that gets their blood up over this business. It's set me thinking.'

Her eyes were raised to his.

'Somethin' as I could understand if you was tellin' me?'

'Of course.'

He smiled encouragingly, but the corners of her mouth quivered a little as she tried to smile back at him.

'Contest,' he said, 'that's a condition of life, of progress – a necessary stimulant. Where there's no contest there's stagnation. It's no good the idealists shutting their eyes to that fact. The problem of civilisation, it seems to me, is how to maintain competition between races and individuals whilst eliminating its present cruelty.'

334

She nodded.

'You are being different from all other folk ever I knew. Maybe others 'll be growin' up like you after a while.'

He smiled, but his face grew grim again immediately.

'Oh, but to you it's just a personal matter. You feel only for the individual. You'd like other men to be more like me because you love me. I'm always thinking of mankind in the mass – this great quarrelsome family of which I am a member – and I'm afraid, Esther, horribly afraid for my people.'

'What's the good o' vexin' yourself about the whole world?'

'What's the good of being anxious about the welfare of one you love? It can't be helped, Esther. Whom we love we suffer for.'

That she understood, as her anguish too plainly showed.

'There were men I met in the army,' he went on, 'Oxford men – fine fellows. They were good to me. They taught me a lot, and I liked their company better than any I'd met before. Some of them shared my views. We loathed the war – the tedious discipline, the dirt, the brutality of it, the waste of life and time. There was one chap, a private like myself at the start, a don or professor or something. He wanted to get back to his books and what he called the sanity of home life. I used to rage about the iniquity of war, although, mind you, I'd enlisted voluntarily just as he had. I remember his pale face, with a sort of tortured look about the mouth, and the quiet way he'd say, "You're right, Lloyd. It's a damnable business, but it's inevitable." Then he'd tell me about old empires before the days of Rome, ages back, and how they fell one after another, and how fire and sword, famine and pestilence had always been the lot of man. "You take to reading ancient history, Lloyd," he would say, "and you'll soon give up hoping for the future of mankind. You'll find life easier when you've ceased to hope." But I never saw a man with such sad eyes. When he was dying, he sent for me in hospital. "Well, Lloyd," he said with a queer twist of the lips – it was meant to be ironical, but it just wrung my heart to see it – "this is an inglorious end, dying of disease in a cause that seems pretty paltry to me now." I don't think he said much more before he died. And he didn't believe in a future life either, poor devil.'

Rhys did not speak for a while, and Esther saw that his eyes were bright with tears. She looked away, fearing that he would not wish her to observe them.

'Is that sort of thing to go on for ever?' he demanded. 'Those cultivated chaps with their gentlemanly resignation – they haven't the gusto for living that a man like myself has. They think it bad form to take life or death seriously. They'll face either with a joke. They're great in their way, but they'll never lead people to better things, for they don't love the people – and I do.'

His face was alight now with the ecstatic fervour which old folk still living remembered having seen in his grandfather the preacher. It seemed that his eyes were deeper set beneath the dark brows, his bronzed cheeks hollower, his lips more determined. Esther was afraid.

''Tis like as if his face did shine as the sun, same as the apostles did see Christ on the mount o' the transfiguration,' she thought.

'The cause of peace,' he was saying, 'is the cause of my child, every child; of every woman who risks her life to bring a new one into the world; of every man who seeks to lead the better, kindlier life for which I crave; it's your cause, Esther – who are so gentle and good, to whom I could not even tell the things that women like yourself have suffered during the war. When I think of it I vow that my life from henceforth shall be devoted to nothing else.'

'Go you,' she whispered with trembling lips, 'go you free to take up your great work.'

Round the ring the sturdy Welsh cobs pounded, while the spectators cheered on their riders, and shouted and hissed when some horse broke its pace and tried to pass another at a canter. Mud, churned up by thundering hooves, flew high in the air. Men waved their hats and women fluttered handkerchiefs.

'Go it, Davies!'

'Well done, Tynpant!'

'Come on, Cefncoed!'

'Stick to it, man!'

'Ah, that's the second time he's broken his trot.'

People were yelling on every side of them, but they scarcely noticed the general excitement. When the cheering was over and the crowd began to disperse, Esther moved away with a heavy heart.

'I must be goin' to look for John,' she said.

'When shall I see you again, then? We have decided nothing about the future, bach.'

The sadness of her expression surprised him.

'I'm going to take you away from that dismal place of yours at once.'

'Not yet awhile. Wait till I do write to you.'

'But Esther...'

'No! No! I can't be talkin' now. I'll write.'

'As you wish, dear. Only don't keep me long in suspense, will you?'

She shook her head.

'My mind is made up a'ready.'

When she looked back a moment later, she found that strangers had hidden him from her sight. But it was not physical distance alone that divided her from the man she loved, nor did she feel merely, as she had felt earlier in the day, that he was too much her social superior to be content for long with her companionship. Now she saw him as a being too advanced, too spiritualised for her to follow; she was of common clay, absorbed in the little things of daily life, desiring children over whose future she would not be more worried than were other ordinary mothers, craving only for tranquillity and comfort and the love of her man. The world to her would be within the four walls of their home.

'I'm not fit to mate with such as he,' she told herself as she trudged along wearily. 'Since he is blind for the while to the distance set between us, I must be makin' it plain to him, though it do break my heart to do so. I've heard tell of women as 'ouldn't marry men as all folks was seein' too good for 'em. People did think as they didn't know their merit, but I do fancy now as they did see it all too well. We are afeard o' what's too high above us, better and bigger nor ourselves. 'Tis the little and weak as we can be motherin', 'tis them as do need us, as do draw us to them. That's how I am bein' made whatever.'

Thus she summed up her character and her life's history.

CHAPTER 9

The show was over and among the occupants of a hundred farms was a dreary feeling that now there was nothing more to which they might look forward. Disappointed cowmen with sacks drawn over their shoulders slouched about the folds staring at their charges that had failed to take some coveted prize. The straight-falling rain of summer was incessant, and within Pengarreg kitchen Esther listened to the steady dropping of water from the eaves. There were rings of shadow about her eyes; her face was colourless and drawn after a sleepless night. The afternoon had been made horrible by the shrieks of a pig, which, having met with an accident, had been summarily slaughtered. Though the last feeble moanings had died away, Esther was still unstrung by the noise. She opened the oven door to see how the flat rhubarb tart intended for Sunday's tea was baking. Beneath the table a cat rose from a basketful of hay and stretched herself. Her newly born litter of kittens set up a tiny mewing. Esther drew the basket gently towards the hearth and lifted up a blind, sprawling creature that lay in the palm of her hand like a small mole. It was still moist and had the crumpled top-heaviness of most babies. As she laid her cheek against the little body that smelled of hay and wet fur, her own troubles receded and she was conscious only of a glow of protective affection. All very young animals gave her a sensation of physical well-being as she handled them, and it was with reluctance that she gave the kitten back to its mother, who had begun to watch it with sudden anxiety and greeted its return with a crooning sound that made Esther stoop and fondle her.

'There, my poor Tibby, you're happy, are you? How pretty you do look with all the funny little mites nestlin' up to you and you watchin' 'em as if they was bein' the world to you.'

She was still kneeling by the fire, running her fingers caressingly through the brindled fur, when John came into the room. He gave her a surly glance, and without speaking clattered into the back kitchen and began to wash his hands at the sink. She could see him through the open doorway as she rose to prepare his tea. His coat was off and his shirt-sleeves rolled up above the elbow. On his forearms grew a thick crop of reddish hair. 'More like a beast nor a man he is,' she thought with a spasm of disgust.

His hands were dyed in blood; she saw it drip from his blunt fingertips and the sight sickened her, although she was no stranger to the slaughtering of the farmyard.

'Maybe John is no worse nor most other men,' she told

herself, but none the less her long-stifled aversion increased, and a flood of hostile memories assailed her. As a boy he had amused himself by brutally tearing down nests full of young birds, and even now his chief recreation was what he proudly called 'a bit o' sport' – to dig out a badger amidst the yelpings of bitten and bleeding terriers or, with dogs, sticks and stones, to chase terrified rabbits that had crept into the diminishing island in the centre of a cornfield at harvest-time.

'Maybe I'm dull,' she thought, 'bein' only an 'oman, but John is seemin' to me no better nor a brute in the things he do take a delight in. He can't have no pleasure but in another's pain. Why, nothin' do make him laugh even but some disgrace or discomfort as do happen to one o' his neighbours. John and I have never once laughed together nor wept together, and 'tis that as do bind folks for life, whether they be kindred or no. Rhys is right, I do believe – blood is not thicker than water. 'Tis only the spirit as do draw two people close, and the spirit as do put them asunder.'

'What are you starin' at me for like that?' John demanded as he strode in, pulling on his coat. He was so busy with it that he did not notice the basket on the hearth and stumbled over it. The next moment he had kicked it deliberately so that it fell on its side. The startled cat sprang out, and the kittens sprawled over the stone-flagged floor.

'What d'you keep them nasty good-for-nothin' cats about the place for? Here, I'm goin' to drown the lot.'

Stooping, he seized the five of them like a handful of dirt. They set up a pitiful little outcry that angered Esther still further against him.

'You leave them poor little things alone,' she cried, snatching them out of his hands.

He stared at her, astonished to see her face flushed and her eyes bright with tears. Her lips were still quivering with indignation when she returned, having carried her pets to a place of safety.

'Whatever's on you, gal? Why don't you look sharp and get my tea?'

'Yes. That's all you do think of, your meals and whatever you do want. You're like father – you're the very spit of him in your looks, and your nature's the same too; there's no pity in it, no thought for others, no care for anyone or anything as is weak or helpless or sorrowful.'

'What 'ould you have me be? Soft and womanish?'

'What I'd have you be is a man like Rhys Lloyd. Yes,' she repeated defiantly as she saw his expression change from contempt to anger. 'Rhys Lloyd. There's a man as is thinkin' o' somethin' besides what he do eat and how he can ruin his neighbour. He's pitiful to the poor and oppressed. He's wantin' women to be treated fair, and children to be given their chanst whilst they're young, and the world to be a better place than you and your father and the likes o' you have been makin' it.'

'Look here,' he shouted. 'My father was your father too, and you did ought to be ashamed o' yourself takin' up with one o' his enemies. He'd rise from his grave to curse you, if he knowed of it.'

'I dare say he 'ould. Revenge and tyranny were all he were thinkin' on, same as you.'

'Aren't you afraid of a father's curse?'

'Not now,' she said. 'If I am tryin' to lead a better life

342

than my father did, why should I heed his wicked, cruel quarrels?'

Their angry eyes met in challenge. Hers were bright, his slowly turning bloodshot.

'I know what it is,' he growled after a pause, 'that villain has been poisonin' your mind with his notions. I've been warned as you was keepin' company with him – but I 'ouldn't believe it. I 'ouldn't believe it,' he repeated, striking the table with his clenched fist. 'You as was havin' the chanst o' marryin' the parson – a parson as is havin' money o' his own; mind you, I 'ouldn't believe as you'd be mad enough...'

He broke off and stood speechless with fury and amazement.

Out in the fold the dogs began to bark. Esther went to the window, started, and turned to him with an attempt at a laugh.

'Here is your parson comin': you'd best go and welcome him in.'

He had more ado to control himself than she had. His face was still flushed and the veins on his temples stood out like string when he opened the door in response to a modest knock. With faintly bitter amusement Esther watched his endeavours to be cordial, and passively extended her hand when Mr Jones approached her. His manner and countenance were grave, but he did not look like a man who had suffered more than transitory disappointment. Since the night of Rhys Lloyd's return she had scarcely spoken to him. When they met at the church door he shook hands with her, reproachfully, she fancied, rather than with warmth as hitherto. But he had the same bland word for

343

everyone and preached the same soothing sermons full of sentimental anecdotes of good Christian homes and lost sheep led back at last to the fold.

'Tea?' he was saying, his heavily lidded glance travelling appreciatively over the table. 'That's very kind of you, Mr Bevan – I shall be delighted.... How are things going? Not very well, I'm afraid. A parson's life has its anxieties the same as a farmer's, you know. Thank you, a little of your sister's excellent cake. Yes, weeds spring up in my field as well as in yours. That library of this eccentric Mr Lloyd's is causing me some uneasiness.'

Esther looked up from the teapot to see two pairs of eyes fixed on her. 'What did I tell you about the blackguard?' her brother's said plainly, but Mr Jones seemed to be uncertain how far he might go and was watching her cautiously for signs of resentment.

'I don't holt with no libraries,' John announced. 'Puttin' a lot o' nonsense into the heads o' young people and causin' 'em to waste time as did ought to be better employed.'

Mr Jones smiled an apology at Esther.

'Oh, of course you're a practical farmer. Personally I'm in favour of judicious reading for everyone. You can't put back the hands of the clock, Mr Bevan. The days of the good old-fashioned farm labourer who could not read or write and thought of nothing but his daily task are over.'

'More's the pity, I do say. This boy I've got now...'

John began a tirade against the 'goin's on' of his farm hand, and Esther lost the thread of his discussion. When the lad himself thrust his tow-coloured head in at the door the interruption came as a shock to her.

'Boss! Boss!' he cried joyfully. 'The old sow is goin' to

farrow. Come you on, quick.' Then, seeing the parson, he giggled and clapped a red hand over his mouth. John rose with alacrity.

'Will you be excusin' of me, Mr Jones, please? Get on out o' the way, boy, don't stand starin' like a stuck scarecrow.'

The door slammed behind them, and the sound of their footsteps died away in the fold. Esther sat with sad indifference, staring at the raindrops that trickled down the window pane.

'They'll never give my Rhys a hearin',' she was thinking. 'The time is not yet ripe for such a prophet as he.'

Her guest shifted in his chair.

'Miss Bevan.'

'Yes, Mr Jones, sir?'

'I came here to have a talk with you on an awkward – that is – a – a difficult subject.'

'Yes, Mr Jones.'

'I want you to understand that I am speaking solely in my capacity as your vicar – that I am not presuming on our personal friendship – though naturally that makes my task still less easy.'

'I understand, Mr Jones.'

'Thank you – thank you. I am sure you will realise how painful it is for me...'

'What is it you do want to say?'

He was disconcerted by her direct question and the steady gaze of her wide-set grey eyes, but he made an effort to come to the point.

'You have been brought up as a Churchwoman.'

'Yes.'

'Well, I should be sorry, more sorry than I can say, to see your faith unsettled by...'

'By?'

Her composure drove him to desperation. He began to speak quickly.

'Miss Bevan, I will be plain. There are rumours afloat. They may not be true. Please do not think me impertinent, but people are talking about this Mr Lloyd and yourself. It is said you may even be induced to marry him, although he is turning your brother out of his farm.'

He waited for her denial, but none came. A spasm of pain contracted her closed lips.

'If you are tempted to do anything rash,' he continued earnestly, 'let me urge you to consider what manner of man he is.'

"Tis what I have been thinkin' on all night,' she answered in a low voice.

'I am glad to hear it. He appears to have no religion. He is a most undutiful son, and from what I can hear quarrelled with the uncle who adopted him as a boy. Even his political views are unsound. He has no more veneration for the State than he has for the Church. He is a revolutionary – a troublesome and dangerous fellow, in my opinion. Do you believe that such a man would make a good husband?'

He waited for her reply, but only the old clock ticked out its invariable comment.

'Miss Bevan,' he asked at length, 'are you going to marry him?'

Slowly she raised her eyes. The shadows beneath them seemed to have deepened.

346

'No.'

He heaved a sigh of relief.

'You are very wise – I'm glad that you have thought better...'

She cut him short: 'Shall I be tellin' you why I 'on't marry Rhys?' Her face was very pale now and her lips quivered. ''Tis along o' his bein' so much too good for me. I'm afraid – afraid in my heart, as I might hinder him. He's havin' a great mission in life.' Her voice rang out suddenly clear and she threw up her head. 'A mission as not one o' you here is big enough to understand. Joseph's brethren you are, sayin' when you do see him, 'Behold, this dreamer cometh.' That is how it has allus been. The man as is better and wiser nor his brethren is bein' hated by them. Maybe as Rhys is come before his time and 'on't meet with honour like what Joseph did at last. But whatever do happen to him in this life, 'tis men such as he as'll be remembered after they are dead – men as is trying to change the wickedness of the world instead o' shuttin' their eyes to it, and passin' by on the other side like what you and your comfortable sort do do.'

She paused and drew her breath sharply. She had been angry when she began to speak, but was angry no longer. This smooth-faced vicar, still young but already growing stout, seemed pathetic in his bewildered resentment, his struggle after dignity. She wondered how she had ever contemplated marrying him.

To his astonishment, she rose and walked out of the kitchen. Up in the raftered room where Gladys had lain through the long months of her illness, she sat down in solitude to write her last letter to Rhys.

347

Her pen moved awkwardly over the paper and a large proportion of her few words was borrowed from the book which, above all others, she knew and loved.

'I cannot be saying as "Thy people shall be my people and thy God my God." For your thoughts are not my thoughts. There is a great gulf fixed between us.' This seemed unsatisfactory; she was afraid that it might suggest disapproval of the change in him rather than her own sense of unworthiness.

But she could make it no better, for she had only the language of outward events. She folded the letter, with a sense of finality that weakened the pressure of her fingers. Then, from the oak coffer, she lifted out the clothes he had bought her.

'They were too fine for me to be wearin',' she sighed as she made them into a parcel. 'I am not fit for the gifts of so big a man. Neither this little one nor the great gift of his love.'

CHAPTER 10

Esther went about her work numbed by a realisation, slow at first but increased by the passing of each monotonous hour, of all that her decision had meant and would yet mean to her. She had begun to see that, so far as her life on earth was concerned, its effects would be continuous; she would grow old beneath their burden, the fires of renunciation would die down, leaving her cold and desolate; she had passed upon herself a life sentence from which there was no reprieve. And she saw herself, with a flash of imaginative terror that her grief made possible, as a parched and shrivelled hag, the contempt of those who would support her declining years, who yet secretly guarded a little hoard of memories which would then be all the surviving riches of her emptying soul. Memories of what might have been. Memories of what might still be, her agony cried, if she had the weakness – or was it the strength? – to recall her letter.

John would now come into meals lowering with disapproval, order what he wanted, and relapse into silence. The hired lad, awed by his master's ill-humour, scampered away whenever he could upon business of his own. Only the animals she had loved so long rewarded her with their companionship. Apart from the consolation – itself almost a hurt – which their friendliness gave her, she fought her battle unaided.

On the eighth day after the sending of her parcel to Rhys, she left the kitchen in the early afternoon and, with the basket containing the men's tea upon her arm, set out for the dingle below the house where they were working. When she reached the gate of the cornfield, she set her basket on the topmost bar and paused. The postman was plodding up the track towards her. She had intended her letter to be final, and at first had expected no reply, but, as the lonely days passed, a traitor hope had sprung up in her, and she could not help watching the approaching figure with a pang of excitement.

Perhaps Rhys would not be satisfied by one refusal. She tried to put the thought from her. He must be free to follow his calling; she had been right to tell him so; if once more he asked her to marry him she could only reply as she had replied and suffer a second agony of renunciation. Better that the postman should come empty-handed from now onward to the end of her days. Nevertheless, her pulses quickened as his hand went to his bag.

'Anythin' for me?' she asked with attempted indifference.

'Not today indeed. There's only one of these old circulars from the Farmer's Co-operative Union – the Llangantyn branch by the postmark. 'Tis for your brother.'

Esther remembered him as he had been on the day when he had brought her the letter which announced Rhys' departure for Canada. More shrivelled and battered by rough weather, lacking now altogether some of the teeth which, so long as she had known him, had been darkened by decay, he was still like a rat, hardy but ageing fast. ''Twas long ago,' she thought, 'for him and for me. Gettin' old, too, he is.'

'Well,' she said aloud, 'I must be gettin' along down with John's tea. Shall I take the circular for you?'

'Thank you, if you'll be so good. 'Twill save me to go down the dingle.' He leant across the gate and shot at her a dark, curious glance. 'I daresay your brother is a bit daunted, like?'

'Over havin' to leave the old place?'

He stood back and looked at her, not doubting that she knew as well as he did what was in his mind. But he admired her skill – close she was and clever, not givin' nothin' away.

'Well, no,' he said slowly. 'I wasn't thinkin' o' that in partic'lar, though that's gone against him too, no doubt.'

'Well, I don't know o' nothing else,' Esther answered, beginning to wonder uneasily how far the conclusion of her affair with the parson had become a subject for pitying or scornful comment. She saw suspicion deepen in the postman's little black eyes.

'Why, this accident! Maybe 'twill cost him a pretty penny.'

'What accident?'

His suspicion vanished; his eyelids went up in genuine surprise. '*What* accident! You don't mean to tell me as he's not mentioned it to you?'

351

'I'm not knowin' nothin'.'

'Well, well, well! Maybe I'd best not tell you, but you'll hear soon enough when Lloyd the library do claim compensation.'

'Lloyd?'

'Yes, yes. 'Tis an ak'ard business, he bein' your brother's landlord now.'

'Why? – why? Is he hurted?'

'By what I do hear his right foot is hurted terrible. The doctor was tellin' Betsy Jones the shop as 'twere a much more painful and troublesome business nor if he'd broken his leg.'

She stared at him stupidly, making none of the appropriate exclamations which a bringer of such news had a right to expect, and asking none of the questions he was itching to answer.

''Twas like this,' he went on at last in a tone of aggrieved determination, having waited in vain for some show of interest. 'By drivin' home from market four days ago, your brother was passin' through Lewisbridge where there's a nasty old narrow bend in the road, as you do know, close to Mr Lloyd's cottage. He were standin' just outside talkin' to some boys. There's allus a lot o' boys about his place after his books or summat, and the pony takin' fright a bit...'

'Yes, yes! Was he knocked down?'

'If you'll wait a bit,' said the postman, encouraged at last by this outbreak of impatience, 'I'll tell you how it did all happen, though, mind you, there's some as do say as your brother was pullin' the horse on purpose to do Mr Lloyd an injury.' He watched her closely. ''Tis terrible

352

what some folks'll say. I've heard tell afore now…'

'Here,' Esther cried, pushing her basket into his hands. 'Do me a kindness – take the tea down to John.'

Without a word of explanation she left him and ran breathlessly up the path to Pengarreg. A few minutes later she reappeared, wearing a hat and coat and carrying a market basket into which she had thrust a few of her belongings. She walked quickly, unaware of the afternoon's heat. Her brother saw her, straightened himself in amazement and shouted as she passed; but she did not hear him. She must go to Rhys; she must lose no time. The joy of swift decision and action had driven all other thought from her mind.

Even when she had reached the valley and was passing through Lewisbridge, she did not check her pace. She knew that it made her conspicuous and that the inquisitive glances cast at her from cottage doors would be followed by heated discussion of her affairs and the possible reasons for her haste. Little she cared, now that at last her mind was made up and her purpose clear. The church and chapel, scowling at each other across the highway, sent her thought back through the years and a smile moved on her lips as she remembered the long struggle, the enduring bitterness, for which, in her own life, those opposing buildings had stood. She could smile because, being ended at last, it had already begun to seem unreal to her.

A riot of flowers in Rhys' small garden put to shame his neighbours' neglected patches. As she knocked at his door she noticed, almost with personal pride, that the paint on his woodwork was a lively green and his walls were freshly

353

whitewashed. That there was no answer to her summons recalled her from a vaguely possessive dream. She knocked again, waited a little, and knocked loudly a third time. A hungry cat ran up mewing to be let in, and a suggestion of loneliness and desertion in its appearance set Esther's heart beating with sudden fear. Had Rhys gone away? An instinct told her that, if he had, he would never return and she never see him again. The cottage would be empty if by some means she could penetrate into it. There would be nothing there to welcome her but the litter of packing and, perhaps, some intimate possession of his that he had forgotten to take with him.

Yet, if he was injured, he could not have made the necessary arrangements for so hurried a departure. The postman, too, had said nothing of his going – but she had scarcely listened to the postman. With lip trembling and cheeks flushed by the approach of tears, she hurried round to the back of the house. 'He can't be gone!' she thought. ''Tis only that he doesn't hear me yet.' On the kitchen door she rapped again, and in the silence that followed courage ebbed from her. The cat, which had kept close to her, clawed at her skirt. 'Poor pussy!' she said, touching its ear, and found suddenly that she could not say even those words again. The cat dropped from her as if aware of her emotion and afraid of it. Leaning against the doorpost, she watched it creep away, slack-tailed and melancholy. 'I've been lettin' my chanst go by,' she thought. ''Tis not comin' again to those as 'ouldn't take it whilst they might.'

Her outstretched hand touched the latch and without thought she tried it. It moved easily. At once her hope of

354

finding Rhys revived and, pushing open the door, she tiptoed into the kitchen.

The fire was almost out, choked by an accumulation of its own ashes, and the clock on the mantelshelf had stopped at five minutes to ten. On the table were heaped the disorderly remains of a meal – the white of the china now clouded by that bluish dust which is deposited by woodsmoke. In a chair drawn close to the hearth Rhys was asleep, his body twisted in grotesque discomfort, his head fallen forward, his arms loosely hanging and a bandaged foot propped up, with no cushion beneath it, on a wooden chair.

Esther was suddenly glad – so glad that her fingers went unsteadily to her throat and she swayed where she stood. His rumpled clothes, his tousled hair, some odd, almost comic looseness of his body gave him the air of a small boy who, spent and miserable, had fallen asleep from sheer exhaustion. Well, let him have his sleep out; he would not be alone or uncared for when he woke.

She unlaced her boots, and put on the slippers she had brought in her basket. Then, having taken off her hat and coat, she silently cleared the table and spread over it a clean cloth. Soon the kitchen began to look cheerfully inhabited, and, as she surveyed her work, she wondered with what strange phrase 'o' fairies or suchlike' Rhys would comment upon the miraculous change when he saw it.

At that moment there was a loud knocking at the front of the house. Rhys was disturbed by it and lifted a hand to his hair, but with a little sigh he let it drop and seemed to be asleep again. Esther ran to the back door and peeped out, to find her brother turning the corner of the house.

'Here,' he said, halting abruptly. 'What's the meanin' o' this?'

'I've come to tend Rhys Lloyd,' she answered.

'The devil you have, when 'twas I as smashed his foot for him – and a good job too. You're come to tend him indeed – you, my own sister!'

'If 'twas you as hurted him, all the more reason for me to tend him.'

'That's right. You go to take his part against me over that damned accident. 'Twas allus your way.'

She looked him steadfastly in the face.

'Was it an accident, John?' He answered with a string of oaths. When they were ended, she asked, 'What have you come here for?'

'To take you home,' he said, striding closer to her so that only a few inches divided their faces. 'D'you think as I'll have my sister whoremongerin' about the countryside?'

'You 'on't take me home save by force, and you 'on't dare use that down here in the village for the neighbours to witness.'

'Have you lost all shame! What d'you think folks'll say o' your comin' here alone to the house o' this good-for-nothin' so soon as ever he'd got rid of his last keepmiss? Why does he skulk in the house there, the coward, instead o' comin' to meet me man to man? He's not so terrible hurted that he need be afraid.'

'I don't care what people do say,' she answered. ''Tis nobody's business but my own.'

''Tis *my* business whatever! I'll tell you onst and for all, you wanton, if you 'on't come home with me now this minute, you shan't never darken my doors again.' He paused to watch the effect of this tremendous threat, but, seeing her unmoved, went on: 'D'you think that man 'ull marry you now you're come to him without, you fool? What are you goin' to do then, when my door is locked on you?'

'I haven't thought,' she said. 'But I'm goin' to stay here now along o' him and nurse him.'

He knew that it was her final word. Looking round him, he saw that the place where they stood was too public for violence. But he would have his last fling at her.

'A' right. Stay you here. Stay you here to be the shame and laughin' stock o' the parish, and when he do turn you out, same as he did do the last one, you can be goin' to the workhouse in Llangantyn for all I do care. You're no true sister o' mine, nor no daughter o' poor father's.'

'No,' she thought when he had left her, 'that's bein' true enough. But I'm shut o' the lot of 'em now.'

When she re-entered the kitchen, she found Rhys awake and staring at her. She stood still at a little distance from him, her fingers curled over the table edge, timidly smiling. But there was no answering smile upon his lips.

'Why have you come here?' he demanded in the querulous voice of an invalid.

'Didn't you hear what I said to John?'

'I heard something. You'd better go after him quickly and make your peace.'

'Rhys! And leave you here uncared for?'

'There's an old woman comes in for an hour or so and does for me, and the doctor will call in some time today.'

'And Megan?'

He pulled himself up in his chair, frowning with pain. 'I told you long ago that I was going to set her up as

357

caretaker of my village institute at Aberdulas.'

'So that's what John did mean by your havin' got rid of your – oh well. You never said as you was sendin' her there all of a sudden.'

'When I told you about it, you hadn't as good as promised to marry me. Afterwards you did, and changed your mind again. Give me down that nice little note of yours off the mantelpiece, will you? I want to light my pipe with it.'

The extreme bitterness of his tone frightened her and she hesitated. But he was ill and tired, she told herself; whatever he said now, she must not heed him; she must first of all make him comfortable and as happy as might be – then they could talk. So she gave him the letter for which he had asked. He lighted his pipe with it, puffing out the smoke with a ludicrous deliberation, and, as he dropped the charred paper into the fire, watching her sidelong with the defiance of a naughty child. She turned from him, secretly smiling.

'I'm glad as you've burnt it,' she said.

'I suppose you think that because it's burnt it's forgotten?'

She busied herself in making the fire burn up brightly, and set the kettle to boil.

'Where's your little 'un?' she asked.

'At school in Llangantyn. He's there for the week now and comes home for Sundays. A nice cheerful weekend it'll be for him this time, poor kid.'

'Oh, come you, I'll be here, and I'll bake him some cakes and summat...'

'Will you?' he interrupted. 'Will you, indeed? I don't

want you here. I won't have you coming to me out of pity if you wouldn't come out of love.'

''Twas love kept me away, bach.'

'A queer sort of love that! You wrote to me that my people were not your people, nor your God my God. If that's how you feel you'd better go home to your precious brother before it's too late. My having a smashed foot doesn't alter the position.'

He fell back, exhausted by his anger. Was that the end? he wondered as his thoughts grew more calm. Would she put on her hat, pick up her basket and be gone, leaving him with nothing but the echo of his own foolish words? Foolish he knew them to have been; yet his pride justified them to himself and he could not recall them. So he lay, staring and waiting; she must decide.

To his astonishment she made no answer, but went on with the work she had set herself – dusting the furniture, washing the dirty crockery, and preparing tea. The room was warm with sunshine that made the firelight an opaque, fixed yellow, and exposed the rustiness of her black dress. Its heavy material scarcely stirred as she moved, but hung in thick, regular folds like the drapery of a primitive statue. Though as clear-eyed and rosy-cheeked as she had ever been, she had now none of the elasticity of youth – only a dignity and power which, having distinguished her when she was a girl, had increased with the years. How odd it was that he, who could admire and love this rare quality in her, should have married a woman so different! His wife's fair, fluffy hair, her light laughter, the scent she had used, the dainty lace and frills she wore, the pert, new-world vivacity of her – how powerful their fascination had been through the tempestuous weeks of their courtship! The shock of his discovery that she was after all no more to him than a hundred other women might have been returned to him now. He had been able to share with her none of his enthusiasms; he had become lonely in her presence, finding in her gaiety only a perpetual irritation.

'It's strange,' he thought, 'how all my life I've been lonely. Only when Esther is near me is the ache of it healed, and yet she never was my intellectual companion, and now, why – she's not even pretty as she was at eighteen. Did she ever set my blood on fire in those days, I wonder? If she did, I've forgotten it. I only remember that I liked to have her near me as I do still, and that some force drove me to tell her all that I thought and felt even though I knew she'd only half understand what I said. I wonder why I never loved a more beautiful and gifted woman? There were smart American girls – but no man' – a smile came with the thought – 'no man who has loved a sing-songing Welsh woman can ever forgive them when they speak. I think it was Esther's voice I remembered in all those years when I'd almost forgotten what she looked like, and still was lonely for her. I've admired women by the dozen, but I've never really wanted but one woman.' He was half-resentful still, and would not praise her, but his eyes opened slowly and followed her as she moved to and fro.

'She's of the land,' he thought, dropping back into the idiom of his own people. 'Maybe as that is how she is bein' so dear to me. My nature is rooted in hers like, same as 'tis rooted in the soil from which the both of us was springin'.

It's a poor hard soil, no better nor that of other countries, but 'tis *ours*. Welsh I was born, and Welsh I was bred. I've tried to make the world my country and all folk my kin, but 'tis to Wales as I've come home, and to my first love.'

Having made everything ready for his comfort and seeing that again he had fallen asleep, Esther sat down to wait, her hands folded tranquilly in her lap. Such peace of mind as had not been hers for many years descended upon her as she considered each line of the face opposite her. Time had not dealt gently with Rhys. His dear face, seen now in repose without the illumination of his bright, daring eyes, was scarred by suffering more deeply than she had realised. His need of her care was greater. 'If I'd been seein' him asleep like this,' she reflected, 'I 'ouldn't have been afeard to marry him. Wiser and better nor me he may be, but for all that he do want me to look after him.'

Rhys the suitor, for whom she felt admiration and awe, had never been so dear to her as was this Rhys, the sick child who had spoken so fretfully, and had fallen asleep in his chair. This unexpected weakness would bind her to him more powerfully than his strength. She could pity him now, and laugh at him a little, and lavish upon him her passion for service. She saw him no longer as a prophet whom she might not hinder in his high calling, but as a childlike creature who could not keep his house or his life as she would keep them for him.

When he awoke from his doze he found her standing over him with a basinful of warm water. A kettle steamed on the hob, and the cat, which she had fed, was purring on the hearth. Off his guard for a moment, he allowed a glow of pleasure to pass through him as he noticed the changed aspect of the room, and his hand moved towards her in gratitude. But the movement awakened him to remembrance of what had passed, a spasm of pain attacked him and, half-fretful, half-disappointed, he let his arm drop loosely to his side and began picking at the splintered wicker of his chair.

'You'll feel more like a cup o' tea when you've washed your face and hands,' she was saying. 'I do reckon as you've sat crumpled up in that old chair all night by the look o' you.'

'You're right. I did. There was no one here to help me upstairs.' Then with an effort he demanded: 'What are you doing still here?'

'Makin' tea. There's the towel. Just you finish washing and I'll take away the basin. Time enough to talk afterwards.'

He obeyed her silently and felt refreshed.

'Esther,' he said, 'what good do you suppose your coming here is going to do me if you leave me as soon as my foot is healed?'

'I 'on't be leavin' you.'

'How am I to know that? You've failed me before.'

'I can't be goin' back to my brother,' she said, handing him his tea. 'So you'll have to be marryin' me to make an honest 'oman of me.... Bread and butter?'

'It's all very well for you to treat it as a joke, but I don't understand you. I never have. You baffle and disappoint me. You can be very cruel, Esther, you who are so kind. Why have you changed your mind all of a sudden just because my foot has been hurt?'

She sat down beside him and stared into the fire.

''Tis difficult to tell you, bach. I do think it has come

between us terrible in the past, my not bein' able to say nor write what is in my heart. Will you be bearin' with me patient?'

In spite of himself he smiled at her.

'Well now, 'tis like this,' she went on. 'When I was writin' to you as your people was not my people nor your Gods my Gods I wasn't meanin' as I didn't wish them to be so. I did allus want to share everythin' with you, but I wasn't able to do so along o' my havin' no education, and bein' no class. But today I have been seein' as maybe we aren't so far apart. You've different ways o' sayin' things to what I have, but we are of one heart and of one mind, after all.'

'How do you make that out?'

Something in his tone reminded her of Aberdulas – of the gentle way in which he had encouraged her when she had tried to make plain to him a meaning, clear enough in her own mind, but for which she could find no words.

'Like this,' she said slowly. 'Isn't it because you can't bear as small little nations should be oppressed that you are wantin' the Great Powers to protect the weak? You are not holdin' as might is right, but as strength did ought to be showin' mercy.'

The old light kindled in his eyes.

'Well?'

'Well, that is what I have been feelin' all my life too; only, bein' a 'oman and not a scholard nor a wonderful thinker like what you are, I have not been seein' it large like. 'Twasn't for me to think o' thousands o' folk unknown to me. All I was able to think on was them as was near at hand. But what I've felt for them you've felt for all mankind.'

'But if you felt for those nearest to you, Esther, why

did you let me wait year after year? Didn't you love me? Wasn't I near to you? And yet you sacrificed me again and again to your notions of duty to your family.'

''Twasn't *that* as I did sacrifice you to. I don't think as it 'ould have made no manner o' difference had poor Mother and Gladys been no kin o' mine. Terrible weak they was. That is why I was havin' to help them rather nor you as was so strong and brave.'

She looked him in the face, her wide-set eyes full of tears.

'Now are you understandin'?' she whispered.

He hardened his heart against her.

'I don't understand any woman treating a man she loved as you have treated me.'

Her tears silently overflowed. For a moment she sat without moving. Then she brushed them aside and stretched out her hand for his cup.

Having set it down, she stood beside him, her grip on his shoulder. She could say no more, and tried to convey in her touch what, it seemed, her words had failed to tell him. Or was it his pride only that held him back now? She didn't know. Perhaps before many minutes had passed his door would have closed behind her and she be once more on her way to Pengarreg.

When at last he turned in his chair, she met his eyes bravely, but with desperate longing, as if she feared never to look upon his face again. But slowly fear and the remembrance of fear died in her heart. She had ceased to think of herself or of what would become of her. If she went, what would become of him? What dark sadness would bespread the dear puzzled face now upraised to

hers? And, as if this swift change of thought had visibly
transfigured her, she saw awake in him an answering
tenderness. He took her hand from his shoulder and
pressed it to his lips.

'Esther, Esther,' he murmured, 'I do understand. I've
always understood – deep down in the heart of my love
for you. But I wouldn't admit it even to myself. You have
been as God made you – strong so that the weak turn to
you and live by your victories. That's how it's been – and
is now, you blessed, gentle one.'

Behind her, as she stooped towards him, the sun
flowed up the wall's grave shadows.

A THING OF NOUGHT

To her neighbours she was known as Megan Lloyd. In my memory she lives as Saint Anne.

Years after I had lost her, I was wandering through the Louvre, and came upon the picture attributed to Leonardo. I stood before it, happy; and my eyes filled with tears. Megan Lloyd, when I knew her, was older than this wise and gracious mother of the Virgin. Her hair was white as lamb's wool; her face, like a stored apple, seamed with fine wrinkles. Yet there was her familiar smile, full of tenderness and understanding.

She is in my mind now, seated, like Leonardo's homely saint, in the open. Often I saw her moving about the farmhouse kitchen, or sitting beside the whitewashed hearth, her fingers, as she stooped to warm them, cornelian red in the glow of a peat fire. Sometimes she had a grandchild in her lap, and another in the cradle that her foot was rocking with slow rhythm. But I remember her best as I saw her often during my last summer in Wales, out of doors, her faded lips parted a little to the hill wind.

She sat on an oaken chair upon the stretch of sward surrounding Cwmbach homestead, where hissing geese paddled to and fro, bobbing their heads on long necks. From the neighbouring buildings, white as mushrooms in the green landscape, came the cheerful noises of a farm-yard and a house full of lusty children. Her eldest son, dark and dour, clothed in earth-brown corduroys, her busy shrill daughter-in-law, her tribe of swarthy grandchildren, to me were present only as a background to Saint Anne. They and their home were like the walled towns, the cavalcades of horsemen, the plumed trees, behind the central figure of the Madonna in some fifteenth-century altar piece. They had no connection with my tranquil saint. Their toil and clatter, their laughter, quarrelling and crying did not disturb us, who were the only two human beings of leisure in the countryside.

I was idle and self-tortured throughout that long hot summer. The harsh gales of spring were raging through my mind, unemployed and as yet empty of experience. She was profoundly calm; serene as an autumn evening after a tempestuous day, when the wind has fallen and the dead leaves lie still. It was with difficulty that she dragged herself abroad. Her fingers were twisted with rheumatism; she could no longer work. She could not even see to read her Bible. So, during these last months of her life, she sat, content to wait for death, with hands folded, while she watched the shadows of the hills on either side of

370

Cwmbach as they stole across the narrow valley. The shade of the eastern hill dwindled behind the house as the sun reached its zenith; that of the western hill advanced when the sun began to sink. Little Cwmbach was so strait that only for an hour at noon was its whole width lit by sunshine. The mountains rose like walls on either side, shutting out the world. Down in the dingle lay the solitary farm and a stern chapel, square and grey, with the caretaker's cottage clinging to its side, as a white shell to a strong rock. An angry stream, hurling itself against boulders, foamed between these two dwelling places, and a thin ribbon of road wound its empty length up over the pass, where the hills converged.

Day after day I climbed across a waste of heather, moss and bog, and, scrambling down the channel of a waterfall, flung myself at Saint Anne's feet. I was eighteen. The universe to me was the stage upon which my own tragedy was being acted. I talked by the hour about myself and my important emotions. She listened with inexhaustible patience. When I told her that no one had ever loved or suffered as I did, she smiled, not with derision, but sadly, as one who knew better.

If I looked up at her and found her smiling in that fashion, I fell silent. Then, after a while, she would begin to talk. It was thus I came to know her lover, her husband and her child. Her words were few, but they had magic to conjure up the dead. I knew so well their looks, their manner of speech, their gestures; it is hard to believe that never in my life did I see them, save through her eyes, or hear their voices except as an echo in her memory.

* * *

371

She was eighteen when she went to Pontnoyadd fair and fell in love with Penry Price, son of Rhosferig. He was tall, broad-shouldered, wind-tanned, blue-eyed. His laughter had reached her, gay and good-natured, so that she loved him before ever she set eyes upon his beauty. She edged her way forward through the press of admiring yokels by whom he was surrounded. He was in his shirtsleeves, hurling a wooden ball at an Aunt Sally. With a superb swing he brought his right arm back and flung the ball with such force that the coconut he aimed at flew out of its stand and broke to pieces. A chuckle of applause arose from the spectators. He turned round to smile at them, displaying teeth white and strong as those of a young savage. Picking up another ball, he threw it with all his might, smashing the target as before. One after another, he brought the coconuts down, until a heap of broken winnings lay scattered at his feet. The owner of the booth watched him with apprehensive admiration, and the murmuring of the onlookers rose at last to a shout. Megan could not take her eyes off him. His cap and coat lay on the ground. The sun on the bright hair gave him the splendour of a warrior in a helmet of gold. His shirt sleeves were rolled up, and the hairs on the back of his freckled arms glinted like a smear of honey. The sweat of exertion made his shirt cling close. She could see his muscles swell. To her, who seldom looked on any young man but her own weakling brother, this hero of the fair appeared a god. She held her breath with joy when he turned round and began to distribute his earnings to the children in the crowd. '*There now!*' she thought, proud as a mother. He was as good and generous as he was strong and handsome! 'Any gal 'ould have been bound to love him,' she was wont to tell me, 'he was such a *man*. There was summat about him of a child, too.'

Soon he caught sight of her brother, who had brought her to the fair, and greeted him with a slap on the shoulder.

'This is my sister as you are not knowing,' announced the boy, pushing Megan forward.

Looking down at her eager face, Penry flushed self-consciously. 'And shy, also, like myself,' she thought. 'Who ever 'ould have guessed it!' Should he treat her to a ride on the roundabout, he asked, stammering. She was too excited to answer, but nodded her head, whilst her colour came and went and her green eyes sparkled, like dew on spring's first grass.

She went with him, elated by the scene – the white tents pitched upon the wet and shining field; the dizzy kaleidoscope of colours formed by roundabouts flashing with brass and gypsies' choice of paint; the throng of country folk, forgetful today of their Puritanism; the discordant clash of three or four organs playing different tunes, of bells ringing and people laughing, talking, shouting; the holiday jostling and fun of it all.

'There's pretty you are,' said a young man, ogling her. She was glad that Penry heard, and marched her off quickly. She glanced at him from under her straw bonnet. Perhaps she really was good to look upon? Devoutly she hoped so. Her hair was parted demurely in the centre, brushed down each side of her oval face, and twisted in a neat coil at the nape of her neck. She wore her Sabbath gown of black alpaca, and the shawl of white cashmere with a red fringe in which her mother had been married. In a new pair of slippers 'her feet beneath her petticoat like little mice stole in and out'. To the front of her tight-fitting bodice was pinned a posy of cottage garden flowers. Her breasts were small and firm as apples; her waist was slim. She looked winsome, and Penry thought so, evidently, for he stayed close to her the rest of the day, and showed her the many delights of the fair: the gypsy fortune-teller, who promised each of them a faithful and pretty sweetheart; the monstrous fat woman in tights and spangles; the shooting gallery where goldfish could be won; the acrobats and jugglers, the wrestlers and daubed clowns. By all these pagan wonders Megan was enchanted. She drove home that evening beside her sleepy brother in the jolting farm cart with her heart beating and her temples throbbing. For nights after, she dreamed of Penry. The sound of footsteps, a knock at the door brought hot colour to her checks.

He came on the fifth day. It was the Sabbath. She was trying to read the Psalms, but closed her Bible quickly as she saw him vault down from his pony. He asked leave to stable it at Cwmbach farm. 'I have come to hear the preacher at your chapel,' he explained to her brother, who grinned.

Penry flushed, and her father replied: 'He's a tidy minister, but I never heard tell as he was noted for his eloquence…. Still, you're welcome, young man.'

So Penry stayed to tea, and at dusk walked over to chapel side by side with Megan. There, in a dream of Paradise, she listened to him singing in his hearty bass voice.

'What a voice he was havin',' she would say. 'Goin' through me it was, deep down into my heart. Onst I had heard him sing, it was as if I was belongin' to him ever after. He was *here* – always.' And she would lay her gnarled hand, with wrinkled skin loose on the knuckles, upon her shrunken breast.

I did not dare look up at her when she spoke of her lover's singing. At such times I knew that tears were trickling down her cheeks. Of all the suffering through which she had passed, she could speak in her old age dry-eyed; but not of that happy voice, to remember which was ecstasy.

'They was all listenin' to him in chapel; and praisin' his singin' after. But *I* wasn't able to say nothin'. Feelin' too much, I was.'

After that first Sunday, he came again often from his father's farm which lay twelve miles away over the wind-scoured hills. He was a general favourite, whom Megan's parents welcomed to a meal and heard with indulgent disapproval when he told of fights, fairings and poaching. They were strict Calvinistic Methodists. A pious gloom hushed their home when Penry was not in it. To Megan he seemed a dazzling shaft of sunshine which had pierced its way into the darkness of a tomb.

'I was livin' in a family vault afore he came,' she said to me once. 'Indeed, he was my Saviour, bringin' me hope o' a glorious Resurrection. God forgive me if I do take His name in vain. 'Tis not in blaspheming. For Penry was my life, as Christ is the life o' good religious Christians.'

She spoke to him seldom, being content to listen to his voice, and to his laughter that made her happy, hot and afraid. It was to her he spoke when he addressed her parents or her brother. His tales of daring escapades were told to them in order to amuse her. When she joined, wholehearted, in their reluctant mirth, he grew still gayer. Sometimes he and she exchanged a glance full of understanding.

So she existed from week to week, going about her drudgery in a trance, waiting for Sunday till she should live again. Monday and Tuesday were hateful days, empty and cold. On Wednesday anticipation began to revive. Was it not already the middle of the week? Throughout Thursday and Friday her impatience mounted. On Saturday she was secretly distraught. Tired though she was by long hours of labour, she could scarcely sleep that night, but lay tossing in the darkness, asking herself again and again: 'Will he come tomorrow? Will he come?' If he came, she was supremely blissful, until the hour of his dreaded departure. If he did not come, the day was leaden with disappointment, and another week of interminable length dragged itself out like a life sentence.

One Sunday Penry knocked at the door of Cwmbach farmhouse.

'There he is,' cried Megan, springing up. She had been trying for hours to hide the fact that she was on the alert for his approach. When her mother looked at her with a smile and a sigh, she hung her head, abashed.

'Come you on in, boy,' her father called, and Penry strode into the kitchen. His manner was preoccupied. He neither laughed nor boasted during dinner. The old people noticed nothing amiss, since he spoke with his usual candour when they asked him any question. Only Megan, who knew every fleet change of expression in his eyes, grew troubled. Watching him anxiously, she pushed away her food untouched. His glance avoided hers, until, as they rose from table, she laid her hand timidly on his wrist. She had never touched him before, and she withdrew her fingers as though the contact had burnt them. He stood rooted, gazing down at her. She could have fainted, fearing that he was about to take her in his arms before them all. For an instant he seemed to struggle with himself whilst she held her timid breath. Then, turning away with a frown, he addressed the others.

'I have been thinkin'. 'Tis like this. A boy as is the youngest o' five and livin' at home like I am, he isn't gettin' no manner o' chance to earn money – not even gettin' the wages of a workin' man, he isn't.' He stared at the stone-flagged floor between his feet. 'Workin' like that for twenty or thirty years maybe, and left with nothin' after.'

Megan's father nodded. 'Yes, yes. When there is more nor one or two sons, 'tis better for the younger ones to get out o' the nest.'

'Well, now, I am havin' an uncle in Australia,' Penry resumed gloomily, and Megan's eyes grew wide with fear. 'Writin' to Mother he was some years ago, and sayin' "send you out one o' the lumpers, and I'll see as he shall do well."' Megan's lips parted, but no sound came from them. 'I've a mind to go out to my uncle,' Penry announced, his tone challenging anyone to stop him. Megan leant for support against the dresser and became aware that the kitchen had grown dark. The speech of her parents and brother had a muffled sound as though it came from a long way off. They were agreeing with Penry, but she could scarcely make out what they said. Her life seemed to be coming to an end. She had turned so white that at last her mother noticed it.

'Whatever's on you, bach?' she cried, and all eyes were turned on the girl where she stood, still as a figure of stone.

'I am all right,' Megan murmured, 'only – 'tis terrible cold in here.' She moved unsteadily towards the door and went out into the pale sunshine of early spring that turned to a sad yellow the stretch of sward before the house. The smell of moist earth and the sound of many streams were in the air. The hills, that had been brown and sombre all the winter through, were beginning to grow green, except where a patch of snow still lingered in a hollow. Everything was awakening to new life. Yet Megan felt as though her blood were ebbing away.

After a while she heard her mother's voice calling from the small window overhead. ''Tis time to get ready for chapel.'

'I am not going,' she answered, and remained motionless, staring at the wide sweep of open hillside across the valley. From the time she was a little child, the vastness of the hills had brought her comfort in distress. At this moment she could not endure to have them shut out from her sight. So she stayed while the little group of black-clad figures came out of the house, and made their way soberly across the valley.

When the landscape was once more empty, and the silence of the hills unbroken but for the voices of wind and waterfall, Penry also came out of the house, and laid his hand on Megan's shoulder. She started and, turning round, looked up at him with eyes full of suffering. He was gazing at her as he had done when she touched his arm in the kitchen, and her heart began to beat again violently.

'Why are you goin' away?' she made bold to whisper, with a catch in her throat.

'Because it was comin' to me, sudden like, when last I

378

seed you, that I couldn't live no more without you.'

She gave a sob of joy and wonder. 'But you are goin' away from me where I 'ont never see you.'

'Only to make a home for you there, Megan bach,' he answered, and his eyes travelled caressingly over her face, the silky, lustrous brown hair around it, the curves of her slender neck. Then, because he could find no words to say, he picked her up in his arms, and carried her into the house. There he set her on his knee. She sat very still for a long while, with her head drooped on his shoulder. Fear and suffering no longer existed for her; nor did time. In a moment she had been raised from the depths of despair to giddy heights of happiness beyond belief. The upward flight had left her weak, and with a queer sensation of dizziness. She clung silently to Penry, and listened to the throbbing of his heart close to her own. The strength of his muscle-hard arms around her was consoling. They gave her a sense of safety. Nothing, she fancied in this hour of ecstasy, could ever take her from him. She was profoundly content.

After a while, his hand stole up to her small chin and raised her face gently to his. Their lips had never met before. They did not soon part.

Penry came again to Cwmbach oftener than hitherto; and, since the young people were from henceforth admitted to be 'courting', they were allowed to sit up together, according to custom, long after the rest of the household had gone to bed. They sat hand in hand in the glow of a peat fire, and talked in whispers. What they said would have conveyed nothing to anyone else, for they had much to tell which neither could put into words. They looked, sighed, smiled and kissed. Sometimes they

379

laughed low, and sometimes they clung together throughout a long silence. They understood each other perfectly. Their love filled the world for them. There was no serpent in their Eden. Even the thought of the impending parting did not greatly dismay them – they passed it over, and looked forward already to the time when they should meet again and be always together. They believed that such love as theirs must needs triumph over poverty, and that neither time nor distance could make it grow dim. Talking thus, they would throw more peat on the embers. The fire would leap up and the light of it flicker on the low ceiling. Wicked little shadows would run hither and thither, as if mocking the lovers and their happy fancies. But they did not heed – being too glad for fear, until their eyelids grew swollen for lack of sleep and dawn looked in upon them, ghostly grey.

'Cold,' Penry would say with a sudden shiver. 'Is it?' Megan would ask. 'I wasn't noticin'.'

It was not until the autumn, when Penry had gone away, that Megan began to realise the meaning of that dread word 'parted'. Then her longing to see him and to hear his voice became a physical torment, and she would be awake at night struggling with her sobs, telling herself in vain that this separation was but for a little time.

The winter set in pitiless. For months the pass at the top of the valley was snowbound, and even the pious few who attended Alpha Chapel in lonely Cwmbach were kept from their devotions. Megan went about her household duties day by day, silent and subdued, finding the weeks and months of waiting, which were to have sped by so swiftly, intolerably long. She wrote to Penry every

Saturday night; but letter-writing was to her a labour, exceedingly slow and toilsome; and when the ill-spelt letters, that had cost such pains, were returned to her long after, with 'Not known at this address' scrawled on them, she abandoned herself to despair. It seemed as though she would never hear from Penry, never be able to reach him, now that the unknown had closed upon him. She tormented herself with the thought that he had died on the voyage out; until at last, almost a year after he had gone away, she received his first letter. It was despondent in tone, but still she hugged it to her as evidence that he was still alive, and not irrevocably lost to her.

He had arrived in Australia, so he wrote, to find that his uncle was dead, and that no work was to be obtained in that locality. There had been a succession of droughts, and prospects were very bad; still, he had managed, after great difficulty, to find temporary employment on a sheep ranch. He feared that making a home for his Megan would prove a longer business than they had thought, but, if she would wait for him, he would never give up the struggle.

Wait for him? What else could he fancy there was for her to do? What was she living for but the time when they should meet again? She laughed at him for imagining that she could ever give any other man a thought. She carried his letter about inside her bodice, and slept with it under her pillow, until it was tattered and crumpled. Then, lest she should wear it out altogether, she put it away in the oak chest where she kept the coloured daguerreotype he had sent her of himself before he sailed from Liverpool. It was her most cherished possession, too well beloved to be exposed; to be taken out and looked at only by lamplight and in secret.

381

Another year went by, and another; and after that, in her loneliness and disappointment, Megan lost count of the seasons that divided her from her lover, and, at length, even from hope. She heard from him at rare intervals. Now he was doing well, and would soon have earned enough to come and fetch her. Now another drought had ruined his employer, and he was again cast on the world, searching for work, whilst his precious store of savings, that meant happiness for them both, dwindled.

He had been gone seven years when she received a short, barely legible letter, written in pencil, much blurred, and in a laboured, childish hand. Luck was against him. She must wait for him no longer. He had been almost starving for the last month, rather than break into the store of money he had laid by. He had enough to come and fetch her now, but where was the good in bringing her out to a country in which he had no home to offer her? Every enterprise he touched failed. He had begun to think that he brought ill fortune with him wherever he went. 'Like Jonah in the Bible,' he wrote. 'I won't never bring you, my love, to ruin, you may be sure. So better think of me as dead.' There followed a cross and his signature.

This was the last letter she ever received from him. With tears dropping on to the paper, she wrote to tell him that she would never give him up. The pathetic, smudged little missive was returned unopened. He had apparently gone away, leaving no address, no indication of his whereabouts. She heard from him no more. She could not hope to obtain news of him, for she knew no one in that far-distant country. He was now utterly lost to her, as though he had passed over to another world. 'Indeed most

382

likely the boy is dead,' her parents told her, and at last she came to believe that it was so.

It was then that the new minister came to Alpha Chapel. He was unmarried, and lived alone with the deaf caretaker in the barnacle cottage clinging to the bleak wall of his house of prayer. The fame of his preaching spread abroad, and people came from far over the hills to be denounced and edified by him.

He was not old; nor did he look young. His aspect was austerely virginal, for he was tall and very thin, with a pale face, and black eyes, in which burned fanatical fire. A spiritual descendant of Savonarola, he loathed the sins of humanity, and saw terrible visions of an avenging God. He would have made a 'bonfire of vanities' and condemned to the flames whatever ministered to the gaiety of life. Religion and self-denial were to him inseparable. He was ready, in the name of his faith, to endure torture or to inflict it. Yet even he was moved to pity by the sight of Megan's pale face. He learned her story from the lips of her parents, at whose house he became a frequent visitor. She herself never spoke to him of her sorrow until one day he met her coming home from market alone, and laid his lean hand on her shoulder.

'My sister,' he said abruptly, 'I know why you are sad.' 'Oh,' she cried, flushing. 'I do hope as I don't let everyone see how 'tis with me. I am tryin' not to hurt others by the sight o' my sorrow. Indeed and I am.' 'Yes, yes,' he answered, looking into her eyes. 'I know. You endeavour to be brave; but you cannot always succeed, is that not so?' She nodded. 'Do you know why?' he resumed. 'Because you are proud.'

383

She stared at him, astonished.

'Proud,' he repeated. 'And spiritual pride is sinful. In your secret arrogance, you strive to bear the burden of your grief alone.' He had intended to preach her a sermon on the duty of casting her care upon the Redeemer, but the grandiloquent words, long premeditated, died on his lips. He found himself saying instead, quite simply: 'Won't you make a friend of me, and tell me all about it?'

She was too overwhelmed to reply; so he took the market basket out of her hands, saying as he did so: 'I can carry this home for you, at any rate.'

Lonely and unused to kindness as she was, she felt her eyes smart with tears of gratitude. 'You are wonderful good to me,' she murmured, 'and you such a great preacher too.'

'We are all alike sinners in the sight of God,' he answered, resuming once more the lofty tone that became his calling.

The following Sunday, Rees Lloyd preached upon the Christian virtue of resignation. His thin fingers strayed along the edge of the pulpit, as though they groped for something to hold fast. His gaze seemed to pierce through the whitewashed wall on which it rested, as if beyond it he beheld a sublime vision. He was in a gentler mood than usual. No longer concerned with death and judgement and the vengeance of an Old Testament Deity, but full of pity for the afflicted. '"Blessed are they that mourn for they shall be comforted,"' he quoted, and again: '"It is good for me that I have been in trouble; that I may learn Thy statutes." Without suffering,' he cried, 'there is no understanding; be not rebellious then, but resign yourselves to the hand of the Lord, knowing that whom

He loveth he chasteneth, that His loved ones may be refined as is gold by the fiery furnace.'

The black-clad congregation sat spellbound, listening to the vibrations of the preacher's voice as it rose to a shout or sank to a penetrating whisper. Down the weatherbeaten face of an old man, who had lost his wife and child, tears fell. A girl who had crept into the back of the building, huddled up in a shawl, shrinking from the contemptuous glances of her respectable neighbours, sobbed unrestrainedly. All who had suffered loss and grief were moved by the sermon. But Megan was afraid, knowing that this eloquence was directed towards herself.

'Did you like what I said today?' the preacher asked her that evening when he came to Cwmbach farm. 'Yes, indeed,' she answered, 'it was beautiful.' 'Oh,' he said impatiently, 'but was it *helpful*?'

They were standing beside the hearth in the kitchen, apart from the others, who were busy at the supper table. Megan gave him a look at once timid and thankful.

'Yes,' she breathed, scarcely above a whisper, 'it do help me somethin' wonderful to know as you are feelin' for me.'

'I would give my life to help you,' he whispered back, with such fierce intensity that she shivered and hung her head. 'Look at me,' he commanded in a low tone, but she dared not raise her eyes to his.

'Supper is ready,' her mother announced, and Megan turned away quickly with a breath of relief.

She could not define her attitude towards Rees Lloyd, his absorption in the things of the spirit, his devotion to his faith, the stirring tones of his voice, the penetrating gaze of his eyes, fascinated her; yet she feared him personally, and was never at ease in his presence. When he was near her she would have been glad to escape; but because he, of all souls in this indifferent world, had offered her his sympathy, she felt the need of him when he was gone. Her hopeless love for Penry was in no way abated; but daily the minister took a larger share in her thoughts.

Soon after this, the caretaker of Alpha Chapel died. The elders who gathered together at the funeral were concerned as to what should be done. It was not easy to find anyone who, for the pittance so poor a community could offer, would live alone in the valley where was only one other dwelling. 'If only the preacher were married,' one of them said, 'he and his wife could have the house by the chapel for theirselves.'

'Yes, yes,' they all agreed. ''Tis pity as he isn't married to a tidy 'oman as 'ould look after the place for us.'

When Rees Lloyd came to Cwmbach farm that night, Megan's father repeated to him what the elders had said. They were sitting round the kitchen table in a circle of light thrown down by a heavily shaded lamp. The rest of the room, with its low raftered ceiling and stone-flagged floor, was in semi-darkness; only a red glow shone from the hearth and was reflected in the gleaming eyes of cats that slunk about in the shadows. All the brightness in the room was concentrated on the open pages of the Bible, which lay on the table beneath the lamp. Rees Lloyd, with his hand resting upon the book, arose. His head and shoulders disappeared in the twilight above the lamp. His pale face was still visible, ghostly, with eyes shining in the gloom. He remained thus whilst the grandfather clock ticked through a whole minute, and all the while he looked fixedly at Megan. The old people sat in hushed expectancy, with faces upturned; but their daughter kept her gaze on the Bible and the taut hand clenched in the harsh light upon its sacred pages. She dared not look Rees Lloyd in the face. At length he turned his burning glance on her parents.

'Behold your daughter,' he said, in slow deliberate tones. 'This is the Lord's call to her.' 'No, no,' she cried, starting to her feet, 'not that.' 'Yes,' he persisted, 'the Lord has need of you for His service. You cannot deny His call.'

She looked about her distractedly, seeking a way of escape. The others remained awestruck, listening to this voice that compelled them in the darkness.

'Here is your appointed task in life,' it continued. 'I am a minister of the Most High; I need your help, and in helping me you will serve Him also. He is calling to you, Megan, to forget yourself and your personal sorrow; to live only for others, and for His greater honour and glory.' She made no reply. 'God is calling to you,' cried the voice, louder and more insistent than before: 'He is calling to you through me, because it shall be given to me to lead your wandering soul into the safety of His fold. Will you not come?'

She turned away into the darkness, and hid her face in her hands. 'Answer,' he commanded. 'I do want to serve God,' she whispered at last, 'but indeed, indeed, I can never be your wife.' 'Are you mad, gal?' cried the old people both together. For answer she wrung her hands. Then the voice from the darkness spoke to her more gently.

'I know what you are thinking of, Megan. You have not forgotten your first love.' She inclined her head. 'But I have need of you,' cried the voice, vibrating with

387

passionate appeal. 'I love you.' And after a tense silence, imploringly – 'Will you not come?'

Slowly, reluctantly, as if drawn towards him against her will, she stole into the circle of lamplight, and placed her cold hand in his upon the Bible.

When they were married she crossed the narrow valley from her old home to her new. There she took up the work of the chapel caretaker, and cooked the minister's meals, and kept his cottage in order, waiting on him day by day. He believed that in doing this she was serving God; and he made her also believe it. Therefore she was content with her lot, and her husband in his possession of her. He had not known carnal love before, and he abandoned himself to it, indifferent to the feelings of the woman who submitted herself to his caresses.

So the weeks wore by, each like the last, marked by Sundays when up the valley and down over the pass the faithful came to worship, black as rooks. When they were gathered together in chapel, they sang their melancholy hymns, set to music in the minor key, older than Christianity, old almost as the race; and Rees Lloyd thundered at them from his high pulpit.

After the people had gone away, the shadow of the western hill stole across the emptied valley, and every trace of the congregation was gone. It seemed to Megan that with the next Sunday might come a fresh generation, for a week and an age were as one to the mountains that had looked down unmoved on the passing of one race after another.

To her husband she did not tell these fancies. It would have been difficult for her to put them into words, though as a girl she had managed to convey all she felt to Penry. But he and she had been as children together, holding hands on the threshold of a darkened room, peering awestruck into the unknown. Rees Lloyd, on the contrary, appeared to her to possess vast learning, gained from his score of theological books, which she dusted reverently every day. His positive assertion and ease of self-expression made it almost impossible for her to converse with him at all. She spoke to him always with hesitation, struggling to translate her thought into the intricacies of language – a language seldom used by the people around her except to communicate the needs of daily life. To have contradicted any of her husband's dogmatic pronouncements would have been open heresy, and she dared be a heretic only in secret. She admired him. She sat demurely listening to his eloquence Sunday after Sunday, aware that his knowledge of many matters was as great as was her ignorance. Yet in the wisdom of her humility, she guessed that he was well instructed rather than wise. His wrath against sinners made her sigh. For his famished lusting after her body she felt a shrinking pity.

He had gone one day to preach at a distant chapel. She stood with arms folded on the stone wall before their home, and mused upon the strangeness of their marriage. Her gaze was on a point where, at a bend in the valley, the road was lost to sight. Something about that lonely road, leading away into a world she had never seen, fascinated her. She often stood thus, staring. Today she felt unable to take her eyes off it, though it was time she locked up the house and crossed over the stream to her former home. Whenever her husband was away, she returned to

Cwmbach farm 'for company'; but this evening the profound stillness held her entranced. As she lingered in the mellow golden sunlight, a speck appeared upon the road and grew presently into the figure of a man. When he had come closer, she saw that he was unusually tall, and was swinging along at a great pace. He carried a stick in one hand, and a bundle slung over his shoulder. He drew near rapidly, and she noticed that he wore no hat and that his fair hair and beard glistened like honey in the sun. Her curiosity was awake now, for a stranger was seldom seen in the Cwm. She leant over the wall, intently watching his approach. As he came closer still, she could see that his face was sunburnt, making his blue eyes appear startlingly light; they were fixed upon her. Something stirred within her breast, as though her heart, long dormant, had awakened, and begun once more hotly to beat. The rugged strength of this strange man's features was familiar. The upward tilt of the chin, though hidden by a luxuriant beard, recalled a favourite pose of *someone* whose face she had once known – someone – who was it? The next instant the ground beneath her feet seemed to have given way.

'Did you ever dream as you were fallin' off of a tremendous high place?' she asked me when she was describing the sensations of that moment. 'That's how I was feelin', and I wasn't wakin' up neither, as you are doin' after a bad dream. I seemed to go on fallin' and fallin' for a long while, and then to hang in the air, as if there wasn't nothin' below me nor above, nor on either side. It was the sound of his voice as brought me back to myself, at last – the same voice, strong and deep as ever, not changed even so much as his face was. Only I was havin' a terrible feelin'

as if I was listenin' to the dead; and I was tryin' to pray –
"God help me, God help me." But there didn't seem to be a
God no longer, seein' as *this* had happened.'

She sat twisting her fingers together when she told me
this. 'What did *he* say to you?' I asked at last, caressing
her knee. '"Megan," he was sayin', coming close up
against the other side o' the wall, "are you rememberin'
me?" I was leanin' against the wall, my strength havin'
gone clean from me, and lookin' up into his face. I knowed
it well, every line of it. It seemed 'twas only yesterday as
he'd gone away – only there was more power in his face
like, and lines round his eyes, as wasn't there before. Very
thin and strong it looked, not so round and boyish; but
handsomer nor ever. I wasn't answerin' him for a while,
but was lettin' my eyes have their fill of what they'd been
weepin' for many a long year. When I could find my voice,
I was answerin': "I am rememberin' you right enough –
diar anwl, could I ever forget you?"

'"You *did* forget me, whatever," says he, "when you
married another man. They told me down in Pontnoyadd
how 'twas; but I 'ouldn't believe them, no, not one of 'em,
till I saw it with my own eyes." He was lookin' at the ring
on my hand, as I held by the wall for the weakness in my
knees. I looked down at it too, and I turned as cold as if
I'd been standin' on top o' the hills in a bitter winter. I
couldn't speak for a long while after, to tell him how I
comed to get married; but we was lookin' at each other all
the time, quite still, and frightened like, same as people
that had seen a corpse candle.'

She could not tell me, but I knew what turmoil of
emotions assailed her during this silence that seemed to her

391

tormented soul to last through an eternity. For she knew, as she looked upon Penry, that here was the man who had possessed her heart entirely from the day on which she had first set eyes on him; and that she had no love for her husband, with whom she must live out her days to the end. She looked back on her own passive calm of a few moments ago, as though she were looking across a gulf of time, knowing that the relative contentment of her first months of married life could never again be hers. *He* had returned. He would go away, no doubt, suddenly as he had come, and she would most likely never see him in this world again. But in these threatened moments, as she stood scrutinising his face, the ecstasy and passion of first love, the yearning of years of hope deferred, reawakened within her; and she knew that never for an instant could she forget him again. The memory of her promise to 'love, honour and obey' another man tormented her. Honour and obey – yes, she could continue to do that, but *love* – was it possible to keep such a promise? Was it right to force anyone to make it? Could she ever again suffer the caresses of Rees Lloyd? At the thought of them she sickened. The future appeared to her so unbearable that she prayed God to take pity on her and let her die, now, whilst she stood looking up at the man whom she adored. But God was without mercy, since He had suffered her to betray Penry's trust. Why had she received no warning that he was yet alive? Why had she not waited for him just a few months more? Wherein had they both deserved this cruel suffering? Was there no compassion, no justice even, in the universe?

I do not know to what depths her soul went down during that long silence. She spoke to me of it once only,

392

and then in broken sentences. She was never quite at home in English, and there are feelings too deep for any language to convey. It was forty years afterwards that she related to me this episode in her life, but as I looked up into those quiet deep-set eyes of hers, I saw such a haunting of anguish that I turned away.

At last they began to talk. Simply, in a few words, they told each other what had happened. Soon after Penry had written her the last letter she received, he had succeeded in finding work with a man who paid him good wages and treated him as a friend. He still had those cherished savings of his. Grown reckless with ill fortune, he sank them all in a speculation into which he and his employer entered together. To his delight and astonishment, the concern prospered. Soon he had doubled his small hoard and wrote to tell Megan that a turn had come in the tide of his affairs, that he would be home within the year to fetch her. That letter, which should have reached her just before her marriage, miscarried.

'Duw, Duw,' she cried, wringing her hands, 'why was I never gettin' it? I didn't hear from you, diar anwl, and the years was passin' by, and they was all tellin' me as you were dead.'

'I do wish as I had died out there,' he answered, 'I can't go back to the place where I've made a home for you; nor I can't bear to stay here where you are livin' as another man's wife.'

'What will you be doin', then?' she asked him.

''Deed and I don't know,' he answered wearily. 'Maybe as I 'on't be livin' long.'

It was then that she clasped his hand in hers. At the

393

contact, fire seemed to run through her veins. Another silence fell between them, but this time there was a different look in their eyes. She forgot all her misery, her dread of the future. She lived exultantly in the present.

A moment, or an hour, may have passed; and then Penry leant across the wall, and taking her face between his hands, he kissed her on the lips. She did not remember when he let her go, nor if any more was said between them. I do not think that they spoke again. It never seems to have entered their heads to go away together. She had married Rees Lloyd, and was bound.

How he left her, Megan could never recall. When she regained full consciousness, after the delirium of that kiss, he was already a long way off, striding up the valley towards the pass. She was still standing where he had found her, leaning against the inside of her little garden wall. Nothing had changed visibly, except the shadow of the western hill, which now lay across the Cwm. As Penry disappeared from sight, the last glint of sunlight vanished from the tops of the hills.

Not until many hours later did Megan re-enter her house. She remained standing motionless until it became too dark to trace the white line of road in its ascent of the distant pass. Even then she stayed on, staring into the deepening gloom. She was not aware as yet of being acutely miserable. The magnitude of the blow she had received had stunned her, and left her unable to act, or even to think.

Perhaps she would have remained like this all night, had not her parents sent their servant girl to enquire why she had not come to supper. 'I 'on't be comin' tonight,' she managed to say, when she became conscious that someone was addressing her. ''On't you be afraid to sleep here alone?' the girl asked. 'No,' she answered, 'I'm not afraid of anything as can happen to me – now.' It was the sound of a human voice, reminding her of a life which must be resumed, that awoke her from her lethargy.

When she was alone once more, she began to pace up and down in the darkness, sobbing inconsolably like a child. Nothing broke the silence of the hills, that loomed above her, black, on either side, but the pitiful sound of her crying, and the faint sighing of the night wind.

For hours she walked to and fro, and cried, and wrung her hands. When dawn was turning the sky to a chill grey, she dragged herself into the house, and up the stairs, and fell, exhausted by suffering, on to the bed. She must have fallen asleep immediately, and have stayed in the drugged slumber of worn-out grief, for it was noon when she was awakened by her husband and her mother.

Rees Lloyd had called for his wife at Cwmbach farm that morning; but she was not there. 'There's odd she was last night, too,' the servant girl had told him, 'like as if she's *seen* something.' He had turned to his mother-in-law anxiously and asked her to come over at once to his home with him. They set off together in haste, fearing that Megan might have been taken ill. On their way across the valley they encountered the postman, who passed Cwmbach twice a week on his rounds. He was excited, and shouted to them from a distance. 'Have you seen Penry Price, son of Rhosferig as used to be?' Megan's mother stared, aghast. 'The Lord forbid,' she cried. 'Isn't he dead this long while?' 'Nor, nor,' answered the postman, coming up to them, triumphant that he should be the bearer of sensational tidings. 'Alive he is, and they do tell me as he was in Pontnoyadd yesterday. The folks there was tellin' him as your gal was married to Mr Lloyd here, but he 'ouldn't believe it. "Megan's not one to forget," says he, so he was comin' up by here to see for hisself.' 'Coming here?' Rees Lloyd interrupted. 'Yes, yes,' the postman affirmed. 'Up this road he did come sure. John Jones as was ploughin' close by seed a great tall man passin' by in the afternoon. Findin' out his mistake he was, no doubt,' the postman added, grinning at the old woman. 'Your gal's done a deal better for herself by marryin' a wonderful gifted preacher like Mr Lloyd here. She's not havin' no cause to look back, she's...' But Rees Lloyd waited to hear no more. He seized his mother-in-law by the arm, and hurried her on towards his cottage. She stole a glance at his white face and thin tight lips, and was so much alarmed that she began to wail: 'Duw, Duw, why has Penry come back to trouble us all?' Rees Lloyd made no reply, but jealousy and fear tormented him, and he hastened his pace, dragging the breathless whimpering old woman after him. When they reached the house, he flung open the door which he found ajar, and called in a harsh voice: 'Megan, Megan, where are you?' There was no answer and, dreading to find her gone, he rushed upstairs, and burst into the bedroom.

There he found her, fully dressed, but with her hair dishevelled, lying asleep upon the bed with shadows under her closed eyes. The lids were swollen with much crying. The fit of murderous jealousy that had possessed him when he heard of her sweetheart's return left him as suddenly as it had come. 'Megan bach, poor Megan bach,' he

whispered, and her mother, who had followed him into the
room, echoed 'Poor Megan bach, she must have seen him;
but indeed,' she added, 'Megan's allus been an honest gal,
and she 'on't think no more about him, now that she's
married to you; only do you be gentle with her, Rees bach.'
'I'll be gentle,' he promised, struggling to quell another
pang of jealousy at the thought that his wife should have
been so deeply affected by the return of Penry.

At that moment Megan opened her eyes. At first she
was only vaguely conscious of great unhappiness; then, as
her mother began to talk, she recalled what had happened
the night before, and turning her eyes away from her
husband, she hid her face in the pillow. 'I do wish as I
might die,' she thought. She lay there too unutterably
weary and miserable to move; whilst Rees Lloyd stood
watching her, with hatred and pity, love, desire, and
jealousy coursing each other through his tortured being.
The old woman rambled on, incessantly repeating the
phrases about duty and the will of God which she had
heard so often in chapel; and outside the little window of
the darkened room, the autumn sunshine gilded the hills,
and the larks and meadow pipits soared up singing
joyfully into a blue sky.

'Let me be,' Megan pleaded at last, 'just for a little
while.' At length they left her alone. Later in the day her
husband brought her a cupful of something to drink,
liquid which might perhaps have been tea, though it had
no flavour. He forced it between her lips. She shrank from
physical contact with him; but this act of kindness on his
part gave her a sort of desperate courage to go on living.

When he left the room, she rose unsteadily, and began

to wash her tear-stained face and arrange her disordered hair. It surprised her to find how easily these things could be done, mechanically, whilst the spirit was far away. Having set the bedroom to rights, with the precision of a machine, she went downstairs, and began, as though nothing unusual had occurred, to cook her husband's supper. He asked her no questions, but his sombre eyes followed her wherever she went, with the devotion and suspicion of an ill-treated, hungry dog.

In the weeks that followed, she often saw this expression in his gaze, invariably fixed upon her; and she grew increasingly to pity the man of whom formerly she had been afraid. In pitying him she found some solace from her grief. So she picked up the broken thread of her life, and was busy as ever about the house and the chapel, all day long. Only at night-time when her husband had fallen asleep was she able to abandon herself to her sorrow.

There came a day when Rees Lloyd was sitting moodily before the fire with a book of sermons lying unread on his knee. Megan had grown so thin that he had sent her to Pontnoyadd to see the doctor. As he awaited her return, forebodings of disaster assailed him. There had always been something elusive about his wife, he reflected bitterly. Even before the accursed return of Penry Price, she had never seemed wholly to belong to himself. Now perhaps she would cheat him altogether by dying, daring to die for love of another man! It was unjust, he swore, clenching his hands in impotent anger. She had only set her eyes on this interloper once since he left her eight or ten years ago. 'Whilst I,' cried Rees Lloyd to himself, 'I am close to her day and night, watching over her, ready to spend all I have on her, if only she would love me as I love her.' And then he added threateningly: 'And I am her lawful husband. I have a *right* to her affection.' It appeared to him dishonest of her to pine away as she was doing, for this Penry – a vagabond, with no claim on her affection.

Rees Lloyd angrily closed his book. He could not read. When Megan was not there to distract him in person, her sorrowful face haunted his imagination. She, who in the early days of their marriage had quenched his desire when need be, and at other times occupied a safe place in the background of his thoughts, had, through this unforeseen catastrophe, forced herself into his every thought and dream, awake or sleeping. He could no longer concentrate his attention upon his preaching or his prayers. He had chosen her for his helpmate; it was her wifely duty to succour and soothe him, that he might the better serve God. Now that she came between him and his devotion she was beginning to assume the aspect of a temptation sent him by the Devil.

He rose, and was frantically pacing up and down the little kitchen, trying to banish her image, when she herself came softly into the room. He turned on her his black eyes full of lustful hostility. For answer she smiled at him, yet he fancied hardly so much *at* him as *through* him, as though she were smiling at another whom she saw in his place. He scowled, suffering from a sense of unreality, wishing that she might fade away, if only he could be released thus from the nightmare in which he had been living. But she laid her hand on his shoulder. 'I am goin' to have a child,' she announced quietly.

For a moment he was too greatly surprised and overjoyed to speak. Then he took her in his arms and triumphantly kissed her. 'Now you will be mine,' he said, 'wholly mine.' She made no reply. 'When you are the mother of my child, Megan bach, you will learn to care for *me* only,' he assured her.

'You are very kind to me,' she murmured, absently. She was thinking of the child she might have borne, had she been the wife of Penry – blue-eyed and golden-haired, splendid to look upon, like himself, and she fancied that she could hear again the infectious happy laugh she remembered so well from her girlhood.

The days passed monotonously, and Megan went about her work as before. But now she wore a mysterious smile, as if she were picturing to herself something which greatly pleased her. She had set herself, scarcely conscious of what she was doing, to form the child of her dreams. Throughout her waking hours she dwelt on her memories of Penry. She rehearsed every word he had spoken to her; she recalled every characteristic gesture, every tone of his voice. They were all stored up in her heart, these precious things. The years had but overlaid them with the dust of lesser matters. When she came to search them out once more, scenes and incidents of her early courtship became distinct again, as on the day when they took place. Her picture gallery of beloved memories grew more vivid as her time drew near.

When her household work was finished, she would put a chair outside the cottage, close to the wall on which she had leant when Penry had returned. She knew the exact spot on which their hands had met; and there, evening by evening in the winter's dusk, she rested her clasped hands, as she sat picturing that last meeting in all its details. Sometimes she fancied even that she felt his parting kiss on her lips. Then, for a long while, she would sit motionless in silent ecstasy, with her eyes closed.

When she had married, she had put away the little coloured daguerreotype of Penry with her other relics of him. She had not thought it right to cherish, yet lacked the heart to destroy them. Now she brought out his portrait, and, carrying it about in her pocket, looked at it secretly a hundred times a day.

Her husband, unsuspecting, watched her covertly, and rejoiced that she should have become, it seemed, not merely content, but cheerful. He was considerate to her in a clumsy fashion. She, in return, was in all things a dutiful, submissive wife. In all things, that is, but her thoughts. These she kept to herself, as the silent hills about Cwmbach have kept the secrets of ten thousand years.

Rees Lloyd and all his kith and kin were swarthy of skin, dark-haired, black-eyed, with the long narrow skulls of a race older even than the Celt. Megan's hair was nut brown, smooth and silky to touch. Her eyes were the colour of the peat streams that ran down her native hillsides, neither altogether brown, nor green, nor amber, but each in turn, according to the light in which you saw them. The child that was born to these two some nine months after the return of Penry was blue-eyed and had a crop of close yellow curls all over his head. When Megan's mother took the crumpled scrap of flesh out of the doctor's hands, she stared at him with grave misgiving; after which she hastened to tell her son-in-law that his firstborn 'favoured' a maternal great-grandfather, the only one of her family whom she could recollect to have had blue eyes. She

401

assured the neighbours that the likeness was remarkable. As the ancestor in question had been dead and buried for half a century, they could not contradict her. Nevertheless, the matrons who went to see Megan's baby whispered about it as they came out of chapel.

Rees Lloyd had a puzzled, incredulous way of staring at the infant; and Megan from the moment when he was put into her arms, as she lay half dead with pain and exhaustion, loved him idolatrously. She would sit for hours in silent adoration of the child in her lap.

Had Rees Lloyd been a Catholic, he might have accepted this miracle, which filled his wife with glad devotion, and have been content to play the role of meek Saint Joseph. But being a Calvinistic Methodist, he indulged in no specially tender sentiment about the Holy Family. Moreover, he believed in no miracles excepting those recorded in the Bible. Such things had happened once; this he was constrained to believe on Divine Authority; but that nothing miraculous could possibly occur nowadays, his common sense assured him.

It was not long before rumours of what was being said by his congregation reached his ears, and he began to brood over the shameful suspicion that tarnished his home. He sat watching his wife in her contemplation of the child, and struggled to put all thought of the slander from him as unworthy. He had, however, been trained in the school of thought which holds the human heart to be full of wickedness and guile; and he was afraid of his own more generous instincts. He dared not trust the evidence of his eyes, or believe in the innocence of a possible sinner merely because she had every appearance of innocence. Megan's untroubled manner towards him, and her frank steadfast gaze, became at last, to his fevered imagination, proofs of her deceitfulness. He said not a word to her of this; but he began to preach sermons more threatening than any of his former ones on the need for repentance and public confession. On the deadly sin of adultery he waxed especially eloquent, and the denunciation of those who transgressed the seventh commandment became his obsession. So great was his fervour and eloquence that women sobbed aloud, and men rose to confess to fornication before a hysterically excited congregation. Strange things came to light in Alpha Chapel. The impressionable young were overwrought; the elders shook their heads. Weak brethren, they declared, committed sins in order to enjoy the notoriety of penitence. Some were even so wicked as to invent sins which they had not committed. But though sober-minded persons disapproved, the chapel collections increased, the groaning and crying of 'Amen' rose louder, and Rees Lloyd thundered ever more savagely his terrible threats of death and judgement and everlasting fire.

Only the woman at whom all this fury was directed, who dominated his every thought, who filled his being with impotent rage, sat beneath his pulpit unmoved and placid, as if in her childlike innocence, above the storm of his anger, she heard the calm music of celestial things.

When the child, whom they had christened Ifor, was two years old, Megan gave birth to another son. He was as swarthy as a gypsy. His mother gave him the same dutiful care which she paid to his father. She spared herself no trouble in the service of these two. Nothing was lacking to them but the warmth of her love. That was all for her firstborn, and Rees Lloyd hated her daily more and more.

He found her one day, seated beside the kitchen fire, giving her breast to the black-eyed baby in her arms. He stood staring down at her in a gloomy reverie, when the sound of Ifor's crying reached their ears from the walled-in space before the cottage. In an instant Megan was on her feet, and taking the baby from her breast, rolled it up hastily in a shawl and left it to whimper in its cradle, whilst she hurried out to comfort her loved one. A gust of fury shook Rees Lloyd. He followed his wife out through the doorway, and the sight of her holding the golden-haired child in her arms drove him to the verge of madness. 'Put down that bastard,' he shouted at her, 'put it down – or I'll kill the both of you.'

She gave him a terror-stricken look, but clung closer to the child. 'Do you hear me?' he cried hoarsely. 'You will drive me to murder, flaunting your shame before me as you do!'

'It isn't true,' she said in a low voice, facing him unflinchingly. For a moment he towered over her, clenching and unclenching his hands as though he would strangle her. Then he turned abruptly away, and strode off bareheaded into the hills. Megan crouched down upon the doorstep with Ifor folded close to her heart; and the wailing of the neglected baby rose unheeded from the house.

When Rees Lloyd returned home that evening after hours of prayer and wrestling with himself in the solitude of the mountains, he came up to Megan and laid his hand on her shoulder. 'I will not blame you,' he said, in a voice from which all the life was gone. 'God knows, we are all miserable sinners, and in danger of hell fire; yet the worst of us may be saved, at the last, by repentance. Confess your sin, and I will forgive you, as I hope myself for pardon.' 'I am not guilty of what you do think,' she answered resolutely.

He turned away from her sharply with a gesture of despair. She followed him across the room, moved to compassion by the sight of his suffering. 'Maybe I have done wrong,' she murmured, 'without knowin' as I did it.' He turned and looked at her with revived hope, waiting for her confession. 'But if I sinned,' she continued softly, ''twas only in thought. I have allus been keeping my marriage vows, and actin' honest by you.' 'Look at the child,' he interrupted her with renewed anger. ''Tis the child of my dreams,' she whispered. He stared at her uncomprehending, and turned away in disgust.

That night he said no more, but throughout the years that followed he returned to the subject which poisoned his mind, with reiterated demands for her confession. 'I am not guilty as you do think,' was all she would vouchsafe him, and he with growing conviction would answer: 'You lie!'

She bore him three more children, all dark as her second, and she listened patiently to his cruel denunciations, his reproaches, his appeals to her to repent. She suffered his moods of passionate desire, and his violent reactions of loathing and self-contempt; and the whole wealth of her love was poured out upon Ifor and the memory of Penry. She was far less unhappy than the man who lived to torment her and himself; for her life was one of resignation, whilst his was a self-created hell of hatred and suspicion.

When the imprisoned winds came howling down the Cwm one night in December, a wizened old man knocked at Rees Lloyd's door. Megan opened it a crack, and a wreath of blue smoke and peat ash went swirling round the kitchen. Rees Lloyd raised his head, as he sat before the fire with a book on his knee. He listened to the whispering of his wife and the man who stood in the darkness outside. Unable to hear what they were saying, he felt an angry suspicion that they were discussing something of which they did not want him to know. He was ready to believe any ill of Megan, since she had so repeatedly lied to him. Presently she closed the door on the storm and the firelit room grew warm and still once more. When she came back into the light he saw that her face was pallid and her lips were quivering. She stared past him with dilated eyes; then caught up a shawl and wrapped it round her shoulders. 'I must be goin' to Graigfawr,' she announced. 'What?' he cried, 'going up to the top of the valley on a night like this?' 'Yes, yes, there is someone dyin' there as do want to see me.'

He asked her no more questions, but let her go out alone into the darkness. Driven by an ill presentiment, he rose and followed her stealthily up the road that was just visible beneath his feet.

The wind came raging down between the hills on either side, and lashed the rain and icy sleet into his face. His hands grew numb with cold; at times he could scarcely draw his breath; still he struggled on, now and then catching a glimpse of the two figures ahead of him. Once the sound of their voices was blown back on the tempest. 'Hurry, hurry,' Megan cried in agonised appeal. 'He may be dead afore we can get there.' The old man shouted at her: 'I am goin' as fast as I can. I can't do no more.' The force of the wind had almost overmastered him and he staggered. She caught him by the arm, and dragged him along. She was endowed with superhuman strength, and would have fought her way through fire and water to the place where Penry lay dying.

Two shepherds had found him lying at the foot of a steep rock, off which he had stepped, blinded by the treacherous mist. They had carried him to a neighbouring farm; and there he lay in an upper room, barely conscious when Megan entered. His eyelids fluttered and lifted slowly at the sound of her voice. His blue eyes seemed to have turned black, for the pupils were dilated to take in the last of light. His face was corpse-pale; but at sight of her, a faint smile hovered over it. She knelt down beside the bed, and motioned away the farmer and his wife who had followed her into the dimly lit room. They stole out on tiptoe. On the narrow landing at the top of the stairs they encountered the minister, with burning eyes fixed upon the door through which his wife had passed. No one had seen him enter the house, and they exclaimed in surprise and fear at sight of him.

'Go downstairs,' he commanded, 'and leave me be. I will keep watch here.'

They obeyed him in awed silence; and when he was left alone in the dark, he crept close to the door through which came a faint crack of light. He knelt down beside it, listening, with murder in his heart.

Megan was speaking in low tones. She was telling the dying man the story of the miracle. Her husband could see her, through the crack in the door, kneeling beside the bed, her eyes fixed adoringly on the white face upon the

407

pillow. The haggard man, with bloodstained bandages about his head, did not stir; but he was fully conscious now, and his wide eyes shone with fever's brilliance in the light of the single candle.

'How is it possible you comed to bear a child like me?' he murmured. His lips hardly moved. The words seemed to form themselves in the air. 'We were never doin' no wrong, you and I, Megan.'

'All things are possible to the spirit,' she answered, 'as we are readin' in the Bible. The old folk too, they are tellin' us stories of things they have seen as aren't of this 'orld. I am not laughin' at the old stories, as some are doin'. Folks as have had a bit of education, they aren't willin' to believe in anything as they can't understand. But the wisest are them as are full o' wonder still, like little children.' And she added: 'There is nothin' so strange but what it may come to pass.' This was the summing up of her faith.

Penry nodded his assent, and there seemed to be no further need of speech between them. They remained silent for a time, gazing at each other with comprehension in their eyes. At length he murmured dreamily: 'Your love is wonderful strong, Megan. I do feel as 'twill go with me where I am goin' slippin' – away...' his voice became barely audible, 'away, into – I am not knowing what.'

She bent over him, but could not catch the last words formed by his lips. They had turned the colour of skimmed milk. Silence reigned. He seemed to have fallen asleep, but when she pressed closer to listen to his breathing she found that it had ceased.

She rose quietly and turned away from the bedside. She was not frightened, nor appalled by any tragic sense

408

of loss, for she had suffered all the agonies of parting with him whilst he was yet alive. Rather, she was glad that she had come in time to say to him what she had said. 'He might never have known,' she thought; and then she added: 'but wherever his soul has gone, it must have known *there*.' To her the things of the spirit were stronger and more real than those of the flesh. Had she not proved it to be so?

In the chill of dawn, when she came out of the room where the dead man lay, she saw her husband seated at the head of the stairs with his head buried in his hands. He rose, shivering, as he heard her footsteps behind him, and turning, looked at her with mournful eyes.

'Forgive me,' he said, and suddenly kneeling down at her feet, he put the hem of her coarse skirt to his lips and kissed it reverently. She drew away with an exclamation of surprise and self-depreciation, and taking his hand in hers, raised him and led him downstairs. He wrapped his own coat round her shoulders and her shawl over her head before he took her home; but he did not speak of what had happened that night.

It lay like a mysterious gulf between them, which nothing could bridge. It had been, for him, a revelation of the inexplicable. A chasm had opened under his feet where had been the solid ground of his harsh and concise beliefs. Doubts of all sorts came thronging up from this abyss, doubts as to the finality of his theological creed, the justice of his denunciations, the infallibility of the Bible, or at least of his rendering of it. From that hour until the day of his death he was assailed by questions innumerable and unanswerable. He became daily more

409

morose and absorbed in uncertainty, but gentle in his manner towards Megan, whom, in the light of the miracle, he had ceased to regard as his possession. He was no longer consumed by the flame of jealousy as when he had fancied her unfaithful; but he regarded her as irrevocably lost to him, a saintly being whom he had no right to touch, and for whose love he dared never hope, in this world or the next.

He died of pneumonia before the spring came. As Megan sat at his bedside, he gasped out: 'You are wiser than I am, diar anwyl. I have been preaching to others about the will of the Lord; but you have kept silent and listened whilst God spoke to you.' 'No,' she said, 'I have only listened to my own heart.' 'Perhaps,' he murmured, 'God speaks to us through our hearts.' He lay still for a time, struggling for breath; his frail hands clenched, and a line between his brows. He was grappling with a difficult, new thought. At last he said: 'I don't know'; and later on he repeated very sadly: 'I don't know... after all...'

These were the last words spoken by the preacher who had gained so great a reputation for fiery eloquence and dogmatic fervour. The minister who preached his funeral oration had much to say on the tenacity of Rees Lloyd's faith, in an age of scepticism. 'He stood fast in the true faith,' cried the preacher, 'he was never, for a moment, troubled by doubts on religion, nor on the right conduct of life. He *knew* the right from the wrong. He never admitted that there could be more than one path, the old and narrow road, to heaven.'

The black-clad crowd that had gathered from far and near to attend the funeral, nodded and murmured 'Amen'.

Only one woman amongst them knew the torment of uncertainty through which Rees Lloyd's soul had passed before it left his body; and she was the wife whom for years he had hated for a sin of which she was not guilty. The tears ran down her face as she sat listening to the sermon; but not, as her neighbours fancied, because she had lost the husband whom she had betrayed. 'I was understandin' him, at the last,' she told me. 'And what you do understand you do forgive.'

Before the year was out she had lost Ifor also. 'When he comed to die, I was like a mad 'oman. Sittin' over the fire in my old home here, where I've been ever since, and rockin' myself back and fore, day and night; not able to eat, nor to sleep, nor even to cry for days together; but moanin' to myself and prayin' God in my heart to let me join him. The light was clean gone out o' my life with his honey-sweet hair and that laugh o' his, for all the 'orld like the laugh o' Penry. Father and mother they was takin' it to heart somethin' terrible. 'Ticing me to eat with this and that, and settin' the other children on my lap to try and make me pay heed to them; but nothin' 'ouldn't rouse me. Dyin' I should have been, for I hadn't no wish to go on livin', if they hadn't got me out one day into the sunlight.

'It was springtime, and everything was fresh, and newborn like. The hills was standin' there as calm and grand as ever; and it comed to me, all of a sudden, that we was like their shadows, as do pass to and fro across the Cwm, and are leavin' no trace of theirselves behind.'

I remember that the shadow of the western hill had almost touched our feet as she reached this point in her story. We were still bathed in the afternoon sunlight, Saint

411

Anne and I, but the grass before us lay dark as emerald velvet in the shade.

'Yes,' I said, looking up in wonder at her tranquil old face, 'but did that make you want to go on living?' She shook her head. 'I did not *want* to live,' she said, 'but lookin' up at those ancient old hills, it seemed to me such a small little thing to live out my short span, patient like, to the end o' my days.'

Those words sent a chill through my being. I remember thinking how endlessly long were her seventy years of life. They do not appear to me so now.

'And then,' the sound of her soft Welsh voice broke the stillness, 'little Emrys, as is a grown man and farmin' here now, was fallin' down on the path by my feet, and cryin' something pitiful. I was pickin' him up, and comfortin' him. And after that I was goin' back to my work. There was four little uns to mind, and that kept me from thinkin' overmuch of the one I'd lost. Not that they was ever the same to me, as he'd been; but they had need o' me none the less.' After a pause, she added: 'They are married and with children o' their own now, all dark-eyed, same as poor Rees. Mother died soon after I was comin' back to live here, and I was lookin' after Father, as was gettin' simple. Then I was keepin' house for my eldest boy, after Father was taken too, until the lad was marryin'. Then again there was his children to see to.... Yes, yes, I've been busy with one thing and another. And now I'm gone old,' she said placidly, watching the shadow of the hills opposite steal across her feet, and creep inch by inch up her dress. 'I am sittin' here day after day, rememberin' all as is past. There is no trace of Penry, nor of little Ifor, they are gone – like shadows o' the hills.'

412

When I raised my eyes to hers again, the sunlight had disappeared from Cwmbach.

* * *

Saint Anne is gone now also. Last summer I tramped up the road that leads through the imprisoned valley. I found it unchanged. The great green hills stood sentinel on either side. There was the square grey chapel, and the caretaker's cottage, and Cwmbach farm, nestling in its hollow on the opposite side of the angry torrent. Nothing broke the well-known stillness but the sleepy trickling of many streams, that in winter are foaming spates, and the sound of my own footfall along the stony track. I came to the fold gate. There I disturbed a tribe of black-haired urchins, swarthy as Spaniards, who were playing upon the strip of sward on which Saint Anne used to set her chair. The sight of these children brought back my own girlhood, so that I called to them by name – 'Gladys, John Owen, Rees bach.' Then I saw that they were watching me with shy curiosity. After a moment they ran away and hid from the stranger.

As I trudged on towards the pass, the shade of the western hill stole across the road behind me, seeming to blot out all trace of my passage; and I remembered the words of the Psalmist that my father had taught me in the Book of Common Prayer: 'Man is like a thing of nought; his time passeth away like a shadow.'

413

Foreword by Fflur Dafydd

Fflur Dafydd is a fiction writer who writes in Welsh and English. Her novel *Twenty Thousand Saints* won the inaugural Oxfam Emerging Writer Prize at the Guardian Hay Festival 2009 and her novel *Y Llyfrgell* scooped the Daniel Owen Memorial Prize at the National Eisteddfod in the same year. She has a PhD on the poetry of R.S. Thomas and lectures at Swansea University.

Cover image by Clive Hicks-Jenkins

Clive Hicks-Jenkins is one of the most powerful figurative painters in Wales. Born in Newport in 1951, he worked for twenty-five years as a choreographer and theatre director before concentrating full-time on painting. His work has now been acquired by all the principal public collections in Wales and his artists books (most recently the first illustrated edition of Peter Shaffer's *Equus*) are in libraries worldwide. He has won the Gulbenkian Welsh Art Prize and a Creative Wales Award and is a member of the Royal Cambrian Academy, the Welsh Group and 56 Group Wales. He has had solo exhibitions at Newport Museum & Art Gallery, Brecknock Museum, the Museum of Modern Art Wales and Christ Church Picture Gallery in Oxford. A major retrospective of his work is planned by the National Library of Wales in 2011. He is represented by the Martin Tinney Gallery.

LIBRARY OF WALES

The Library of Wales is a Welsh Assembly Government project designed to ensure that all of the rich and extensive literature of Wales which has been written in English will now be made available to readers in and beyond Wales. Sustaining this wider literary heritage is understood by the Welsh Assembly Government to be a key component in creating and disseminating an ongoing sense of modern Welsh culture and history for the future Wales which is now emerging from contemporary society. Through these texts, until now unavailable, out-of-print or merely forgotten, the Library of Wales brings back into play the voices and actions of the human experience that has made us, in all our complexity, a Welsh people.

The Library of Wales includes prose as well as poetry, essays as well as fiction, anthologies as well as memoirs, drama as well as journalism. It complements the names and texts that are already in the public domain and seeks to include the best of Welsh writing in English, as well as to showcase what has been unjustly neglected. No boundaries limit the ambition of the Library of Wales to open up the borders that have denied some of our best writers a presence in a future Wales. The Library of Wales has been created with that Wales in mind: a young country not afraid to remember what it might yet become.

Dai Smith
Raymond Williams Chair in the Cultural History of Wales,
Swansea University

PARTHIAN

A Carnival of Voices

www.parthianbooks.com

LIBRARY OF WALES
FUNDED BY

Llywodraeth Cynulliad Cymru
Welsh Assembly Government

CYNGOR LLYFRAU CYMRU
WELSH BOOKS COUNCIL

SERIES EDITOR: DAI SMITH

WWW.LIBRARYOFWALES.ORG